THE
BAKER'S
STORY

Alan Reynolds

Fisher King Publishing

THE BAKER'S STORY
Copyright © Alan Reynolds 2021
ISBN 978-1-913170-96-7

Published by
Fisher King Publishing
The Old Barn
York Road
Thirsk
YO7 3AD
England

fisherkingpublishing.co.uk

A huge thanks to Rick Armstrong for his
unstinting support, guidance, and friendship,
also to Samantha Richardson and
Rachel Topping at Fisher King Publishing,
thank you for your patience and great artwork.
Thanks also to Jane Wheatley, and to Lisa Slater
at Make Your Copy Count, for editorial
and proof-reading support.

I would also like to thank the
Keighley Historical Society for their
invaluable assistance.

Dedicated to my family and friends, and to all
those who have supported me in my writing –
your encouragement has been inspirational.
Much love

Also by Alan Reynolds

Flying with Kites
Taskers End
Breaking the Bank
The Sixth Pillar
The Tinker
The Coat
Smoke Screen
Valley of The Serpent
Twelve – a date with obsession
Exfil
Trent Island

'The lamps are going out all over Europe; we shall not see them lit again in our lifetime.'
Sir Edward Grey, British Foreign Secretary, 1914

Chapter One

Five a.m., Saturday June 27ᵗʰ, 1914.

Arthur Marsden was in the back yard of his bakery waiting for the daily delivery of flour, dressed in his normal work attire - overalls, clogs, and flat cap. He pushed his cap back momentarily and scratched his forehead; the sun was already making its presence felt.

The side gate was open, and Arthur looked out, scanning the horizon.

Keighley, a West Yorkshire wool town, prosperous and thriving, the myriad of mill chimneys exuding the residue of fifty or more furnaces, creating a dark haze in the still summer air. It had been Arthur's home for his nineteen years.

To the left of the yard was the blacksmiths. Although motorised transport was increasing in popularity, there were still many working horses needing to be serviced. The road outside the yard showed evidence of their presence, the droppings creating a hazard for unwary pedestrians. The smell of horses hung in the air.

Arthur looked right along the cobbles of West Street. A short distance away was James Street, the main thoroughfare. The baker's shop had had a prominent presence on the corner for over fifty years and was etched in the town's history.

Just then, the sound of Buxton's lorry could be heard, and Arthur watched as it turned from the main road and headed towards him. The driver waved as he parked up. There was a clunk and grind as he applied the handbrake. The side of the lorry was emblazoned with ornate scrolling script, 'Buxton's Flour Mill'; the family-run enterprise which supplied many of the bakeries around the Keighley area.

It was a drop from the cab to the pavement and an

ungainly descent by the man.

"Eh up, Arthur," said the miller in his thick Yorkshire accent. He was an avuncular man but as strong as an ox and nearly as big.

"'Ow do, Edward, fine day."

"Aye, tis indeed. Six today, right?" enquired the miller.

"Aye, busy day Saturday; our Agnes and Grace will be rushed off their feet."

The miller walked towards the trailer, chatting as he went. "I hear strike's been called off today."

"Is that right?"

"Aye, just been chatting to a few of the lads on t'corner. Mind you, seems t'foundry owners called police in. All sorts been going on. Some of 'em were saying they wanted to go back afore but were being threatened by t'ringleaders."

"Nay! That's bad. So what's going to 'appen, you reckon?"

"Most're going back to work... But some of 'em's got themselves into trouble and been arrested, you know, going to prison an' that. If you ask me, I reckon one or two've been getting some grief from their womenfolk."

"Aye, we've had a few of 'em in t'shop asking for credit. I've had to tell our Agnes we can't do that; we've got bills to pay an' all. 'Appen they weren't best pleased."

"Aye, I bet... anyways, I'll get on."

The trailer was a flat-bed, piled with thirty or forty sacks of flour, each weighing a hundredweight. Edward Buxton's hair was already white from earlier deliveries.

Lifting a hundredweight of flour safely was an art and one that the miller had mastered over thirty years. He backed against the trailer; grabbed the two top corners of a sack and slowly eased it away; his upper-back taking the load. He was wearing a modified leather apron which ran across his shoulders to take some of the strain of the heavy bags.

Arthur's frame did not suit him for such a job. Although approaching six feet tall, he was painfully thin. His older sister, Grace, would often tease him about his physique. "Blow over in a gale," she would say. His mother told him he would fill out in time.

Arthur counted the bags as Buxton carried them into the baking shed at the back of the shop. He paid the miller the nine pounds for the delivery. Then he escorted him back to the lorry and bid his farewells.

"Sithee Monday, Arthur," shouted Buxton as he got into the cab.

"Aye, tarra, Edward, take care of thissen."

Arthur watched as the truck lurched and bounced away down the cobbled street to his next call.

Marsden's Bakery had a good reputation in town for fair prices and excellent bread. Queues would regularly form before opening time at eight o'clock. Arthur's father, Albert, and his father before him, Benjamin, were master bakers prior to Arthur taking over the mantle. His father was now infirmed, a consumptive caused by years of breathing in flour. Arthur's mother, Mildred, was now a nurse to her husband as well as a mother to their five children.

Arthur was the only boy. His sisters, Grace, and Agnes, served in the shop; Molly and Freda were still at school. Taking over the family business, following his father's confinement two months ago, was a huge responsibility for Arthur. Not just in providing the income to keep the family fed, but also in serving the local community that depended on the bakery.

In the baking shed, the fire that heated the large oven had been lit; it was the same oven that had baked the bread since the bakery opened. Its brickwork was soot-marked and

3

crumbling in places, evidencing the years of use, but it had served the family well and would continue to do so for the foreseeable future.

The walls of the baking shed were white-tiled to aid cleaning, but many were cracked now, and the crazy patterns provided an unintended decoration. The room was dark and gloomy, despite the bright morning outside, and the air was thick with flour-dust and grime.

Two long-handled, shovel-like tools with elongated blades were resting against the wall; they were used to load the uncooked mix into the oven and then remove the finished loaves. A large vat was in the corner, cleaned and ready to be filled with the ingredients. Arthur knew the amounts without the need for scales. Traditional ingredients of flour, salt, yeast, and water were mixed with the expertise and care of a master baker.

Arthur used metal moulds, twenty at a time, for those wanting the traditional 'loaf' shaped bread. He also made batch-loaves using just the dough-mix, and baps, smaller bread-cakes, which were his most popular produce.

It was skilled work, much of his knowledge learned since he left school four years earlier. He had been a regular helper to his father in the baking shed as soon as he was old enough to be able to lift one of the shovels.

He went to work and was soon stirring the mixture in the vat. The container could easily double as a bath; it was just a little bigger than those facilities enjoyed by the gentry.

Within a few minutes, the unmistakeable aroma of freshly-made bread had permeated the shop as well as the family living quarters on the first floor.

Arthur walked along the short corridor, which linked the baking shed to the retail outlet. Halfway along to the right, there was a flight of stairs. While the dough was baking, he would collect his breakfast.

Upstairs, above the bakery, there were two bedrooms, a kitchen, and a parlour, which housed Arthur and his family. The larger bedroom was shared by the five children. There were two three-quarter sized beds for the girls and a single bed for Arthur which was screened from his sisters by a large sheet.

As Arthur entered the parlour, his mother greeted him with a plate containing two slices of bread, coated with a thick layer of home-made dripping, and a glass of milk. The two elder sisters were at the wooden table eating their sandwiches.

"Thanks, mam." Arthur took the plate from his mother. "'Appen strikes off, according to Edward Buxton."

"Eh, that's some good news… It's been terrible for the families. I've been telling our Grace to give 'em some of the pig scraps; right grateful they were too," said Mildred.

"Mildred!" A voice bellowed from the bedroom.

"I'll just go and see to your father."

Albert Buxton was a difficult man, particularly after he had consumed alcohol. After a hard day in the bakery, he was a frequent visitor to the Malt Shovel, the alehouse down the street. It was for medicinal purposes he would say, to clear the tubes from the dust. Ironic given his present condition.

Beatings were commonplace, and the children would hide from him in the bedroom when they heard his footsteps clomping up the stairs on his return from the pub. Mildred was the recipient of most of her husband's frustrations, although Arthur had received many a lashing with his father's leather belt, even for the most trivial of misdemeanours. Over the years, the treatment had affected Arthur's development. People would describe him as an 'anxious lad'; his hands could often be seen shaking as he went about his daily chores.

While Arthur finished his breakfast and returned to his bread-making, Mildred attended to her husband in the bedroom.

"Clean it up, woman," commanded Albert.

She looked at her husband. Part of her wished that his inevitable death would arrive sooner rather than later to relieve her of this burden. Albert wheezed and slowly removed the bed sheet; he had soiled himself again. There was a jug of water in a basin on the dresser and Mildred went to work without complaint while Albert continued to berate her.

"What are you putting in my food, woman? Are you trying to kill me?"

Irrational rants had become commonplace as his brain deteriorated, unable to control his bodily functions.

Mildred said nothing, but deep inside, she cursed her mother's choice of suiter. "A master baker – you'll never go hungry," she had said. Although that part was true, it was a high price to pay for the regular rapes and beatings Mildred had been subjected to during their marriage.

Twenty minutes later, with the soiled clothing and bedlinen piled in the corner waiting to be washed, Mildred returned to the parlour. The four girls were now at the table eating; Arthur had returned to the baking shed.

"It will be busy today if the rumours are true," warned Mildred.

"What rumours, mam?" said Grace.

"They say there's going to be shortages."

"Why's that?" asked Grace.

"Might not be able to get flour… That's what I heard."

"What will us do?"

"I don't know, Grace, I'll need to speak to Arthur."

By eight o'clock, Molly and Freda, the two younger daughters, were off to school. It was Molly's last term. Grace and Agnes served behind the counter in the shop. Grace was the eldest sibling, at twenty, a year older than Arthur, Agnes a year younger at eighteen, Molly and Freda, fourteen and twelve.

Grace and Agnes were dressed in their aprons and white caps, the serving uniform since Victorian times. The queue of people waiting for the bakery to open stretched up James Street almost to the butcher's, some hundred yards or more. Arthur was helping his sisters bring the large wicker baskets of loaves from the baking shed and placing them on the shelves awaiting sale.

There was a beaded curtain separating the shop from the corridor that led to the baking shed, a necessary but frustrating barrier when trying to move the product from the bakery. Arthur had pegged it back to stop it getting in the way.

The shop itself was a good size; it would comfortably hold twenty customers. There was a serving counter split in two with a gap in the middle where the expensive NCR cash till took pride of place. The girls would serve either side to avoid getting in each other's way. Behind the serving counter were the shelves of bread and at the end, a table with a set of scales on top. Poorer customers who could not afford a whole loaf would buy their bread by the ounce.

The first woman in the queue started knocking on the glass door, the only other entrance to the store.

"Wait tha hurry, woman," shouted Arthur, as the three continued to stock the shelves. The woman knocked again; Arthur ignored her.

Five minutes later, the shelves had been suitably replenished with the results of Arthur's labours. He returned to the baking shed to start again. He would continue until the flour was gone; there would be nothing left over today.

Agnes went to the front door. The clamour behind it was getting ugly as women jostled each other for position. One had seemingly pushed in and had been knocked to the ground.

Agnes stopped. "Arthur," she shouted. "Can you come?"

Arthur answered the call and returned from the baking shed; he could see the mayhem outside.

He took over from Agnes. "Get back and get in line or there'll be no bread today," he shouted through the glass.

His voice seemed to carry some authority, and gradually the crush subsided.

He unlocked the front door. There was a loud 'clang' from the bell, which would indicate a customer in normal times; these were not normal times. He would leave it open today.

The pandemonium started again. The first three women at the head of the queue barged in trying to pass through the door together, jostling to get to the counter first. It was not wide enough, resulting in an ungainly entrance. After six customers had entered the shop, Arthur put his arm across the entrance preventing anyone else from entering. He spoke to the next woman waiting. "It's one out and one in from now... or I fetch the constabulary, pass it on." The word went back.

Looting, in the present climate, was a real concern; a crowded shop increased that risk and Arthur waited by the front door until the chaos had died down and the queue had started to move more orderly. Grace and Agnes were at full tilt dispensing the loaves. "One each, no more," instructed

Arthur as he went back into the baking shed to start the next mix.

There were many arguments about the imposed rationing. Several women had large families and complained bitterly that one loaf was not enough to feed everyone.

"We open again on Monday," said Agnes in an effort to placate the first complainant.

"Aye, and I'll be queuing afore dawn again," was the bitter response.

James Street was a wide thoroughfare on an incline, north to south, with a mixture of horse-drawn and motorised transport. Crimson and white trolleybuses with their overhead umbilical cords, and balcony cars that would hold over fifty people, would pass the bakery at regular intervals. As the morning progressed, the traffic increased. The parade of shops stretched the length of the street to the top where it joined the High Street, the main road through the town, at a busy junction. Next door to the bakery was a florist, then a butcher's, a greengrocer's, a haberdashery and, finally, a general store and grocery on the corner with the main road.

Marsden's Bakery's signage gleamed in the mid-summer sun with its elaborate gold script, a testament to the sign-writer's art. Throughout the morning, the store continued to dispatch bread non-stop, although the queue had been reduced to a steady trickle.

One or two women had re-joined the line in an effort to beat Arthur's rationing, hoping that Grace and Agnes wouldn't recognise them. Given the numbers passing through the shop, that was a distinct possibility. Others had enlisted the help of their children to join the queue in different places.

Wednesdays and Saturdays were half-day closing at one o'clock and, at three minutes to one, Agnes called Arthur to close the doors. The shop was still full. He had finished baking and had started washing down.

He walked into the shop and looked at the shelves; they were almost empty.

"We'll stay open till it's all gone; it'll be barely use for pigs by Monday. There's not much," said Arthur.

He went outside and looked up the street. He could see other proprietors closing their doors. The fruit and vegetables normally on display outside the greengrocer's had gone, and the proprietor was pushing back the awning with a long pole.

By one-fifteen, the shelves were completely empty; Grace and Agnes had served the last of the customers. Arthur retrieved the awning pole and echoed the task recently completed by the greengrocer.

"Eh up, Arthur, how be tha?" said a friendly voice as he was about to return inside the shop.

"'Ow do, Wilfred, aye grand."

"Tha coming for a pint?"

"Aye, give us ten minutes will tha? Come in and wait."

Wilfred Stonehouse was known to all as the 'butcher's boy', but, like Arthur, had taken over from his father on his untimely death a year ago, managing the family business. The parallels were striking. Wilfred had an even larger number of siblings, six; he was the eldest. There were two younger brothers and four sisters. The boys and two of the girls all worked in the butcher's shop. The two remaining girls were at the same school as Arthur's sisters. Wilfred was a year older than Arthur, but they had been friends since primary school.

"How's tha morning been, Wilfred?" said Arthur as he locked the door.

"Aye, grand, Arthur, been rushed off feet today."

"Aye, same here, you'd think the world were going to

end… Why do tha think?"

"Well, I think it's the strike, now it's over… pub'll be busy an' all."

"Aye, tha could be right… Give us a minute, I'll check the girls."

Grace and Agnes were cleaning down the shelves before tackling the baking shed. Arthur went to the till and took out all the money and put it into a cash bag.

He turned to his sister, who was rinsing out a cloth. "Grace, are tha ok? I'm just taking cash upstairs, then off to t'Shovel with Wilfred; be back later."

"Aye, Arthur, sithee later."

"Shan't be a minute," said Arthur to Wilfred and he disappeared through the curtain and up to the parlour.

A few minutes later, Arthur and Wilfred, identically dressed in the fashion of the day, waistcoats, trousers, hobnail boots, and flat caps, left the shop. It was a scorching hot summers day, and they were both thirsty after their morning's labours. They crossed West Street, skipping over the flattened horse dung which littered the road. There was a bank on the corner where Arthur would be depositing his money on Monday. Next to the bank was The Malt Shovel.

The outside of the alehouse was tiled in shiny mottled-brown, green, and yellow terracotta which glistened in the bright sunshine, giving the establishment a garish look. The name was emblazoned across the top in bold black lettering, a swinging sign hung just above the entrance depicting a shovel and two sacks of barley.

The pair went inside; it was heaving with men. Some were standing in the corridor which ran down the centre of the pub to the outside yard at the back where the toilet was situated. The word 'toilet' was a euphemism. It was an old out-building with the left-hand wall used to pee against and the run-off channelled by gravity down the length of the structure and through a hole to an outside drain. The pitted floor would be awash with urine. The stench meant that few ventured there for any length of time.

There was a 'sit-down' facility in an adjacent shed or 'the hut', as it was known. Inside there was a large wooden box with a circular hole cut out of the top, placed over a four-foot deep pit. Scraps of newspaper tied with string were suspended from a hook screwed into the wall.

The entrance to the bar was just along the corridor to the right. To the left was another room, the lounge or 'snug' as it was known. Every seat was taken and a blue fug hung in the air from the smoke of pipes and cigarettes. Glasses and empty ale bottles littered the tables.

Arthur and Wilfred turned right into the bar, a much larger room but, again, heaving with men engaged in discussions, most of which seemed to be about the ending of the strike. Arthur elbowed his way towards the bar where Thomas Fielding, the portly landlord, was dispensing beer at an alarming rate. There was no finesse; the glass was placed under the tap of the barrel; it was turned, and gravity did the rest. There were six barrels in a line, each with pools of beer on the floor beneath. On the shelves above the barrels, rows of pint bottles of ale - brown ale, pale ale, stout; slightly more expensive than that from the barrel and, therefore, less popular. The ale arrived daily by horse-drawn wagon, straight from the Knowle Spring Brewery and Malt kilns.

"Eh up, Arthur, Wilfred, what'll tha have?" said the landlord recognising the new arrivals.

"Aye, two pints of best, Thomas, ta," said Arthur.

Arthur had taken to visiting the pub after work since he turned eighteen, continuing the routine of his father. Mildred had tried counselling him on the dangers, but the advice fell on deaf ears. For many local men, a visit to the pub was more than a social occasion. The quality of the local drinking water was notoriously poor, causing stomach upsets and worse. As a result, men generally preferred to get their liquid intake from the cask.

Thomas presented the two pints. "Sixpence, Arthur."

Arthur put the coins on the countertop. Both lads picked up their beers and took a long slug. Arthur's prominent Adam's Apple bounced up and down as the beer disappeared down his gullet. Within seconds it had gone. Wilfred was not far behind. He took out some coins. "Same again, Thomas."

The barman smiled. "Busy morning I see, young Wilfred."

"Aye, and it's right warm today; builds up a thirst," replied Wilfred.

Thomas served the second pints, and Arthur and Wilfred supped at a more leisurely pace.

There was a lull at the bar, and the landlord started washing a few glasses in the sink under the counter. Just then, his wife, Maisy, came into the bar from the back. There was a flight of stairs leading up to the living quarters over the pub. She took over the glass-washing while her husband took a breather. He had also been awake since five a.m. The licensing laws were generous at this time. There were no restrictions on opening time; many men would enjoy a pint before going to the mill. Closing time was set at eleven o'clock; it was a long day for the licensee. The landlord poured himself a half pint and went to the end of the bar to join Arthur and Wilfred.

"So what's t'news on strike, Thomas, have you heard owt?" asked Arthur.

"Aye, seems all but over. Back to work on Monday. Mind you, there's still unrest in town. Some of the foundry lads up at Prince Smith's place are still bitter. I vouch we've not heard last."

"I heard constabulary were called," said Wilfred.

"Aye, some broken heads an' all. Feelings are still running high," replied the landlord.

While the men continued to debate the news of the day, Mildred was at home preparing Albert's lunch; Grace and Agnes were still cleaning in the baking shed, and the two youngest had gone out for a walk. There was no school today.

"Mildred, where's us lunch, woman?" hollered Albert from his bed. There was the sound of violent coughing.

Mildred ignored the shout and continued her preparation. Five minutes later, she left the kitchen with a tray containing a bowl of home-made soup and some bread.

As she reached the bedroom, Albert appeared to be struggling for breath. His eyes were wide and he was making a strange gasping sound. Mildred put the tray down on the dressing table and watched as her husband wheezed and gesticulated for some kind of help, pointing at his throat.

He had had these seizures before and normally she would just bend him forward and slap his back. His breathing would quickly recover. But this time, she just watched him as his actions became more desperate.

Gradually the gestures slowed, his hands dropped to his side and his eyes closed. His breathing was shallow. Without a moment's thought, Mildred picked up one of the pillows, knelt on the bed and leaned down on her husband's face, completely covering it with the pillow. She stayed there for what seemed an eternity but in reality, was just a few minutes.

Slowly, she removed the pillow. Albert's mouth was open, his lifeless eyes staring at the ceiling. It was no different to putting down a dying dog, a kindness in its own way; she felt no remorse.

She returned the tray to the kitchen and went downstairs to the bakery and called her daughters. "Grace, Agnes, can you come?"

The two girls followed their mother up the stairs.

"What's wrong, mam?"

"It's your father, he's had another seizure. He's gone."

"Oh, no," said Grace.

"Yes, Grace, I need you to go down the Malt Shovel and get our Arthur."

Grace left the bakery, ran across West Street, past the bank and into the pub. She looked around the bar through the smoke and at all the male heads; the conversation suddenly died, and men were staring at her.

"Arthur," she called.

Arthur heard the voice. He was still at the far end with Wilfred and the landlord.

He put down his pint and walked towards her. "Grace…? What are tha doing in here?"

"It's our dad, tha better come."

Arthur went back, picked up his drink and supped up. He bid farewell to his drinking companions. "Summat's up, I'll sithee, Wilfred… Thomas."

He placed the empty glass on the counter and joined Grace.

"What's up?" said Arthur as they left the darkness of the alehouse into the street. He squinted until his eyes became accustomed to the sunlight.

"It's our dad; mam says he's gone… had one of his seizures."

They walked at pace back to the bakery. Mildred was

waiting with Agnes in the shop.

There was a clang of the bell as they entered.

"Eh up, mam, what's happened?" said Arthur.

"It's your dad, he's gone, Arthur… Can you run and get Doctor Adams?"

"Aye, will do."

Arthur left the shop and turned right up James Street trying to take in the news. For some reason, he was not overtaken with grief, more a sense of relief.

It took him fifteen minutes to reach the large house which also served as Doctor Adam's surgery. He rang the bell at the side of the door, then again, then a third time. He couldn't hear anyone and knocked with his knuckles on the glass pane.

It took a few minutes before a figure approached the door.

"Yes," said a matronly-looking woman, sternly, as she opened the door.

"Is Doctor Adams there? It's me dad."

"Wait here," said the woman.

There was another delay.

Doctor Adams had been the family physician since before Arthur was born. His hair was now whispish and white, but he still maintained the bearing of someone in authority. He opened the door and looked at the visitor.

"Arthur Marsden…? What's the problem?"

"It's me dad… mam says he's gone."

"Oh, right, well you get back, young Arthur, I'll be down directly."

Arthur returned to the shop. James Street was still busy; the opposite park full with families enjoying the hot summer weather.

The girls were upstairs, and Arthur used his keys to get

in; the clang heralded his entrance once again. He walked through the shop and up the stairs. His shirt was sticking to him, and there were sweat marks around the brim of his flat cap.

His mother and two sisters were in the parlour. As with Arthur, there seemed little emotion, certainly not the grief you would expect at the passing of a close relative.

"Doctor's on his way, mam," said Arthur as he entered the room.

"Aye, thanks, Arthur," said Mildred.

"What happened, do you know?" asked Arthur.

"Aye, Arthur, he had another one of his turns."

It was half an hour before the doctor rapped on the shop door with his cane. Arthur went downstairs and let him in. Seymour Adams was wearing his three-piece suit, bowler hat and carrying his medical equipment. A pocket watch hung by a chain in his waistcoat.

They went upstairs to the parlour; it was a familiar journey for the doctor who had been maintaining a weekly visit since Albert had taken to his bed.

They entered the parlour, and the doctor took off his hat and placed it on the table.

"Hello, Mrs Marsden… Arthur tells me your husband's gone."

"Aye, I'll take you through."

Mildred had laid out Albert, and he was lying peacefully with his arms across his chest.

Doctor Adams pulled out a stethoscope from his Gladstone bag and checked Albert's heart, then his pulse.

"Can you tell me what happened?"

"Yes, he had another one of his seizures. I came to help him, but he stopped breathing and went limp."

"I'm sorry to hear that Mrs Marsden, my condolences, but it was to be expected. Frankly, I'm surprised he lasted this long. I'll give you a death certificate and you can take it up to the Town Hall on Monday to get it registered. Have you thought about the funeral yet?"

"No, doctor, I haven't."

"That's alright, I can recommend Josiah Rombold of Parish Road. Do you know them?"

"I've heard of them."

"They are very good… Just mention my recommendation and you will get excellent service… or, I can call in on them on the way back if you prefer. It's not out of my way."

"That would be a kindness indeed," said Mildred.

The doctor opened his bag and returned the stethoscope then took out a pad of certificates. He completed the details with Mildred providing the information. Death was stated as 'consumption of the lungs'. The doctor signed with a flourish.

"Now don't forget, you must register the death as soon as you can, else you won't be able to bury your husband."

"Yes, I'll see to it Monday," replied Mildred.

"I'll bid you good day," said the doctor and he picked up his hat.

Arthur escorted him down the stairs. As they reached the door of the shop, the doctor turned to Arthur. "Tell your mother I'll send my account on Monday."

"Aye, will do," replied Arthur and watched as the physician walked back up James Street.

Arthur returned to the parlour. "Doctor Adams said he will send the account on Monday." Mildred looked concerned.

"Are we alright, mam? For money I mean, for Doctor Adams."

"Yes, Arthur, don't worry; your father put away enough

for that and for the funeral. I'll need to go to the bank on Monday and let them know. You better come with me; there'll be forms to sign, I don't doubt."

"Aye, mam, will do... What about t'shop? Do we open?"

"Yes, Arthur, business as usual. It's what your dad would want. Can't be letting folks down. We can go after you've finished baking... Wait here, I need to sort out a few things; I don't want to be disturbed."

Mildred returned to the bedroom.

Arthur and the two girls remained in the parlour. Agnes was cross-stitching, Grace reading a book.

Just then, the two younger sisters arrived back.

"What were the doctor doing? I've just seen him leaving t'shop." asked Molly as she started to take off her shoes.

Grace looked up from her book. "'Appen our dad's died. Don't go in t'bedroom, mam doesn't want to be disturbed."

Molly looked at Freda. They both sat on the sofa next to Grace.

"What'll happen?" said Molly.

"Nowt, tha should worry about. 'Appen we'll manage."

Arthur was quiet, deep in thought, starting to come to terms with being head of the family. He went to the drawer and took out the cloth bag containing the takings from the morning's trade and started to count it ready for banking on Monday.

Chapter Two

It was late afternoon, around five o'clock, when there was another knock on the shop door. It was Jeremiah Rombold, dressed in his funereal black suit.

Arthur opened the door; there was the usual clang from the bell.

"Jeremiah Rombold," announced the man.

He removed his bowler hat, which he always wore when he wasn't on formal duty and held it to his chest in a dignified fashion. He spoke with due solemnity. "I understand from Doctor Adams there has been a bereavement and I might be of service."

"Aye, 'appen tha can… Follow me."

Arthur led Rombold up the stairs where Mildred was waiting. Molly and Freda had joined their elder siblings in their bedroom. There was a great deal of chatting.

The undertaker shook hands with Mildred with an obsequious bow. "Jeremiah Rombold, at your service, madam, please accept my condolences for your loss."

"Thank you... Yes, it's my husband Albert, taken from us earlier today. Doctor Adams has attended; he said you would need to see this."

She handed the man the death certificate, which the undertaker examined then handed back.

"Thank you," said Rombold. "Would you like me to arrange for Mr Marsden to be moved to our chapel of rest this evening or do you wish to keep him here?"

"No, no, you can take him," replied Mildred, rather too quickly. The truth was she wanted him out of the house as soon as possible.

"Good, good, I will arrange that. Had you discussed any

funeral options?"

"No, not really. Nothing fancy, like. Albert wouldn't want much fuss."

They spent an hour discussing arrangements. His costs would cover the standard oak coffin, pallbearers, and horse-drawn hearse – the mourners would walk behind the cortege to the church. Then there were the burial and vicar's fees in addition. Mildred made a note of the details. The funeral would take place on Friday, July 3rd, at one o'clock. The undertaker agreed to arrange the availability of the Methodist Church and vicar. The bakery would close for two hours as a mark of respect.

Once the business had been concluded, Rombold arose from his seat in a stately fashion. There was an elegance about the man; each action appeared deliberate and rehearsed as if he had a programmed behaviour for each movement. Arthur was tasked with escorting Mr Rombold to the door. The undertaker would return in an hour with the hearse to take Albert to the chapel of rest.

Arthur watched him restore his bowler hat to its rightful position and stride off up James Street.

Outside the bakery, a boy of about twelve was stood clutching a pile of newspapers. He was standing next to a board leant against the wall just below the shop window. It was headed, 'Keighley News'; underneath was a headline in black ink, *'Foundrymen Strike over'*. Archie Slater was a familiar presence on James Street, his pre-pubescent voice shrill in the evening air.

"Get tha News, get tha News," like a battle cry, he called to passing pedestrians to attract a sale.

"I'll take one, Archie," said Arthur to the lad. He took out a penny coin from his pocket and gave it to the young vendor who put it in his pocket.

Arthur returned to the parlour with his newspaper and started to read. He was not an educated person in the literal sense, but he did take an interest in the local and international news and was starting to form political leanings. He was becoming increasingly concerned about the poverty around him in what was ostensibly a prosperous town. He sympathised with the plight of the foundrymen and mill workers, many of whom he knew from the Malt Shovel. They complained bitterly about their working conditions and poor pay while the owners lived in large houses away from the urban sprawl.

Arthur started reading the paper. It detailed the treatment of the strikers by the police. Mildred watched her son with a degree of pride; there were many men who were unable to read or write.

"Anything in the news, Arthur?" she asked.

"Aye, mam, they're talking about the strike. Did you know the constabulary charged at the men with batons? Put two in hospital, it says here; arrested the leaders an' all… No wonder there's a lot of bad feeling in town. There'll be riots if they're not careful."

"Yes, that's true enough, but I'm still pleased to see them back at work. The wives have been desperate."

"Aye, we'll be busy again on Monday, I warrant."

Mildred did not speak in the strong local dialect used by her deceased husband and children. Her parents were both teachers, and she had been schooled in the importance of elocution from a young age.

The first-floor accommodation stretched over the shop and the baking shed, so it was a good size. The two bedrooms were at the back, reached by a short corridor. To the left, the larger bedroom where the children slept; to the right the smaller room where Albert was laid waiting to be collected by the undertaker.

The living area was originally one big room, but it had been partitioned off many years earlier with a brick wall and plaster to make the parlour and the kitchen. The premises were lit entirely by gas; Albert had it installed five years earlier. There were three gas-lamps in the parlour, one in the kitchen and one each in the bedrooms. The bakery and shed had their own lamps. The light provided by these lanterns was notoriously poor, creating an eerie atmosphere and long shadows. Luckily, this time of year, they would not be needed too often. A coin-operated gas meter was in the kitchen. Mildred kept a tobacco tin of change on top of it to ensure the supply was always maintained.

The kitchen itself was functional. There was a large square sink, just under the only window, with a hand-pump to the side to draw the water; its green paint flaked, and the metalwork was worn. A tin bucket was housed under the sink and was in regular use. The window was open, enabling house flies to enter at will. The kitchen was plagued by them.

Next to the sink, was the range – a substantial affair of traditional dark ironware with a heavy black kettle on top. The range also had an oven and a small boiler which would hold around three buckets of water. The fire was lit making the room stiflingly hot on this balmy summer evening. The mantle above the range was blackened from the constant heat. A flue took the smoke from the range through the ceiling and out of the building.

Next to the range was a basket of wood and coals, and then a brass container, resembling a shell casing, holding two pokers.

Cupboards and shelves containing plates and other crockery and utensils were attached to three walls. There was a bench-style table next to the sink where much of the preparation was done. The kitchen also had a small pantry in the corner, used for storing food.

The family had taken their evening meal; Mildred had cooked a meat pie with potatoes. The girls were washing the dishes in the sink; Arthur was still reading. There was a rap on the front door.

Arthur left his newspaper and went down to the shop. It was the undertaker with four burly assistants. He could see the horse-drawn hearse parked on the road outside. Jeremiah Rombold removed his hat and entered; the pallbearers followed, suitably attired in their sombre suits. They carried an empty coffin.

"Eh up, Arthur, how be tha?" It was George Harness, one of the two younger assistants; he had been at school with Arthur.

"'Ow do, George… Aye, I'm well enough, thanks."

"Sorry to hear about tha dad."

"Aye, thanks George."

The undertaker turned and scowled at the lad for delaying the group.

Arthur led them to the parlour; their hob-nail boots clomping up the wooden staircase.

There were more greetings as they reached the living area. Mildred had placed five glasses and two bottles of beer from Albert's stash on the table.

"Will you take a drink before you start your work?" asked Mildred as the men entered the room.

"Yes, that would be very welcome indeed," replied the undertaker. "It's thirsty work, it is."

Arthur opened the bottles, poured the drinks, and handed them around. The men made quick work of their stout.

Within a few minutes, they had removed Albert from the

bedroom, and the four lads were walking solemnly through the parlour and towards the stairs. It was hard work; Albert was a man of some weight, and it would take some skilful manoeuvring to get him to the bottom of the stairs with due dignity.

Sunday morning, the bakery was closed. The traditional day of rest was observed by the shopkeepers of Keighley. Although not particularly religious, Arthur had been brought up as a Methodist and, as was tradition, by eleven o'clock, he was sat in one of the pews in the church on Cavendish Street with his family. It was a large building; popularly known as the 'cock chapel' due to its unique weathervane on top of the spire, the tallest in Keighley.

The family were dressed in their Sunday best but were wearing black armbands as a mark of respect for Albert's demise. Several parishioners, having heard the news, had extended their condolences. Mildred was gracious in her acceptance of the good wishes. She still felt no remorse or guilt at her actions in accelerating her husband's passing, just a huge sense of relief. It was a secret she would carry to her grave.

But it was the events elsewhere which would shape the future of the baker and his family.

As the congregation in the Methodist church were giving their all in praise of the Lord, a young student called Gavrilo Princip in the Bosnian capital of Sarajevo, made the most of an unexpected opportunity.

June 28th happened to be a national holiday. The visiting heir-presumptive to the Austrian throne, Archduke Franz Ferdinand, and his wife were riding in an open motor-carriage through the streets of the City. A bomb had already

25

been thrown at the car but missed. Despite this, the Archduke completed his official duties, whereupon the governor of Bosnia suggested they deviate from the planned route on the return trip for safety's sake. But the lead driver in the procession took a wrong turn, the cars stopped momentarily, and at that moment the 19-year-old emerged from the shadows and fired his revolver, killing both royal passengers.

The event would warrant little more than a footnote in the local daily newspapers, and as Arthur prepared his bread for sale on Monday morning, his thoughts revolved around his flour supplies. He had spoken to Edward Buxton, the miller, that very morning following his mother's concern, but Arthur was assured that deliveries would be delivered as normal for the foreseeable future.

He was deep in thought as he mixed his ingredients in the vat ready for the oven when a friendly voice disturbed his meanderings.

"Eh up, Arthur, how be tha?"

Arthur jumped and looked around to see Wilfred in his butcher's apron stood at the baking-shed door. Arthur usually kept the door open while he was working to allow some fresh air and disperse some of the flour dust. The temperature was already reaching seventy degrees outside.

"'Ow do, Wilfred, I'm well, thanks."

"Sorry to hear about tha dad. I were going to call 'round yesterday, but mam said you would be busy."

"Aye, there were bits to do, like, sorting out me dad's things and that."

"Well, I just wanted to give my condolences, like. Do you want to join us for a drink after work?"

"Aye, we'll be finished by four today."

"Grand, I'll see tha later."

Wilfred left the baking shed and Arthur continued with his duties.

The opening of the shop at eight o'clock saw none of the chaos of Saturday. This was due in part to the return to work of the striking foundrymen. There was also a rumour that the bakery would be closed following Albert's demise. However, once it was established that the shop was indeed open for business as usual, people started to arrive in higher numbers.

Mildred had draped some black ribbon around the front door as a mark of respect, but that was the only indication of her husband's passing.

Mid-morning, Agnes had an errand to run; Arthur would briefly cover in the shop. Mildred needed her to call at the bank during her break to secure a one-fifteen meeting with the manager for her and Arthur. Then she was to go across the park to the solicitors to make a similar appointment for three o'clock; this time Arthur would not be required.

By lunchtime, Arthur had finished the day's baking, and the shelves were stocked for the afternoon trade. The bakery closed for an hour at one o'clock, as did the rest of the shops along James Street. It was eerily quiet as Grace and Agnes joined their brother in the parlour.

It was another scorching hot day again; temperatures were expected to be in the nineties according to the newspaper. It was considerably hotter in the baking shed, and Arthur washed himself down in the kitchen sink to cool off.

Having freshened up, he changed into his Sunday best ready for the visit to the bank.

The Bank of Liverpool had been on the corner of West Street and James Street since 1840. Formerly known as The Craven Bank, it changed its name after its takeover in 1906.

Like most banks, it was an impressive building. The name 'Craven Bank' could still be seen at the top of the frontage in faded script.

Arthur and Mildred left the bakery, crossed the street, and entered the bank.

The banking hall was dark and gloomy despite the bright sunshine outside. There was a cashier at one of the tills, his head down counting money. There were no other customers. Behind the counter, three staff were busy sorting cheques and adding columns of figures.

Despite its proximity, Arthur had not set foot in the bank until his father's confinement and he still felt uncomfortable; it was as though he didn't belong. In his mind, it was a place of mystery frequented by the gentry. Albert would normally settle his accounts in cash and visits to the bank were usually confined to get change for the till. Arthur continued the tradition but would also deposit surplus cash on Mondays to cover other bills. Mildred had no idea of her late husband's business affairs or financial state.

In 1914, women, generally, did not have bank accounts; they were not considered trustworthy to manage money. Those that did tended to be wealthy or well-connected; they would also need permission from their husband who would be responsible for any debts the spouse might incur.

Mildred did have her own account, however, and was known to the bank manager as a shrewd woman, so obtaining an appointment had not proved an issue.

Mildred approached the cashier, who appeared oblivious to her presence, and she rapped sharply with her knuckles on the counter in front of him.

"Mildred Marsden for Mr Boothroyd, young man," she exclaimed.

The cashier looked up and jumped to attention. "Yes,

Madam, take a seat; I'll let him know you are here."

A few minutes later, the door to the manager's office opened, and Arthur and Mildred were ushered in.

Cecil Boothroyd stood there, a squat, bespectacled man, about five-foot-three or four, dressed formally in a three-piece suit, despite the oppressive weather. Mildred nudged Arthur and he took off his cap.

"Mrs Marsden and Mr Marsden, come in and take a seat. Can I just say on behalf of The Liverpool Bank, how sorry I was to learn of your husband's passing? He has been a valued customer for many years, and his father before him, I believe, when we were still the Craven Bank."

"That's very kind, Mr Boothroyd... You've met my son Arthur, I think?"

"Not formally, no. Pleased to meet you, Mr Marsden. Taken over the baking, I hear?"

"Aye, sir," replied Arthur nervously. "Since my Dad was taken to his bed."

The pair were ushered to two seats in front of the manager's large oak desk. There was just a blotter and inkwell in the middle and to the right, an empty wooden tray. Boothroyd appeared to disappear in his large ornate chair.

"And business is brisk, it would appear... judging by the queues I saw."

"Aye, sir," replied Arthur again.

He was finding the whole experience intimidating. It was stiflingly hot and his mouth felt dry; beads of sweat were starting to form on his forehead. He could murder a glass of Taylor's best ale right now. He fidgeted in the seat, clutching his flat cap.

The manager looked at them both.

"So you have come to attend to the late Mr Marsden's affairs?"

"Yes," said Mildred. "I believe you need to see this."

She produced the death certificate from her handbag and passed it to the manager.

"Yes, thank you... I'll just get it registered. Please excuse me for a moment."

Boothroyd rose from his chair and opened an adjoining door which led directly to the bank's back office. He called one of his assistants who took the document. The manager shut the door and returned to his seat.

"What about Mr Marsden's will?" asked the manager.

"It's with Drummond Peacock, the solicitors. I'm calling there later."

"Ah, yes... we will need details of probate and then we can transfer the late Mr Marsden's assets to you as next of kin. If you need any money for funeral costs we can make this available to you."

"Thank you, that's very helpful," said Mildred.

There was more polite discussion as they waited for the administration to be completed.

"We won't be a moment," said the manager.

Sweat continued to drip down Arthur's face and he was removing it with his sleeve. He turned to his mother.

"'Appen, I'll get off, if tha don't need me anymore," said Arthur, seeing his presence was no longer required. He felt uncomfortable and was desperate for a drink.

"Yes, very well, I'll see you later."

"I'll let you out, Mr Marsden, we won't be much longer," said the manager, looking at Mildred, and he got up from his chair and escorted Arthur out.

A minute or two later, there was a knock on the inner door. The clerk handed the manager the document which had been duly registered.

"Thank you, Mrs Marsden. I think that concludes our

business; no doubt Peacock Drummond will send a copy of probate in due course."

"Yes, I will mention it to them," said Mildred.

She looked at the manager, unsure of the protocol. "Can I ask the amount of money he has here?"

"Why, of course, Mrs Marsden. Let me see." He picked up a ledger sheet from his desk.

"Five hundred and forty-eight pounds three shillings and sixpence."

"How much...?" It was an exclamation more than a question but the manager repeated. Mildred quickly composed herself, not wishing to disclose her surprise at such a large sum.

Mildred left the bank, still reeling at the amount of money at her husband's disposal. She couldn't understand why he had left them in poverty all these years.

The solicitor's premises were the other side of the park. There was a row of smart Victorian townhouses overlooking the green, inappropriately known as Rotten Row, and the solicitor's address was number one. The remaining properties also housed professional tenants. A cobbled road serviced the premises. Mildred had an appointment with the senior partner, Nevil Drummond, himself. As Mildred made the short journey along the footpath traversing the park, she couldn't help noticing the number of people making the most of the unusually hot weather. Some men had even taken off their waistcoats.

The offices were stone-built on two floors. Each floor had two large wooden lattice windows, probably five feet tall. The street-level windows had been lowered halfway to allow in some air.

Mildred walked up to the front door. A gold plaque adorned the wall to the side with the name 'Drummond Peacock, Solicitors and Commissioners for Oaths', etched in copper-plate script. There was a bell-push below it which she pressed.

The door was opened by one of the clerks, dressed in a three-piece suit, his black hair oiled down, reflecting the latest trend. He was wearing a white shirt with a detachable collar and tie, tightly knotted at his neck, and looking extremely uncomfortable on this steaming hot day.

"Mildred Marsden for Mr Drummond," she announced.

"Certainly, Madam." The young man moved to one side to allow Mildred to pass. "Please take a seat. I will let Mr Drummond know you are here."

There was a small reception area. The only female in view was working on a type-writer behind a glass screen.

The clerk knocked on the door immediately in front of them and it was opened by Nevil Drummond.

"Mrs Marsden, please do come in." said the man. The clerk opened an adjacent door and returned to the office.

Nevil Drummond was a distinguished-looking individual, as befitting a pillar of society. Tall with a prominent nose, his pate was bald, but a small half-circle of white hair ran around his head above his ears. He had a large white moustache and was wearing half-rimmed spectacles.

He led Mildred into his office. As one would expect, it was well-presented, with wood-panelled walls and a large portrait of an older man behind the solicitor's desk. To the left was one of the lattice-windows which was lowered about six inches. A butterfly had ventured in and was trying to find its way out, flapping frantically at the glass. The open window had done little to diminish the oppressive heat, but it meant the room was light without the need for additional illumination. The solicitor beckoned for Mildred to be seated and walked around to his own chair behind the desk.

"Would you like to take some tea, Mrs Marsden?"

On the desk in front of the solicitor was a tray on which stood a bone-china teapot, with matching cups and saucers, a delicate milk jug and a bowl of sugar. There were silver teaspoons and a tea strainer.

"Yes, Mr Drummond, that will be most kind."

The solicitor placed the tea strainer over the cup, poured in the tea and passed it to Mildred. "Please help yourself to sugar and milk."

Mildred applied a splash of milk; it was sparingly used in the Marsden household. Sugar was a luxury they rarely had.

"Can I just say on behalf of Drummond Peacock how sorry I was to hear of your husband's passing. He will be much missed in the community."

"Much missed in the Malt Shovel, more like," replied Mildred. "But thank you for your kind thoughts, Mr Drummond."

Mildred had her teacup and saucer in her hand as if nursing it. She lifted the cup to her mouth with her right hand. Her little finger was at ninety degrees to the rest of her fingers, as all the fine women would do.

The solicitor peered over his spectacles. He opened his desk drawer and pulled out an envelope.

"I have your late husband's will here." He opened the envelope and skim-read the contents. "The estate is straightforward enough. Everything goes to you, including the freehold of the shop and bakery. He had some investments which have done rather well over the years. Your late husband has left you and your family well-provided for. You should be quite secure financially; I'm pleased to say."

Mildred nearly dropped her tea, but just about maintained

her composure. Drummond noticed the reaction.

"You seem surprised, Mrs Marsden."

"Albert always looked after the money; I have no complaints." She took another sip from her cup; her hands were shaking. A drop of tea fell from the bottom and landed in the saucer.

"We have also been holding a deed box which your late husband kept here for safe-keeping. We don't have the key, of course. Did you by any chance come across one when you were going through his things?"

"Yes, as it happened, I did, but I had no idea what it opened. It was in his wallet together with his money."

"Do you have it with you?"

Mildred put down her cup on the tray, opened her handbag, and took out her purse. There were several pound notes neatly folded in one of the compartments and numerous coins which had been transferred from her husband's wallet. She removed the key.

The solicitor took it from her and placed it on the desk in front of him.

"Just one moment."

There was a second door to his office. The solicitor got up and opened it and spoke to someone.

"It's in our safe; one of my clerks will bring it."

Drummond returned to his seat and continued to scan the will. "I need to discuss some of these investments with you in light of the international situation."

"What do you mean?"

"Most of the stocks are trading companies and given the present situation in Europe, I think it might be wise to transfer them into Government Bonds."

"I will leave it to your discretion, Mr Drummond; I have no knowledge of such things."

"No, quite," replied the solicitor.

There was a knock on the door and the clerk entered with the black metal deed box; the name Marsden was painted in white on the side. He put it on the table in front of the solicitor and left. The top was covered in dust. Drummond tutted. "Sorry about the condition, Mrs Drummond. It has not been opened for some years."

Drummond picked up the key and opened it. Mildred stayed in her seat watching the solicitor as he took out the contents and placed them on the desk.

"Hmm, these are the share certificates it would seem. We will need to go through and list them."

He showed Mildred a wad of parchments bound by a ribbon.

There was another large bundle similarly tied. "Yes, these are the deeds to the shop by the look of it."

He also placed them on the desk and peered inside. "There are some letters here..."

He took out the items. There were about thirty letters encased again in a ribbon, all in the same handwriting; just addressed to Albert Marsden. There were no stamps, so they had been delivered in person.

"Wait... There are some more deeds here." The solicitor removed another bundle. "Blossom Cottage... Oakworth."

"Oakworth? But I don't know anyone in Oakworth."

The solicitor checked the deeds. "Purchased August 19th, 1894."

"That's twenty years since."

He scanned the will once more. "Wait a minute; there's a codicil here at the end."

"A codicil?" queried Mildred.

"Yes, it's something added on to an existing will. It's dated January 1911, three years ago. I have to say, I don't remember it, but it could be that one of the clerks dealt with it."

"What does it say?" asked Mildred, her mind hardly able to take in the revelations.

"It's a bequest to… a Kitty Bluet."

"Kitty!" exclaimed Mildred.

"Yes, Miss Kitty Bluet… for five hundred pounds… and the property known as Blossom Cottage, Oakworth." He peered over his glasses. "You know this woman?"

"Yes, indeed I do." She looked anxious; she fiddled with her handbag, which was on her lap. "It was a dreadful scandal. She was our shop assistant many years ago around the time our Grace was born. She was with child and left. I had no idea what happened to her. We never talked about it, Albert and me."

Mildred was considering various scenarios, but certain events were beginning to make sense. For the moment, she would keep her own counsel. She was desperately trying to stay calm.

"So what happens next?" she asked.

"Well, as executors, it will be our responsibility to apply your late husband's wishes in accordance with the will. I will arrange for the deeds of the bakery, and the shares to be transferred into your name. As I was saying, it might be a good time to review the portfolio."

"Whatever you say, Mr Drummond. I will leave it up to you entirely."

"Very well, I will get the paperwork underway… Oh, have you brought the death certificate?"

"Yes," said Mildred. She produced the document from her handbag and passed it to the solicitor.

"I will just get this registered… You know you will need to go to the Town Hall with this?"

"Yes, I'm going there after we have concluded our business."

Drummond got up from his chair, opened the door to the office and called to one of his clerks.

"It won't take a moment, Mrs Marsden. Can I get you some more tea?"

"Thank you, no."

There was an uneasy silence as they waited for the routine to be completed by the clerk. Mildred was deep in thought; Drummond continued to scan the will. A few minutes later, the young man returned with the death certificate, which was returned to Mildred.

Drummond stood up. "Thank you for calling Mrs Marsden. Again, please accept my condolences. I will write to you shortly."

"Thank you for your time Mr Drummond; I will leave everything in your hands. Oh, I'll take the letters if you don't mind."

"Yes, of course." He handed Mildred the small bundle, and she opened her handbag and dropped it in.

Mildred left the solicitors and stood on the pavement outside. She waited for a moment as a pony and trap went by, the cobbles making it difficult for horse and passenger, then she crossed over the road. It was still very warm; many women were fanning themselves vigorously. There was another footpath that led through the park; the Town Hall was opposite. She checked the time by the clock on the top of the building; three fifty-five; they closed at four-thirty. She would have enough time. Her mind, though, was in a fuzz.

She would hardly remember walking into the grand reception area of the Municipal centre. It was busy with flat-caps and ladies' hats bobbing together like flotsam on the incoming tide. That's how Mildred could see it, like some dream. There was a sign, 'Birth, Deaths and Marriages', directing her upstairs to the first floor. She ascended a wide staircase and followed the signs to the right, eventually arriving at the appropriate department. A clerk greeted her politely; she handed him the death certificate. He went away, then a few minutes later, returned and handed the document back.

She had one more errand before she headed back to the bakery.

Along the street from the Town Hall stood the offices of the Keighley News. Five minutes later, Mildred was at the reception desk.

"It's for the Obituary column," she said, solemnly to the clerk at the enquiry counter and handed in a letter detailing Albert's demise that she had written the previous evening. "Funeral's on Friday; it's all there," she said, as the man scanned the contents.

It was approaching five-thirty as Mildred returned to the bakery. Archie Slater was calling the news again. The headline on his Keighley News board said, *'Strike leaders gaoled'*.

Mildred ignored him and walked into the bakery. Grace and Agnes had cleaned and washed down. The baking shed was eerily quiet.

Upstairs in the parlour, Grace and Agnes were sewing; Arthur was reading the newspaper. The outside window was open, allowing in some air. It also provided an entrance to insects, and numerous houseflies zig-zagged around the room, settling on a surface then flying away again.

"Shut that window Arthur, the place is swarming with

flies." Mildred was swishing them away with her hands.

"Aye, Mum, it's the horses next door."

"Yes, as maybe but they're full of germs. You know that."

She picked up a newspaper from the table and rolled it up, then tried to swat as many as she could, squashing them wherever they landed.

With the window shut and several flies succumbing to Mildred's frustrations, she retired to the bedroom.

"Grace, Agnes, can you start on tea; I'm going to be busy for a few minutes?" she said as she walked down the corridor to her bedroom.

She changed out of her 'Sunday best' and hung the clothing on a peg to air; it was damp with sweat.

Wearing more comfortable attire, she sat at her dressing table and opened her handbag. She took out the bundle of letters, put them down in front of the mirror and stared at them.

Slowly, she undid the ribbon. The small pile expanded as the tension from the fastening was released. She picked up the first one and opened it.

It was not dated; it looked more like a quickly scribbled note.

'My dearest Albert, Mrs English is out this evening and I will be alone from seven-thirty. I do hope you can get away. Much love, Kitty x.'

Mildred dropped the letter; her mind returning to twenty years earlier. Kitty, she remembered, lodged above the cobblers on Peel Street. Emily English was the landlady. Her recollection of Mrs English was hazy, but she was a very dominant woman and would certainly not allow any trysts in her establishment.

Mildred reached for the bottom letter.

'My dearest Albert, I am deeply grateful for everything

you have done for me. I could not have wished for more. I know we will not be able to see each other again and it is only right that I move away. Blossom Cottage sounds very nice. I will bring up our child to be God-fearing and respectful, I will make you proud whether it's a girl or boy. I will never forget you and your kindness. Yours forever. Kitty x'.

The writing was smudged as though some water had dropped on the page.

Chapter Three

Mildred said very little after returning from her meeting with the solicitor. As soon as the evening meal was finished, she retired to her bedroom; she didn't feel like speaking to anyone. She lay awake for hours contemplating the day's revelations.

She had no idea what to do about Kitty. Her natural instincts were to let sleeping dogs lie; after all, it was in the past and couldn't be changed. But there was a part of her that was curious. The revelation that her husband had a mistress did not come as a complete surprise. Twenty years ago, he had been an attractive man, despite his brutish behaviour. But a child? Now that was unexpected.

It was one of those nights where it seemed there was just no air; it was stiflingly hot. Mildred had lowered the window, but it seemed to make little difference. Flies buzzed around the room. The heat, coupled with the thoughts surrounding her husband's infidelity, had made sleep difficult.

A distant clock chimed the hour, five am. It was daylight.

She could hear Arthur moving about and she got out of bed; the new day had started. It was pointless trying to sleep now.

Arthur was in the parlour, eating a slice of bread at the table.

"Eh up, mam, I hope I didn't disturb you."

"No, Arthur, I was awake. I'll make us some tea and bring it down."

"Aye, that's grand, thanks. I best be going; t'miller will be here any minute." He tied up his work overalls. "You were quiet last night, is there owt wrong?"

"No, Arthur, I just needed to be on my own, but tonight I do need to speak to you and the girls."

"Aye, right you are, sithee later."

By five-twenty a.m., the temperature in the baking shed was already well over a hundred degrees. Arthur's order was for just four bags of flour today; Tuesdays tended to be less busy. He waited by the gate for the miller's truck. Birdsong filled the air as starlings and house sparrows battled for some sort of supremacy – the pecking order. In the distance, industrial noises could be heard; jack-hammers from the foundry, and the rattle-tattle of the weaving frames in the mills. The factories bought wealth and prosperity to the chosen few and misery and drudgery to the many who laboured fourteen hours a day for a pittance.

Later that morning, Arthur's predictions proved to be correct; the customer queue was steady rather than manic as it had been the previous day.

He took the second batch of bread into the shop around midday. Grace and Agnes were on duty, but the shop was empty.

"Are you still going to your meeting tonight?" he said.

Grace looked at him. "Of course, Annie Kenney's speaking. Should be a good turnout."

"Well, mind you take care; Edward Buxton says there might be trouble."

"Aye, we're hoping so... 'Appen we'll be in t'papers. It all helps our cause."

Arthur ignored the comment; she was becoming too opinionated.

"Will that Minnie Glyde be going?"

"Of course, she's still our secretary."

"Ney, she's nowt but a wool-winder."

"Aye, you say that, but you mark my words; change is going to come."

Arthur looked at her, taken aback by her venom. "What do you want the vote for anyhows? You know nowt about politics."

Grace replied with prompt contradiction. "I know as much as you, Arthur Marsden. The only opinions you have are those of your drinking pals from the Malt Shovel; you have not a thought of your own."

Arthur knew better than to get into any sort of philosophical argument with her; deep-down, he admired the passion of his elder sister.

"Aye, well, you be careful, that's all I'm saying." He left and returned to the baking shed to mix the next batch of bread.

That afternoon, Arthur closed the bakery at four o'clock; there was very little bread left on the shelves and even fewer customers. Wilfred Stonehouse was waiting for him outside. Arthur went upstairs to his bedroom and changed into a shirt and trousers. He would wear one of his father's waistcoats that was still hanging in the wardrobe along with the rest of Albert's clothes. It was a little on the generous side, but it looked quite fashionable, so Arthur would put up with the ill-fit. Not that Arthur was interested in fashion; it was a tribal thing among his pals. He would not be seen dead in the flannels and open-necked collars of the gentry.

As Arthur had feared, the main topic of conversation in the Malt Shovel was about that evening's Women's Social and Political Union meeting. He could hear it at the bar as men came for their ale. Thomas, the landlord, nodded sagely but would not be drawn on an opinion about women's suffrage. Not with the indomitable Maisy in earshot.

There was a hooligan element that frequented the alehouse, and it was obvious they were hell-bent on causing trouble. Arthur said nothing as he stood at the bar with Wilfred, the main discourse being the weather. Neither could remember such a hot period in their lifetime.

Arthur left the alehouse around five o'clock, and he and Wilfred walked back to the bakery. The atmosphere was still oppressive, the heat hardly dissipating despite the late hour. The hot sun had caused horse urine to evaporate from the streets, creating a nauseating acidic smell that hung in the air. Some more well-to-do women held posies to their nose.

Outside the shop, Archie Slater was giving his usual clarion call, pleading for more sales of his newspapers.

"Get tha news, get tha news."

His voice rose in the light breeze and carried along James Street and over the road into the park, cutting through the noise of the thoroughfare. A tram went by, packed with workers from the nearby wool mills; it stopped opposite the bakery disgorging many of its passengers.

Wilfred said his goodbyes and Arthur purchased his evening newspaper. The headline on Archie's board said, 'Suffragette leader to speak tonight'.

Mildred had prepared a meal of rabbit stew and potatoes with bottled damsons to follow, and the girls were setting the table where they would all sit to eat. Once dinner was served, Mildred had their attention.

"I need to tell you something." The children stopped eating and looked at her expectantly. "As you know, I saw Mr Drummond yesterday about your father's will." She paused to consider how she would express herself. "It seems he has left us well-provided for." She used the same words her solicitor had done.

"What do tha mean, mam?" said Arthur.

"Mr Drummond told me your father has invested wisely, and once everything is settled, we should be able to live comfortably. He is going to arrange an income for us."

"So, we don't need the bakery, mam?" said Arthur.

"No, but we must keep the business going; people depend on us. We don't know what's around the corner. I do want to arrange for you girls to have some new clothes though; you've had to make-do for long enough. And you, Arthur, can get yourself down to Cappers and get yourself a new pair of boots. You can see your feet in those you're wearing."

Arthur looked at his mother then at his feet and smiled. "Aye true enough, but 'appen they'll wear a bit longer."

Like many women, Mildred had learned the skills of a seamstress; most of the clothes that the girls were wearing were the result of her hand. They were passed down the line as the children developed; nothing was wasted. Even Arthur's clothes had once belonged to his father; stitched to Arthur's frame as he grew. His pants were too short for his gangliness, almost wearing like britches.

"Things are going to change." she continued. "I'm also going to make enquiries about the electric lighting; they say it is so much brighter than gas lamps. We could even get one of those telephones. It would be of use for the business."

"Sounds costly, mam," said Arthur.

"Aye, but we'll manage."

The girls talked animatedly about this revelation and the fact that they could have new clothes. The excitement was like Christmas morn.

By seven o'clock, Grace was ready for her meeting

wearing her 'Sunday best'. She looked into the bedroom mirror and unthinkingly cocked her head to one side. The reflection was pleasing and she retired from the bedroom into the parlour.

Agnes was continuing her stitching, Mildred reading. The two youngest were sat quietly playing in the corner. Arthur was slumped over the newspaper.

He looked at Grace. "Eh up, Grace, you look fine you do... but best tha take care tonight."

"Aye, Arthur, don't go worrying; I'll be safe enough. They reckon there could be five hundred going tonight."

"Aye, but many with trouble in their heads, especially with a brew or two inside the'selves."

Grace gave the sigh of someone who didn't want to listen.

She said her goodbyes and left the bakery. Arthur's warnings still echoed in her head, but she would pay no heed.

Annie Kenney, although not as famous as the Pankhursts, was nevertheless a prominent figure in the Suffragette movement and had been an inspiration to Grace for some while. Earlier that year, she had been imprisoned for her views and force-fed whilst on hunger strike. Only now was she well enough to speak in public.

The meeting was programmed to be chaired by Norah Dacre-Fox, the WSPU general secretary, who would be travelling from London with Miss Kenney with the sole purpose of appealing to the women of Yorkshire.

The venue, Central Hall, was just a short walk across the park and close to the Town Hall. It was another Methodist property, but thoughts of religion would not be at the forefront of minds tonight.

It was another warm, balmy evening as Grace started to walk across the park. The smell of horses still lingered. The trees were at their finest – sycamore, beech, horse-chestnut, even a solitary oak. The benches under the bowers were populated by elderly gentlemen with walking sticks, pipe-smoking, passing the time, and watching the world go by. Grace noticed others on the move; women in their finery, heading in the direction of Central Hall.

At the end of the walkway traversing the park, Grace reached the main road. The area was buzzing with people. The building was just opposite the park exit and queues had formed at the entrance snaking back along the pavement. Grace dodged her way across the busy thoroughfare and joined one of the lines. She waved to one or two people she knew. Trams and trolleybuses continued to spew passengers onto the pavement inflating the queues even further.

Back across the road on the edge of the park, a more sinister group was beginning to emerge. Maybe twenty or thirty men, youths mostly; some holding bottles of ale, chanting unflattering slogans.

A police vehicle drew up alongside the queue, and Grace watched as eight officers with truncheons drawn, appeared from the back. They crossed the road and started to remonstrate with the group, demanding that they disperse. Most of the youths slunk away into the shadows of the park and regrouped; the chanting continued, echoing among the greenery.

Eventually, the doors of the hall opened, and the waiting women pushed forward determined to get a seat. Inside it was mayhem, as the audience jostled to get a chair. Grace managed to get seated and looked around; there was not a spare space. Women were standing two abreast around the sides, eager to hear the speakers.

At the front of the hall, a stage had been erected. On top stood a bare wooden table in front of four kitchen chairs which looked as though they had been supplied from someone's house. Behind the make-shift podium were several banners designed to inspire the audience – '*Votes for Women, NOW!*', '*Deeds not words*', '*Thro' thick and thin, when we begin*', '*Arise! Go forth and conquer*'.

Grace soaked up the emotion around her; it gave her tingles inside. Goosebumps ran down her arms, despite the incredible heat. Many women were fanning themselves with leaflets that had been distributed by supporters at the hall entrance. It was inspiring stuff to an impressionable twenty-year-old.

It was almost eight o'clock. The audience was getting impatient at the delay, and a crescendo of noise echoed around the cavernous hall. More chanting could be heard from outside, soprano, female voices from those unable to find room inside.

Then there was a great cacophony as the guest speaker and her small entourage took to the stage. Hoots and chants, slogans unfamiliar to Grace rose from the gathering. The lady-chair, as she was known, raised her hands as a gesture for silence. Grace was on tenterhooks waiting for Annie Kenney to speak, the anticipation in itself was electrifying. Her pulse increased; if truth be known, she needed to relieve herself.

Norah Dacre-Fox waited for the noise to abate and then started her own oratory. Minnie Glyde, the local secretary, was also on the top table and was seated proudly next to Ms Kenney. Rapturous applause rang out at every positive statement; it felt similar to the variety halls where the support acts warmed the audience for the main event. By the time she announced the guest speaker, the listeners were in her thrall.

If it were possible to lift the roof with sound, then this

was the occasion, as Annie Kenney rose unsteadily to speak. Accounts of her suffering during her incarceration had spread around the country, and she was greeted like a Messiah.

Grace was on her feet with the rest of the followers.

Annie spoke for about ten minutes; you could hear a pin drop as she recounted her experiences at the hands of her gaolers.

Then Grace noticed movement to her left. A man, scruffy in appearance, and ungainly in movement, clearly the worse for ale, was walking towards the stage. He stood in front of the dais, took out a bag of flour and hurled it at Annie Kenney; it landed on her chest and scattered its contents in all directions. Then another protagonist of similar appearance and, presumably, background, appeared behind the flour thrower. This time the man was carrying a large paper bag filled with horse manure. He grabbed a handful, then another, then another and threw it at the three women in turn.

There was pandemonium. Women rushed to the men, the anger palpable, seething, a basic instinct of a mother protecting her brood. Like a pack of hungry wolves on prey, they descended on the men. Parasols were being used, not as clubs but as swords, poking, prodding, gouging. Then more noise. Police whistles.

The speaker and her two companions were quickly ushered away from the stage. Inside the hall, more police entered trying to make their way to the stricken attackers. Truncheons landed randomly, like an explorer clearing a jungle path. Hats were knocked to the ground and trodden into the floor. Heads were broken; blood was spilt.

Grace was experiencing a different emotion - fear. There was a primaeval need to escape, fight or flight; she would fight but for the absence of a weapon. She saw friends being felled to the ground by hefty blows. A couple of policemen had reached the stricken men and were trying to escort them out of the hall, barely conscious. They themselves were coming under attack and fended off blows with vicious swipes of their billy-clubs.

Women were fleeing in all directions like a stampeding herd. Chairs were overturned, women prone on the floor, devoid of movement but not of life. Grace just watched and then felt a blow to her shoulder. She winced in pain and turned around. A constable with hate in his eyes, or perhaps it was fear, aimed another blow. Instinctively, Grace moved her arm to protect her head.

"Get off, leave me be. I've done nowt wrong," she bellowed at the man.

His nostrils seem to be extended like a stallion; spittle sprayed from his mouth. Grace ducked as more blows came down on her, but she managed to crawl away as the policeman found another innocent victim to bludgeon.

She eventually reached the exit, stooping, crawling, clambering over other women with the same mind. Blood was oozing down the side of her head, her hat long-gone. Her forearms bore nasty defensive welts, painful to the touch.

She stood, then suddenly she felt hands around her waist; then moving higher, above her corsetry.

"Come on, my little beauty, you're going for a ride." It was another policeman; rough-looking with a large dark moustache. She could feel his hands on her breasts as he dragged her to the pavement outside the hall where a police-van was waiting, its doors open. Several other girls were sat inside, all bearing the scars of this uneven battle.

"Nice tits, tha has," said the brute and laughed, as he forced Grace up the four-rung wooden steps that had been placed to allow access into the wagon. Twenty women had been crammed inside before the heavy door was forced shut.

The vehicle drew away.

Through the barred window at the back, Grace could see the brutality continuing as more women were forced to run the gauntlet of batons. More prison wagons arrived to be loaded with protestors. The group of men had reappeared from the park and were laughing and heckling at the scene being played out before them.

Back in the parlour, by nine-thirty, the two youngest girls were in bed. Arthur, as he was accustomed to doing, was scanning the newspaper. Mildred was reading quietly under the gas-lamp, although her mind was elsewhere. Agnes continued her embroidery, which all the girls enjoyed doing; although it was Molly who was showing real talent. The ambient light was beginning to fade as darkness descended. In the distance, they could hear shouts and screams. The noise had begun earlier, rhythmic cries of protestors; a cacophony that echoed around the empty streets, drowning out the rattle of the trams as they made their way along James Street. But now the sounds had changed, the timbre different, screams, shouts, whistles.

Mildred looked at Arthur. "Can you hear that, Arthur?"

He looked up from his newspaper. "Aye, mam."

"Something's wrong. I'm worried about our Grace; can you go and see if you can find her?"

"Aye, mam, will do." He got up from the table and fetched his jacket and cap from the bedroom.

"Don't fret, mam; I'll find her."

Outside the bakery, people were milling about. The bus stops were busy with people awaiting trams to take them home. The bakery door clanged as Arthur walked out to the street. The noise was much louder now.

A friendly face approached him, crossing the road from the park.

"Eh up, Arthur, I was just coming to find tha."

"'Ow do, Wilfred, what's about? There's a lot of noise t'other side of the park."

"Aye, it's them protestors, up at Central Hall; there's been a riot."

"A riot?" repeated Arthur. "What d' tha mean?"

"I was just talking with Peter Granger, from t'grocery; he says there's all sorts going on. Police have been arresting the women. Scraps going on all over. He says he saw your Grace being carried off."

"Our Grace... how...? Where?"

"I don't know, but I suppose it will be the police station. What do tha want to do, Arthur?"

"I need to find her, Wilfred. I best go there, see what's happening."

"Aye, I'll come with tha, if you want company."

"Aye, 'appen it'd be most welcome, Wilfred."

The pair strode off up James Street. With a stout march, it would take them a good fifteen minutes to reach the imposing offices of the local constabulary on North Street.

Arthur had never been inside a police station. They had an air, an unmistakable air, one of fear and uncertainty. Why he should fear such a place, he didn't know; it was something embedded in his subconscious. Police stations represented incarceration, the removal of basic freedoms. He thought himself an honest person, fearful and respectful of the law; the thought of being taken to the police station filled him with dread.

Yet here he was, quickened of pace, heading in that

direction.

As the pair reached the building, the sight before them was unexpected, and they stopped for a moment to survey the scene.

Three police 'Black Marias' were parked outside surrounded by a dozen officers with their truncheons drawn. They were supervising the transfer of women from the vehicles into the police station. Every now and then, a degree of encouragement was issued with a swift deployment of the baton. The buttock area seemed a favourite place which resulted in hoots of laughter from the supervising officers.

Several of the women, Arthur noticed, were blooded; others were crying. Some were belligerent and resisting their gaolers and became the targets of the swinging truncheons. This was not the constabulary's finest hour.

Arthur just looked at Wilfred in disbelief.

They waited for a few minutes for the melee to die down before walking closer to the building. The officers were inside, the vehicles empty and unattended.

Cautiously, the lads skirted the three wagons and reached the entrance. They could hear the cacophony inside. Raised voices, language not usually associated with women of class, for that's what many were, not just spinning Jennies from the wool mills. A collective sisterhood, drawn with one accord.

Arthur and Wilfred stopped at the entrance and waited for those inside to be taken to another part of the building, presumably the cells.

The reception area was still populated by probably twenty folk, some seated, some standing, around the perimeter of the office with glum, concerned expressions; no-one appeared to be talking. Arthur and Wilfred walked in, making eye-contact with some of those waiting. One or two nodded in recognition; customers who Arthur couldn't recall by name.

They approached the officer manning the desk; his head was down concentrating. They stood for a moment and watched, not wanting to disturb the man.

In front of the constable was a ledger book in which he appeared to be logging names from a paper list. He picked up the paper several times and squinted at the pencilled script then went back to his pen and ink.

He was a large man with impressive whiskers which turned up at the margins. His uniform was specked with what looked like spittle. His undertaking was being carried out with a degree of pride and care. The deliberate flow of his ink-charged nib completed with a flourish.

He looked up, suddenly aware of a presence.

"What can I do for thee?" he said, looking at Arthur who was stood a little in front of Wilfred. The officer's demeanour was intimidating.

"Ah'm looking for someone," replied Arthur anxiously.

"Aye? And who might that be?" replied the officer menacingly.

"Grace Marsden," replied Arthur.

The officer scanned his list, moving up the column; then turned back a page and repeated the process.

"Marsden, you say?"

"Aye," repeated Arthur.

He flicked the page back a further time, then stopped, halfway down the column of names.

"Aye, here we are…" He looked up. "She's been arrested; she's in custody."

"On what charge?" enquired Arthur, shock etched over his face.

"Riotous assembly," replied the officer, gravely.

"Riotous assembly? Nah, that can't be right. She's gentle

as a kitten, our Grace."

"That's what it says here, so it must be right."

Arthur thought for a moment. "What will happen?"

"She'll go before the magistrate tomorrow, be fined two pounds and released if she can afford the fine. Otherwise, she will be gaoled for two weeks."

"What time will she be in court?"

"Difficult to say... there be two hundred of 'em. I hear there's an early sitting at eight o'clock."

"Aye, right you are. Thank you for your time; we'll be off then."

Arthur doffed his cap, believing good manners were appropriate. The constable looked surprised at the civility; the first respect anyone had shown that evening.

Arthur and Wilfred headed back to James Street, talking nineteen-to-the-dozen about the evening's events.

"What'll tha say to tha mam?" said Wilfred.

"I'll just tell her what we've seen. 'Appen she'll go to the magistrates tomorrow to pay Grace's fine."

"Aye, it's a rum do, sure enough," replied Wilfred.

They reached the butcher's shop and stopped. Wilfred put his key in the door but then turned to Arthur.

"I were just thinking, do tha fancy t'Picture House this week?"

"Aye, can do... What's on?"

"'*The touch of a child*', it said in t'news."

"What's it about? Sounds more like our Grace would fancy."

"Aye, you may be right... Anyhow, it's on all week, but the Picture House is closed next week for repairs."

"Aye, I'll give it some thought... Thanks for thar company tonight. Sithee tomorrow, Wilfred."

"Aye, Arthur, sithee."

Wilfred unlocked the butcher's shop door and disappeared inside.

Arthur continued the short distance to the bakery, still thinking about what he should say to his mother. She had just lost her husband; she didn't need more anxiety, but the truth needed to be told.

He let himself in and headed upstairs to the parlour. It was just Mildred, still seated under her lamp, reading; the three girls had gone to bed.

Mildred looked up and dropped her book to her lap.

"What's happened? Where's our Grace?" she exclaimed, seeing Arthur unaccompanied.

"Don't tha fret, mam, there's been some trouble up at Central Hall."

"What trouble? What's happened?"

"I don't know full story, but Grace is in t'police station."

"Police station?"

"Aye, she were arrested, along with a few others."

"So, what was she doing to get arrested?"

"I don't rightly know, mam. 'Appen it were a mistake, I think. I went to the police station, me and Wilfred, and spoke to one of the constabulary and he said she'll be before Bench in t'morning."

"Oh, dear God!" exclaimed Mildred. "I feel quite faint. Get me some of your father's brandy, quick."

Arthur went to one of the kitchen cupboards and retrieved the brandy and a glass, then returned to the parlour.

With Grace unavailable, Wednesday was going to be difficult in the shop. It was seven-thirty, the bread was ready for the shelves; Molly had been excused school for the morning and would cover for the absent Grace.

Upstairs in the parlour, Agnes was already in her serving attire and was helping Molly, who was trying to fit into Grace's uniform. Mildred had supplied clips to bring the outfit to the appropriate size.

Mildred's mind though was elsewhere. Grace was a concern right enough; she would go to the Magistrates this morning and pay her fine. Then, she had other things to do, a trip to Oakworth.

By eight o'clock, all was ready, and Molly and Agnes were stacking the shelves with bread ready for the morning's trade. Agnes was explaining the workings of the cash register. Just two customers were waiting outside as Arthur opened the store with the familiar clang. Molly stood behind her allotted half of the counter space, looking a little anxious. Agnes was giving her encouragement.

With the customers now being served, Arthur was about to return to his baking duties when a man in the uniform of the postal service appeared at the door proffering a letter.

"For Mrs Marsden, Arthur," said the man who handed it to him and went on his way.

Arthur acknowledged and stared at the elaborate script, a testament to the art of calligraphy.

"I'll just take this up to mam," shouted Arthur to the girls, just as three more customers entered the shop.

Mildred was getting ready for her journey to the Magistrates Court. She had soon discovered Albert's secret cache, where he kept most of his money. She had seen him at one of the drawers on several occasions, and he always behaved surreptitiously, as if she had caught him in the act of something wrongful. Occasionally, he would become aggressive. "What are you staring at, woman? Go about thar business," he would shout. She could still hear his voice.

He was not an avaricious man but careful and miserly; the tin box behind the false back of the drawer revealed the extent of that shrewdness. A hundred pounds or thereabouts, a pretty penny that Mildred had plans for.

She had taken five pounds for today's business; first a visit to the Magistrates Court, then the other journey which she had in mind.

Arthur entered the parlour and handed his mother the letter.

"I'll be off to the Magistrates shortly, Arthur. Can you see if you can find me a cabbie?"

Arthur looked surprised; he couldn't remember his mother ever taking a taxi before; it was always a tram or trolleybus for longer journeys, or, most usually, a walk.

"Aye, mam." Arthur left the parlour to do his mother's bidding.

Mildred looked at herself in the mirror and straightened her hat. Then she took a knife from the table and slit opened the letter.

It was headed 'Peacock Drummond, Solicitors and Commissioners for Oaths' in Copperplate lettering, '1 Rotten Row, Keighley, in the West Riding of Yorkshire'.

Beneath that in typed characters – *In the Estate of Albert Henry Marsden deceased'*.

There was a message of condolence from Nevil Drummond and then followed a detailed inventory of her husband's estate. Mildred's eyes were immediately drawn to the total at the bottom. She felt her legs go and had to hold onto the table to stop herself from falling to the floor.

Eighteen thousand, four hundred and twenty-three pounds twelve shillings and sixpence, and that excluded the bakery. At a time when the average daily wage for a man was two shillings and sixpence, it was a substantial sum of money.

She stared at the figure; she wondered how he had amassed such a fortune. Some, she knew, was from his own father, who was also foxy when it came to money. There were also details of pending transactions which would transfer the stocks into Government Bonds.

Her attention was disturbed by Arthur's shouting to alert Mildred that the cabbie was waiting outside.

Mildred folded the letter and returned it to the envelope, then into her handbag. She checked her hat once more, then left the parlour.

Mildred said goodbye to the girls, Arthur was back in the shed, and she left the shop. The taxi was waiting right outside the bakery. It was a grand vehicle, square-shaped with open-spoked wheels and gaslights on the side of the driver's window. Leaving the engine running, the driver escorted Mildred to the rear door, and she got in. There was a distinctive smell of leather and petrol.

It took less than ten minutes to make the journey, not much shorter than a brisk walk, but Mildred intended to make a statement after a life of penny-pinching and going without.

She paid the driver the sixpence and was helped from the carriage. For the first time in her life, she felt like somebody.

Chapter Four

The entrance to the Magistrates Court was packed with people trying to enter; Mildred joined the queue. All around her were concerned faces, nervous talking and gabbling, as she waited her turn to be allowed in. Once in the reception area, she had a better idea of what was happening. The prisoners were being led into court six at a time, asked to make a plea, and then sentenced accordingly, along the lines of the constable's description to Arthur the previous evening.

All the women had pleaded guilty but refused to pay the fine; thus, they were returned to the cells.

Mildred waited in the public gallery for Grace, but it was over an hour before her daughter's name was called and the charge read. She was led into the courtroom up a flight of stairs behind the dock with five other women escorted by a policeman.

Mildred watched her in the dock standing together with her co-defendants. Mildred squinted in an attempt to see her more clearly. There appeared to be blood on the side of her face; her hair was dishevelled, and she was not wearing her hat.

"How do you plead?" asked the foreman to each of the women in turn.

"Guilty," replied Grace when addressed.

Mildred gasped again.

"Very well, your plea has been noted, and you are hereby sentenced to a fine of two guineas," said the Magistrate.

"I refuse to pay," shouted Grace defiantly.

"Very well, you will be sentenced to a term of imprisonment for the duration of two weeks from today."

Mildred stood up.

"No, wait, that is my daughter; I will pay the fine."

She had everyone's attention; a low murmur echoed among the gathering.

The Magistrate stared from the bench at the interruption. He was wearing half-rimmed eye-glasses and peered over the top into the distance.

"Mrs Marsden... the baker's wife? Is that you?"

"Aye, sir, and that's my headstrong and foolish daughter. I need her in my shop right now; these are hard times." She rustled around in her handbag, took out two-pound notes and held them up towards the bench. "I can pay."

"Your credit is not in doubt Mrs Marsden, but let me say, your daughter's behaviour is."

"Aye, sir, and you have my word it will be the last. She's nowt but a slip, barely twenty; what do they know, eh?"

"Yes, Mrs Marsden. Very well, on condition that you control your daughter in the future, then that will be the end of it. Pay the clerk on your way out."

The Magistrate turned to Grace; her defiance had evaporated at the sight of her mother.

"Miss Marsden, if you are before me again, you will not be spared a visit to Armley. Do I make myself clear?"

Grace looked at the Magistrate like a fawn caught in a beam. "Aye, sir," she managed to whisper.

He slammed down his gavel with an enormous crack making everyone jump, such was the drama being played out. "Next!" he bellowed.

"Leave me be," protested Grace as a constable grabbed her arm to escort her from the dock to the side door. The remaining five girls returned down the staircase.

Grace stopped, calmed herself and raised her head in a last act of defiance before exiting the courtroom.

Overnight, she had been imprisoned with ten other

women in a cell designed for no more than two. She had been seated with her back to the wall for most of the time with little chance of sleep. The only other furnishing was a bucket in the middle of the room. During conversations it was clear that many of her fellow incarcerates were much more militant and were describing tales of past meetings with a degree of pride, swearing to refuse to pay the fine and embark on a hunger strike whilst in gaol. Grace had been inspired to follow this example but had bowed to family pressures.

Mildred called at the cashier's window, paid the fine and was waiting for her outside the door to the courtroom.

There was no immediate show of emotion as Grace appeared. "Come, let's get you away from this place; you don't belong here."

There was reluctant acquiescence as Mildred took Grace's arm and they left the courthouse.

Outside was busy. Two Black Marias with barred windows were parked adjacent to the side exit; one was already loaded with prisoners being transferred to the gaol in Leeds, its engine running. The women were chanting protest slogans. The other wagon was waiting for its passengers. Grace felt a sense of guilt, seeing her 'sisters' in their cause célèbre being taken away.

Mildred looked about and raised her arm to attract a vacant taxi parked opposite the entrance. The driver acknowledged the gesture. He put down his newspaper, started the engine with a swift swing of the handle, and turned the cab around to the waiting passengers.

"Hey, mam, what's us doing with a cabbie? We can't afford one of them; we can walk."

"Now watch your words, my lady, you have done enough

already causing your mother so much worry."

Grace reacted defensively, realising she had not heard the last of her recent trauma.

The sun was halfway to its zenith and its rays reflected from the glistening chrome of the vehicle's shining carriage-work as it pulled up. The driver got out and opened the door for the women to enter. Inside it was hot and uncomfortable.

"Marsden's Bakery, James Street," said Mildred authoritatively, as the driver closed the door.

As the cab pulled away, Mildred started to examine Grace's wounds more closely. There was congealed blood down the side of her face and nasty bruises on her arms.

"Oh my, Grace, what have they done to you?"

Grace suddenly started crying, the emotion of the last twelve hours overtaking her,

"There, there," said Mildred. "Don't fret so; you are with your family now. Let's get you home, and you can tell me all about it."

The cab made its way down James Street. Mid-morning, and the thoroughfare was buzzing with activity. The shops were busy, trade brisk. Trolleybuses were filled with people going about their business; the community appeared to be thriving.

They pulled up outside the bakery, and the driver opened the door, allowing Grace and Mildred to alight. Grace had, by now, composed herself.

Mildred paid the man and led Grace into the bakery. There was only one customer, being served by Agnes. Molly was tidying around sweeping breadcrumbs off the floor. She saw Grace and immediately dropped her broom. "Grace, Grace, how be tha? We've been so worried." She raised the wooden flap that allowed access behind the counter.

Mildred and Grace walked through. "What's happened to tha?" said Molly with concern, seeing the blood on the side of Grace's face. Agnes finished serving her customer and joined the family group.

Arthur, hearing the commotion, came in from the baking shed. "Eh up, our Grace, we've been right bothered about tha."

"She's well now... Leave her be," said Mildred. "Let's get upstairs."

The party ascended the stairs, leaving Molly to serve the customers.

In the parlour, Grace was being overwhelmed by her concerned siblings. Arthur was looking at the wound on her head, which had raised a bruise the size of an egg.

"Who done this to tha?" asked Arthur.

"It were the constabulary," said Grace. "They were like wild animals, clubbing everyone in sight. There'll be many in t'infirmary, you mark my words."

"But why? They must've had cause," asked Arthur.

"Nay, 'appen they don't need no cause. I heard from some of the other women. They're always being attacked by the Tiggies."

"Tiggies?" enquired Arthur.

"Aye, that's what the girls call 'em. Brutes every last one of them with their club sticks."

Mildred took charge. "Right, Agnes, go back downstairs and help Molly; she can't be left on her own. Arthur get down and fetch the bath will you? I'll see to Grace."

Arthur went downstairs and retrieved the bath from the yard and returned to the parlour. "Run us some hot water, Arthur, and Grace remove your outer garments."

In a few minutes, Arthur had filled the bath with all the

hot water in the range and was topping it up with cold from a bucket.

"Arthur, go down to your baking; I'll look after Grace."

Arthur returned to the baking shed while Mildred helped Grace remove her clothes. Her arms had stiffened and she had trouble raising them over her head. There were three large bruises on her forearm where she had defended her head from the constable's blows.

As her mother bathed her, she recounted the evening. "They just came at us, mam, we was just listening to Annie Kenney; we were doing nowt wrong. Some fellows came in and threw flour at her, and that's what caused the bother. We were doing nowt wrong."

"Well, it's them that wants locking up, if you ask me."

"Aye, they did worse things too, the constabulary... Touching up the women and that, they were... me and all."

"What?!" exclaimed Mildred.

"Aye, one of them grabbed my chest, giving it a right good feel he were, and my backside."

"Oh, dear Lord, but that's terrible." Mildred looked at her with concern.

"Aye, it were, but there's nowt we can do about it. No one'll believe us against the constabulary."

"Yes, dear, unfortunately it's the way of the world."

"Aye, but why should us women suffer?"

"As I said, dear, it's the way of the world."

Half an hour later, Mildred had finished bathing Grace, and she was recovering gradually from her ordeal. Her mother had made her drink some tea, and Grace was now in bed resting.

Having sorted out that issue, Mildred had another task to

attend to.

Earlier that morning, a letter with the same elaborate script as the one delivered to Mildred had arrived at Blossom Cottage, Oakworth.

Kitty Bluet was in the kitchen when the uniformed man knocked on the door and handed her the missive. She read the envelope. It looked official; she rarely received such correspondence.

She went back to the kitchen, retrieved a knife from one of the drawers and slit it open. She removed the letter inside and started to read, then dropped to a nearby seat for fear she would fall. She read it again. She had heard that Albert had taken to his bed, but his death was still a shock. Then there was the revelation that she had benefitted from the will. Blossom Cottage was hers; could it be true? She said a silent prayer.

She considered the implications; the financial bequest would cover some long-needed repairs to the cottage with some to spare. With her income as a seamstress and the contribution from her son from his wages, they had managed well enough, but now, she was a woman of property. She made herself a pot of tea and mused.

It was after lunch when Mildred made the finishing touches to her appearance. Before leaving, she went to her husband's drawer, removed a small box, and dropped it into her handbag. One last check on Grace who was still sleeping, then she descended the stairs to the shop,

Agnes and Molly were serving, but the shop was quiet.

"Agnes, I'm away. Make sure you see to your sister until I get back."

Agnes turned from her customer and acknowledged.

"Aye, mam, where are you going?"

"Just some business of your father's I need to attend to."

Mildred left the bakery and walked up James Street to the main road. The trolleybus stop was on the opposite side. The main mode of public transport was track-less trolleybuses; the Corporation had eight of them, and there was a direct service to Oakworth. There was also a railway line, but the station in Oakworth was a much further walk.

Mildred crossed the road, the conducting wires that provided the power for the buses were high overhead, a set in each direction.

Six or seven other passengers were waiting at the stop. Two elderly men with walking sticks and impressive moustaches talking to each other as good friends would do; the rest were women, looking uncomfortable in the oppressive heat. One was holding an ivory fan frantically wafting at the air in an attempt to stimulate a cooling breeze. There was none.

After five minutes, the cream and crimson liveried vehicle approached. From a distance, the trolleybuses had a flimsy appearance. The top deck was open to the elements and, without pantographs, a thick wire, the size of a good rope snaked upwards from a pole outside the driver's cab and attached itself to the overhead wires by what looked like a large upside-down coat hanger.

There were probably twenty or so passengers preparing to get off, less than the thirty-three it could carry. The waiting group stood to one side. There was a jostle to get the preferred seat; the elderly gentlemen waited in good manners for the women to board.

The stairs to the top of the vehicle looked as though they had been nailed onto the back of the bus resembling a child's slide but with steps. Mildred gingerly held onto the handrail to ascend.

She had decided to sit on the top-deck as the temperature in the cabin below would be well over a hundred degrees. But it was not an easy manoeuvre to reach her seat. She made herself comfortable; only two others had made the perilous journey to the top deck. She pulled down her hat to protect her face from the scorching sun. There was not a cloud in the sky.

Mildred had a panoramic view across the town as the bus pulled away. To her left, the park was still busy with people sat enjoying the sunshine; there were some with hampers enjoying a picnic. On the right, they passed the Central Hall, the scene of the Suffragette Meeting.

There were a few stops on the way along the Worth Valley, passing through the village of Ingrow and its numerous woollen mills, before reaching Oakworth. Mildred paid the conductor and got off just outside the general store.

She was now in a dilemma, unfamiliar with the village and not knowing the area, just an address. She decided to make enquiries at the store.

A galvanised steel washing-tub hung outside the emporium on a hook. There were displays of plants, ladders, buckets, everything the village-folk of Oakworth would need. She entered.

The village store was an Aladdin's Cave with all manner of items for sale in addition to the usual food and cleaning materials. She walked to the counter where a man in a light-brown overall was restocking shelves. He turned, hearing a customer.

"Aye, madam, 'ow do, what can I do fa tha?"

Mildred replied in a voice as refined as she could do.

"I am enquiring the whereabouts of Blossom Cottage; I have business with the occupant."

"Aye, 'appen I knows Mrs Bluet."

'Mrs' Bluet? Now, that had Mildred confused.

"Yes, Mrs Bluet." Mildred decided to go along with the man; it was clearly the same woman.

"Aye, it's not far, seven, eight-minute brisk walk. Turn right outside 'ere, cross the road and down about two hundred yards. Turn left; that be Slaymaker Lane, Blossom Cottage on tha right. Tha can't miss it."

"Thank you, my good man; You have been most helpful."

Mildred, now someone of substance, was determined to play the role of a gentry woman.

She thanked the man again and left the store.

Following the proprietor's instructions, Mildred soon reached her destination.

Slaymaker Lane was rural in appearance. All the residences were individual cottages seemingly from a by-gone age. The front gardens had been cultivated as allotments where vegetables and other crops were growing.

The third cottage on the right-hand side was bordered by a neatly-trimmed, three-feet tall Box hedge which ran the length of the front perimeter. There was a wooden sign at the end of the crazy-paving path that led to the front door. 'Blossom Cottage' it said.

Mildred stopped for a moment, hesitating, wondering if she had made the right decision to pay a call, particularly unannounced. Maybe she should have sent a letter.

But she was here now.

She looked at the house. It was a black and white thatched cottage, probably two-hundred years old. It was set back about forty yards from the lane. Either side of the crazy-paving footpath evidence of someone's labours which would provide fresh produce for the owner; the white and black flowers of broad-beans, the red of dwarf runner beans, potatoes, cabbage; enough to last a winter.

Mildred took a breath, opened the small white wooden gate, and walked slowly towards the front door, the uneven surface a possible trip hazard for the careless. Tall Hollyhocks stood either side of the cottage entrance providing a visually stunning guard of honour; their flowers bulging with colour. Numerous bees were sipping their nectar.

Mildred composed herself, trying to decide what to say. Then she knocked against the wooden door, an assertive knock, but not aggressive. A knock that would say, 'I mean business'.

A minute went by, and Mildred knocked a second time, a little louder.

Then a noise from within indicated someone was at home. Footsteps coming closer; then a click as the latch was raised. Inside it was dark and, for a moment, Mildred couldn't see the occupant; then the door opened wider, allowing the daylight to enter.

"Mrs Marsden!?"

"Hello, Kitty, I believe we may have matters to discuss."

For a moment there was a stand-off as Kitty recovered from the shock. "Aye, you're right; you best come in."

Kitty opened the door further to allow Mildred to pass. "Go through to the parlour." Kitty indicated a room to the right. "Would you like some tea or some lemon; it's fair stifling today?"

"Yes, it is… as you say. That's most kind; it was very hot on the bus; a glass of lemon will be most welcome."

"You've come on the trolley? And there was me thinking you would have your own driver."

"No," said Mildred. "I don't know why you would think so."

She looked at Kitty, trying to remember her from almost

twenty years earlier. The fresh face had gone, replaced by a mature countenance, gently lined, reflecting the ageing process, a kind look. She was dressed in a fashionable smock, giving a casual appearance; her auburn hair tied back in a bun and secured from her face with a scarf. It was the appearance of someone at work.

Mildred gazed out of the window to the rear which overlooked fields and distant hills.

"My, my, what a wonderful view you have."

"Aye, thank you. Please take a seat. I'll be with you directly," said Kitty. She left the room feeling anxious at the arrival of her visitor, wondering what she wanted.

Mildred looked around the living room; a chaise longue, a bureau, a dining table, a large Welsh Dresser with plates displayed, two adjacent armchairs facing an empty hearth with gleaming fender. It was all very tidy and well-presented. Mildred chose the chaise longue. She was sat upright, her hat in place, and her handbag in her lap. She, too, was feeling the tension.

A few minutes later, Kitty returned carrying a tray with a glass jug filled with a green-grey liquid and two glasses.

"Would you like a bite to eat at all? I have some cake that was fresh this morning."

"No, that won't be necessary; the drink will be fine, thank you."

Kitty filled the two tumblers with lemon juice and handed one to Mildred. She took the daintiest of sips then put it down on the table.

"I expect you are wondering why I have come to see you after all these years."

"Well, I wasn't expecting you, but I think I might have an idea."

"Then you'll be aware that my husband passed away

recently?"

"Yes, but not until this morning; I received a letter from a solicitor in town. I'm sorry for your loss."

"Thank you," said Mildred. "And I believe you are a beneficiary in his will?"

"Yes, it was in the letter."

"I had cause to see Mr Drummond, the solicitor, and he acquainted me with the contents of my late husband's will." Mildred took another sip of her drink, not wishing to rush her revelation. "My husband also had a box lodged with them for safe-keeping in which he had retained certain items."

She was also deliberately using the term, 'my husband', as an indication of ownership.

Mildred rummaged in her handbag and retrieved the letters. "I believe these belong to you."

She handed the ribboned package to Kitty. She looked at them in horror.

"I have read them. I know what was going on."

Kitty took the letters and looked down, her expression one of deep sadness. "I am at a loss, Mrs Marsden; I really am. I was nothing but a lass."

"It's alright, Kitty, I'm not angry."

"You have cause, Mrs Marsden."

"Probably, but I know my husband. What were you... seventeen?"

"Yes."

"And my husband was such a dominant man."

"Yes, that he was."

"Difficult to refuse."

"Yes, that was true."

"The last letter mentioned a child."

"Yes, Freddie."

"Freddie?"

"Yes, Frederick, but everyone calls him Freddie."

"And how old is he?"

"Just nineteen, last month."

"And he is Albert's boy?"

"Yes, but Freddie does not know his father. I told him he died when he was little. He thinks I am a widow woman."

"I see," said Mildred. "And you have done alright by my husband?"

"Yes, I have. He has provided for Freddie and me, right enough."

"Good, that's one thing at least." Mildred took another drink of her lemonade. "Tell me, how long did your affair continue?"

"Not long, three months maybe. Your husband would visit my lodgings once a week when my landlady was out, but I fell pregnant, and that's when I left," said Kitty. She was finding it difficult to remain calm. "I live with the shame of it every day, Mrs Marsden. I should have been stronger."

"What's done is done, Kitty. It has long passed. Keep the letters… and, I have something else for you."

Mildred retrieved the small jewellery box from her handbag and passed it to Kitty.

"What's this?"

"Open it. It's a gift; it belonged to Albert. I thought you could hand it down to your son."

Kitty opened the box; a set of gold cuff-links. She looked at it in amazement, then at Mildred.

"I don't know what to say. I don't deserve this."

"Well, maybe not, but I bear you no bad will, Kitty Bluet. My husband was a very persuasive man. You were a victim, same as I for all those years by his malicious nature. Tell me about your son; where is he?"

"He works at the mill, in the combing shed down at

Providence. He used to be at Lockwood's until the fire last month."

"Lockwood's, you say. I heard about that, most unfortunate. All those men losing their jobs."

"Yes, it was terrible. Freddie and one or two others got took on by Providence, but he doesn't like it. Says they treat the people like dogs. With what they pay 'em, he's nothing but a slave; that's what he says. Fourteen hours, he's there."

Mildred was now holding her glass, drinking more frequently until it was empty. Kitty took the glass and refilled it without asking.

"And what about you, Kitty, what do you do?" asked Mildred as she watched her host refresh the drinks.

Kitty looked down, unsure how to reply; there was a long pause.

"After I left the bakery, your husband arranged for me to stay here with Mrs Juke; he said she was a cousin."

"Mrs Juke? I don't recall such a person... by what name was she called?"

"Elizabeth... She was a seamstress, hereabouts, and while I was in confinement, she taught me her skills. Then after Freddie was born, we worked together; fourteen years, or more, it was."

"Is she here? I must make her acquaintance, Kitty, I would like to meet her. I had no knowledge of the woman."

"But that I could; she died some four years since.... pneumonia. If it weren't for her, I don't know what would have been my fate, the poorhouse, I reckon. She wrote to your husband before she died explaining her condition. It was then your husband bought the cottage, so I didn't have to leave."

Mildred was taking in every word, enthralled at this new disclosure. She took another drink; Kitty continued.

"Mrs Juke was always so kind… and godmother to Freddie."

"Godmother you say?"

"Yes." Mildred could see the sadness in Kitty's face.

"So, you met him again, my husband?"

"No, not so!" Kitty replied rather indignantly. "Mrs Juke made the arrangements. I've not seen your husband since I left the bakery. I said I would not; I made a promise."

"And did he know about your son?"

"Yes, Mrs Juke told him. He used to send money to her on Freddie's birthday. When she died, Mrs Juke bequeathed me her sewing machines and all the furnishings and jewellery. I have a workshop at the back. I have a good number of regular customers in Keighley and around, even Leeds and Bradford. Come, I will show you." She stood up. "Would you like more lemon… or a tea, perhaps?"

"Yes, I think a cup of tea would be most welcome."

Mildred followed Kitty into the kitchen where a fire was heating the range; it was stiflingly hot. Kitty placed a teapot under the range tap and drew two cups worth of boiling water, then added two teaspoons of tea.

It was a long room, with a pantry to the right. Under the window, next to the range, there was a deep, square sink with a solitary tap. There was a rustic table against the wall with three accompanying lathe-back chairs. Around the room, were various shelves holding cooking utensils and crockery. Kitty made the tea on the draining board. "Do you take milk?"

"Just a little, please," replied Mildred.

Kitty went into the pantry and returned with a milk bottle. She removed the cardboard top and poured measures into two cups, then returned the milk bottle to the pantry.

They continued their discussion over tea, seated at the

kitchen table; Kitty was keen to hear about Mildred's family and life at the bakery.

Once they had finished their teas, Kitty gave Mildred a guided tour. Mildred found herself fascinated by Kitty and her life. At the back of the cottage, the original scullery had been converted into an atelier. There were two pedal-driven sewing machines and three dressmaker's mannequins, two with pinned fabric. A needlework box of pins, needles and scissors lay alongside. Rolls of material were lying around the room. There were two completed garments hung up on hangers and suspended from a rail. Mildred viewed them with the eye of an expert.

"My, my, these are beautiful, Kitty; the stitching is exquisite, most pleasing." Mildred continued examining them. "I have a proposition for you."

"Yes, Mrs Marsden, and what might that be?"

"I promised my daughters a new dress, and I would like to employ you to make them."

"I don't know what to say… Yes, of course, I will be glad to."

"When will you be able to start?"

"Directly, if you wish… I will need to take measurements; it will mean a visit unless they come here."

"No, of course, you can visit; you can come after the bakery is closed… I will arrange a cabbie for you."

"A cabbie, no that's not necessary, I will take the trolley."

"I insist," replied Mildred.

"That's most kind of you, Mrs Marsden. What day shall I come?"

"Tomorrow, you can come tomorrow if that suits. I will arrange a cabbie for four o'clock, and please call me Mildred."

"Yes, thank you… er, Mildred, that will suit, perfectly.

I'll need to return for six o'clock to cook Freddie's tea."

"Yes, of course. That should be plenty of time. I will ensure the girls are ready."

Mildred and Kitty left the workshop and walked towards the parlour.

"Now, I must take my leave. Your hospitality has been most generous. I am glad of your acquaintance."

"Yes, and I am sorry for my foolishness."

"Pay no heed, it's all in the past now... I will see you tomorrow," said Mildred.

Mildred said her goodbyes and walked back to the trolleybus stop. It was the terminus, and a bus was waiting to make its journey back to Keighley. Ten minutes later, they were on the return journey. There were just two other people on board, but it would pick up many more passengers on its way. By the time it reached town, it would be standing room only.

As Mildred viewed the scenery, she considered her visit to Oakworth. She was pleased she had made the journey; it had been cathartic.

She watched the vista change from fields and hills to mill factories, dominating the skyline with their ugly beauty; the smoke from their chimneys choked the air, hanging in layers over the town. It was still stiflingly hot and, sitting on the top compartment, there was no shade. The atmosphere was heavy; 'maffin' the locals would call it – a familiar word with the workers in the mill. It would not be in Mildred's vocabulary.

It was gone five o'clock before Mildred arrived back at the bakery. The girls were in their bedroom, Arthur reading his newspaper having recently returned from The Malt

Shovel with Wilfred.

"Eh up, mam, where's tha been?" asked Arthur, looking up from his newspaper.

"Oakworth," replied Mildred as she removed her hat.

"Oakworth? That's a way. Why there?"

"Just some business to see to."

Just then the girls returned to the parlour, hearing their mother had returned. Mildred immediately went to Grace.

"And how are you, Grace? Let me look at you."

"I'm alright, mam. Don't fuss."

Mildred ignored the comment and checked Grace's head where she had been struck. It was in the thick of her hair, and Mildred had to pull the strands apart to examine the wound.

"Yes, it looks well enough, but I'll bathe it again with some Witch-hazel before you go to bed tonight. What about your arms?"

Grace slowly raised her arms and winced at the effort. The three welts were still angry-looking.

"We'll dress those as well. Have you managed to sleep?"

"Aye, a little."

"Good… I just hope you do not intend to go to any more rallies."

"No mam."

"Good… Mind you, those policemen should be locked away."

She addressed the girls, as a school ma'am might.

"I have some news for you. I have found a seamstress who is going to make your new dresses. She will be coming tomorrow afternoon after the shop has closed to take your measurements."

The girls looked at each other with excited eyes. Even Grace smiled for the first time in a day.

Arthur looked up from his newspaper. "Don't worry

Arthur, you won't be left out. I'll give you some money and you can go down to Cappers, as I promised."

"Thanks mam."

Mildred could see Arthur concentrating on a piece in the newspaper.

"What's that you're reading?"

Arthur looked up. "Nowt special... 'Appen some Austrian Duke's been shot, him and his missus. Reckon there's going to be trouble over it, it says here."

"Aye, well I'll get us some tea and you can tell us more."

79

Chapter Five

As she lay in bed that evening, Mildred considered her meeting with Kitty. Despite everything, she felt no ill-will, in fact she had an admiration for her; the way she had laboured to provide for herself and her son. She was trying to remember Elizabeth Juke, but there was no recollection; it was a name her husband had never mentioned. She couldn't understand why.

Albert was an only child and, like Arthur, had been raised in the bakery under the tutelage of his father, Benjamin. Albert's mother had died in childbirth at the age of thirty-five when he was just seven years old and he had been brought up by his father, a strict disciplinarian according to rumour. Mildred only had a vague recollection of the man, as he too had died early.

Mildred and Albert had been courting at the time but were not betrothed. When his father died, Albert suggested they got engaged to be married. Mildred took a job in the baker's shop and moved into the flat above following the nuptials a few months later.

Albert had never discussed his family – grandparents, aunts, uncles – and Mildred felt no right to intrude. Her role in the marriage soon became increasingly subservient. She couldn't count the number of times she'd heard the command, "Speak when thar spoken to, woman!"

Mildred couldn't settle. Despite the open window, the atmosphere in the room was heavy. She could hear houseflies buzzing around the room, attracted by food, and sweat.

But the insomnia was giving Mildred time to reflect. There was something else.

She had not visited Oakworth before and had been taken

by the countryside, the greenery, the fields, the trees, the fresh air. That's what her family deserved. She would make an appointment to see Mr Drummond.

The following morning, Grace had recovered sufficiently to return to her shop-keeping duties, leaving Molly to return to school with Freda. There was only one topic of conversation at breakfast, the measuring for the new dresses. The girls jabbered excitedly about colours, fabric, and styles they would choose.

At ten o'clock, with the early-morning queue of customers having passed, Mildred asked Agnes to walk over to the solicitors and seek an appointment with Mr Drummond for after lunch.

Arthur was well into his second batch of bread for the morning, his mind considering matters of the day, random thoughts bouncing around his head. It kept his mind alert and passed the time. It was something the miller had said about supplies of flour. Some of the producers had been warned of shortages if problems in the Balkans escalated. What that was about, neither Arthur nor the miller could fathom; he'd read 'nowt' in the papers, but for now, his daily delivery would not be affected.

Agnes secured the meeting for her mother with Mr Drummond. She had been quite taken by the young clerk that opened the door; she found herself blushing for no reason as she requested the appointment.

By ten to three, Mildred was crossing James Street on the way to Rotten Row for her appointment with the solicitor. She stopped briefly at the cabbie stop opposite the bakery and ordered a taxi to collect Kitty at four o'clock.

The heatwave continued unabated; the temperature

searing; over ninety degrees it had said in the News. The smell of horses had not receded. Despite the backdrop of the trolleybuses and cabbies traversing James Street and the main road, the noise from the foundry was clearly audible in the still air, thrumping its rhythmic pounding across the valley.

The park was again populated by those with a mind not to work. Women with children, elderly men with their pipes and cloth caps, the occasional drunk who had given up on life; the park had become their place in the sun. People on bicycles, using the footpaths as a short cut to the High Street, proved an additional hazard for the unwary. Mildred paid them no heed but went about her business with purpose.

She reached the solicitor's office, its gold signage glowing in the mid-afternoon sun. Mildred pressed the bell-push and waited.

"Ah, good day, Mrs Marsden." It was the same clerk who had welcomed her on her previous visit. "Mr Drummond is expecting you."

"That he is," replied Mildred.

"Please take a seat, he will be with you directly."

Before she could get properly comfortable, Mr Drummond opened his office door and appeared before her.

"Mrs Marsden, a delight to see you again, please come in. I have arranged for some tea."

Despite the incredible heat, the solicitor was still dressed in his three-piece suit and adorning fob-watch, the chain snaking from his waistcoat pocket and affixing to his middle button-hole.

"That's most kind, Mr Drummond, and my thanks to you for accommodating me at such short notice; it's most generous of you."

"It's of no consequence, Mrs Marsden, please take a seat.

Norman will bring through the tea momentarily."

Mildred took 'Norman' to be the clerk that had answered the door.

The solicitor was sat erect, not showing any reclining casualness. "How can I help you today?"

"I'll come directly to the point, Mr Drummond. I want to buy a property."

"A property?"

The solicitor imbued the air of a sage, as an old schoolmaster might, knowledgeable and worldly. He steepled his long narrow fingers in front of his mouth.

"Yes," replied Mildred, without elaboration.

Before the solicitor could add to the debate, there was a knock on the door and Norman entered with a tray and accoutrements. He placed it on the desk in front of Drummond who proceeded to pour.

"No sugar, I recall, Mrs Marsden."

"Yes, that's correct." Sugar had been an unnecessary extravagance; although that might change, she thought to herself, as she took her first sip.

"Had you a property in mind?" asked Drummond.

"No, I know nothing about property and the like; I need your guidance on such matters."

"Of course, of course, it will be my pleasure. Have you a district you wish to consider?"

"Yes, Oakworth would be my preference. It is on the omnibus route, and the air is much fresher there."

"Yes, of course, Blossom Cottage."

"Indeed," replied Mildred.

He was curious but didn't enquire further. "I do have occasion to contact house and land agents from time to time. I can make enquiries on your behalf. Do you know Josiah Springett?"

"Only by reputation, Mr Drummond," replied Mildred taking another dainty sip of her tea.

"Well deserved, Mrs Marsden, a fine man and quite knowledgeable in property matters. I can highly recommend him."

"I will leave that entirely at your discretion, Mr Drummond."

"Tell me, what kind of dwelling were you seeking if I may ask?"

"One that the gentry might use. I have the wherewithal."

"Indeed you have, Mrs Marsden; indeed you have. Very well, let me make some enquiries and I will write to you as soon as I have some information."

Over tea, they continued discussing the financial implications and the process of purchasing property, which Mildred was completely unacquainted with.

Once they had finished their drinks, with a polite pause, the solicitor stood and escorted Mildred to the door.

"I will write again shortly as promised with some recommendations, Mrs Marsden. Meanwhile, we remain at your disposal."

Mildred offered her hand which the solicitor touched fleetingly as required in gentile circles.

She felt as if she was walking on air as she returned through the park. A woman of property, as well as a businesswoman; who would credit it? She had so much on her mind.

Archie Slater, the shrill-voiced newspaper vendor, was at his usual post, his voice cutting the atmosphere like a knife through butter. "Get thar news. Get thar news." Mildred could hear him before she could see him.

As she approached the bakery, she noticed the headline board, leaning against the shop wall. *'Women's Rally, Police injured, several arrested.'*

Mildred recoiled for a moment; Grace's name would be among those arrested; she hoped none of her acquaintances would recognise it.

She ignored Archie and his beseeching and entered the bakery. It was four o'clock, the shop was closed, and the four girls were together in the parlour eagerly awaiting the arrival of Kitty. Arthur was in the Malt Shovel with Wilfred discussing world affairs and politics, but with money in his pocket from Mildred, he would visit Cappers, the bootmakers, later. It was just a short distance down James Street.

The girls greeted their mother. Mildred turned to Grace. "I see you've made front-page news, you and your rally."

Grace looked at her mother. "What do tha mean?"

"It's on Archie Slater's board: police injured, it says; there'll be much talk about it, you mark my words," replied Mildred. "Arthur will have a copy when he comes in; you'll be in there, I warrant."

"I'm sorry mam," said Grace and started to cry.

"Now then, Grace, compose yourself; you've cried enough."

Mildred put a comforting arm around her, the other girls looked on. "Let's have a look at your welts."

Grace showed her mother the injuries on her arm, then Mildred parted her hair to view the contusion to her scalp. "Yes, they're looking a lot better. Now get yourself together for the seamstress."

She turned to her other daughters. "Agnes, go set out the best china; there are some cakes in the pantry. Molly, Freda, go put on your Sunday smocks."

It was twenty-to-five when there was a rap on the bakery door. Mildred left the parlour and descended the stairs.

With the afternoon sun blazing through the large window, the temperature in the shop was oppressive, and Mildred subconsciously fanned herself with her hand as she walked to the door.

"Kitty… it's so lovely to see you again. Did the cabbie arrive on time as I directed?"

"Yes, Mrs Marsden, much appreciated, I'm sure."

"Mildred, you must call me Mildred, I insist."

"Yes, of course… Mildred, sorry, just habit."

"Get thar news… Get thar news…" Archie Slater's voice penetrated the air as Mildred stepped to one side to allow Kitty to enter. Mildred locked the door and could see Kitty staring at the counter, then she looked around the shop, deep in thought.

"It's like turning the clock to a time long passed, but warm in the heart… So many memories, so many memories." she mused and turned to Mildred. "There were happy ones too. They weren't all bad."

"Come up to the parlour, the girls are waiting," said Mildred, as she watched Kitty in her reminiscences.

Kitty was carrying a large hessian bag, not heavy but with bulk.

"Can you manage, Kitty?" asked Mildred as they reached the foot of the stairs to the parlour.

"Yes, it's fine… Mildred."

"Oh, I want to ask… did you give the boy the gift?"

"Yes, I did. He was most grateful. I told him I had found it in some of my things and was waiting for the right time to give it to him."

"I am pleased it gave him pleasure… Come through, let's meet the girls."

They reached the parlour and Mildred's four daughters

were lined up in their orphan-smocks. They looked at the visitor with excited eyes; even Grace was smiling now.

"Girls, this is Kitty, the seamstress from Oakworth. I have asked her to make your new dresses. Kitty, this is Grace, Agnes, Molly and Freda."

Kitty looked at them. "My, you have such a fine family, Mrs Marsden." Kitty was finding it hard to call Mildred by her first name, and this time, Mildred did not correct her.

"Thank you. Would you like some tea, Kitty, before we start?"

"Yes, that's very kind of you, most welcome."

"Agnes, can you bring the teas?" Mildred ordered.

Agnes went into the kitchen and returned with a tray holding the teapot, milk jug and two cups. There was also a plate piled high with buttered scones, a luxury rarely experienced.

"Agnes made these; she takes after her mother for her baking skills."

Mildred poured the teas and handed Kitty the cakes. She took one and handed back the plate.

"Help yourself, girls, but save one for Arthur," said Mildred.

Kitty had started drinking her tea and taken a bite from her scone. "Why, these are so delicious, Agnes, you certainly have a talent," she said, moving a crumb from the side of her mouth.

After ten minutes, the teas were drunk and the scones eaten. Kitty got up from her chair, reached into her large bag and pulled out a tape measure. Then a note pad and pencil.

"Right, let's have a look at you. Who wants to go first?"

"Me, me, me," said Freda, excitedly. As the youngest, she was used to being spoiled by the others and they were happy to let her.

"I have some magazines which you might want to look at to give a thought of what style you would like me to make." Kitty handed out the magazines.

"What's this?" asked Grace.

"It's French, *'Au Bon Marché'*, a fashion magazine from Paris."

"Paris!" exclaimed Grace.

"Yes, I can make your dresses look like them… or something else. Most of my gentry customers like the French styles; they are very much in favour in London, I believe," said Kitty.

Grace was speechless.

"I can make them suitable for the younger lady; the girls might prefer something more simple," added Kitty looking at Mildred.

Mildred was also taking an interest, and while Freda was being measured had taken charge of the fashion publication.

"Kitty, while you're here, maybe you can measure me too; I would like one of these."

"Of course, it will be my privilege. Here… look through this one too."

Kitty handed Mildred the latest edition of the *'Ladies Home Journal'*.

So, after an hour, the four girls and Mildred had been measured. Kitty had made notes and taken details of their preferences based on the pictures in the two magazines. There was much to do.

Kitty put her chattels away and looked at Mildred.

"I can have something pinned up by Sunday; I have fabric enough. You will need to come to my studio for me to take more measurements. Would that be acceptable, Mrs

Marsden?"

"Yes, it would be very acceptable, Kitty. What time would you like us to call?" Mildred was also feeling a touch excited but was maintaining her decorum.

"Afternoon... around four, if that's suits."

Mildred looked at the girls. "Yes, that suits," she said. She had not seen such joy in her children's faces before.

Kitty made her farewells and Mildred escorted her down the stairs to the shop just as Arthur was returning from the Malt Shovel. He opened the shop door clutching a copy of the news and a large brown paper bag.

"Eh up mam."

"Oh, Arthur, this is Kitty, the seamstress from Oakworth."

"Oh aye. Been to measure up, I hear."

"Yes," replied Kitty. Immediately, she could see the resemblance to Freddie.

He doffed his cap and headed for the stairs. "Sithee, nice to meet tha."

"Yes," said Kitty, but Arthur had his back turned and was through the curtain. Mildred was not impressed by his manner.

"I apologise for my son's rudeness; Been down the Shovel, forgot his manners."

"Pay no mind, Mrs Marsden... boys are boys."

"Aye, but he's been brought up better."

Kitty stepped toward the door.

"Oh... Kitty... before you go, I have something to say. It's the funeral tomorrow. I have been giving it some thought. You are welcome to join us if you would like."

"That's most kind of you, Mrs Marsden. I know you mean well, but that's in the past and I have no mind to return. I hope you understand."

"Of course, Kitty, and I respect your wishes."

They left the bakery and Mildred walked with Kitty across the road to the taxi stand. She paid the cabbie and watched as Kitty left for the journey back to Oakworth.

Mildred returned to the parlour; the girls were buzzing. Arthur was already slouched over his newspaper. The paper bag was next to him.

"Now then, Arthur, you were quite rude with the seamstress."

He looked up, his eyes were glazed, and momentarily she saw Albert looking at her.

"Nay, there were no rudeness intended."

"That's as maybe, but you could have been more polite."

He looked at her but not in an adversarial way; he respected his mother. "Then if that be so, I am sorry."

He turned to the news again. "What does it say about the rally?" asked Mildred, deciding not to pursue it further.

"It says there are three constables in the infirmary."

"What about the women?" interrupted Grace.

"Nowt about any being hurt; fifty arrested for riotous behaviour, it says here," his voice sounded slightly slurred.

Grace looked angry. "Really! Well, that's most typical, that is. It's what Annie Kelley were saying, t'newspapers are in association with the constabulary. Women in this country don't get a fair hearing."

Mildred looked at Grace. "Yes, but it is what it is; one day things will change."

"Aye, but not while Mr Asquith is Prime Minister. We must keep fighting."

Mildred looked at her daughter. "You have done your share of fighting, young lady; there are things to take care of here." She turned to Arthur. "Is there owt about Grace in there?"

Arthur scanned the article. "Nay, mam, nowt I can tell."

"Thank goodness. Now we have a new standing, we don't want any scandal."

"What's this about a new standing?" asked Arthur, looking at his mother quizzically.

She gathered her daughters together and wrapped her arms around, a pair each side.

"Listen, girls, and you, Arthur… I have some news."

Arthur looked at his mother, there was a serious countenance about her, but the turn of her mouth suggested joy.

"I have been to see Mr Drummond today and made enquiries about the purchase of a fine house."

There was a considered silence. The girls glanced at each other.

Arthur looked at his mother, his eyes now more focussed. "What does tha mean?"

"I have asked him to enquire about a suitable house, for us… for the family."

"But we have a place to live… here," said Arthur.

"Yes, I know…" She looked at him in a matriarchal way. "But now things have changed. We can have a better life after all the years of struggle."

"But mam, *this* is our home," countered Arthur. "And what about the bakery? What will happen to the business?"

"Don't worry yourself, I have no mind to close the bakery. We can even find lodgers for the living quarters."

The girls looked at each other, trying to work out the ramifications. Arthur was sceptical about the proposed change.

"So, where will this house be?" asked Arthur.

"Mr Drummond is looking for us, but in the country

somewhere… Oakworth, maybe."

"Oakworth!? But there's nowt to do in Oakworth; there's not even an alehouse," said Arthur.

"Yes, and that'll be no loss," said Mildred, disappointed at her children's antipathy. She addressed her eldest. "What do you say, Grace? We'll have a proper bath and indoor privvy like the gentry."

"Aye, but we have friends here."

"But you will still see them; it's only half an hour on the trolley."

Arthur had thought of another objection. "But how will us get to work? There be no trollies at five in the morning, and in t'winter, they can't get up the hill. Anyhow, we have all us need here."

Mildred was now feeling cornered. Her daughters had moved from her side.

"I don't understand. Don't you want to make something of your life?" said Mildred looking disappointed at the reaction.

"Aye, that I do," said Arthur. "But 'appen tha's getting above thar station."

"And what station is that? The trouble with you, Arthur Marsden, you wear poverty like a badge of honour. Well, it doesn't have to be like that, not anymore. We have money now, and it has been honestly earned."

"Honestly earned! Tha said it were stocks an' stuff. It's all profit earned on the backs of slave labour; that's what it be. I don't call that honest."

Mildred didn't want to get into an argument and ignored the remark, not wishing to inflame the situation. "Very well, yes, I can see there are matters to discuss, but we must take this opportunity your father has given us."

"'Appen he's cursing us," said Arthur.

"There'll be none of that talk, Arthur. There's no cursing."
She needed to change the subject.

"Are those the new boots?" she said, looking at the large paper bag.

"Aye." He opened the bag and took out the footwear.

"Let's see," requested Freda, showing more excitement than Arthur. He passed them to his sister, who proceeded to hand them around.

"Right, I'll make us some tea," said Mildred, seeing the topic of the new house had been exhausted for the moment. There was work to do there.

The children's bedroom was quiet; it was one-thirty and they had been asleep for three hours despite the oppressive heat. The window was open, allowing the occasional buzz of a mosquito and more houseflies. The long, dark fabric curtain that separated the girls' beds from Arthur's sleeping quarters was in place.

Suddenly a scream. "Get off…! Get off…! Leave me be…!"

Agnes turned over in bed. There was a home-made bolster between her and her sister; Agnes leaned across. "Grace, Grace wake up; you're having a nightmare."

Then, the gaslight illuminated. "Whatever's the matter? Grace, dear, are you ok?" It was Mildred at the curtain. Arthur was still sound asleep.

Grace suddenly woke and sat upright.

"Are you alright, Grace?" said Agnes.

Grace was breathing deeply and unable to speak. Mildred went to her and placed a consoling arm around her shoulders. "Agnes, fetch a drink of water, there's some cold in the scullery."

Agnes left the bedroom. The two younger girls were

beginning to stir. "What's happening mam?" said Freda, rubbing her eyes to acclimatise to the dim illumination provided by the gaslight. Moths started to flap around the light source.

It was twenty minutes before Grace had settled and the family returned to sleep; tomorrow was going to be a busy day.

Friday, July 3rd, 1914, the funeral of Albert Henry Marsden.

The horse-drawn hearse containing Albert's coffin drew up outside the bakery at twelve forty-five, pulled by two black stallions suitably adorned in funereal tack. The shop was closed with a sign in the window indicating the break in service. It would reopen at three-thirty it said.

Jeremiah Rombold looked immaculate in his morning suit and top hat. The four pallbearers, dressed in smart suits, were immediately behind the hearse. The family were in their Sunday best, including Arthur who was 'breaking-in' his new boots. His old flat cap was already moist where it touched his forehead. He was also sporting a black armband on Mildred's insistence.

Before they left, Mildred had taken Arthur to one side. "I have something for you," she said and handed him a small box, about three inches square. "It was your father's; I thought you should have it."

Arthur opened the box and saw his father's gold fob-watch. He looked at his mother with an expression of surprise. "Thanks mam," he said and attached it to his waistcoat pocket with a degree of pride.

The procession turned around and moved slowly up James Street with Mildred and the children walking behind the pallbearers and the hearse. Traffic in James Street was reduced to a crawl as the cortege slowly headed for the church, much to the chagrin of the trolleybus passengers and the cabbies who had been forced to follow at a similar pace. Shoppers on the pavement stood in deference; men doffed their caps as the funeral procession passed by.

The weather was on the change; the oppressive heat was still there, but the atmosphere was heavy, as if the air lacked oxygen, sapping strength, and energy. The fug in the valley from the mill chimneys hung like a grey-brown shroud; the smell of horses was at its worst.

To the south, large cumulonimbus clouds billowed like sails in the sky as if some portent.

By the time the procession had reached the church in Cavendish Street, the walkers were sweating profusely. Mildred was fanning herself, although making little impact on the temperature. Arthur's face was red and clammy, his throat dry; he was desperate for an ale to quench his thirst.

As had been announced in the obituary, the burial would take place in Utley Cemetery following the service at the Methodist church. The graveyard was two miles away, and Mildred had arranged for a motorised hearse and two vehicles to transport the mourners to the cemetery.

The church was busy, over a hundred, according to the Church Elder, who conducted the service. Many of Albert's former drinking companions from the Malt Shovel were there, including the landlord, Thomas Fielding, as well as regular customers of the bakery.

The funeral procession entered the church and moved mournfully down the aisle behind Albert's coffin carried by the four pallbearers. A simple wreath was laid on top. The congregation stood in silence; just the sound of an organ playing a sad refrain. Mildred glanced to her left and noticed a familiar face in the back row; it was Kitty. Mildred nodded in acknowledgement and raised her eyebrows in surprise as she walked solemnly by. Nevil Drummond was also there behind the front row where the family were seated. White Lilies decked the altar and surrounds.

The Elder gave a befitting eulogy; hymns were sung in remembrance, but the family seemed unmoved. There was little outpouring of grief. It wasn't that the family were undemonstrative; the overwhelming feeling was one of welcome relief.

After the ceremony, while the coffin was being transferred to the hearse, Mildred waited in the vestibule of the church to thank the mourners. The children were outside in the car, waiting while their mother carried out her social duties.

Mildred noticed Kitty approaching.

"Good day, Kitty."

"Good day, Mrs Marsden. I hope you don't mind me attending. I was mithering about it most of the night."

"No, no, of course not; in fact, it was good to see you."

"I'll not come to the grave if it's all the same. I just wanted to pay my respects."

"No, I understand. Thank you for coming."

Mildred noticed Kitty's dress, clearly one of her creations. It was beautiful.

"And how are things with the dresses? It's all the girls can talk about."

"Well, the dresses are pinned and will be ready for fitting by Sunday."

"Yes, you mentioned you would like us to come to the cottage?"

"Yes, if you wouldn't mind. I thought four o'clock; they

should be ready by then."

"Yes, of course, I will tell the children; they will be most pleased."

They said their goodbyes. Kitty left the church and walked towards the trolleybus stop.

After ten minutes, the church had emptied and Mildred joined the children in the car for the trip to Utley. She gestured to the undertaker, who was next to the driver in the hearse, indicating she was ready to leave. They slowly pulled away.

At the cemetery, the family watched as the coffin was lowered into the grave. Mildred picked up a small handful of earth and, as was the custom, threw it into the hole. It sprayed over the oak coffin with its gleaming gold-plated plaque: Albert Henry Marsden, April 19th, 1867 - June 27th, 1914.

As the dirt hit the coffin, a clap of thunder sounded. It was not a distant rumble; it was loud and frightening. It started with a crack and reverberated around the valley. Mildred held onto her hat; the girls jumped, startled by the noise.

Then, from nowhere, the rain, torrential rain. It was mixed with hailstones the size of pigeon eggs, which bounced off the coffin.

Mildred looked at the Elder who was conducting the graveside service, then at the children who were showing signs of consternation. Even Arthur was displaying concern.

The Elder increased the pace of his delivery and uttered "Amen," although whether the service had been completed, no-one would rightly know, or probably care for that matter. Shelter had become a priority.

A bolt of lightning zig-zagged its way across the blackened skies; more thunder sounded. The girls hurried towards the carriages. Water dripped off the peak of Arthur's cap.

Mr Rombold walked from the awaiting cars carrying an umbrella which he opened and used to shield Mildred.

Just as they reached the vehicles, there was an almighty crack, and a flame seemed to appear from nowhere; electric sparks, chips of wood, descended to the ground. The bough of one of the ancient oaks surrounding the cemetery, not twenty feet away, had been struck and was now on the ground, blocking the track to the cemetery entrance, its sheared end blackened and smoking. The rain was bouncing off the surface of the gravel track from the main road. The Elder and the grave-digger were sheltering under a large beech tree close to the stricken oak.

The minister had intended to walk the distance back to the church, half an hour by foot, but Mildred beckoned him to join them.

The Marsden family were in the first car, their clothes darkened by the rain; their hats ruined, hair bedraggled dripping water down their backs.

Mildred held open the door for the Elder to get in. It would barely hold the passengers. Rombold and the pallbearers had made it to the second car. Two of them ran to the large branch that was blocking the lane and moved it aside to allow the vehicles to pass. Another flash followed almost immediately with an enormous retort that shook the car. The rain was coming down in torrents, the ruts in the track were filling with water. Hailstones continued to hit the car, rattling on the roof, then tumbling to the ground.

Arthur was in the front with the driver, his cap dripping with water, his clothes, wet and uncomfortable. He took off his cap and shook it on the floor to expunge the excess water. The driver looked at him with some displeasure.

The vehicle started to move, but the flimsy windscreen wipers just couldn't cope with the deluge, making it almost impossible to see. As the driver pressed the accelerator, so the wipers stopped altogether. The car moved forward at walking pace. The driver squinting to improve visibility but not with any success. In the back, the girls were watching with concern; the priest was muttering something; it seemed like a prayer.

Behind the lead car, the undertaker and his team were fairing no better. Another clap of thunder rocked the car as they reached the main gate at the end of the cemetery track. The trees that guarded the entrance, full with leaves, were bending under the weight of water.

Traffic on the road into town was at a standstill. The gutters weren't able to keep up with the flow of water, and large pools were now forming across the road. It was ten minutes before the line started to move and a polite motorist allowed them to join the queue in front of them. Still it cascaded down, like someone had opened heaven's sluice gate.

Lightning continued to skit across the sky followed by the crack and rumble of deafening thunderclaps. It was as if the storm had become trapped in the valley and was trying to escape, wreaking its anger on the town.

James Street was awash, the water pouring down the gutters. Fallen leaves, branches and horse droppings blocked drains. Debris was being swept down the hill in a torrent, creating large lakes in the undulations in the road.

It was nearer quarter-to-four before the funeral car finally reached the bakery, having dropped off the Elder at the church. One or two customers were sheltering under the awning, water cascading off the sides from the large pool that had formed on top. Water dripped through holes in the fabric, causing people underneath to dodge.

Arthur looked on with some concern.

Chapter Six

The family exited the car and dashed into the shop. The waiting customers filed in as soon as Arthur had opened the door. Grace and Agnes went behind the serving counter without bothering to change or remove their hats, just putting aprons over their damp clothes.

Mildred, Molly and Freda went upstairs while Arthur checked the baking shed.

He couldn't believe his eyes.

The shed was flooded with water, at least six inches deep, and it was still pouring in. Water lapped the base of the oven; luckily, it had not reached the fire itself, which was still giving off heat. The mixing vat was surrounded by floating horse droppings, carried in from the street. Arthur's work boots were submerged on the floor in the corner, but worst of all, his stock of flour was ruined. The two spoiled sacks were on the floor, one on top of the other; the bottom sack was not visible at all.

He cursed himself at his stupidity for not closing the outer gates to the shed. He left them open during the day as the temperature became too hot with the oven lit. He would close them again when he had finished for the day, and everything had been cleaned.

He waded through the flood to the back yard, which was open to the elements. The water had cascaded down West Street, and the storm drain just outside the gate had become blocked, the over-flow pouring directly into the yard and then into the shed. He stood for a moment; his new boots totally immersed.

Arthur looked up at the sky; it was as black as he had ever seen. The hail and rain were unabated, heavier if anything.

Another bolt of lightning flashed across the sky followed immediately by a clap of thunder. Arthur grabbed one of his long-handled shovels and went to the yard gate. Water was dripping off the peak of his cap and down his face.

The flooded drain had created a large lake across the street, mini whirlpools swirled in the torrent. He reached the drain and manoeuvred the shovel trying to clear the leaves and other debris that was blocking it.

Like someone pulling the plug out of a bath, as soon as the detritus cleared, water poured down the gulley, freed of its dam. Arthur threw the debris onto the footpath out of the way of the torrent. To his left, he could see the entrance to the farrier's. The gate had been closed, but he could hear the sound of agitated horses and the voice of the blacksmith trying to calm them.

There was still water flowing down the slope into the yard but a lot less. He walked back through the shed and along the corridor to the shop. Fortunately, there was a step at the start of the corridor which had prevented the water from reaching the bakery itself.

The customers had gone and the store was empty.

"Grace, Agnes, lock the door… I need some help; there's been a flood."

The girls left their posts; Grace went to lock the door, Agnes followed Arthur.

"Arthur, thar's soaked to the skin," said Agnes. They reached the baking shed; Agnes's jaw dropped at the sight.

"Flippin 'eck, Arthur… What's happened here?"

"Rain's flooded in, all t'flour's ruined. We need to get rid of the water."

"How's us going to do that? It's pouring in."

Grace joined them and could see the flooded baking shed.

"By 'eck, Arthur, it's a right mess; what's tha gonna do?"

"Nowt much we can do till rain stops; it can't go on much longer… I think I'll get out of these wet clothes… I think you girls should do t'same."

"Aye, tha's right, Arthur… Agnes and me can lend tha a hand, can't we, Agnes?"

"Aye, I need to change first though."

The three left the baking shed to the will of the Gods of rain and went up to the parlour where Mildred was waiting with Molly and Freda. The room was bathed in the dim lighting of the gaslights; it was as dark as night outside.

"Goodness Arthur, look at the state of you. Take off those wet things; you'll catch your death," said Mildred.

She looked at him and noticed his new boots, saturated, and covered with mud and horse manure.

"Just look at those new boots; have you seen the state of them? Take them off, now; I'll put them next to the range to dry."

Arthur sat down and started pulling at the laces.

"Mam, tha should see the baking shed; it's full of water," said Grace as she pulled her hat from her head and shook her hair.

Mildred looked at Arthur with concern. "What's this, Arthur?"

"Aye, shed's flooded almost t'bottom of the oven; flour's gone; it's a right mess. Nowt we can do till rain stops."

"Well, the three of you remove those clothes quickly, and let's see what needs to be done."

They went to the bedroom and changed into their day clothes. Mildred gave them a towel-cloth each to dry themselves. Arthur had completely forgotten about his newly-acquired pocket-watch, but as he removed it from his waistcoat pocket, it seemed non-the-worse for wear. The hands were still moving.

Arthur returned to the parlour wearing his ordinary day clothes, the ones he would wear for baking, and a pair of clogs. He was carrying his wet things. There was another rumble of thunder, but more distant.

The temperature had dropped by ten degrees. Arthur went to the parlour window and looked across towards the park. The wires carrying the electricity for the trolleybuses were swaying in the wind threatening to break. James Street was almost deserted; the rain had now eased to a steady shower. Two taxis were marooned, one with its bonnet raised, the cabbie looking at the inner workings with some concern. Water was still gushing down the gutters.

Further in the park, several tree branches had come down as a result of the weight of water on the foliage, some possibly caused by lightning strikes; it was difficult to tell from a distance. It resembled a battle zone.

"Seems like it's stopping," said Arthur.

Mildred joined him at the window. "In my life, I can't remember such a storm," she said.

Grace and Agnes were also looking at the carnage outside.

Arthur looked at his mother. "'Appen, I'll call on Wilfred, see if he has a bucket or two."

"Yes, good idea. We'll go down to the shop and see what needs to be done."

Arthur went downstairs and into the bakery. Archie Slater was stood in the doorway, calling for customers.

Arthur opened the door with a 'clang' which made the lad jump.

"Eh up, Archie, tha'll not sell many papers in this."

"Aye, Arthur, that's a fact."

"You best stand inside a minute; I need to pull back the

awning."

Archie picked up his board and stock of newspapers and moved in the doorway while Arthur negotiated the winding machinery with his pole. It was as if someone had emptied a bath as the water that had caught in the awning came gushing down. Arthur jumped out of the way to avoid getting drenched again. The skies were beginning to brighten; to the north, the departing storm was still visible, the sky as black as night.

Archie resumed his calling as Arthur walked up to the butcher's. The street was almost deserted at a time it would normally be busy with people going about their business. All the shops had closed and their awnings were pulled in.

Arthur knocked on the butcher's door, and it was Wilfred who answered.

"Eh up, Arthur, what's wrong?"

"The shed's flooded; I need buckets and tha help if tha has a mind."

"Aye, of course... I'll come down directly; 'appen I'll need my wellingtons."

"Aye, that tha will."

Arthur looked down at his wooden clogs. They had served him well enough; wellingtons were a luxury that he had not been able to afford.

He returned to the shop and joined Mildred, Grace, and Agnes at the baking shed. They had not ventured into the water but were discussing ways of clearing the mess.

"Rain's stopped," said Arthur as he walked towards them.

Mildred turned. "Yes, that's a blessing. We need to get this cleaned up if we're going to bake any bread tomorrow."

"'Appen there won't be any bread unless we can get us flour. Look at sacks over yonder; they're covered." He pointed at the submerged bags of flour. "Wilfred says he'll be down directly."

"That's kind of him," said Mildred. "What do you want us to do?"

"Well, I can't see no point in us all getting wet. Wilfred's bringing his wellingtons and is going to help me get rid of the water. Then you can help us clean."

"Yes, very well, come on girls, let's leave the men to it."

Just then, the clang of the shop door sounded, and Wilfred entered with his eldest sister, Ivy. They were carrying brooms, mops and buckets, and a strange-looking contraption that Arthur didn't recognise.

"Eh up, Wilfred, what's tha got there?"

"What, this?" he said, holding up a long handle with two planks of wood on the end set at right-angles. "It's what us use for clearing snow. 'Appen it'll shift water an' all."

"Aye, that it could."

Seeing Ivy had arrived, also wearing wellingtons, Grace and Agnes decided to stay around and help; Mildred returned to the parlour.

Agnes turned to Grace. "What about yer arm?" she said with a concerned look.

"It's much better today. 'Appen I can move a broom," replied Grace.

Arthur rolled up his trousers, and he and Wilfred waded out into the yard. There was another, smaller drain in the middle which would normally deal with any excess water, but this had also become clogged with debris. The two lads set about unblocking it. The mini-lake started to slowly drain away, taking some of the water in the baking shed with it. Using brooms and Wilfred's snow-clearing invention, after half an hour, the shed was clear of water, but the floor was covered in horse manure and other material swept in by the storm.

The clean-up operation could commence in earnest.

Around seven o'clock, Mildred brought a plate of Agnes's scones and handed them out to the clear-up team.

Arthur had managed to start a fire in the oven. The pile of coal in the yard was wet, but the kindling was dry enough. The heat started to help the process, and by nine o'clock, the walls and mixing vat had been scrubbed.

Arthur took stock. He had enough yeast and salt; they were on higher shelves and had not been affected by the water. The main problem was the flour; Saturday was his busiest day. He would see what Buxton's could do in the morning; he was due a delivery.

With the baking shed clean and clear of water, Arthur closed the gate and outside door to the baking shed. The oven he would leave to burn out; the heat would continue to aid the drying process.

"Do tha fancy a pint or two, Wilfred? I've a right thirst, I have" said Arthur.

"Aye, that would be most welcome," replied Wilfred.

Arthur thanked Ivy; he had been impressed by her industry. She went back to the butcher's carrying a couple of brooms and a bucket. Wilfred would carry the rest later. Grace and Agnes returned to the parlour.

Outside the bakery, Archie had gone and the street looked deserted. Rubbish carried down by the storm was everywhere. Although it was not yet properly dark, the streetlights were not illuminated; the storm had cut the electricity, which meant the trolleybuses had no power. One was stranded just opposite the alehouse.

"By 'eck, Wilfred, I've not seen owt like this before," said Arthur, as they walked the short distance to the Malt Shovel.

The following morning, Arthur was in the baking shed. He felt tired and rotten; the previous day had taken its toll; that, and the four pints he had consumed the previous evening. There had been only one topic of conversation in the alehouse with everyone having tales of destruction and upheaval. There were rumours of people being killed by lightning and fallen trees.

He opened the doors to the shed and started collecting the coal for the oven; it was just after five o'clock. He was waiting anxiously for Buxton's lorry.

Six o'clock, the oven was lit, but there was still no sign of the miller. Arthur was getting concerned. He would need to start mixing soon if he were going to be ready to open at eight o'clock.

He looked across the yard; there were still signs of the storm everywhere. The air was much cooler and fresher, the smell of pollen almost as potent as the aroma of horses. He could see the occasional vehicle moving along James Street. He went across to the other side of the yard and started picking up more debris. He examined the two sacks of flour wondering if they could be dried and recycled, but they were still sodden and the flour totally unusable.

The temperature in the baking shed had risen with the heat from the oven, and the floor was now dry. He was wearing his old boots; his new ones were still drying out in the kitchen next to the range.

It was quarter to seven when he heard the trundle of the lorry and the familiar clank of the handbrake.

"By 'eck, Edward, I was about to give tha up," said Arthur as he went out to greet the miller. He stopped in his tracks when he saw the trailer.

"Aye, Arthur, sorry, but there's been some right bother. The mill chimney were struck by lightning in the storm;

right mess it were, bricks everywhere. There's no flour at the moment. I've had to get all t'lads working to clear up t'mess. These I have were t'last in stock. It's one for each customer; it's all I can manage."

"That's bad, Edward, right bad. I don't know what us'll do, I had two sacks, but they got ruined by the water."

"Aye, I'm right sorry, but there's nowt I can do."

"Can tha just give us another? I can make it worth thar while."

"I'll be in trouble if t'other customers find out."

"Well, I'll not say owt."

"Aye, fair enough, but keep it to thaself, eh?"

The miller lugged the two sacks into the baking shed, and Arthur paid Edward an additional half a crown for his troubles.

"Thanks, Arthur, 'appen things'll be back to normal on Monday."

"Aye, Edward, let's hope so."

The miller left, leaving Arthur with a big problem. The two bags of flour would hardly last the morning, certainly on a Saturday.

Grace and Agnes came down to the baking shed about seven-thirty to see how Arthur was managing.

"I'll not be ready for eight o'clock; miller's only just come and there's not enough flour for the day unless we can find some from somewhere."

"What about Granger's?" said Grace.

"I doubt they'd spare us any even if they had some."

"No harm in asking."

"Aye, that's true enough. Can you go and see?"

Granger's store was the large grocery business on the corner of James Street and the main road. They were not competitors as such but did sell a wide range of cakes and also the ingredients that went into them.

Arthur told Agnes to put a sign on the door to say that due to the storm, the bakery would not be open until eight-thirty. That was the earliest Arthur thought he would have the first batch of bread ready.

Fifteen minutes later, Grace returned from the grocery.

"I spoke to George Granger; he says he'll sell you a bag, but it will be at the retail price."

"Aye, I guess it might be. He's as cunning as a fox is George. That'll be nearly twice what I pay Buxton's I'll warrant."

"Aye, he said one pound nineteen shillings and fourpence."

"What!? That's robbery." Arthur had no idea where Granger bought his flour; he didn't think it was Buxton's. Arthur's normal price from them was one pound ten shillings a hundredweight.

"That's what he said. It's what he would make from selling it by the bag, by all accounts... He said to take it or leave it."

"Aye, I'll give it some thought; let's get this mixed and baking."

By eight o'clock, several customers had arrived for their bread but left disgruntled as soon as they read the message. Half an hour later, the queue stretched up James Street halfway to the butcher's.

As Arthur brought in the first batch of loaves from the shed; he could see the queue outside the door.

"We'll have to give 'em one loaf only today to make it go 'round."

"They won't be happy with that," said Grace.

"Aye, but it's fairest way; tell 'em we'll be back to normal on Monday, and best get Molly down to help." Agnes went upstairs to fetch her sister.

Arthur opened the door at twenty-to-nine to be greeted by numerous rumblings of complaint. "It weren't my fault," he shouted at one woman. "It were the bloody storm."

Grace witnessed Arthur's rant. It was the first time she'd heard Arthur use any sort of expletive. She chuckled to herself as the customer shrank forlornly into the waiting line.

With Arthur at full throttle and the three girls serving, by nine-fifteen the queue had gone and it was back to the usual trickle of customers. There were many complaints about the enforced rationing.

Outside the shop, James Street was busy. Corporation workmen were starting to clear up the gutters and drains. The electricity supply had been reconnected, so the trolleybuses were working again. There seemed to be more horse-drawn carriages about, Arthur noticed.

At around eleven o'clock, a young gentleman with slicked-down dark hair, and wearing a smart suit, arrived in the shop causing a stir among the sisters who were jostling to serve him.

"How can I help you, kind sir?" said Agnes, coquettishly, before the other two could respond. She recognised him from her visit to the solicitors.

He handed a letter to her. "Can you give this to Mrs Marsden please, it's from Mr Drummond, Peacock Drummond."

"Aye," said Agnes. "It will be my pleasure."

She turned her head slightly to one side and blinked several times. The young man looked flustered and turned to leave.

"What's your name?" said Agnes.

He turned back to face her. "It's Norman, Norman Hoskins... I... I'm an Articled Clerk working for Mr Drummond," he stammered.

"Nice to meet you, Mr Hoskins. I'm Agnes. I hope we'll see you in here again," she said, dropping the local dialect.

"Yes, yes, I expect so," he replied nervously.

He pulled the door with a clang and left hurriedly, crossed James Street, and headed towards the park entrance.

Agnes giggled to herself and looked at the letter. "I'll take this upstairs to mam," she said gesturing to Grace. There was another clang as the next customer entered the bakery.

Mildred was in the kitchen busy washing out the wet clothes from the previous day. The dresses were hung next to the range to dry out; there was a degree of warmth from the oven. Arthur's boots were on top but had white marks where the leather was stained from the water. They would need further attention with some boot polish.

"Mam, there's a letter for you," called Agnes.

Mildred dried her hands and went into the parlour. "Who's it from?" she asked, taking it from her daughter.

"It's from Mr Drummond."

"Oh, right... How are things in the shop?"

"Arthur's not much flour left, and it's barely eleven o'clock. 'Appen we'll run out in less than an hour."

"What's to be done?"

"Mr Granger said he would sell us a bag, but it will be very pricey."

"Did he indeed? I think I'll have a word with George Granger. Let me get my hat."

Mildred, with hat in place, followed Agnes down to the baking shed where Arthur was finishing the last of the flour.

"Eh up mam, 'ow be tha?"

"Agnes tells me Granger's will sell us some flour. What's he say?"

"Aye, Grace called up this morning. Wants one pound nineteen odd for a bag."

"And what do we pay Buxton's?"

"One pound ten shillings."

"Right, let me have a word with George Granger."

Arthur went back to his mixing and Agnes to the shop. Trade had quietened after the earlier rush.

Mildred strode business-like up James Street. It was a great deal cooler than the previous week and rain clouds were present but not with the anger of those of the previous day.

All the shops were open, and the pavement in front of each establishment had been cleared of mud and horse effluent brought down by the storm, although many people were wearing Wellington boots. Trade seemed to be brisk. Mildred passed the greengrocer's and butcher's, and there were queues at each.

She reached the corner and walked into Granger's Grocery store. It too was busy inside, with a queue at the long glass counter. There were six girls serving.

Mildred looked around the store. It always appeared dark and gloomy, she thought; the daylight was obscured by the large awning, but the array of stock was impressive, illuminated by electric lighting. Tins of all manner of produce were piled high. If it could be canned, then Granger's appeared to supply it. Toiletries, an excellent cheese counter, cakes and scones, confectionery, pressed ham, and other meats were also on display. Mildred had shopped there for many years and was one of Granger's best customers.

She saw George Granger cutting some corned-beef at the

end of the counter. He was a round, portly fellow with a white moustache; a flat cap was hiding his bald head. He finished using the hand-powered bacon-slicer and passed the meat to one of the serving girls. He looked up and saw Mildred hovering over him like a hawk stalking a lapwing.

"George Granger, I need a word."

"Eh up, Mrs Marsden, aye, what can I do fer thee?"

"George Granger; I'm disappointed in you."

"Why's that, Mrs Marsden?"

"I hear you won't sell us a bag of flour."

"Nay, I'll sell thee a bag."

"Yes, at one pound nineteen shillings. How are we going to make a profit on that? We keep our prices low so people can afford them, you know that."

"Aye, aye."

"So, I expect a bit of support; these are hard times with flood and all. Come on, George, what do you say?"

Mildred meant business; there was no doubting that.

"Aye, aye, alright." He pushed his flat cap off his brow, revealing more of his bald head, giving the matter some thought.

"One pound fifteen shillings."

"One pound thirteen shillings, and you'll still make a good profit," countered Mildred.

She opened her purse and took out a pound note, then a ten-shilling note and put them on the glass counter in front of Granger; then started looking for the coins.

"Tha'll put me out of business, Mrs Marsden."

"Nothing of the sort. You're not short of a penny or two, George Granger."

Mildred found the three shillings and added them to the notes. "There you are… cash in hand. What do tha say?"

George's cap was nearly at the back of his head and in

danger of falling off.

"Aye, go on, seeing as it's tha."

"And you can that get that lad of yours to bring it down directly; we're near run out."

"Aye, right away, Mrs Marsden."

"Thank you, George, I'll bid you goodbye."

Granger picked up the money and called the lad.

Mildred returned to the bakery with news of her negotiations with the grocer. Arthur was in the shop.

"Thanks mam."

"You just need to be firm with these tradesmen, Arthur; you're too weak."

"Aye, I'll have it in mind."

Mildred returned to the parlour and remembered the letter from the solicitor. She examined the elegant hand-written script on the envelope. She opened the letter and sat down to read it.

'Dear Mrs Marsden

Following your recent visit, I have had cause to speak to Josiah Springett and I am pleased to say I think he has just the house you were looking for. It has recently been brought for sale following the death of the owner, Sir James Springfield, of whom you may be familiar.

I have enclosed Mr Springett's sale notice which provides more detail of the property.

If you would kindly study the same, perhaps you can let me know if you would like me to arrange a viewing.

Yours most sincerely

Nevil Drummond, Solicitor.'

The sale notice dropped on the floor and she bent down to pick it up.

Sir James Springfield was a name with which she was

acquainted, a mill owner with a reputation among his workers for bullying and mistreating. Few people mourned his passing.

Mildred started to read.

Springfield Hall was described as a 'fine country residence', former home of the late Sir James Springfield, Wool Mill owner.

She looked at the specifications: six bedrooms, bathroom, toilet, entrance hall, dining room, library, study, kitchen, scullery, various outbuildings and three acres of land. 'Electric lighting has been installed', it said.

Mildred felt a strange sensation, partly excitement, partly nervousness at the possible undertaking. Could this really be mine, she asked herself. She would contact Mr Drummond on Monday and arrange a viewing. In the meantime, she needed to persuade the children of the viability of her intention.

All morning, she couldn't stop thinking about the new house and found it difficult to settle. She picked up the previous evening's newspaper and started to read. Her eyes were drawn to a theatre production. She had never been to the theatre before but had always wanted to go. She had passed the Hippodrome many times and watched the audience going in wearing their finery. She read the programme; 'The London Actress', it said, the last day. It started at seven-thirty; she would give it some thought. She knew Nathaniel Hepworth, the general manager; he was a customer. She was sure she would be able to be accommodated. The thought, at least, had distracted her mind from any potential house purchase.

Back in the baking shed, Granger's lad had carried down the sack of flour on his back, and Arthur was already using the contents. This would be the last mix of the day; there would be an early closure.

By twelve-thirty, the shelves were empty and all the flour gone. There would be no more bread today.

Arthur went outside with the pole and pulled in the awning, then locked up and displayed the 'closed' sign. The three girls started cleaning.

"I'm going to see Wilfred," said Arthur, leaving the bakery.

It was good to get out; he breathed deeply as he stepped onto the pavement. Traffic seemed to have recovered its normal urgency and people were milling about among the shops which were enjoying some welcome trade after yesterday's storm.

He was still feeling the effects of the previous day's trauma and the consumption of ale. For some reason, he felt angry at the world. Although he would never admit it, he was becoming an inveterate drinker and in danger of ending up like his father.

He reached the butcher's and could see Wilfred cutting joints on the wooden block behind the counter. Six customers were waiting to be served.

"Eh up, Wilfred," said Arthur, trying to attract his attention.'

The butcher turned around.

"'Ow do, Arthur, tha's a bit early. How be tha?"

"Aye, 'appen we're out of flour; nowt to be done now. I'm going t'Shovel, fancy joining us?"

"Aye, I'll be down directly. Just need to finish here."

"Aye, ok... sithee soon," said Arthur and left the shop.

Arthur walked back down James Street. Old Walter

Nugent, the greengrocer, was starting to take in his produce from outside. Arthur doffed his cap. Walter had been a fixture on James Street for as long as anyone could remember. No-one knew his age for sure, but into his eighties was the popular belief.

Arthur thought about this as he walked by. Did he want to be still serving bread from the bakery when he was Walter's age, if of course, he survived that long? He had no answer.

It was turned three o'clock before Arthur returned to the parlour and, as he took off his boots and cap, announced that he and Wilfred were going to the Picture House to see 'Thor, Lord of the Jungle'.

"What's it about?" asked Grace.

"Not sure… the jungle, I think…. Kathlyn Williams is in it. There's one of that Charlie Chaplin's films on too. Some of the lads in t'Shovel went on Thursday and thought it were good. It weren't on last night cos of the storm. All t'lights were off, they said."

Hearing about Arthur's night out, made up Mildred's mind.

"Well, I'm going to the theatre," she said with a degree of triumph.

"You're going to the theatre?" said Grace.

"Yes, I've wanted to go, and tonight I shall."

"What, on your own?"

"I don't see why not."

"Well, if Arthur's going out, 'appen I can come with tha to the theatre," said Grace, who was a keen reader of stage magazines.

Mildred looked at Agnes. "If you don't mind looking after Molly and Freda."

"No, I don't mind. Tha must tell us what it's like." Agnes

was also interested in the stage, particularly the songs of the music halls and would regularly be heard singing around the flat.

"That's settled then. We will leave at quarter-to-seven."

Mildred was biding her time to announce the contents of the solicitor's letter.

"Any more news on the storm?" she asked. She wanted to keep Arthur engaged.

"Aye, it were bad. Bradford was worse than here, so they said. Forster Square was underwater."

"My, my… It's a long time since I went to Bradford. Maybe we should go one day."

"Aye, 'appen it won't be tomorrow; the railway line's blocked."

"Goodness, I've never known a storm like it," said Mildred, not for the first time.

She couldn't wait any longer.

"I need to say something to you. Molly, Freda, you come and listen too."

With the family together, Mildred opened the letter from the solicitor.

"I've had a letter from Mr Drummond this morning and he has found a fine house for us."

Arthur looked at Grace, but before he could say anything, Mildred started reading the details from the sales inventory.

"Aye, sounds grand right enough… Where is it?" said Arthur.

"In Oakworth… Springfield Hall."

"Is that owt to do with James Springfield?"

"I don't know, I suppose it might be," said Mildred, not wishing to disclose her knowledge.

"Folks 'round here spit on his grave. We should have nowt to do wi' it," said Arthur, who went to get up.

"Now then, don't be too hasty, Arthur. It's of no consequence whose house it was, what matters is how we behave."

Arthur couldn't think of an argument.

"I'm going to get a paper," he said and left the parlour.

Chapter Seven

Arthur returned with his paper a few minutes later to find he was now outnumbered. Mildred had persuaded the girls to visit the house with her as soon as it could be arranged.

Arthur felt cornered. He opened his newspaper on the table, completely ignoring the rest of the family. It was Grace who took the initiative.

"Now then, Arthur, it's no use getting narky. Mam's doing her best for us and tha should be more respectful. It won't hurt for us to visit the house... or do you want to spend your life as a backstreet baker with just your drinking friends for company?"

"What do you know, you and your women's movement? Tha don't know tha place."

Grace was furious.

"Arthur Marsden, how dare you say such things. You go on about workers' rights; 'appen you pay some account to how women are treated in this country, second class citizens, every one."

"Now then, now then, you two, stop arguing," said Mildred, seeing emotions were running high.

"Arthur, don't talk like that to your sister. If you don't want to come to the house, that's up to you, but we are going; I'm not staying here for the rest of my life. You're just like your father, stubborn to a fault."

Arthur looked up from his paper. His sisters were staring at him, Grace had her arms folded and was still angry. "Come on Arthur," said Agnes. "We need to be a family together."

Arthur sighed in resignation and reluctantly agreed. "Aye, go on then, I'll come with thee and look at t'place."

"Good, that's settled then; I'll write back to Mr

Drummond."

"I can take the letter for you, mam," said Agnes rather eagerly.

"Yes, that will be most kind."

"Only wants to see her fancy man," Grace teased. Agnes playfully smacked her arm.

"Ow!" said Grace. "Mind my arm; it's still sore." She pulled back her sleeve to reveal three yellowy-purple marks.

"Oh, sorry," said Agnes.

"What's this about a fancy man?" said Mildred.

"I think our Agnes has a heart for a certain gentleman there," replied Grace.

"I do not!" exclaimed Agnes.

"And who might that be?" asked Mildred now intrigued.

"His name is Norman, he's clerking there," said Grace. "He delivered the letter; right smitten she was."

"I was not," said Agnes.

Mildred remembered the young man. He would be a good prospect for one of her daughters.

"Don't tease, Grace... Agnes, you can deliver the letter Monday morning. I'll write it this afternoon."

Agnes smiled.

"You won't forget we're going to Oakworth tomorrow. I've ordered a cabbie for three-thirty."

Arthur looked up. "Don't worry Arthur, you don't have to come."

"'Appen he'll still be in t'Shovel," said Grace.

Arthur ignored the remark and went back to the newspaper.

"Anything interesting today, Arthur?" asked Mildred.

Like most newspapers, the front page was taken by advertisements and announcements. Keighley Cricket Club was holding a garden party, the Central Chiropody Surgery was offering services for warts, bunions, and calluses; then there was the cinema and theatre programme. There was an advertisement for Black Cat Cigarettes. The news was inside, which Arthur was scanning.

"Aye, mostly about t'storm. 'Appen Bradford were hit bad. Says here a shop were hit by lightning and burnt down. They reckon damage's in city's over a hundred thousand pounds."

He continued digesting the news. There was more about the assassination of Archduke Ferdinand which had attracted a great deal of sympathy around Europe, but nobody could yet predict its eventual effect. Arthur took little more than a passing interest.

A report of the inquest of an unfortunate fifteen-year-old shuttle-maker called Ronald Laycock did catch his eye. He had been killed in one of the factories when the Emery Wheel he was working on burst. Graphic details of his injuries were described. The verdict of 'Misadventure' meant Thomas Burwin and Co, his employer, would escape any formal sanction.

Arthur recoiled at the injustice; it was another example of how the working class were being treated.

Emotions gradually cooled. Mildred and Agnes retired to their bedrooms to get ready for the theatre. Arthur eventually left his newspaper to prepare for his evening at the 'pictures'.

Mildred was seated in front of her mirror, applying the merest hint of makeup. Her black-lacquered Japanned box containing her cosmetics was open on the dressing table. She would use some lemon juice to maintain a light complexion and a touch of lip rouge, recently purchased from the pharmacy in North Street; too much and she would belong more on the stage, or the street.

For the first time in her life, she felt a sense of empowerment and entitlement after years of being shackled by an invisible yoke, a yoke that had choked the very lifeblood from her, sucking out her very spirit.

For Mildred, tonight was an adventure. The many times she had listened to customers' accounts of theatre visits, so refined, so civilised, so... gentrified. She was determined to make the most of the experience. She was also pleased to share it with Grace, who, she felt, was now mature enough to appreciate the finer things in life.

Mildred and Grace said goodbye to the girls and left the parlour around six-forty; Arthur had already left to meet Wilfred.

Two taxis were waiting for custom. Mildred crossed the road towards them, skipping over more horse droppings; she walked to the first one with Grace close by. A red-faced cyclist pedalled past, making heavy weather of the James Street's gradient.

Mildred gave the address to the cabbie and he helped them inside in turn. Grace felt like a lady sat in the back of a taxicab; she couldn't remember such an experience before.

The driver stopped directly outside the theatre entrance and opened the door for the ladies to exit. Mildred paid the fare and tip. She looked up at the impressive building and then at the people making their way inside, dressed in their finery. She would soon have a wardrobe to be proud of, she vowed.

The Hippodrome was an impressive four-story building on the corner of Queen Street and Adelaide Street and stretched the length for almost a hundred yards. The façade of the theatre featured ornamental carvings, with an iron veranda fitted with coloured glass, running the whole length of the frontage. This was where queuing customers took shelter in the event of inclement weather. Its old name, 'The Queens Theatre', was still displayed next to the new name.

Mildred and Grace entered the theatre and joined the queue at the box office; the prices were displayed behind the cashier.

Grace turned to her mother and whispered. "Are you sure we can afford this?"

"Aye, and a lot more besides," replied Mildred.

Mildred managed to buy the last two tickets in the dress circle; it was a popular show she was told. They walked up the stairs to the entrance and entered the auditorium. Mildred looked around to see if she could see anyone she knew. The pit stalls, dress circle, and balcony all had tip-up seats covered in crimson velvet. The curtain was down; Mildred marvelled at the ornamental proscenium. She could see the orchestra pit, which was empty for tonight's production; there was no music. It was a whole new experience.

The theatre was full and, just before seven-thirty, the lights dimmed and the curtain opened. Mildred felt a shudder inside; she had never experienced such delights before.

Violet Vaughan played the leading role, the guest 'London Actress', as advertised in the newspaper. Applause broke out as she took to the stage. Mildred and Grace were engrossed as the play unfolded.

The show finished at nine-thirty to a rapturous ovation. Mildred looked across to Grace; the joy on her face had made the excursion all the more worthwhile. "Enchanting," said Mildred. It was the right word to describe her emotions.

They made their way out of the theatre and Mildred was looking for a taxi. "Let's walk," said Grace. "It's not far and the fresh air would be welcome."

"Yes, that's a good idea. What did you think?"

"It was wonderful," replied Grace. "My best time, ever."

Mildred thought for a moment and had to agree with Grace; it was probably her best time ever too.

The following day saw growing excitement among the Marsden ladies, anxiously waiting for their trip to Oakworth. At breakfast, Grace was recounting her theatre excursion to her sisters, still gushing about the experience.

Arthur was becoming more morose. He almost fell asleep during the church service and had to be nudged by Agnes more than once when snores emanated from his open mouth. Truth be told, he was still hungover from his night at the Picture House with Wilfred. The Mason's Arms, close by, was the venue for the imbibing afterwards, not their regular haunt, but perfectly acceptable in that it sold ale.

After the service, the family returned to the bakery; Arthur announced he was going back to bed. Mildred made some lunch and, after cleaning up, the girls got themselves ready for their trip to the seamstress.

Arthur was still sleeping, and Mildred decided against waking him. "He'll be of better spirit when he wakes up," she told Grace.

At three twenty-five, they left the parlour; the taxi they had ordered was waiting outside the shop. Across the road, the taxicab bays were empty. A trolleybus went by but with few people on board. The park was also less busy with the cooler weather. It was cloudy but no threat of rain. There was still plenty of debris on the ground from Friday's storm.

Apart from Grace, the girls had not ridden in a taxi before, and the trip was almost as exciting as the much-anticipated dress fitting. On the journey, evidence of the storm was everywhere, mud and effluent across the road, broken branches, flooded fields, fallen walls, all victims of the torrential rain.

Mildred sat in the front next to the driver and struck up a conversation. He proceeded to point out places of storm incidents. "Aye, a man were stood under yonder tree there and was struck down; it were like the fist of God, I heard. Dead afore he touched t'ground, that's what I was told." He pointed to a large elm, on the corner of a junction in the road.

It was just after four o'clock as the taxi turned into Slaymaker Lane. Inside the cab, the excitement was mounting.

The taxi stopped outside the Box hedge in front of Blossom Cottage. The driver alighted and opened the doors for the passengers to get out. "Can you return at six o'clock, please, to take us back to the bakery?" said Mildred and paid the man.

With the return journey secured, Mildred opened the small picket gate in the gap in the hedge and walked down the crazy-paving path to the front door. "Mind your step on the paving," warned Mildred.

It was wise words as Grace had become very distracted as she followed her siblings towards the front door. A few yards to her left, a young man was tying up canes supporting runner beans which appeared to have fallen in the storm. Grace stopped for a moment and stared. His discarded shirt was strewn on top of a blackcurrant bush. His breeches were hung at his hips; his white trouser braces were hanging down from their buttons, his torso gleamed with sweat, not from any great heat but from his exertions. He left his labours and walked towards the visitors.

"Come on, Grace," shouted Agnes.

Grace turned and caught her shoe on one of the raised paving slabs, sending her sprawling. The young man was just a short distance away and had seen the slip. He jumped forward and caught her before she had chance to hit the floor.

Grace was more embarrassed than hurt.

"Eh up, that were quite a tumble, are tha alright?" he said.

"Aye, thank you, just caught my shoe."

The ground was still wet, and Grace's hands were covered in mud. Immediately the lad took out a handkerchief from his pocket and handed it to her. "Here, wipe thaself down; it is clean."

Grace took the cloth and wiped her hands, then returned it.

Agnes had seen the fall and rushed to her sister. Mildred and the two youngest had reached the front door, unaware of the mishap.

"Are you alright, Grace?"

"Aye, right enough, just a trip." She looked at the man. "Thank you. That was very kind."

"My pleasure, I'm sure… I'm Freddie."

"I'm Grace," she said, repositioning her hat which had become displaced.

"I'm Agnes," said her sister, quickly introducing herself to the chivalrous lad.

"Come on t'cottage. 'Appen tha've come for the fitting. Mam said we were expecting visitors this afternoon."

Freddie stopped for a moment and slipped his braces over his shoulders, then walked along the path towards the front door. The two eldest siblings followed, giggling to each other.

By the time they had reached the door, Kitty was there greeting her guests. Mildred had already been invited inside. As he approached, Kitty looked at her son.

"Freddie, where's your shirt? You can't come in the house looking like that."

"Aye mam."

He turned and walked back to the blackcurrant bush, retrieved his shirt, and put it on.

The girls followed Kitty and Mildred into the parlour.

"Please, be seated… I've made some cakes and kettle's on we can have some tea before we start the fitting," said Kitty.

She left Mildred and the girls and headed into the kitchen. The room went quiet; the four daughters taking in their surroundings, too shy to start a conversation.

The front door opened and Freddie walked in, now suitably dressed; he joined the women in the parlour. He looked at Mildred and the two younger daughters. "I'm Freddie."

Mildred was struck dumb for a moment, unable to think of an appropriate greeting. She just stared at her late husband's son, looking for resemblances. She replied, almost subconsciously. "Hello… Freddie, I'm Mrs Marsden… oh, and this is Freda, Molly, Grace and Agnes." She introduced her daughters in turn.

"We've already met," said Grace.

"Aye, it were quite a tumble… are you sure tha's alright?" he said looking at Grace with concern.

"Aye, 'appen I should look where I'm going." She dropped her gaze, demurely, unable to maintain eye-contact.

"Nice view you have here, Freddie," said Mildred, trying to make conversation but not knowing what to say. The other girls looked out of the back window. The hills and trees were remarkably green against the grey sky.

"Aye, but 'appen I'm used to it; I don't take a mind anymore."

Kitty walked in carrying a tray containing a large china teapot with matching cups and saucers; she placed it on the table, then returned to the kitchen to fetch the milk, sugar, and a plate of cakes.

"I see you've met Freddie," said Kitty as she poured the tea.

"Yes," said Mildred and looked knowingly at Kitty.

"He's been out all day repairing damage in the garden; the storm's fair flattened everything."

"Yes, we had a flood at the bakery, a dreadful mess," responded Mildred.

The teas were handed around.

"We'll just finish our tea, and then I'll take you through to the workshop. The dresses are all pinned. I just need to make sure they fit before I start sewing," said Kitty. "And Freddie, you best go and make yourself presentable now we have visitors."

"Aye mam," said the lad and left the parlour. Grace's eyes followed him out of the room.

There was more polite conversation.

"Oh, I do have some news," said Mildred, after a few minutes, seemingly as an afterthought but something she was dying to share.

Kitty looked at Mildred in anticipation.

"I have a mind to buy a property."

"Really, and what property do you have in mind?" replied Kitty.

Mildred opened her handbag and pulled out the sales inventory she had received from Josiah Springett.

"This one," she said and handed Kitty the flyer.

Kitty read the heading.

"Springfield Hall!?" It was half statement, half question. "But that's not a mile away."

"Yes, quite close, I think." The girls were eating cake and drinking tea, just watching the discourse. Kitty was reading the inventory.

"My, but this is a grand house, Mrs Marsden. I am sure you'll be very happy there."

"Do you know it at all?" asked Mildred.

"Well, I've not been inside, but folk say it's magnificent. You can see it from Howarth Road..." She took a sip of tea. "The late Sir James was not a well-liked man 'round here. No respect for people, I heard. Oswald Jessop up at the store, his wife worked there as housekeeper for a while, but left because of his rudeness."

"Really? That's unforgivable, there's no room or need for rudeness in this world; it's a harsh enough place without."

"Yes, that's true enough. So what will happen?" said Kitty.

"Well, we hope to view it this week if the agent is amenable."

"You must call in and tell me all about it."

"Yes, most certainly, we will," said Mildred, who took a final sip of her tea.

Just then, Freddie returned looking refreshed and smart in his 'Sunday best'.

"Oh dear, tea's cold," said Kitty. "Go and make some fresh; I expect the girls could drink another cup." There were polite nods from the girls. Grace kept looking down, unable to make any eye contact with Freddie.

He left the room with the teapot and returned a few minutes later with the contents replenished.

Kitty refilled the cups.

"So, Freddie, you work at the Mill, I hear?" said Mildred.

"Aye, Providence, up on t'lane."

"In the combing shed, your mam was telling me?"

"Aye."

Mildred was not the only one taking more than a passing interest in the young man. Grace could hardly take her eyes off him. Mildred was doing her own assessment. He had some of the features of his late father, but there was a softness to him which was an alien trait to the late baker.

With their afternoon teas finished and the plate of cakes empty, Kitty led the girls out of the parlour and through to the studio where five mannequins were stood, each with pinned-up garments dressed on them.

"I have had to borrow two more mannequins; I don't normally do five dresses at one time," said Kitty as they approached them.

The girls couldn't believe their eyes seeing their dresses coming to life.

"Kitty, these are wonderful," said Mildred, examining hers minutely.

The girls hovered around the mannequins, checking their individual designs, chatting excitedly as they compared notes.

"I just need you to try them on but be careful, they are only held together with pins and tack stitching," said Kitty. "You will need to take off your outerwear, don't worry, there's no one about."

Grace had a wicked thought that Freddie was watching her take off her dress ready for the fitting. Oh, how she would love that, she thought to herself. She was blushed and flustered, but no one would notice.

It took a good hour before Mildred and the girls had tried on their dresses and adjustments were made. The atelier was alive with chatter and energy. Kitty was fussing about her charges like a doting mother, feeling somehow one of the family. A point not lost on Mildred, not with any sense of ire, but with inward joy; Kitty <u>was</u> one of the family.

Mildred noticed the clock on the small table in the workshop; it was almost six o'clock.

"My, look at the time, how it has flown. The cabbie will be here directly; we must take our leave, Kitty."

"Of course, Mrs Marsden. The dresses should be ready by the weekend if you have a mind to visit again on Saturday."

The girls looked at each other; the joy on their faces obvious.

"Yes, that will be perfect, perfect indeed, Kitty. Bakery closes at one o'clock; shall we say three o'clock?"

"Yes, three will be most convenient…"

Kitty looked around the parlour and the hallway; there was no sign of Freddie. She called upstairs, still no answer. "He'll be back in the garden, I warrant," she said.

She opened the cottage door to allow her visitors to leave and, sure enough, Freddie had returned to the errant runner bean canes; his shirt was still on. Grace was taking more than a passing interest.

Just then, the taxi pulled up at the end of the footpath and Mildred and the girls said their farewells to Kitty. Freddie saw they were about to leave and walked over to them.

"It's been nice to meet you Freddie," said Mildred. Freddie removed his cap.

"Aye, you too… Have a safe journey."

He looked at them in turn and stopped at Grace. "Mind how you go up t'path, Miss Grace. Don't go stumbling again."

"No, Master Freddie, that I won't, but 'appen you'll be there to catch me."

"Aye, that I will," said Freddie.

"Grace, stop flirting with young Freddie," said Agnes, hearing the discourse and breaking the atmosphere. Grace gave her sister a withering look.

"Come on, girls, let's not keep the cabbie waiting," said Mildred, not hearing Agnes's remark.

With a final wave, they walked up the path to the waiting taxi. As the driver opened the door for them to alight, Grace turned for a final look at Freddie. Instinctively she waved; Freddie waved back.

The homebound journey to the bakery was as exciting as the earlier one to Oakworth; the talk and comments about each choice of garment was incessant.

"I think our Grace has taken a shine to young Freddie," said Agnes as they reached the outskirts of Keighley.

"How can you say such things?" said Grace, defensively.

"I saw the way you were looking at him."

"I was just being polite; he was very gracious in helping me when I fell."

"'Appen you did it on purpose to get his attention, more like," said Agnes, teasingly.

"Now girls, stop arguing. You can help with the tea when we get back; Arthur will be hungry," said Mildred.

"Aye, if he's not in t'Shovel," said Agnes.

But Mildred was distracted; Agnes's words were a concern. She couldn't afford any liaison between Grace and Freddie; it would cause no end of problems.

When they got back to the bakery, Arthur was in the parlour reading the previous day's newspaper; there were no editions on Sundays. The return of the girls had disturbed his solitude.

"Eh up, Arthur, tha's got up I see," said Agnes, the remark

clearly one of sarcasm.

"Aye, seems like," replied Arthur, his mood had not improved.

"Have you eaten?" asked Mildred.

"Not as yet," said Arthur, his demeanour impatient.

"There's some meat pie in the pantry." She looked at the girls. "Grace, Agnes, can you prepare some potatoes? We can eat together. Molly, Freda, you can wash the dishes"

After dinner, Arthur announced he was returning to the alehouse.

"I don't know why tha don't take tha bed there," said Agnes.

Arthur ignored the remark.

"Leave him be," said Mildred.

Arthur left the bakery and headed up James Street to call on Wilfred.

The Malt Shovel was busy with several mill workers taking a post-shift pint or two. Arthur and Wilfred joined a group who were complaining bitterly about the treatment they had been subjected to for supporting the recent strike. Arthur listened to their grievances.

"Did you read about them two men in t'paper begging for the strikers?" said Arthur.

"Aye, it were a bad do that," said one of the men.

"What happened?" asked Wilfred.

"Two lads, both strikers, went begging for children's clogs and pocketed the money the'selves."

"Nay, who would do such a thing?" said Wilfred.

"Aye, it's right enough, over Addingham way. Up before the magistrates, one got bound over t'other got fined a pound," said Arthur.

"Well, I'll tell tha this much," said the mill worker, lifting his pint; his face twisted with hate. "If they show their faces around here, there'll be trouble, make no mistake."

There were shouts of concurrence from the group.

Back in the parlour, Mildred was reading by the dim light of the gas lamp. The words were not registering, staring at her in a meaningless jumble as her mind tried to make sense of recent events.

Her main concern was Arthur. He had changed over recent days, and she was beginning to wonder if running the bakery was getting too much for him, especially now her husband was not around to give him guidance. For all his abusive nature, he had been a good mentor to Arthur in baking matters.

Then there was Grace. Mildred was desperately hoping that the attraction of Freddie Bluet would be just the fleeting fancy of an impressionable young lady. She would need to keep them apart at all costs. The good news was that Freddie would be working on their next visit.

These concerns were balanced by the excitement she was feeling about the proposed house purchase, but all served to ensure sleep would not come easy.

The following morning at five a.m., Arthur was waiting for the usual delivery of flour. It was a bright morning, the sky crystalline with a turquoise rim; the hum of industry echoed around the valley.

He had been thinking about his flour supply a great deal and had decided to replenish his stock with some extra bags to ensure he would not run out in the future.

The miller was late again; it was turned five-thirty when the usual rattle of Buxton's lorry bounced down West Street and parked outside the baker's yard.

"'Ow do, Edward, how be tha?" said Arthur. He looked at the trailer and could see it was less than half what he would normally expect to see.

"Not too bright, Arthur, as it 'appens." He got down from his cab, the engine was still running.

"What's up? Still problems at mill?"

"Aye."

"What, with the chimney?"

"Aye, in part. T'lads've cleared rubble and that, but we need to build a new one. We're managing for now with a pipe. But we're not getting us supplies of grain, that's t'real problem. They say the Government is buying up all the supplies, and millers in Bradford and Leeds are stock-piling, so I've heard."

"Aye? Never... I don't trust any of 'em. Asquith and all his Liberal cronies have no mind for working folk," replied Arthur, with some concern.

"Aye, 'appen thar right there."

"So, what can tha do for us? I wanted six if tha can spare."

"Nay, Arthur, lad. I can't do six. I've got other customers to see." The miller looked at the sacks piled on the trailer. "I'll tell tha what... I'll let tha have three."

"Aye, if that's tha best tha can do."

"Aye, sorry, young Arthur." There was a pause. "'Appen I need to change t'price an all."

"How's that?" said Arthur with a look of surprise.

"It's what I've got to pay for t'grain. It's all going up... price, like. I've got to cover that."

"Aye, so, what're tha wanting?"

"One pound twelve and six a bag."

"So that's seven and six more for three bags."

"Aye," replied the miller, looking down, somewhat

embarrassed.

"It seems I've no choice in the matter, do I? We'll be going out of business at this rate. I can't put up my prices, can I? Tha knows that." Arthur was getting angry and his voice was getting louder.

"Aye, I knows that; I knows… but what can us do?" He pushed his cap back on his head.

"Aye, go on then, if tha must. I don't have an option, do I? I'll take the three. Put them in t'shed, I'll need to go upstairs to get extra."

Arthur went to the parlour. His mother was in the kitchen preparing some food.

"Arthur… is that you?"

"Aye mam, I need more money for flour. 'Appen Buxton's putting t'price up. Says there's a shortage."

Mildred came out of the kitchen wiping her hands. "How much?"

"Seven and six."

"Seven and six? But that's robbery."

"Aye, but what can us do?"

"Wait, I'll fetch the money." She went into the bedroom and returned with three half-crowns, then handed them to Arthur.

"We need to think of changing millers, Arthur. I'll speak with George Granger and ask where he gets his."

"Aye, but 'appen he'll be in t'same boat."

"Maybe, but no harm in asking," said Mildred.

Arthur returned to the baking shed and paid the miller.

It was the usual busy morning in the bakery. Grace and Agnes were serving in the shop, and Molly and Freda were at school.

At eleven o'clock, Mildred left the parlour and went down

to the shop carrying a letter addressed to Mr Drummond. The bakery was quiet. Grace turned as she walked in.

"Are you still intending to go to your Suffragette meeting tonight?"

"Aye, mam," replied Grace, rather anxiously.

"Well, you mind you don't get into trouble again."

"Nay, it's just a normal meeting; there'll not be many there."

"Well, even so."

"Don't worry, I will take care, don't you mind."

Grace turned her back on her mother and started wiping down the counter.

If truth be known, it wasn't the Suffragette meeting that was exciting Grace. She had hardly slept thinking about the young man at Blossom Cottage. She hoped desperately to make his acquaintance again.

Mildred sighed and turned to Agnes.

"Agnes, I have the letter to go to Mr Drummond."

Agnes was clearing some of the empty trays ready to return them to the baking shed.

"Aye mam," she said excitedly. She had been waiting all morning to run this errand.

She took off her apron and put on her hat and left the shop. It had clouded over since the dawn brightness, but it was still reasonably warm – a typical summer's day.

The park was still showing the scars from Friday's storm. Corporation workers were sawing up large branches that had been brought down. There were one or two spectators, but otherwise the park was fairly empty.

Agnes reached the solicitor's and knocked on the door. It was opened as usual by Norman Hoskins, the articled clerk. Agnes felt herself blushing as he stood there looking at her.

"Hello," he said, a little nervously when recognising the

visitor.

"I have a letter from my mother for Mr Drummond," said Agnes.

"Aye, I'll see he gets it," replied Norman. He paused momentarily.

Agnes looked at him. "I have a mind to go for a walk come dinner time, here in the park."

"Aye, maybe I will be of a similar mind," replied the clerk.

"Sithee then perhaps, one o'clock."

"Aye," said Norman. "I'll see Mr Drummond gets the letter." He smiled and closed the door.

Agnes skipped back to the bakery.

Chapter Eight

In the baking shed, Arthur was worried.

With the lack of flour restricting Arthur's production, he had already imposed another limit of one loaf per customer to much complaint, but even with the rationing, the supply of bread would not last the day. He was getting increasingly concerned that trade would suffer. He needed to do something but was unsure what.

By one o'clock, he had finished what would be the final mix of the day. He took the last basket of loaves into the shop and placed it on the floor ready to restock the shelves. He walked to the front door and dropped the latch for the lunchtime break. The girls were taking off their aprons.

"There'll be no more bread today; that's the last of it," said Arthur.

"What do us tell customers?" said Agnes as she started to leave the bakery and return upstairs.

"Tell 'em what tha like; there's no more to be had once that lot's gone," replied Arthur, sharply. "I'm going down t'Shovel," and he left the shop, slamming the front door.

Agnes looked at Grace and shrugged her shoulders. They stocked the shelves and then headed for the parlour.

Mildred was waiting with some sandwiches.

"Not for me. I'm going out," said Agnes.

"Where's tha going?" asked Grace, intrigued.

"'Appen I'll get some fresh air in t'park."

With Mildred in the kitchen, Agnes sneaked into her mother's bedroom and found the lip-rouge on the dressing table. She quickly undid the lid, smeared a small amount on her finger, then applied it to her lips, checking the result in the mirror.

Happy that it had achieved the right effect, she returned to the parlour.

"I'll be back shortly," she shouted to Mildred, who was still in the kitchen.

Grace was seated at the table, eating a sandwich, and looked up. "Agnes, are you wearing makeup."

Agnes put her finger to her lips. "Shh, say nowt," she whispered and left the parlour before anything else could be said.

Agnes felt nervous as she crossed the road and entered the park. The numerous tree-surgeons were continuing their remedial work. The footpath was strewn with leaves and puddles making walking treacherous. She found a wooden bench close by the Rotten Row entrance to the park. The seating was still damp, but dry enough to be sat on.

She made herself comfortable and looked around; there was no sign of Norman, just workmen and the occasional dog-walker. Just then the front door to the solicitor's office opened and he appeared. Agnes wanted to wave to attract his attention but restrained herself. She was, after all, a lady.

Norman entered the park and spotted Agnes straightaway. He walked briskly towards her.

"Hello, do you mind if I join you?"

"Aye, if tha's a mind," said Agnes and moved along the bench to give him space.

She suddenly became conscious of her speech; it was a condition of the vernacular. She needed to speak more like a lady, she decided. She'd often listen in admiration to some of the gentry that had occasion to visit the shop and was trying to mimic their tone.

"What have you been doing this morning?" she asked, as refined as she could manage.

"There have been plenty of things to do," he replied.

He reached in his pocket and took out an envelope. "Can you give this to Mrs Marsden; it's from Mr Drummond."

"Yes, I will see that she gets it," said Agnes and took the envelope.

Norman seemed, not anxious exactly, more bashful, which Agnes found somewhat endearing. She would need to take the initiative.

"So, how old are you, Norman?"

"Uh… twenty-two."

"I'm eighteen, just last month… and where do you live?"

"Utley."

"Utley?"

"Yes," said Norman. "I live in the rectory."

"Your father's a vicar?"

"Yes, vicar of Utley for twenty years since."

"And you have many paramours I expect, a good looking fellow like yourself."

"No, no, whatever gave you that idea?"

Agnes looked at him, resplendent in his three-piece suit, fob-watch chain in his waistcoat, leather shoes. He had a fresh face and pale complexion. It looked like he was trying to grow a moustache, but it had yet to make its presence define his face as whiskers tended to do. He epitomised the young professional class.

"Just asking," she replied decorously, dropping her gaze momentarily.

"And you work in the bakery?"

"Aye, tha knows that," she said, unconsciously slipping back into her normal speech. "My Dad owns it or did. It's me mam now."

"Yes, it must be hard losing your father like that."

"Aye, but we will manage. Do you fancy a walk, Master Norman?"

"Yes, why not."

They both got up from the bench and walked towards the main road. A trolleybus went by towards Oakworth. There were many on the upper-deck, making the most of the drier weather. The sound of men sawing wood predominated the backdrop to the park. With the weather warming, the puddles in the footpath were starting to crust with mud.

"Have you ever been to the theatre, Norman?" She had decided to drop the 'master', despite her upbringing; it sounded too subservient.

"Yes, but not for some time; it was the Christmas pantomime. My father took us, myself and my sisters."

"You have sisters?"

"Yes, two."

"I have three... oh, and a brother, Arthur. He's the baker now... So, you like the theatre then?"

"Well, it was only the once."

"I've not been... but I have a mind to. Grace has, my sister. She said it was wonderful." She turned and caught his glance, hoping for a reaction. "I couldn't go on my own though," she added, not the most subtle of hints.

"You think I should accompany you?"

"Aye, if you've a mind."

There was a pause; another trolleybus went by in the opposite direction. There was more motorised transport around; Keighley seemed to have recovered from Friday's drenching.

"Yes, I would like that," said Norman.

Norman agreed to find a suitable production and contact her again.

Agnes was walking on air as she returned to the bakery after their walk.

"Where's tha been?" said Grace as Agnes entered the shop. Grace was wearing her apron and ready for customers.

"Just for a walk. I have a letter for mam. I'll just go and give it to her."

Agnes walked briskly up the stairs; her shoes clomping up the wooden steps.

Mildred was in the parlour and looked up as Agnes opened the door.

"I've a letter for you… from Mr Drummond."

"My, that was sooner than I expected."

"Yes, as it happens, I was taking some air, and I saw Mr Norman leaving the solicitors. He was on his way to deliver it, so I said I would save him the journey."

"That's most kind of you, Agnes."

Agnes returned to the bakery for what was going to be a short afternoon shift; there were just two small shelves of bread left.

In the parlour, Mildred opened the letter and sat down to read it.

'Dear Mrs Marsden

Following your recent letter, I have conveyed your desire to purchase Springfield Hall to Mr Springett and he has suggested an early meeting. He explained there has been a lot of interest in such a fine property.

He will be available tomorrow afternoon if that is convenient, at three-thirty. He will meet you at the house.

If you would kindly confirm the same, I will advise Mr Springett accordingly.

I remain, yours most sincerely.

Nevil Drummond, Solicitor.'

Mildred felt anxious. She read it again. *'A lot of interest'*, what did that mean?

She took out her writing pad and immediately replied,

agreeing to the time. She took the letter down to the bakery. There were three customers in the shop, all complaining at the imposed rationing. Agnes and Grace were doing their best to placate them.

Mildred waited for the shop to empty. "Agnes, can you run another errand?"

"Aye, mam, there's no bread left."

Mildred handed her the letter and Agnes's eyes lit up.

"It's to Drummond's, we can view the property tomorrow afternoon," replied Mildred.

Agnes took off her apron, put on her hat and made the journey back across the park. She rang the doorbell; again, it was Norman who answered. He seemed pleased to see her.

"Miss Agnes, it's a pleasure to see you again."

Agnes dropped her gaze. "Aye, you too. I have a letter from my mam for Mr Drummond."

She handed over the envelope.

"I'll see that he gets it."

"Will you be taking the air, tomorrow dinner time, Norman?" said Agnes.

"Yes, I certainly will," said Norman with a smile.

"'Appen, I'll sithee then," said Agnes, completely forgetting her desire to appear more scholarly.

"One o'clock," said the clerk and closed the door.

Agnes's smile brightened the grey afternoon. Rain threatened again.

Back at the bakery, the door was closed and a sign, 'No Bread', displayed. The girls were in the bedroom.

Arthur was back from the Malt Shovel but was in no better humour. The anxiety he was feeling about the flour problem was reflected in his behaviour. He turned to his newspaper but was hardly concentrating.

Mildred was close by and could smell the drink. Reminiscences of his father came to her, the same physique, facial expression, mannerisms. It was starting to worry her.

"What's the latest news from Buxton's?"

Arthur looked up; it was that same look that had haunted Mildred for so many years.

"Nowt different, 'appen there'll be no bread tomorrow."

"Why do you say that?"

"If there's no flour, there'll be no bread," he replied sharply.

"Has he said there will be no delivery tomorrow?"

"Nay, he's not said owt, but he was talking about the big millers taking all the supplies, so Buxton's will be left short... and they've lost their chimney."

"Why can't we find another supplier?"

"There'll be nowt round here, just Buxton's."

"What about the mills, they bake their own? They must get theirs from somewhere."

"Aye, I asked around at t'Shovel, but no one knew owt."

"Well, we can't sit here and do nothing. I'm going to see George Granger, see what he says."

"Aye, if tha think it will help."

"Well, I don't know, but it's a start. And in the meantime, I would be obliged if you would show more respect to your sisters and me. You are becoming quite ill-tempered these days."

"Aye, 'appen I have cause."

"And what good will all that sulking achieve? You're creating a bad feeling in the house. I had enough of that from your father. I don't want you turning into him."

Arthur was avoiding eye-contact, but the words were registering.

Mildred put on her hat and headed for the door. "I'll be back shortly," she said as she left the parlour, leaving Arthur with his newspaper. As he looked at the words, the typeface might well have been in Chinese for all the sense they were making. His concentration level was negligible.

He got up from the table just as Agnes entered the room.

"Where's mam?" she said.

"Gone t'grocery to see George Granger." He put on his cap and started lacing up his boots.

"And where's tha going?"

"Down t'Shovel; 'appen I'll get some peace there."

"But you've only just got back."

"Aye. Company's better and I don't get mithered."

"What about supper? I was about to start cooking."

"Don't fret none; I'll get something later."

He finished lacing his boots and left the parlour. Agnes could hear his heavy steps descending, clomp, clomp, clomp.

Outside the bakery, Archie Slater's echoing call rose above the passing traffic but with limited success; customers seemed few and far between today. Arthur acknowledged him and turned left in the direction of the alehouse.

Meanwhile, Mildred had walked in the opposite direction. As she passed the greengrocer's, old Walter Nugent, came out of the shop and started stacking the trays of fruit and vegetables to be taken indoors. His movements appeared laboured.

"Afternoon, Mrs Marsden," he said as she made eye-contact.

"Good day, Mr Nugent, I trust you are well?" acknowledged Mildred.

"Aye, as well as can be expected," he replied as he struggled to lift a pallet of apples.

She continued up James Street. Wilfred Stonehouse was

just negotiating the awning mechanism outside the butcher's with his long pole. He didn't see Mildred.

She reached the grocers. Five o'clock, and it was busy with women buying food for the evening meal; 'dinner' as it was called by the gentry, 'supper' to normal folk. It would be another half an hour before George Granger had his.

The cold meat counter was doing a good trade, and the proprietor was busy at his slicer, carving a large joint of brisket into wafer-thin slices.

He looked up and saw Mildred approach. Had he seen her enter the store, he would have escaped into the outside toilet, but it was too late; he was cornered.

"Mrs Marsden, a pleasure, how can I help thee?"

"Flour, Mr Granger, I would like to talk about flour."

"Ee, I can't help tha, I'm sorry, I've barely a bag left meself."

"No, Mr Granger, I'm not after buying some from you. Although I would happily take any spare off your hands. It seems Mr Buxton has a problem at the mill, his chimney came down in the storm apparently, and he can't get his normal deliveries out. I was wondering about the source of your supply."

The grocer pushed his cap back on his head, as was his habit.

"Aye, I heard that. I gets mine from wholesalers in Bradford."

"What's their name?"

"Ruskin's, it's where I get most of me stock."

"And do they deliver?"

"Aye, 'appen they do. I have the van here three times a week."

"And when's next delivery?"

"Aye, it will be Wednesday now, Mondays, Wednesdays

and Fridays. Friday is biggest delivery… for the weekend."

"What time will he be here on Wednesday?"

"Any time before ten; depends on what deliveries he has."

"Can you ask him to call at the bakery on Wednesday after he's finished here?"

"Aye, I don't see why not."

"That's very kind of you, Mr Granger, much appreciated. While I'm here, I'll take six slices of that brisket you're slicing. Can you make them a little thicker? You can see the tray through those you've just cut."

"Aye, right you are, Mrs Marsden."

He cut the slices to Mildred's satisfaction and she paid. The grocer put them in a brown paper bag and handed them to Mildred.

"Now, you won't forget, Mr Granger, will you?"

"Nay, nay, Mrs Marsden, I'll remember."

Mildred took her provisions and left the shop feeling happier about the flour situation. Maybe this was the lifeline they needed.

She returned to the parlour and straightaway noticed Arthur's empty chair and unattended newspaper open on the table.

Agnes came in from the kitchen, and Mildred handed over the beef. "We can have this for supper with some potatoes and lettuce."

"Aye, I'll see to it."

"Where's Arthur?" said Mildred.

"He's gone back to Malt Shovel."

"Has he indeed?"

Mildred checked her hat, turned, and left the room.

James Street was much quieter now. Archie Slater was still pleading with passing pedestrians to buy a newspaper but, with footfall diminishing, he was considering closing for the day and returning to the Keighley News office with his meagre takings.

Mildred crossed West Street. She could see the clerks in the bank, busying over their ledgers by the dim gaslighting. It seemed such a dreary existence.

She reached the alehouse and went inside. There was the usual buzz of conversation. Visibility was impaired by the blue haze of tobacco smoke. The smell of beer was so strong you could seal it in a jar. She turned right into the main bar and looked around for her errant son.

Heads, male heads, turned as she walked towards the bar counter. Then she spotted him in the corner; his back was towards her. He was with three other lads. The one facing Mildred nodded to Arthur to attract his attention to the interloper. He turned around, holding a pint glass with what was left of his beer.

"Mam? What are tha doing here?" To his knowledge, his mother had never set foot in a drinking establishment before.

"I need you back at the shop; there're matters to discuss."

Arthur was in a quandary. On the one hand, he didn't want his drinking pals to think he was at his mother's beck and call; on the other hand, he certainly didn't want to face her wrath.

"Aye, I'll be there directly." He turned his back and continued talking to his pals who were looking decidedly uncomfortable at his behaviour.

"Now, Arthur… this won't wait."

He turned and deliberately downed the dregs of his drink in front of her, mockingly. Mildred was furious but remained calm. If he had been a twelve-year-old boy, she would have dragged him out by the hair and clipped his ear.

"If you want a job tomorrow, you'll come now!" She walked towards the exit; the bar went quiet.

Arthur put down his pint glass and meekly followed his mother.

As she exited, she took in a large gulp of the evening air to clear her lungs of the fug of the alehouse.

She faced Arthur, her expression one of anger; a look Arthur hadn't seen before. She turned and headed back to the bakery. Archie Slater had finished his shift, and the front of the shop was clear except for some pieces of paper and other litter swept in by the wind. Mildred ignored it and went inside, still angry.

They ascended the stairs and entered the parlour.

Mildred turned around; Arthur knew he was in trouble.

"Right, Arthur, my lad, sit down; we are going to have a serious discussion."

She turned to Agnes and Grace, who were both reading. "Agnes, Grace, go to your room." They obeyed without question.

Arthur took off his cap and started undoing the laces on his boots.

Mildred looked at him sternly.

"I've just come back from Granger's and I might have found a solution to the flour situation."

"Aye, and what might that be?" Arthur slurred.

"He says he gets his supplies from a wholesaler in Bradford called Ruskin's."

"I don't know 'em," said Arthur.

"Well, you're about to become acquainted. I've asked Mr Granger to get them to call here on Wednesday morning to discuss getting us some flour."

"'Appen we may not have any tomorrow."

"If that's the case, you can take a cabbie to Bradford and get some."

Arthur didn't respond.

"We will find a way," continued Mildred. "This business has been here for nigh on a hundred years, and we're not giving up now, but you need to change your ways. You're drinking to excess and it's turning you into your father and you saw what it did to him with your own eyes."

Arthur was just staring into space, not sure how to respond. He had never heard his mother speak like this before.

"And there's another thing," she continued. "We're going to see the house tomorrow afternoon, and I want you to be there; you can go down the alehouse when we get back."

"Aye, whatever tha says," replied Arthur.

That evening, Grace, not without some anxiety, made her way to her monthly meeting of the Women's Social and Political Union. This time it was held in a church hall and had attracted no external interest. There was a great deal of discussion about the Annie Kenny rally. Several of the members were still in prison and refusing food. Their treatment nothing short of barbaric according to Minnie Glyde, who was chairing the event. She stirred emotions again and there were various suggestions of direct action which she was going to pass to the central committee for consideration. She urged members not to take any isolated action which might damage the cause.

Grace came away fired with the injustice and ready to take whatever action was decided by the local committee.

The following morning, Arthur walked through the baking shed and opened the external doors. He stared up at the skies; there was no sign of the rising sun, just a dark umber. The throb of distant machinery seemed louder unable to escape the misty canopy. His mouth was dry and his head throbbed.

He opened the gate to the yard and looked along the cobbled road towards James Street, wondering what Edward Buxton would bring today. He was feeling anxious as he prepared the oven, hoping that there would be something to bake. The fire was well alight as he heard the trundle of the wagon and the clank of brakes.

He walked to greet the miller.

"'Ow do, Arthur, how be tha?" said Buxton.

"Fair to middling," replied Arthur. "What've tha got for us?"

"Well, better news, we were able to get going again yesterday afternoon; temporary chimney seems to be holding, and we had three ton of grain delivered. I've got one of our lads to go up to Leeds on t'train to try and get some more delivered for tomorrow."

"Aye? Well, that's good news. Can tha let us have five bags?"

"I can do tha three today, Arthur... until I know what's happening."

"Aye, Edward, if that's the best tha can do. At the new price I suppose?"

"Aye, Arthur, if tha don't mind."

So the delivery was done, and the exigency had been abated for the time being. At least he would have enough for today's demand.

Unfortunately, rumours of shortages had spread like wildfire, and, by eight o'clock, a queue had formed outside the shop. On seeing the demand, Arthur quickly stepped in and imposed a quota which he hoped would see the supply last the day.

The flow of customers was incessant, Agnes and Grace were rushed off their feet. Then, around eleven o'clock, Agnes glanced up and noticed a friendly face. She felt her legs wobble and her hands were shaking; her face felt flushed. Eventually, he reached the counter.

"I can see you're busy, Miss Agnes; I just wanted to give you this." He passed her an envelope. "I'll see you in the park later; if you have a mind."

"Aye, Norman, that you will." She smiled at him and put the letter in her apron pocket. Her expression lit up the dismal morning.

She waited for the queue to calm and excused herself for the toilet.

"I'll not be long," she said to Grace.

"Aye, don't be," her sister replied.

Agnes walked through the baking shed. Arthur was mixing another batch of bread.

"Eh up, Agnes, how's it going?" he said, seeing his sister.

"Aye, we're managing, queue's died down a bit." She brushed by him and headed for the toilet at the corner of the yard.

Inside she took out the envelope and quickly read the note.

'Dear Agnes,

Since our meeting yesterday I have not been able to think of anything else, I think I am lovestruck. You are so beautiful and to think you would like me to accompany you to the theatre has made my heart jump summersaults in celebration. I have taken the liberty of visiting the Hippodrome box office this morning and purchased two tickets to see the variety show next Monday night. I do hope it meets with your approval.

Yours most respectfully,
Norman

It was Agnes's turn to skip a heartbeat. She returned to the bakery; her mind firmly fixed on lunchtime.

The next two hours or so seemed to drag. There was a large clock behind the counter; white-faced with a black surround and roman numerals, similar to those seen at railway stations. The hands seemed to have little momentum, but eventually, one o'clock arrived, and Arthur dropped the catch on the front door and turned around the hanging sign to indicate 'closed'.

Agnes rushed upstairs and went to her bedroom; Mildred was in the kitchen preparing food.

"Is that you, Agnes? I've made some sandwiches," she called.

"I'm going for a walk; I'll collect one when I get back," Agnes called back as she positioned her hat. She snuck into Mildred's bedroom again for another smear of rouge.

Grace was in the parlour as Agnes returned from the bedroom.

"'Appen, tha's going courting, Agnes," she said as her sister slipped on her best shoes.

"I'm just promenading," replied Agnes.

"Aye, with a certain clerk, I reckon."

Mildred walked in with a plate of sandwiches. "What's this about courting, Agnes?"

"Nothing, mam, just going for a walk."

"Well, you take care, young lady," said Mildred.

"Aye, I will," said Agnes as she turned and headed out the door.

Agnes crossed the road and walked into the park. The weather had brightened, and it was quite busy. The clearing up operation had been completed, but many of the trees bore the scars of the storm.

Agnes approached the bench and could see that Norman had arrived before her. She quickened her stride.

Norman stood up as she reached him.

"Hello Agnes, you're looking fine this morning."

"Thank you, kind sir. You look fine yourself."

"So did you read my letter?"

"Indeed I did, and I would be very happy to accompany you to the theatre next Monday."

"Then, you make me a happy man indeed. I also have another proposition for you."

"Aye? And what might that be?"

"It's the annual garden party on Saturday at the rectory and it would be an honour for me if you would attend as my guest."

"Saturday, you say?"

"Yes."

"What time?"

"It starts at two and finishes about eight."

"Hmm, I have an appointment Saturday afternoon," she said with a sense of frustration.

Norman looked crestfallen. "What time will you finish?"

Agnes could sense his disappointment. "I don't know, four-thirty or five o'clock, I believe. I will be in Oakworth."

"Well, you could always get a taxicab. Don't worry, I will see to the cost." Norman was not giving up.

"Aye, I'll speak to my mam and let you know." Agnes thought it would be a great opportunity to wear her new dress.

Meanwhile, back at the Malt Shovel, Arthur was enjoying

a lunchtime pint with Wilfred the butcher and several of his drinking pals. The talk was sombre. Far from being finished, the foundrymen's strike had boiled over again. The bosses had sacked several of the 'trouble-makers' who had been convicted of rioting, leading to another walkout. Feelings were running high.

"Eh, it's a bad do, right enough," said Wilfred.

"'Appen some of the lads are meeting up tonight and walking t'foundry to support the strikers. Tha coming, Arthur?" said Henry King, a millworker and one of Arthur's regular alehouse companions.

"Aye, 'appen I'll join tha, what time?"

"We can meet here at eight o'clock. What about tha Wilfred?" said Henry.

"Aye, I'll be there," the butcher replied.

The early afternoon trade continued to be steady and, by two-thirty, Arthur had taken the last of the bread into the shop. Agnes had not had the opportunity of talking to her mother, but Saturday's garden party was on her mind. She wasn't about to miss that opportunity.

The shop closed at two forty-five with the last of the bread being sold, and Agnes and Grace returned to the parlour. Arthur was sat at the table reading last night's paper, baking had finished for the day.

Mildred was getting ready for the viewing of the property and could hardly contain her excitement. Arthur was showing complete disinterest.

With the two youngest daughters returned from school, the family left the bakery ten minutes later. The cabbie was waiting outside. The family squeezed in the back and Mildred gave the address to the driver.

Transport by taxi was still a new experience, and the family spent most of the journey in silence looking out of the window at the countryside. Arthur seemed to be in a world of his own. It was just over half an hour before the taxi drove through the village and turned right just after the village store. Mildred noticed the proprietor outside rearranging fruit pallets.

A short distance down the lane there was a white gate on the left-hand side flanked by two enormous horse-chestnut trees. The gate was open, and the cabbie steered the taxi through and along a compacted dirt track. It was only a short distance, fifty yards or so, surrounded by huge rhododendron bushes on both sides providing a guard of honour. Then the track opened, and the magnificent house was in front of them. Mildred was peering over the cabbie's head trying to get a better look.

The space in front of the house was a gravelled area large enough for a car to turn in a circle. The taxi stopped outside and the family got out.

"You can wait for us if you wish; I will pay for your time," said Mildred to the cabbie. He touched his cap and returned to the driver's seat and took out a newspaper. He appeared to be studying the horse-racing pages.

There was another car parked in the forecourt and a man got out from the driver's seat and walked towards them. The children were staring at the impressive frontage of the house. It was an alien world.

"Mrs Marsden? Josiah Springett, at your service."

The man was wearing a bowler hat which he removed as he offered his hand to Mildred. She eyed the land-agent, tall and slim, military-looking, with a fine set of whiskers and sideburns. He was immaculately turned out in a fine three-piece suit; his voice was confident with a deep timbre, definitely gentry thought Mildred.

"Yes, and this is my family." She named the children even though the man would never remember them.

"A pleasure to meet you. Let me take you inside. I have to say you have made a splendid choice. It's an ideal property for a family such as yours."

Chapter Nine

Springfield Hall was everything Mildred had dreamed of.

Actually, it was more than that, for she could never in her wildest dreams imagine being able to live in such a residence. The children too, were carried away by the sheer size, space, and grandeur. Not the grandeur of a stately home, maybe, but compared with the bakery, it was a palace.

Each room was furnished, clearly to the specifications of the late Sir James Springfield, a mill owner and hated employer. Mildred couldn't understand how someone with such elegant taste could have such a cruel reputation.

From the large entrance hall, they examined the various downstairs rooms and then ascended a wide staircase. Upstairs, the bedrooms were beautiful, the back ones with views of the grounds and surrounding countryside. There was a bathroom with a gleaming white porcelain toilet and matching bath.

After the first floor guided tour, the agent led them back to the ground floor.

"Here's something I think you will like, madam," said the man.

They reached the kitchen and Mildred couldn't believe her eyes. Hanging utensils, pots, dishes, colanders, and a large double sink, and then what looked like a range in the centre of the back wall. Mildred was intrigued.

"My, what a fine range," she said as Springett looked on. He had never seen such a reaction before; the pure joy was uplifting and he couldn't fail to be moved. "But where's the fire?" said Mildred.

"Ah, yes. Sir James loved his contraptions; he had several motor vehicles, you know. It's a gas oven. He had it installed last year... the very latest model."

"Gas?" queried Mildred.

"Yes, it's the only one I know of in the area. There are a few in Keighley, of course. The ladies I have spoken to who have one say how clean they are."

"Yes, I can see that." She walked up to it and stood in wonderment. She was joined by the girls.

"What do you think?"

"Aye mam, it's very fine, indeed," said Grace. The three other daughters started exploring, opening drawers. Agnes turned on the tap and watched the water flow.

Arthur was less impressed. He was stood at the door holding his cap.

"Come on Arthur, don't you want to have a look?" said Grace.

"Nay, I'll wait outside, for tha." He turned and headed to the front door, then left the house. Grace and Agnes watched him.

"What's wrong with our Arthur?" asked Agnes.

Mildred was still examining the range with the land agent close by. "What was that Agnes?" she asked, only half concentrating.

"Our Arthur, 'appen he's not interested in t'house," said Agnes.

"Oh well, don't pay a mind. He's still worried about the flour, I reckon," said Mildred.

The land agent stepped in, not wishing to lose any chance of a possible sale. "The Springfield estate have agreed to leave the furnishings, carpets and curtains with just a small adjustment to the price."

"Really, that would be wonderful. It would save so much inconvenience."

"'Appen you'll need a housekeeper, mam," said Agnes.

"Aye, and a gardener," added Grace.

"So, what is your opinion, Mrs Marsden? Is it to your satisfaction?" asked the agent.

"Oh yes, Mr Springett, most certainly."

"Do you want me to tell the vendors that you would like to proceed?"

"If you would be so kind. I will speak to Mr Drummond tomorrow morning."

"Excellent, most excellent." Springett appeared to be wringing his hands.

The cabbie was still outside, sat in the driver's seat, seemingly quite content at being paid to read the racing pages. Arthur was pacing up and down, waiting impatiently for the visit to conclude. He was dying for a beer.

Mildred had one last admiring glance at the building before getting into the taxi. Arthur sat next to the driver allowing the rest of the family to get in the back. The chatter was incessant; the women unable to contain their excitement. As the journey progressed, the babble slowly died down; Agnes had a question she had been dying to ask her mother but had bided her time, waiting for the appropriate moment.

"Mam, I have a question to ask."

"What's that, my dear?" replied Mildred, her mind still elsewhere.

"Norman, you know, the clerk from t'solicitors, has asked me to go with him to the theatre next Monday. You don't mind, do you?"

"What? Eh? The theatre?"

"Aye, he has two tickets and has invited me to accompany him."

"That sounds so romantic, Agnes," said Grace.

"Well, yes, then you must go. I hope he will pay you due

respect," replied Mildred.

"Yes, mam, 'appens his dad's a vicar."

"A vicar?"

"Aye, in Utley, and he's invited me to the garden party on Saturday after we collect our dresses."

"Has he indeed?"

"Aye."

"And how are you going to get there?"

"Norman says he will pay a cabbie."

"My, well, it seems it's all been arranged."

"No, mam, only if you allow me. I told Norman I needed your approval," said Agnes.

"Very well. A vicar's son, you say?"

"Aye mam."

"We must invite him to tea once we've moved."

"Aye, that we should."

Agnes couldn't wait to tell Norman. She would compose a message for him and deliver it by hand.

Arthur had remained locked in his own thoughts during the journey. The whole thing seemed wrong. His father's inheritance was nothing short of blood money, the result of investment in capitalist ventures with dubious pedigree. He thought about his pals in the Malt Shovel, the foundrymen and mill workers and their fourteen-hour shifts for subsistence-level pay. Then the customers who bought bread by the ounce. Where was their mansion?

They arrived back at the bakery. Mildred paid the cabbie, and the girls skipped inside, still buzzing with excitement. Archie Slater was back on post; his notice board read, '*Provisional Government in Ireland threat.*' His shrill voice echoed the headline.

Arthur would buy a copy after his visit to the alehouse.

It was nearer six when he returned to the bakery, and Mildred was finishing preparing the evening meal. Agnes and Grace were in the parlour reading while their younger sisters were in the bedroom.

Mildred heard his heavy footsteps clomping up the stairs and went into the parlour; she needed to speak to him.

He entered the room; the stench of ale preceded him. He was carrying his newspaper.

Agnes took issue with him. "Arthur, why are you drinking all the time?"

He took off his cap and boots and stared at his sister. "It's of no concern to tha?"

"Arthur, don't speak to your sister like that; have more respect," interjected Mildred.

He ignored the comment and opened his newspaper on the table.

"Arthur, put that paper away, we need to talk. There are some important things we need to discuss."

"Aye, 'appen there is because I'm not moving to no posh house."

Agnes looked at Grace. "But you have to come, Arthur, tha's family."

"It's alright, Agnes, let him speak," said Mildred. She turned to Arthur. "So why this attitude? What are we working for if not to improve our situation?"

"Aye, but that's the point, we ain't working. 'Appen it's blood money."

"Blood money?" said Mildred. "Why would you call it so? Your father worked his life for this, and his father before him."

Arthur had difficulty in countering the argument. "Aye, but it's not honest money."

"Not honest money?! Of course it is."

"Aye, earned off the backs of real workers."

"Your father worked hard, the same as you do now. Do you not call that honest money?"

"Aye, but how come we've been poor all these years, then? How come I've had just one pair of boots and Agnes and Grace one dress apiece."

Grace looked at Agnes and shrugged her shoulders.

Mildred continued. "It was your Dad's way, I suppose. Maybe he wanted us to be looked after when he was gone. Who knows what passed in his mind?"

"Well, I want none of it."

"But tha must come with us Arthur, tha must," said Agnes.

He turned to his sister. "And who's going to look after the bakery?"

"We can work something out," said Mildred.

"Aye, a cabbie? Or we going to have our own chauffeur... is that it? We'd be just like them."

"Them?" asked Mildred.

"Aye, the gentry... in their posh frocks and houses. Just like 'em. I despise them, leaches to a man. 'Appen there'll be a revolution one day, see off the lot of 'em."

"Well, 'appen tha don't know tha mind, Arthur," intervened Grace. "This is our family, we'll not be gentry, never will."

"Aye, that's what tha says, but tha wait... look at tha now, going to theatre already."

"There's nowt gentry about the theatre, Arthur, thar mind's muddled," said Grace. "'Appen tha spends too much time in t'Shovel, it's addled tha head."

Arthur was feeling the pressure of being attacked from all sides. Mildred wanted to find some common ground.

"So what do you want with your life, Arthur?"

"'Appen I'm happy as we are."

"So you want to spend all your life in a backstreet bakery, is that it?"

"Aye, it's where we belong."

"Goodness Arthur," said Mildred. "You sound just like your father. It could be him sat there."

She paused for a moment to collect herself. "Well, if your mind's made up, I'm not forcing you, but I am taking the girls to the house. If you want to stay here, you can. I will even transfer the bakery into your name if you wish, or will that go against your principles?"

Arthur was stunned for a moment.

"I'll think on it," he said and went back to his newspaper.

Mildred returned to the kitchen with Agnes and Grace to finish preparing their evening meal.

"What'll us do?" said Agnes. "We can't leave Arthur here."

"Well, we can. I'm not missing this chance of the house. I will instruct Mr Drummond tomorrow. Agnes, you can take a letter for me." Agnes smiled.

The mood around the table was strained as they ate their meal. Arthur finished his food without making any eye-contact, and once he had cleared his plate, he got up.

Mildred sighed as he started to lace up his boots. The girls looked at each other.

"So, tha's off sulking down t'alehouse, Arthur?" said Agnes. She was always the more outspoken of the daughters.

Arthur ignored her.

"Tha's splitting up family; hope tha's happy," she added.

Arthur put on his cap and walked out of the parlour, just the clomp, clomp, clomp of his boots as he descended the stairs.

Archie Slater had finished his shift and Arthur breathed deeply as he stood on the corner. He looked across to the park; it was quite busy with evening walkers. Cyclists criss-crossed the paths taking shortcuts from the main thoroughfares. A trolleybus went by, dragging its overhead cable like a dog on a lead. It was a bright evening and the top deck was full. He crossed West Street; the bank was in darkness. He could see people outside the Malt Shovel with pint glasses in their hands.

Arthur went in and could see Henry York in the corner; he was with another regular, Samuel Tanner, a moulder.

"'Ow do, Arthur," said Henry as Arthur approached the table. "What's tha 'avin'?"

"Ney, tha's alright. I'll get these. Pints both?"

With drinks duly dispensed, Arthur returned to the table just as Wilfred walked in and joined the group. Another pint was ordered.

"So, how many of us tonight?" asked Arthur.

Henry looked at Samuel. "Dunno exactly, some from here and a group from Ingrow. They'll come in on t'train. We'll meet 'em at station for eight o'clock."

At just before eight o'clock, Arthur and his three pals were walking the half a mile to the meeting point. Others from the Malt Shovel had also joined them. Then, as they approached the station, about thirty men exited; some were carrying banners. All were shouting raucously. Arthur felt a stirring, an adrenaline rush, seeing the passion of the marchers; he was soon alongside with his pals joining in the protests.

It was a two-mile walk to the foundry and, as they passed alehouses, more men joined. Fuelled with alcohol, the shouting became more abusive. Someone threw a brick through a window which was greeted with cheers and more stone-throwing. Herd mentality was propelling the behaviour, a collective mindset driving them forward, built on years of frustration. Arthur had felt nothing like it before; it was like a high.

They were about two hundred yards from the foundry gates when several constables appeared from a side street carrying batons. The group stopped, and then someone from the middle of the crowd threw a brick. Others started pulling at street cobbles trying to garner missiles.

Wilfred turned to Arthur. "Eh up, Arthur, there're troublemakers here. We best get out before us gets in bother."

Henry and Samuel were alongside; the group had stopped and there was a momentary stand-off. Howls of abuse and more stones were thrown towards the police line.

"Aye, tha's right," said Henry. "Quick down here."

Arthur was suddenly shaken from his 'high' and followed the other three along a small ginnel, a worn path separating the back yards of two rows of terraced houses. Behind them, the march had turned ugly, disintegrating into small skirmishes as police charged the protestors swinging their batons.

The path was about a hundred yards long and the four were now running away from the trouble. The sounds of yard-life emanated, toilet flushes, dog's barking, even pigeons cooing.

They reached the end of the ginnel entering another side street with more rows of terraced houses, left and right; it was like a maze. In the distance, behind them, the noise of the protestors' confrontation with the police masked the usual industrial hum.

Across the road was another street which would lead them back into town. Suddenly, a Black Maria appeared at the junction.

"Quick, run!" shouted Henry.

"Nah, hold tha'selves, we've done nowt wrong," said Arthur.

Henry stopped in his tracks.

Arthur led them across the road in the direction of the police vehicle and nonchalantly turned left at the junction. The driver watched them carefully, then turned and shouted something. The door of the van opened and six constables leapt out with their truncheons drawn; they immediately ran across the road towards the four pals.

They circled the lads menacingly. Then, without warning, the leading officer, a brute of a man with large sideburns, slammed his baton down on the side of Wilfred's knee. He dropped like a stone, screaming in agony.

"Eh, you can't do that; we've done nowt wrong," protested Arthur.

"You want one an' all?" said the burly sergeant. The officer pinned Arthur to the wall with the baton pressed on his neck.

"Ay, go on, it's right what they says; tha's all pigs."

Without warning, the officer repeated the treatment he had administered on Wilfred. Arthur didn't flinch and the officer hit him again.

"Secure 'em and get 'em in the wagon," said the sergeant.

"Right, come on you lot, in the back," ordered another constable.

Protests of innocence were followed by abuse as the four were bundled into the back of the van. Wilfred and Arthur were both having difficulty walking.

Inside the wagon, one of the officers produced some of the newly-designed handcuffs and secured Arthur and his three pals.

Four of the officers left the scene to join their colleagues and face the protestors; the other two sat in the back with the four pals, their batons drawn. They pulled away and headed back to town to the police station on North Street. The pain in Arthur's leg was excruciating; Wilfred was in a similar way. Henry and Samuel just stared blankly ahead in the confines of the Black Maria, all four restrained with their hands behind their backs.

By ten o'clock, Mildred was getting worried. Despite his drinking, Arthur, with a five o'clock morning start, was not in the habit of staying out late. She wondered if it was just a mind game to prove a point, but she discounted that; Arthur took his baking very seriously. It was the one thing that kept him together.

She read for a while. The daughters were all in bed, but she couldn't settle. She put a shawl around her shoulders, left the parlour and headed down to the alehouse.

It was still busy, another half an hour till closing time. The tobacco smoke hung in the air like a blue fog as Mildred made her way to the bar.

Thomas Fielding, the landlord, was serving while his wife was washing glasses. Again, there were strange looks at the presence of a woman. It was Maisie who spotted Mildred first. She was a customer at the bakery and knew her.

"Mrs Marsden, I've not sin thee in here afore."

"No, Mrs Fielding, I'm looking for Arthur; he's not arrived home yet."

"Aye, he were in here earlier, but 'appen him and three of the lads went to the protest. He said that was where they were going."

"Protest?" queried Mildred.

"Aye. Foundrymen's strike; there was a march."

A man in workman's clothes was stood next to Mildred and had heard the conversation.

"Tha asking about the march?" he interjected, looking at Mildred. His face was unshaven and his eyes narrow; his hands gnarled from years of hard graft.

"Yes, it would seem my son was there."

"Aye, well there's been a bit of a to do; I've just come from there. All sorts going on. Police charged wi' batons; there's broken heads everywhere. It were a right mess; I don't mind saying. Mind you there were troublemakers from Silsden mixed up wi' 'em. T'were them that started trouble, chuckin' bricks and stuff."

"Oh, my Lord," said Mildred, her hand at her mouth in a demonstration of surprise.

"Aye, reckon some'll be in t'infirmary… or locked up. T'police rounded up dozens. Just pulling them out they were. Any they could get their hands on. If tha's lost someone, 'appen they'll be at North Street or in t'infirmary."

"Thank you, let me buy you a drink."

"Aye, go on then, that's most kind."

Mildred paid Maisie for the drink and left the alehouse. She took a breath of fresh air and thought for a moment. Across the street, opposite the bakery, a lone cabbie was parked; the driver stood next to it with a cigarette in his mouth staring into the park.

Mildred had a choice, the hospital, or the police station; for some reason, her instincts told her it would be the latter.

She walked up to the man, who appeared irked by the incursion into his daydream. A young couple were strolling towards the park exit; she, a pretty young thing and possibly the object of his gaze.

"Can you take me to the police station in North Street, please?"

The man threw his cigarette into the gutter. "Aye, get in," replied the cabbie and held open the passenger door for Mildred.

North Street police station was again busy. It was different from the Suffragette rally – the constables didn't mind that, there were fringe benefits. But keeping the peace among anarchists and drunken strikers was a different proposition entirely.

As Mildred left the taxicab, a group of men were being led from a van into the reception area. The abuse was appalling; Mildred had never heard such language.

Several constables with their batons drawn provided a corridor from the van to the entrance to the police station. The truncheons were used numerous times to maintain compliance.

She waited a few minutes until the noise had died down before entering the building. She arranged her hat and approached the desk sergeant.

He looked up, his knuckles were grazed and there were specks of blood on his chin and tunic, clearly not his own.

He was writing in a ledger and looked up as Mildred approached.

"I'm looking for my son," she said before he could enquire.

"Aye, we have many sons in tonight."

"Arthur Marsden, master baker of James Street."

He looked at her and then started scanning his ledger.

"Aye, he's here; he's in the cells."

"So, I've come to take him home; I'll see that he's no trouble."

"Aye? Well, it's too late for that; he's already in trouble."

She opened her purse and took out a pound note. "Is there

a way we can come to some arrangement?"

She looked at the man; her expression was stern. The sergeant could see she was someone who meant business.

"Aye, I'll speak to the inspector. Wait here; take a seat."

Mildred looked across the reception area. The floor was awash with vomit and blobs of blood. She decided to wait at the desk while the sergeant disappeared into an adjoining room.

Ten minutes later, he returned, accompanied by another officer.

"Mrs Marsden?" asked the man.

"Yes."

"I'm Inspector Fairchild. I'm afraid your son was involved with the riots earlier this evening."

"Riots, what riots?"

"At Lawson's Foundry, Ma'am. We have made a number of arrests, of which your son was one."

"Hmm, I see. So, what's to be done. You're not keeping them here I take it?"

"That depends. I would be prepared to consider bail, but I would need an assurity, given the serious nature of the crime."

"How much?"

"Two guineas," replied the officer. The sergeant was stood next to him with a smirk on his face.

"Very well, two guineas it is."

Mildred opened her purse and pulled out a five-pound note. The inspector had probably never seen one before; the sergeant definitely hadn't.

Mildred gave it to the man. "You have change, I take it."

"Yes, ma'am," replied the inspector. He turned to the sergeant and said something that Mildred couldn't hear.

A few minutes later, the inspector returned with Mildred's

change. "He'll be along directly. He'll still need to attend court though."

"When will that be?" asked Mildred.

"Depends on the Magistrate's diary but not for a few weeks, I wouldn't think. The cells are full."

Ten minutes later, a heavy door to the side opened, and Arthur appeared, escorted by a heavy-set officer. Arthur saw his mother and staggered towards her dragging his injured leg.

"Oh my dear Lord, what have they done to you, Arthur?"

"I'm alright." He hobbled next to her. She looked at him. His clothes were dishevelled; there was blood on the side of his head, and his face was pale and drawn.

"Wilfred's still here. Can we get him out? His mam doesn't know he's here; she'll be going mad with worry."

"Yes, very well."

She returned to the desk sergeant, who was in discussion with his superior. There appeared to be some levity. She wrapped on the counter with her knuckles to draw his attention.

He turned in attendance and Mildred explained the situation. Again, there was some negotiation and a further two guinea payment. After another ten minutes, Wilfred was brought up from the cells. He looked worse than Arthur if anything.

"Come on, you two; let's get you home."

It was turned midnight as they left the police station and there would be no cabbies, so it was a twenty-minute walk back to the bakery. Both Wilfred and Arthur were limping badly, which slowed the journey.

They reached the butcher's and Wilfred thanked Mildred. He promised to repay the bail money. "There's no rush," said Mildred.

Five minutes later, they were back in the parlour, and Arthur recalled the events of the evening.

"We were doing nowt. We left the march when trouble started; we were walking home."

"What about your leg; what happened there?"

"Were a constable's baton." He undid the buttons on his trousers and pulled them down to his ankles. There were two huge bruises at the side of his leg and his knee was swollen like a balloon.

"Goodness." She placed her hand on his leg in a mother's healing motion. "Wait, I'll get some witch-hazel."

Mildred went to the kitchen and collected the brown medicine bottle she kept in her cupboard, then applied the clear, sweet-smelling liquid with a cloth. Arthur winced at the remotest pressure.

"Animals, nothing short of animals, they did for our Grace too," said Mildred.

"We weren't doing anything, mam, I swear. We were just walking home."

"Hmm, unfortunately, the police have the support of the magistrates and, if it's your word against theirs, they'll believe the police."

"Aye, that's not right, though."

"No, it isn't. What about the baking tomorrow? Will you be able to manage? I can get Grace to help. I'll take Molly from school, she's not doing much there now anyway, and she can serve in the shop."

"I'll be right enough."

"You best get some rest then."

Arthur hitched up his trousers and held them in his hand, then walked into the bedroom. He would use the chamber-pot; he had no energy to walk out to the outside toilet.

Five a.m., Wednesday morning, somehow Arthur had managed to summon enough energy to make it to the baking shed. His left knee was still badly swollen and he was in agony. Despite the fatigue, he had found it difficult to sleep.

Edward Buxton turned up around five-thirty and was able to deliver two bags of flour. There was still a great deal of uncertainty about future deliveries he explained. According to the miller, the news of the protest march and the subsequent violence was all around town, twenty-six arrests and about the same number in the infirmary according to rumour.

Arthur described his treatment by the police, still protesting his innocence. "We were just walking home, Edward, we weren't doing owt."

"Aye, 'appen constabulary takes pleasure in causing suffering. So, what's going to happen?"

"We'll be up before bench I suppose, no idea when. Me mam paid us bail."

An hour later, Mildred brought Arthur a much-needed cup of tea and some sandwiches. "You won't forget, Ruskin's are coming at ten o'clock."

"Aye," he replied but, in truth, he had forgotten. "'Appen, I'm going to have to put price of bread up."

"Oh dear, is that really necessary?"

"Aye, it is if we're not to go bankrupt."

"Hmm, well it's your decision, Arthur, but you know what folks are like around here, it won't be welcome."

"I'll see what Ruskin's say, but I reckon they'll be dearer than Buxton's."

"Yes, I'm sure you're right, Arthur."

"I just can't make no sense of it. Summat's going on, that's for certain, but there's nowt in t'paper."

The bakery opened at eight o'clock, and there was the now usual rush to buy bread. Arthur had explained to Grace and Agnes that the price was to go up by a halfpenny a loaf which was greeted by howls of protest from the shoppers. Arthur had been called on two or three occasions to placate irate customers. They had little time for his excuse of the cost of flour.

At just turned ten o'clock, Arthur was busy mixing the second batch of bread when the sound of a small wagon entering the yard broke his concentration. The name 'Ruskin's General Grocery Wholesalers' was emblazoned on the side in gold script.

Arthur went to greet the visitor.

"'Ow do," said Arthur in greeting.

"Percy Ruskin, Mr Marsden, I understand you might be in need of our service." He took off his cap.

Arthur weighed up the man. Shorter than Arthur, late forties-early fifties, judging by the facial lines, bald head, and some serious grey whiskers; he was wearing an apron over his brown overalls.

"Aye, 'appen I might if price is right."

"Flour, is it you want?"

"Aye," replied Arthur.

There was a sharp intake of breath by the grocer to indicate the difficulty of the request.

"Aye, I can let tha have a bag or two."

"Aye, at what price?"

"One pound fourteen shillings."

"How much?!" Arthur looked at him incredulously.

"That's the price if tha wants it… flour's getting scarce to get hold of."

Arthur thought for a moment; he might have to increase his bread prices yet again.

"Aye, go on then; give us two bags. I'll be a minute; put them down in t'corner."

Arthur went up to the parlour to collect the money. Mildred was in the kitchen but came out when she heard Arthur's footsteps.

"Ruskin's are here, I need some money for flour. Three pound eight shillings."

"That's very expensive," she said, looking at Arthur with some concern."

"Aye, 'appen they've got same problem as Buxton's."

"Hmm, do you want me to speak to them?"

"Nay, won't do any good; they've got us good and proper."

"Oh dear, yes, you're right."

Arthur returned to the bakery with the money and paid Ruskin. He would return on Friday with another supply.

Back in the parlour, Mildred was compiling another letter to the solicitor confirming her agreement to buy Springfield Hall; Agnes again volunteered to deliver the missive. She had one of her own.

Once the bakery was quiet, Agnes put on her hat and slipped out. Five minutes later she was at the door of Drummond Peacock. Her heart skipped a beat as the door opened. Norman's eyes also lit up.

"Miss Agnes, it's a delight to see you."

"I have a letter for Mr Drummond."

"I'll see he gets it," said Norman and took the envelope.

Agnes looked around then took out another letter from her apron pocket and handed it over; it was just addressed to 'Norman'. "I'll sithee lunchtime," she said as she walked away.

Two hours later, Agnes returned to the bench near the solicitor's office. She felt a wave of excitement as he appeared at the door and walked towards her. It was something she had never experienced before, the electricity of first love, that fathomless emotion embroiling her.

He smiled as he approached. Agnes had sat in the middle of the bench to ensure no one else would be tempted to rest there and she shuffled to one side to allow him to sit.

"Hello, Miss Agnes." Agnes detected the bashfulness again, his posture and hesitancy in speech.

"Hello, Norman," she said and moved closer to him.

"Thank you for your letter." He managed to say. He looked down and started wringing his fingers. "I read it until my eyes were sore. I've not been able to concentrate on anything. Mr Drummond caught me daydreaming, and he wasn't best pleased."

"Oh, I don't want to cause you any bother."

"Please, no matter, it's of no consequence. So, you will join me at the theatre… and the garden party?"

"Aye, that I will," said Agnes.

Chapter Ten

Arthur made his usual visit to the Malt Shovel after his baking duties had been completed. There was only one topic of conversation.

Henry, Samuel, and the remainder of those arrested, had been released after a night in the cells. There would be a court case to follow.

"We should fight this," said Henry, who had joined Arthur; Wilfred was still working. "We were doing nowt wrong!"

"Aye, 'appen you're right but who's going to believe us?" said Arthur with a degree of resignation.

The mood was sombre, the alehouse unusually quiet.

By four o'clock, conversation in the bar had ceased to be a priority, and Arthur decided to leave. Outside, the weather had changed, and it matched his mood – grey and dismal. He squinted through the murk; the wind was blowing litter along the pavement. A discarded newspaper wrapped itself around his legs. He kicked it away and then winced in pain. The litter continued its journey rolling down James Street.

Archie Slater was in his usual spot. Arthur heard his calls before he saw the headline on his board. "Protest march violence," he called out to anyone who would listen.

Arthur bought a copy and entered the bakery.

The shop was eerily quiet. All the shelves were clear, and the floor had been swept. His boots left damp footmarks as he limped his way to the stairs.

Upstairs, Mildred was in the kitchen doing washing in the sink. The four girls were scattered around the parlour in various pursuits. Agnes was deep in concentration,

181

composing something on letter-paper.

There was no acknowledgement of Arthur's presence as he took his usual place at the table and opened his newspaper. The reading didn't help his mood; his recent arrest, the flour situation, the family move, were all on his mind. He felt like Sisyphus pushing the boulder up the mountain only for it to roll back on him again.

There was little support from the Keighley News for the protestors.

The banner headline; *'Deplorable Demonstrations'*.

'The most deplorable feature of the renewal of the strike is the outbreak of rowdyism and lawlessness that has accompanied it... marked by some very regrettable incidents which we feel are as much deplored by the more responsible and level-headed men who are standing out for an improvement in Keighley wages as by any other citizens. Such manifestations tend to harm any cause with which they are associated.'

The editorial continued for a full page. It was a fair assessment but did little to serve the wider purpose. Public opinion was not on their side. The sense of injustice mounted, but there was nothing Arthur could do.

Mildred came in from the kitchen. She had hung the finished washing on an airer in front of the range to dry. She noticed Arthur deep in thought. Although he was like his father in many ways, there was one trait he had inherited from her, a vulnerability and lack of confidence. Only now had Mildred began to find her voice, away from the shadow of her late husband. She went to him.

"Girls, can you go to your room? I want to speak to Arthur." The girls complied, and Mildred sat opposite him.

"Arthur, we need to talk; put your paper away for a moment."

Arthur pushed the newspaper to one side and looked at his mother with his arms folded.

"I know things are difficult for you at the moment what with one thing and another, but whatever your thoughts we are still a family; you're not on your own."

"Aye? 'Appen it don't feel that way."

"Yes, I can see why you feel so, but there are others I need to consider too; the girls' futures are just as important as yours. You spend all your day locked in your thoughts, in your own world without a mind about others."

Arthur looked out of the window, unable to maintain any eye contact with his mother. The wires powering the trolleybus swayed as they took the strain of another vehicle heading up James Street.

"Tell me why you are so against us moving from here?"

"Tha knows why, it ain't right, that's the bottom end of it."

"But why is it not right? There's no God-given rule that says we have to stay poor. Your father worked day and night; you know that. It killed him in the end."

A fleeting flash of guilt swept across Mildred, but it was gone in a blink of an eye.

"If you are content to stay here then we need to make arrangements. I said before I am willing to transfer the bakery to you and you can stay here, but you'll need a housekeeper; you can't manage it on your own. Or I can sell the bakery."

Arthur looked at her incredulously.

"Tha can't do that."

"Yes, I can; it's in my name… and if that were to happen, you could end up at one of the mills. They have bakers there."

Arthur looked down, unable to respond.

"Why don't you move with us… for a fortnight, perhaps,

to see how it goes; if it doesn't work, we can think of another way?"

In truth, Arthur was tired, isolated, and very depressed. Part of him felt he was being abandoned, betrayed even, but the thought of being on his own was even more frightening. Mildred's suggestion seemed a reasonable compromise.

"Aye, I'll give it some thought," he replied and put his head in his hands.

From nowhere, tears rolled down his cheeks. Weeks of pent-up emotions, that had built and built since he had taken the responsibility of the bakery, surfaced like a giant wave and came crashing down onto the shore.

Mildred went around the table and comforted him as she did as a child. His sobs were deep and alcohol-fuelled.

The release of emotion had a cathartic effect, and after a few minutes, he gradually calmed down.

"So, what we need is a plan… yes?" said Mildred trying to engage him. "There will be lots to do and so much to think about… and don't worry about your court case; we can pay the fine, and that will be the end of it."

"Aye," said Arthur, still composing himself and not really able to contribute to the discussion.

"What about the flour? Now you have Ruskin's you'll be alright, won't you?"

"Aye, should be, although we ain't making much money… not enough to live on anyhow."

"Well, that isn't a problem anymore. If we can just cover the costs, we can manage without putting up the prices again. Let's call it our contribution to the poor people of Keighley?"

"Aye, 'appen that'll work. I just wish I knew what were going on. Edward Buxton reckons it's the Government stockpiling, but there's nowt in t'paper."

Saturday, 11ᵗʰ July 1914.

Arthur's breakdown had been a turning point. Since his discussion with his mother, his relationship with his family improved considerably. His sisters had noticed the change in his demeanour; his drinking had also lessened. His flour deliveries were maintained, albeit at lower levels and most days the bakery had run out by the early afternoon. This had resulted in long queues at opening time.

His deep concern at the social injustices hadn't changed, but he needed to channel his energies in a different direction. He was being drawn to the increasing influence of the Labour Party who appeared to be championing his cause. He had read an advertisement in the Keighley News, announcing a meeting, and he decided he would attend. It would be at seven-thirty that evening.

Before that, however, there was the question of the dresses. Mildred and the four girls were ready to leave by two o'clock, which would give them sufficient time to make their two-thirty appointment. Arthur had retired to bed.

Agnes and Norman had continued their lunchtime trysts and exchanging of love-letters. The excitement she felt was doubled by the thought of the garden party after collecting her dress.

Mildred had ordered a cabbie to Oakworth, and it was waiting for them outside the bakery. The driver opened the back doors for them to get in. Everyone was excited; Freda and Molly giggled continuously during the journey.

It was just turned half-past two as the taxicab pulled up outside the cottage. The weather had changed again, and it was a glorious summer's day with not a cloud in the sky. The driver helped the four girls and Mildred alight from the cab.

"Four-thirty, if you would be so kind," said Mildred as

she paid the cabbie his fare and a tip.

They entered the narrow footpath through the gap in the box-hedge. The garden looked immaculate with rows and rows of produce on display, a mixture of greens and flowering vegetables. A figure was toiling away in the far end to the left. He had a spade in his hand and appeared to be digging a trench for planting. Grace spotted him immediately.

"Look, there's Freddie," she said with excitement. "Freddie!" she yelled at the top of her voice and she started waving before Mildred could stop her.

Freddie looked around and put down his spade. His shirt was hung on the handle of a fork that had been embedded in the ground next to the trench. He dropped his trouser braces from his shoulders and put on his shirt, then replaced the braces. He started to walk towards the party.

Mildred was concerned; she had expected him to be at work.

Kitty, meanwhile, had seen the taxi pull up; she had been at the window waiting for them to arrive.

They reached the front door of the cottage just as Freddie joined them. He immediately stood next to Grace. "I see tha didn't fall this time," he said and smiled.

"And would you have caught me again Master Freddie?"

"Aye, that I would."

"'Appen I should have fallen then," replied Grace and smiled.

Mildred was busy greeting Kitty, who kissed her warmly on the cheek, and neither heard the exchange. Agnes did.

"Stop flirting you two," she said which resulted in a playful slap on the arm from Grace.

"Hello," said Kitty, addressing the girls. "Come in, I've made some tea and scones for you."

"That's most kind," said Mildred. "I see Freddie's here; I

thought he would be at the mill this afternoon.

"Aye, so he should be… Have a seat," she said as they walked into the living room. The girls found chairs; Freddie went upstairs to change.

"The union have called them out on strike in support of the Keighley workers. There's such a lot of bad feeling about. It's so worrying; I don't know where it will all end. Oswald Jessop up at the store reckons there's going to be a war, but I have no idea where he gets that thought from; he can be an alarmist. He was saying the storm was a portent or some such nonsense. Make yourselves comfortable."

Kitty left the room and returned a few minutes later with a large tray that held a teapot, cups, and saucers. She placed them on the table and left to fetch the scones. Grace was waiting for Freddie to return and was staring anxiously at the doorway that led to the first floor.

Her eyes lit up as he appeared, wearing a newly-pressed pair of trousers and a clean shirt. He sat down opposite Grace and immediately looked in her direction. She was unable to hold his gaze and looked down demurely; she could feel her face start to blush; a point not lost on Agnes.

"Hey, 'appen our Grace is smitten, her face's gone as red as a beetroot," she said to Mildred.

Grace looked up. "What nonsense, just feeling warm, nowt else," she countered.

Nevertheless, it did concern Mildred. It was a liaison that couldn't happen.

Kitty returned with the rest of the tea-making accoutrements and started handing out the scones.

"So, tell me about the house," said Kitty. "Are you still intent on moving?"

"Oh yes," replied Mildred. "We've been to view it with Mr Springett; it's a fine house indeed."

"Aye, it was rumoured around the village that someone had been to see it. And you have agreed on it?"

"Yes, I instructed Mr Drummond to proceed on Wednesday. I don't know how long these things take."

"There will be a lot to think about," said Kitty.

"Yes, indeed," replied Mildred.

"'Appen we'll need a gardener," said Grace interjecting and looking at Freddie. "Freddie could do it, couldn't tha, Freddie? Tha has the touch it would seem."

"Aye, that would be just grand. I hate it at mill, and now strike's on, there's no work. There's going to be more trouble, tha mark my words," commented Freddie.

"Well, I'll have to think about it, Freddie; it's too early to make any decisions just yet."

It was a stalling tactic by Mildred; she needed to speak to Kitty. She would need her help in managing the situation.

The tea and scones were consumed, and Kitty led the girls into the studio. For the next hour, they were trying on their dresses, with Kitty making minor adjustments.

"Kitty, you are surely a magician. How do you make such beautiful clothes?" said Mildred, admiring her new frock in the full-length mirror.

"Thank you, it's been a real pleasure; it really has," said Kitty, still adjusting Agnes's dress.

After everyone was satisfied with their outfits, Kitty produced five large boxes. "I have these, they will keep them clean until you get home."

"I want to keep mine on, please," said Agnes.

"Yes, of course, the garden party," said Mildred.

"What's this about a garden party?" said Kitty.

"She's courting, aren't you Agnes," teased Grace.

"I am not so," said Agnes indignantly. "Norman is a very respectable gentleman. Anyway, I saw you flirting with

Master Freddie."

"I was doing no such thing," replied Grace, similarly indignant.

"Now girls, stop squabbling," intervened Mildred. "Agnes can wear her dress if she wants. You can put your other one in the box."

There was a honk from outside; the taxicab had arrived for the return journey.

There were fond farewells. Mildred invited Kitty for tea whenever she was free. They would exchange letters to confirm.

Freddie was chatting to Grace out of earshot. No-one seemed to notice.

Again, there was excited chatter on the return to the bakery. They were all delighted with their dresses and Mildred had already mentioned she would return for another once the house was settled.

On their arrival, Mildred paid the cabbie and instructed him to take Agnes to Utley.

Agnes could hardly contain her excitement as the cab retraced the route made by her father's funeral cortege just two weeks earlier. The rectory was only a short distance from the cemetery and on the other side of the road. Fallen trees and branches were still in evidence along the roadside, victims to the storm.

On the approach, Agnes could see bunting fashioned in an arch at the gateway. The cabbie made the turn under the arch, then on to the front of the house. There were several cars parked as well as three horse and traps; their drivers tending to the horses and chatting to each other.

The building reminded Agnes of their new house; it was

slightly smaller but similar in design. There was a large circular driveway in front of the rectory bordered by lawns and shrubs.

The taxi stopped outside the frontage. The cabbie went around to the passenger door and opened it for Agnes to alight, just like a duchess. She stepped out anxiously to the sound of a brass band playing somewhere in the distance. Then suddenly she became aware of a presence beside her.

"My, Miss Agnes, how pretty you look." Norman had been eagerly awaiting her arrival. His fob watch was hardly out of his hand all afternoon willing the time to pass more quickly.

"Thank you Norman, you look mighty fine too. What a lovely house," she said, viewing the exterior.

"Thank you… Come 'round to the garden; there are lots of people here."

She took his arm and instead of entering the front door, they skirted left along a gravel walkway at the side of the house. Under the windows, magnificent flower beds of begonias, fuchsias, and geraniums added colour to the stone façade. They reached the boundary wall and a large arched gate, guarded on both sides by two huge rhododendron bushes. Bunting and Union Jack flags hung everywhere, giving the event a festive feel. The gate was open and they walked through. Agnes was feeling anxious; this was her first venture into what she would deem as gentry territory. She held onto Norman's arm.

As they entered the garden, Agnes could hardly believe her eyes. The splendour of the garden mirrored that of the house. The lawn, probably half the size of a football pitch, was crowded with people dressed in their finery. Various stalls were positioned across the grass, enticing people to part with their money for the benefit of the community. The brass band was performing on the veranda that led from a large picture window at the back of the house.

"Let me introduce you to Papa and Mother and then we can enjoy ourselves at the stalls," said Norman.

Agnes was still feeling nervous as Norman walked up to a tall man wearing a dog-collar, lean and immaculate, every inch the gentleman. He was surveying the scene, ensuring all was well.

He turned as they approached. "Ah, Norman... and you must be Agnes. Norman has been telling us a lot about you."

"Nice to meet you sir," said Agnes, she felt her knees shaking under her dress, but given its length, nobody would notice.

"You work at the bakery on James Street, I understand."

"Yes."

"And this is the family business... Marsden's?"

"Yes."

"A good reputation for fine bread, I hear."

"Yes, thank you."

"Norman tells me your father has been recently taken from us."

"Aye... Yes," she corrected herself.

"I was very sorry to hear that; you have my condolences."

"Thank you," replied Agnes.

"Welcome to our house. I do hope you enjoy the garden party. Mrs Hoskins is in the kitchen supervising the food, but I'm sure she'll want to say hello. Now, if you'll excuse me, I must circulate with the guests."

Norman looked at Agnes as the reverend walked towards a group of people.

"He likes you," said Norman.

"Really? I hope so," replied Agnes.

"Yes, I can tell... Come on, let's go to the stalls." Agnes

took Norman's arm and walked across the lawn to the nearest attraction.

For the next half an hour Norman entertained Agnes, demonstrating his prowess at skittles, and throwing cloth balls at tin cans. He also bought two tickets for the tombola. The prizes, generously donated by the parishioners, were laid out on a trestle table, mostly homemade produce - jams, chutney, as well as small embroidery items. Agnes was filled with joy as Norman handed her a knitted doll courtesy of a winning ticket. Just six inches long with felt eyes and mouth, it seemed to be smiling at her as she cuddled it to her cheek. She had never experienced such an occasion before.

Around seven o'clock, an announcement was made that sandwiches and cakes, all home-made, were available. Several helpers were ferrying plates from the house onto more trestle tables set up on the veranda. The brass band that had been playing continuously since Agnes's arrival had taken a break and all of the musicians were now consuming pints of ale, kindly donated by Taylor's brewery who had constructed a temporary bar on the side of the terrace.

"Come on, let me introduce you to Mother," said Norman and led Agnes up three wide steps to the veranda where the food was now being presented. A queue had formed, and around twenty people were stood patiently waiting to collect something to eat. A small donation was requested to cover the costs.

A middle-aged woman, stood at the French windows that led into the house, was directing operations. She had the air of confidence of someone 'in charge'; she was slim and dressed stylishly, with grey hair tied in a bun at the back. Norman approached the woman. Agnes suddenly felt inadequate.

"Hello Norman… and you must be Agnes, Norman has

been telling us all about you. My, you do look handsome… and what a fine dress." She eyed Agnes with a great deal of interest.

"Thank you, Mrs Hoskins, and what a wonderful house you have," replied Agnes, not really knowing what to say.

"That's very kind my dear. We thank the Lord for blessing us." She continued her scrutiny. "And you're a baker's daughter, Norman tells us?"

"Yes," Agnes confirmed, but was unable to elaborate. Norman intervened recognising Agnes's anxiety.

"Her mother owns Marsden's on James Street… and very good bread it is too." He looked at Agnes fondly; she smiled.

"That's excellent, we must try it sometime. I'll ask Norman to place an order for me."

"That will be a pleasure, Mrs Hoskins."

"I do hope you are enjoying the garden party; it's been a good turnout this year."

"Yes, very much," said Agnes.

The vicar's wife surveyed the scene. Most people had congregated around the veranda and the food; the donations seemed to be thriving.

"Well, help yourself to some food. You must excuse me, there are a lot of guests I need to check on. You must come to tea so we can talk some more. Norman will arrange something, won't you Norman?"

"Yes, Mother," said Norman, and his mother went to circulate.

"It seems Mother has taken a shine to you as well."

While Agnes was being entertained at the rectory, Arthur was back in a sombre place. The newspaper did not make good reading, with more condemnation of the 'deplorable conduct' of the strikers. It seemed the Suffragettes were also being maligned by the press after a series of failed bomb attempts.

His idea of an egalitarian society seemed nothing but a pipe dream.

He was, however, looking forward to attending the Labour Party meeting. If stories about their activities were true, maybe this was a chance to change things.

He left the bakery around seven o'clock and walked across the park to the Central Hall, the same venue that had held the earlier Suffragette meeting. As he approached, he saw a long line of men outside, waiting to enter. Arthur joined them and soon made conversation with those around him.

"Do tha know who's speaking?" asked the fellow behind him, a big lad with wide shoulders. He was wearing a traditional flat-cap, and beneath it, his head appeared to be shaved at the margins giving him quite a sinister look.

"Nay, this is my first meeting," replied Arthur.

"'Appen Robert Young might be speaking, I heard," interjected a man standing next to the first enquirer.

"What, from Union?" asked Arthur.

"Aye," replied the man.

"He'll be a brave man if he shows up here; there's many a family would take issue with him," proffered Arthur.

Robert Young was the General Secretary of the Amalgamated Society of Engineers who had called for the strike.

"Nay, I can't see him being here. He'll have sent a local man," observed the first chap. "I'm Herbert Draper," he said.

"Frank Cheetham," said the other. They shook hands and Arthur introduced himself too.

As they waited, they continued their discussions on all things of a socialist nature – striking, poverty, poor wages.

Arthur was among like-minded people.

"Do tha think this lot'll make any difference?" asked Herbert as they reached the entrance.

"Aye, we'll have to see but can do no worse. T'Liberals are fighting among themselves, and the Unionists serve none bar the gentry to my mind," replied Arthur.

"Aye, you're right there," said Herbert.

By 1914, the fortunes of the Labour Party were on the rise. It had done well in the 1911 General Election with forty-two Members of Parliament and had over four hundred councillors up and down the country. In Keighley, the standing MP, Sir Stanley Buckmaster, was a Liberal and had held the seat since a bi-election in 1913. The Labour Party had come third in that poll but was the only party to increase its share of the vote. Politically, it had the momentum, and the meeting was going to be well-attended.

By the time Arthur and his two new friends had got inside, there were no seats to be had so they joined about a hundred others stood around the periphery of the hall.

On the stage, the platform was set out with several chairs and a rostrum. Behind the chairs, colourful banners from Trade Unions were on display. The Amalgamated Society of Engineers ensign was prominent.

The meeting was rowdy with many in the audience worse for ale which led to several confrontations with the speakers. The local chairman had difficulty in maintaining any sort of order. Arthur observed the proceedings with a degree of disappointment. There was no sense of common purpose. Some wanted militant action to force the mill and foundry owners into providing better pay and conditions for their workers, while others were more conciliatory.

The announcement that Robert Young couldn't attend due to other commitments was greeted with howls of derision from the audience. Some were carrying banners which were hurled onto the stage towards the speakers. It took some strong intervention by the chairman to recover some sort of order by threatening to close down the meeting.

It was the local Labour Party election candidate, William Bland, who managed to command a modicum of respect. He spoke fluently and articulately without creating rancour among the different factions in the audience, calling for unity and shared purpose and to put away personal grievances.

The meeting lasted until nine-thirty, and as they filed out of the hall, Arthur noticed one or two fights breaking out. He and his two new friends managed to escape the violence and headed for the nearest alehouse.

The garden party in Utley was a far more gentile affair, and the affection between Agnes and Norman was growing with every minute.

Agnes had been introduced to many of the invited guests who were friends or acquaintances of the vicar. The event was also open to the general public which had swelled the numbers significantly. Some of the children were getting bored and spent the time running around, causing mayhem as they expunged their pent-up energy. But for all that, it was a joyous occasion, and Agnes felt a degree of sadness as the vicar stood on the veranda and announced the end of the event.

"Can I help with anything?" she asked, as volunteers started dismantling the stalls and piling up chairs which were being stored in an outhouse ready for next year.

"Well, we can help put the chairs in the summerhouse, if you don't mind," suggested Norman.

"No, I would like to help," she replied. She picked up two chairs and walked towards the large shed, with Norman following, similarly loaded.

After a few minutes, the volunteers had cleared the garden and it looked strangely deserted. Agnes and Norman were carrying a small table between them. They manoeuvred it into the back of the shed against the wall. The sun had dropped below the horizon, replaced by the dusk of a July evening. Inside the summerhouse visibility had dropped; it was just the ambient light from the open door.

Agnes looked around. The guests and visitors were making their way towards the archway gate at the far end of the garden. Agnes grabbed Norman's hand.

"Wait up Norman."

Norman turned and Agnes wrapped her arms around his neck, pulling him down to her waiting lips.

The kiss was soft and gentle at first but soon grew in intensity. Agnes felt a wave of emotion sweeping over her, a totally new feeling as if she were being swept along like a twig in a stream.

"Norman!" A woman's voice called from the direction of the veranda.

Norman jumped and the moment was gone. "I better see what Mother wants."

"Aye," said Agnes. "We best go."

Agnes and Norman left the summerhouse together and walked to the veranda where the vicar's wife was saying farewell to the remaining guests who had been helping with the clearing up. It was still warm, but now the dusk had given away to darkness. Stars twinkled; the crescent of a new moon was in ascendance. It was a magical evening and Agnes couldn't remember being this happy; she felt her life was changing.

"Ah, Norman, there you are. I have asked one of the cabbies to return to take Agnes back; he shouldn't be too long. It's much too far for her to walk on her own. You can come and wait inside."

"Thank you, that's very kind," replied Agnes before Norman could answer.

Inside, the illumination was considerably brighter than the normal gas lighting Agnes was used to.

"My, what a lovely room," said Agnes, as the three entered the house via the French window that led to the veranda.

"Thank you, my dear," replied Norman's mother, as she shut the doors and pulled across the curtains. "And you are going to the theatre I hear."

"Yes, on Monday." Agnes turned and looked at Norman and smiled.

"Hmm, I can't say it's something I endorse, a little bawdy for my taste."

"No, Mother, it's not that kind of show," said Norman.

"I should hope not. Anyway, please sit down, you can wait here in the drawing-room; the cabbie shouldn't be long."

Mrs Hoskins left the room. Norman and Agnes made themselves comfortable on the settee. Agnes looked around. It was very, 'tasteful'; that would be the word she would use - large sofa and matching chairs, a writing desk, various cabinets with ornaments on top, a globe. There was an ornate ceiling light above them, illuminating the whole room.

"It's so bright in here," said Agnes as she looked around.

"Yes, we had electricity installed last winter; the church paid for it."

"Our new house has electricity too; I can't wait to move," said Agnes. "Do you know how long it will be?"

"It shouldn't be too long," replied Norman. "I know Mr

Drummond has been speaking to the agent about it."

Norman held her hand and looked around, then leaned forward and kissed her.

"Norman, the cabbie's here," came a voice from outside.

He pulled a disapproving face, then smiled at Agnes. "Coming Mother," he called back without looking away from her.

Agnes and Norman walked from the room into a large hall with wood panelling around the perimeter. The front door was open at the far end.

The vicar had joined his wife. "Thank you very much; it's been very nice," said Agnes as she shook hands with the pair. Then turned to Norman. "See you on Monday."

The waiting cabbie escorted Agnes to the taxi and opened the door for her. Agnes turned and waved to Norman who was stood in the doorway.

Norman closed the door; his mother and father were still beside him. "You look after that girl, Norman; she could be the making of you," said his mother.

"Yes, I intend to," he replied.

Chapter Eleven

Monday morning, Arthur had taken his delivery of flour, and the first batch of bread was being placed on the shelves. Grace and Agnes were in their work overalls preparing the shop for opening. A queue had already started to form.

Agnes had hardly stopped smiling all weekend, and Grace too was in a buoyant mood. She had a letter to post having spent the previous evening huddled over a writing pad, scratching away with her nib pen and bottle of ink.

It had not gone unnoticed; Mildred had spotted her and was concerned she might be writing to Freddie. She also had a letter to write.

'Dear Kitty, I wanted to say how satisfied we were with the dresses, they really are fine and you are a very excellent seamstress. I think I should also mention that it seems Grace has taken a fancy to Freddie. She appeared to be writing a letter this evening and I fear it might be to him. It would be wise to hide such correspondence should you receive one in the hope any ardour will fade. Perhaps we can discuss it over tea. I hope you will take up my offer to visit; it will be lovely to see you again. Yours most sincerely, Mildred.'

She would post it Monday.

With the morning queue served, Grace announced she needed to post a letter and excused herself. She checked her pocket and left the bakery. The nearest postal facility was at the top of James Street, just outside Granger's grocery store, and a few minutes later, she was stood at the familiar red pillar box. She looked at the address, just a final check; *Freddie Bluet, Blossom Cottage, Oakworth.* She had added the postage stamp and gave it a kiss for luck before pushing it into the slot. Her first love-letter. She couldn't wait to read

Freddie's reply; she felt sure he shared her feelings.

While Grace was out, the bakery had a visitor. It was Norman with a hand-delivery for Mildred. The shop door was wedged open with a wooden peg to provide some fresh air and to avoid the constant 'clang' of the bell. Agnes was serving a customer as he entered the shop. A feeling of excitement came over her as she saw him waiting in the short line.

"Hello Norman," said Agnes as he reached his turn. He handed over a letter. "This is for your mother from Mr Drummond, can you give it to her, please?"

"Aye, I'll see to it directly when Grace gets back. Shall I sithee lunchtime?"

"Yes, I'll be there. Oh, while I'm here, I would like some bread. Mother insisted I buy some today."

"It will be a pleasure. What would you like?"

Arthur's rationing rules went out of the window as Agnes supplied Norman with two large loaves and six baps. Luckily, the shop was now empty, and there were no witnesses to the transgression.

"I'm looking forward to the theatre," he said, as she handed him his produce wrapped in tissue paper and a large carrier bag.

"Yes, me too," she replied and giggled just as another customer entered.

Once Grace had returned from her brief excursion, Agnes went upstairs to the parlour to deliver Drummond's letter. Mildred was in the kitchen. Agnes could hear her mother and called, "There's a letter from the solicitor's. I'll leave it on the table."

She left to return to the bakery; there was a queue building.

Mildred wiped her hands, went into the parlour, and opened the letter.

'Dear Mrs Marsden, I am delighted to say that the vendor has accepted your offer to buy Springfield Hall with an early completion. I have taken the liberty of reserving a meeting time at three-thirty this afternoon for us to discuss the purchase. If it's not convenient, kindly let me know. I remain at your service. Yours most sincerely, Nevil Drummond.'

Mildred exhaled. She was beginning to realise the enormity of what she was doing, but she was not going to pass up this opportunity; she owed it to her family.

Downstairs, the postman arrived later that morning with another letter; it was addressed to Arthur. In a lull in the queue, Grace called him and handed him the envelope. Arthur shuddered anxiously as he saw the originator stamped on the envelope – 'Keighley Magistrates Court'. Was it a deliberate ploy to intimidate the recipient, he wondered; if so, it had succeeded.

He went back to the baking shed and nervously opened it. As he had feared, it was a date for his court appearance – Friday, August 7th.

He had hoped that by some miracle all would be forgotten, or he would be let off with a caution. But then he remembered the reaction to the strikers' protests in the Keighley News. There was a lot of pressure to make examples of those involved, and the magistrates were of a bellicose mind.

He sat for a moment, then left the baking shed and went upstairs to the parlour. Mildred was in the bedroom and heard his boots clomping up the stairs.

"Arthur? Is everything alright?" she asked as she went into the parlour. It was not usual to see him away from the baking shed at this time.

He stood there in his work-stained overalls; his hair

flecked with flour. He handed Mildred the envelope. "Nay, 'appen not. This just came. It's from t'magistrates."

Mildred read the letter. "Well, we can afford a solicitor now. I'm seeing Mr Drummond this afternoon. I can get his advice; I'm sure he will know someone. We can't risk you going to gaol, especially as you were doing nothing wrong. It's time someone stood up to these bullies."

"Nay, I don't want no solicitor. None of my pals've got one. I'll stand with them."

"But Arthur, you may go to prison. You know what they've done with the others?"

"Aye, but 'appen I'll tell the truth and take my chances."

"But you need proper justice; they'll just treat you like the real trouble-makers."

"Aye, 'appen they might, but there's nowt I can do about it. I don't see why we have to pay for justice. It's not right."

Arthur left the parlour with Mildred still holding the letter. She would still speak to the solicitor and take his advice.

At lunchtime, Agnes was taking her usual walk across the park to meet Norman. It was cloudy but bright and quite pleasant. The oppressive heat of just a few weeks ago was a distant memory.

Arrangements were made for the theatre. Norman would be waiting at the foyer at seven-fifteen and gave Agnes a sixpence to cover the cabbie.

Once the baking for the day had been completed, Arthur made his usual excursion to the alehouse. Since his discussion with his mother, he had cut back significantly on his drinking but would not miss his lunchtime session. Despite the proximity of the shop, his work was solitary; most of his time spent in the baking shed alone with his thoughts. This daily routine was a chance to unwind and meet his pals, away from his normal isolation.

As he reached the bar, Henry King and Samuel Tanner were sat at one of the tables and beckoned him over. There was an empty seat with a pint of beer in front of it.

"'Ow do, Arthur," said Henry. "Sit theeself down; I've got a drink in for tha."

"Nah then, Henry… Sam, ta for that. 'Ow be tha?" he responded, looking at the lads in turn. He sat down, lifted his glass, and took a large gulp.

"Did tha get a letter this morning?" asked Samuel.

"Aye, 'appen I did. August 7th."

"Aye, same here," said Henry.

"Aye, me too," added Samuel.

"What about Wilfred? Have tha seen him today?" asked Arthur.

"Nay, he'll still be working, but 'appen it'll be the same," replied Henry.

"What'll they do, do tha reckon?" asked Samuel.

"Who knows the minds of magistrates? But newspapers are full of letters asking for examples to be made," said Arthur who was almost at the bottom of his glass.

"Aye, I read that," said Henry.

"Do tha think they'll send us to prison?" asked Samuel.

Arthur looked at him. He was only a couple of years older but looked beyond his age; his face already lined. He was wearing a cap and a white collar-less shirt showing the dirt and grime of several days' wear, and a waistcoat. His hair was closely cropped at the sides in line with the latest trend, courtesy of his father and an open razor. He was not someone who would seek attention and was always on Henry's coat-tails, but a loyal and valued friend nonetheless. His question was etched with concern.

"Aye, it's possible," replied Arthur.

"What'll us do?" asked Samuel.

"Nowt much us can do," interjected Henry.

Henry was the opposite of Samuel, cocky and full of opinions, particularly when it came to workers' rights; he had been a big influence on Arthur. His appearance reflected that persona. Henry's father also worked at one of the mills, so, without a family to support, unlike Samuel, he had been able to invest in better clothes and was, by comparison, a sharp dresser.

"Aye, that's a fact," said Arthur, and the atmosphere turned sombre.

"Have tha got time for another?" asked Arthur, trying to change the mood.

There was a large clock on the wall in the bar which looked like it had originated from a station. The words, 'North East Railway Company', appeared on the bottom of the clockface; one twenty-seven it said.

"Nay, ta, on two-till-ten, best get off," said Henry and finished his pint.

Samuel did the same. "Aye, me an' all," he added.

He bid farewell and watched his pals leave. Arthur sat with the remainder of his pint deep in thought. He would walk up to the butcher's to check on Wilfred.

Later that afternoon, Mildred was getting ready for her three-thirty appointment with Drummond's solicitors. She was wearing her new dress together with a hat she had bought to accompany it.

She left the parlour and walked down to the shop where Agnes and Grace were cleaning the shelves. Arthur had returned from the Malt Shovel and was in the baking shed.

"Hey mam, are you off courting again?" said Agnes as Mildred walked through the bakery. Grace laughed. "'Appen

Mr Drummond will take a fancy to tha," added Grace.

She looked at the girls and smiled. "One's got to look one's best when dealing with professional matters. Oh, and I think Mr Drummond is far too old, even for me."

With that, she turned and left the shop with the two girls giggling.

She arrived at the solicitor's and rang the bell. It was Norman who answered, maintaining his role as the doorman. "Mrs Marsden, please come in; Mr Drummond is expecting you."

"Thank you, Norman." She entered and turned to him. "And make sure you look after my daughter tonight," she whispered.

"Of course, Mrs Marsden. I'll make sure no harm comes to her. Please take a seat, Mr Drummond will be with you shortly."

A few minutes later, the door to Nevil Drummond's office opened, and he greeted his client courteously.

"Mrs Marsden, so good of you to make the appointment. Please do come in."

He ushered Mildred into the room. As on her previous meeting, there was a tray with tea settings for two people.

"I've taken the liberty of providing some refreshment. I find it exceedingly stimulating this time of day."

"That's most kind, Mr Drummond,"

"Please take a seat and, if I might be so bold, say how handsome you look this afternoon."

"Thank you," said Mildred, slightly taken aback by the lack of his usual formality.

Once the solicitor had finished dispensing the teas, it was down to business.

He picked up a letter. "As I said in my correspondence, I've had confirmation from the vendors that they have accepted your offer and would like to complete by 4th August. Is that acceptable to you?"

"Yes. Yes, of course, most acceptable." She was trying to contain her excitement.

"Good, well, I will make preparations and withdraw the necessary funds from your holdings. Do you have any preferences which stocks you would like to dispense with?"

"Goodness no, Mr Drummond, I must leave that to your discretion."

"Very well, I have taken the liberty of drawing up some forms for your signature." He opened a file and removed several pieces of paper and three stock transfer forms then passed them across the desk. There was a large blotter in front of him with an inkwell and two pens in holders. He took one of the pens, dipped it in ink and handed it to Mildred. She signed the documents without having an idea of their meaning; she trusted the solicitor entirely.

"Thank you," replied Drummond as she passed the documents back and placed the pen in its holder. "I must say it seems a fine property, judging by the descriptions."

"Yes, it's ideal for my family. It even has a bath and one of those new ranges run on gas."

"Yes, I saw that. You were aware there is a charge at the moment for owning a bath?"

"No, I didn't know that."

"Yes, it's scandalous. There have been many representations in the newspapers about it. It's due to the water shortage in this area."

"After all that rain we had?"

"Yes, unfortunately. The council need to raise money for a new piping system, so they're charging everyone who owns a bath."

"That doesn't seem right, Mr Drummond."

"No, I agree with you, Mrs Marsden. There's going to be a debate on the matter at the next council meeting, but for the moment, there will be an extra cost." Mildred responded with a look of resignation. He changed the subject. "What are you going to do about the bakery? Have you decided?"

"Well, Arthur is keen to continue, but there are problems with transportation. He starts before the trolleybus service. He wants to stay in the property, but I am not sure he can look after himself."

"Have you thought about a housekeeper?"

"Yes, I have that in mind; it might be a solution. I have discussed transferring the property to him. What are your thoughts?"

"That is your decision, Mrs Marsden, but it can be easily achieved once he's reached his majority. How old is he now?"

"Nineteen."

"Hmm, well, we can put the property into a trust for him so it passes to him when he's twenty-one."

"Very well, I will give it a great deal of thought, Mr Drummond." She took a drink of tea.

"While we are talking about Arthur, there is another matter on which I would like your advice."

Mildred described the circumstances of Arthur's arrest and his pending court appearance. "He is adamant he was not involved in any of the riotous behaviour and was on his way home when he was arrested."

"In which case, he will need some legal representation."

"Yes, I have told him that, but Arthur takes after his father; he's a proud and very stubborn lad. He says that if his pals can't have a solicitor, then he's not having one either."

"Hmm, well, does he know he could face imprisonment?"

"Yes, he does, but he says he will take his chances."

"And he is adamant about representation?"

"Yes, he is."

"Hmm... Well, we can't have an innocent master-baker imprisoned, can we?"

"But I don't know what to do; it is such a worry."

"Leave it with me, Mrs Marsden; I know the Magistrate. I may be able to put in a good word."

"Could you? I would be so grateful."

"Well, I can't promise anything, but it won't do any harm."

The solicitor concluded his business and escorted Mildred to the front door.

Mildred had mixed feelings as she retraced her steps through the park back to the bakery. She was excited by the house purchase, of course, but her concern for Arthur was still at the forefront of her mind. Maybe if Mr Drummond were to put in a good word for Arthur, he would escape a term in prison. She would hold on to that thought.

As she approached the store, Archie Slater was again at his pitch. The headlines had changed from the local industrial relations issues to the banner headline; *'Irish problem – latest'*. Mildred nodded to him as she went past.

Upstairs in the parlour, Agnes was getting ready for her theatre date and had been given access to Mildred's Japanned makeup box, the contents of which had been expanded over the last week or so. Mildred joined her in the bedroom and gave her some help. Applying makeup was a new experience for Agnes; it was a luxury enjoyed only by the gentry or the girls of the night. The right amount was essential if she didn't want to get mistaken between the two.

By seven o'clock, she was ready. She walked into the

parlour; Arthur was at the table reading his newspaper, Grace was helping the two youngest with some schoolwork on the settee.

"My, look how grand you look," said Grace. She stood up to take a closer inspection. Mildred followed holding the hat she had recently purchased.

"Here, wear this; it will match your frock perfectly."

Agnes placed the hat on her head and examined it in a hand mirror. "What do you think, Arthur?" said Agnes.

He looked up from his newspaper and glanced at Agnes.

"Very gentrified," he said, and went back to his paper.

"Now then, Arthur, be more respectful to your sister," admonished Mildred.

"Aye, 'appen I'll get some peace down t'Shovel," he said. He picked up his newspaper and started putting on his boots.

"Why's tha being so horrible to Agnes? Tha don't want to spoil her evening do tha?" said Grace.

"I mean no disrespect, but 'appen tha's let the money go to tha head. There's millworkers out there can't put bread on t'table and here's thee wasting money on posh frocks and going to the theatre. It ain't right; that's all I'm saying."

"Now don't you go saying things like that, Arthur Marsden. There's no fault in bettering ourselves," replied Mildred.

Arthur ignored the comment and left the parlour. They could hear the sounds of his boots clomping down the stairs.

"Now you pay no mind, Agnes. Arthur has different thoughts, that's all," said Mildred.

"Aye, he has, but he can't go round saying such things. 'Appen he spends too much time drinking with millworkers and not enough time thinking about his family."

The atmosphere had changed, and Arthur's rant had taken some of the shine off the evening.

"Now you pay no heed, Agnes," said Mildred. "Here's some money for the taxi and maybe some refreshments if you so choose." She handed Agnes a two-shilling piece.

"Thank you," said Agnes. She would add that to Norman's sixpence.

She kissed her mother on the cheek and then Grace and the two girls in turn. "Have a lovely time," said Grace.

Agnes left the bakery and walked across the road to the cabbie stop where a taxi was waiting. The thought of taking a taxicab just a couple of weeks ago was out of the question and it still felt strange, but special, nonetheless. She gave the driver the address and sat back in the seat; her thoughts of Arthur had been replaced by more pleasant reflections on the evening ahead.

She had read the programme on the front page of the Keighley News; 'Dare-Devil Dorothy', and a full chorus of London review girls. She wondered what that meant, but frankly, she didn't care. She was with Norman; that's all that mattered.

The taxi pulled up outside the theatre and the driver opened the door for her to step out. There was the usual queue waiting to get in, and one or two people had seen Agnes vacate the taxi. She noticed them whispering to each other. She smiled; she was clearly a topic of conversation.

Norman had been waiting a few minutes and strode over to the car. He took her hand.

"Agnes, my, how pretty you look and what a wonderful hat, if I may say."

"You may, Norman, and thank you. You're looking mighty handsome yourself."

Norman was wearing his best suit complete with a white shirt with a detachable collar, and tie.

They stood in line for a short time as the queue shuffled towards the entrance. Just inside to the right, was a confectionery stall. Agnes spotted bars of Fry's Turkish Delight for sale, a new product and very popular, although she had never tried one.

"Oh, Norman, look," she exclaimed and took out her purse.

"I'll get you one," said Norman and he handed the vendor a threepenny bit. "Two please."

Ten minutes later, they were taking their seats in the balcony. Agnes had difficulty in absorbing it all, the grandeur, the elegance, the… she had run out of superlatives. And then the orchestra struck up, the curtain opened in a blaze of light that took her breath away. A line of chorus girls dancing and high-kicking; Agnes's jaw dropped. She had never experienced anything like this. The glamour, stuff she had only seen in magazines.

It was traditional music hall entertainment with speciality acts, including Dorothy, the headline, who performed amazing feats on a trapeze which had the audience holding their breath. It was the songs, though, that really enthralled Agnes. Some of the songs she knew and sang along. Then there were the costumes; she thought the girls looked so beautiful.

Two hours later Agnes was exhausted with clapping, singing, enjoying every second. Once or twice, Norman would take her hand and squeeze it. It had been a magical evening; even the chocolate bar had added to the occasion, and when the curtain finally closed, Agnes was on her feet applauding the performers.

Norman looked at Agnes as people around them stood up and started making their way to the exits. "Did you enjoy the show?"

"Oh, yes. Thank you Norman; I have had such a wonderful time."

They got outside the theatre. "I'd like to walk," said Agnes. "It's a beautiful evening."

Nine-thirty, and it was a warm summer's night. "Yes, alright. I can get a cabbie outside your shop."

So, arm-in-arm the couple walked the mile and a half to the bakery, talking animatedly about the show, swapping highlights. Agnes loved the glamour; she suddenly wanted to be a singer. She imagined herself up on stage with the spotlight shining on her while everyone watched. If only!

Twenty minutes later, they had reached James Street. Just past the butcher's, there was an alleyway leading to the side entrance where deliveries were made. Agnes looked at Norman. "Quick, in here, no-one will see us."

Norman followed her into the shadows, and they were soon locked in a kiss that seemed to go on and on. Agnes could feel new sensations; a desire she would only experience in private moments. She suppressed her natural instincts, as convention said she must.

"We best be going," she said after ten minutes. "Mam will be fretting."

"Yes, of course," said Norman, but there was a reluctance in his tone.

They composed themselves and returned to the pale glow of the streetlights and continued the short distance to the bakery. As they reached the shop doorway. Norman looked at her.

"I have a thought; would you like to go to see 'Robin Hood and Maid Marian'?"

"The picture show?"

"Yes, it's on at the Oxford Hall Picture House on Wednesday,"

"Oh yes, I would like that very much."

"I'll find out about the times and tell you tomorrow," replied Norman.

They said their farewells and Norman walked across the road to the taxi rank to wait for the next cabbie.

In bed that night, Agnes was finding it hard to sleep. The evening had made a lasting impression on her. Throughout her childhood, she would entertain her sisters, and Arthur occasionally, with her singing and play-acting. She had a good voice according to her family, and she would read passages from books with dramatic postures and voices. The theatre visit had conjured up all kinds of dreams.

The following morning, in Oakworth, two letters arrived at Blossom Cottage. Kitty was in her studio working on another commission when the postman called. She took the letters; one was addressed to her. The other to *Freddie Bluet, Blossom Cottage, Oakworth*. She examined the handwriting, definitely a woman's hand. It was an artistic, flowing script, suggesting someone creative.

She put Freddie's missive to one side and opened the other. She read Mildred's warning. She had not spoken to Freddie about any attraction with Grace, and now she was in a dilemma. It went against her nature to hide things from Freddie; they had enjoyed a close relationship, but this was different.

As she sat at her sewing desk, Freddie's letter was leant against the wall at the back of the table where she was working. The light seemed to be illuminating the delicate handwriting. Inside, she guessed, was the outpourings of feelings of a young woman. She wanted to read it to see if her assumptions were correct, but then what?

She was considering her options. She could destroy it; no one would know, letters frequently got lost. Or, of course, she could confess everything, the affair with the baker, the years of lies to keep it secret. Would Freddie understand? Despite his time working at the mill, he was still naive when it came to life and relationships. Kitty had sheltered him from the harshness of the world. Then there was Mildred; it would have considerable implications for her too, if the truth were to come out.

She picked up the letter, opened one of the drawers to her needlework box and placed it at the back. It would give her time to think.

Back at the bakery, Tuesday morning, and trade continued unabated. By mid-morning, the queues had lessened, giving Grace and Agnes a moment's breather. As they tidied the shelves ready for Arthur's next batch of bread from the baking shed, both were deep in thought. Grace was wondering what Freddie's response would be to her first-ever love-letter; she was sure her feelings were reciprocated.

Agnes had been in a dream since her theatre visit the previous evening. On her return, Mildred was waiting for her and listened intently as Agnes recounted every detail. Agnes couldn't sleep for the buzz of excitement, tossing and turning as she replayed the events in her head. She dearly loved Norman, but it was the theatre that had enthralled her. She wanted more.

At three in the morning, she suddenly remembered an advertisement in the Keighley News, only a couple of days earlier. She had read it with interest at the time but quickly discounted it; what did she know about singing? But fired with the thrill of the theatre, she would read it again and maybe, just maybe...

With the bakery in full swing, Agnes had not had time to read the article again, but she had put the newspaper to one side in case her mother used it to light the range. She would speak to Norman at lunchtime.

Agnes was still on a high as she walked across the park to meet the solicitor's clerk. It was a warm summer's day and the birds seemed to be singing louder for some reason. Norman was on their usual bench, waiting for her. He stood as she approached and smiled.

"Hello, how are you today?"

"I'm very well Norman, thank you. What a glorious day it is too." They sat down and immediately held hands.

"I've been thinking about you all morning; it has been difficult to concentrate."

"Aye, me as well; I had such a good time. Thank you."

Agnes was far more relaxed in Norman's company now and was less concerned about her style of speech. After catching up and reminiscing about the evening's events, Agnes posed a question.

"I've been thinking on something and would like your thoughts on the matter."

He looked at her inquisitively.

"I saw an advertisement in the newspaper about an audition for singers for a show at the Hippodrome."

Norman's expression changed. "You want to be a singer?" he said with a frown.

"Aye, well, I don't want to work in a bakery all my life and I've been singing since I was a little girl."

"What will it mean?"

"I don't know; I don't have all the details, but it said they were having auditions later this week for a new production and are asking people to apply."

"But you have no experience of such things."

"Aye, that's true, but I have a good voice; my mam always said."

"Well, if it's what you want."

She looked at him; his body language seemed to indicate a different emotion from his voice.

"Aye, it is. But if you think I should not, then I won't apply."

"No, no, I would not want to stand in the way."

Norman looked in front of him. The park was busy with promenaders; as usual, several older men were seated on benches smoking, just passing the day; women trying to control small children. He was considering the implications, thinking about the showgirls from the previous evening. He didn't think his mother would approve.

Agnes could sense his unease. "You don't seem keen on the idea."

He turned and looked at her, then took her hand. "If it is your dream, then you should do it; whatever you choose, I will be with you."

"Thank you," she said and smiled. "Then I shall send a letter this afternoon."

They continued chatting until just before two o'clock when they both resumed work. Norman confirmed the picture show on Wednesday and arranged to meet Agnes outside the cinema at seven-fifteen.

Later that afternoon, Agnes found the advertisement in the newspaper and composed a letter requesting an audition.

Earlier, Arthur had made his usual journey to the Malt Shovel. His two friends, Henry, and Samuel, had left to start their two o'clock shift, leaving him on his own. He was on a barstool staring into his glass.

In a break in customers, Thomas Fielding, the landlord, joined him.

"Eh up, Arthur, tha looks deep in thought."

"Aye, Thomas, 'appen I've a lot on my mind. You heard about the court case?"

"Aye."

"We could go to prison."

"Aye, there's a few more besides coming in here saying same thing. A lot of worried lads."

"Aye, true enough. Mam says I should get a solicitor, but 'appen I'll take my chances."

"Well, there's nowt more to be done, if that's thar mind."

Arthur finished his beer. "Put another one in there will you, Thomas?"

The landlord took Arthur's glass and replenished his beer.

"Have you been following what's going on in t'papers, overseas, I mean?" asked the landlord.

"Only what's in news."

"I read things are getting worse; one paper reckons there could be a war."

"Nay, that's just t'government trying to cause problems for workers. You mark my words; they do anything to support t'mill owners."

"Aye, you could be right, Arthur."

Chapter Twelve

The landlord was right. By mid-July, the political climate in Eastern Europe was deteriorating rapidly. However, the threat of war wasn't totally appreciated in the UK, and there was little reporting of events, even in the national newspapers. Problems in Ireland were dominating the headlines as the question of home rule would not go away.

As Arthur made his way back to the bakery, thoughts of foreign conflicts were far from his mind. He shared his pals' rage against the mill owners, the functionaries that supported them, and the machines that were clanking away in the distance, a constant reminder of life's inequalities.

The clock on the Town Hall struck four times. It resonated across the park and along James Street. He stopped to get a paper from Archie Slater, then walked upstairs to the parlour where Molly was embroidering and Freda crayoning. Grace and Agnes were in the kitchen with Mildred.

Mildred heard him arrive and left the kitchen; she needed to speak to him.

She could smell the drink and the stale odour of unwashed clothes. He put his newspaper on the table and took off his boots.

"Before you start reading, I have some news."

"Aye, thought you might," replied Arthur. He sat down and folded his arms.

"I went to see Mr Drummond this afternoon."

"Aye, you said."

"I have signed the papers to buy Springfield Hall, and we will be moving on August 4th. We need to discuss what you want to do."

"And I have a say in the matter?"

"Yes, of course you do; I have been thinking a great deal about what the best thing would be for you. What do you want to do?"

"I want to stay here as a family like us always have."

"You know that cannot happen. I am not missing this opportunity for the family to satisfy your personal class war." She spoke with some vigour which momentarily shook Arthur. He stayed silent.

"You want to stay here and continue running the bakery, yes?"

"Aye, 'appen I knows nowt else."

"And you don't want to give the new house a try like we discussed?"

"Nay, there's no point as I see it."

She looked at him and sighed. "Very well, I will speak to Mr Drummond about changing the bakery into your name. Mind, you won't be able to own it until you're twenty-one but he said he can put it into a trust for you, or some such, until you are of age. Then it will be yours to do what you like with... You realise it will also mean you'll be able to vote?"

This had Arthur's attention. This was another issue that grieved him; only men who owned property or paid 'substantial' rent enjoyed suffrage.

"Aye, mam, I suppose." Arthur was trying to take everything in.

Mildred continued.

"Grace and Agnes will be able to catch the trolley in time to start work so that won't change, but have you thought how you will look after yourself?"

"Nay, can't say I have."

"Well, I'll speak to Mr Drummond to arrange everything. I can try to find a housekeeper for you and you can pay for her out of the takings; the girls won't be needing anything."

There was a glimmer of acquiescence in Arthur's eyes. He was beginning to see the logic and played the idea in his mind. Suddenly, there was some much-needed motivation.

"Aye, 'appen that'll work."

"I can pay for some improvements here too. I'll arrange for electricity and water to be put in, and we can get a new bathroom. I'll ask Mr Drummond to recommend someone to come and see what needs to be done. You can think on it."

Arthur sat for a moment, taking it all in, considering whether he could reconcile it with his social conscience. All the years of hard labour working from five o'clock in the morning, he was entitled to some recompense he reasoned; it was not incompatible with his ideals. He remembered some of the Labour Party committee members from the recent meeting; good socialists, one and all, and most of them were property owners and some even owned motor cars.

"Aye, mam, I think that will work well enough."

Mildred looked at him, slightly taken aback; she was expecting a more difficult battle.

"Good, good, I will direct Mr Drummond to draw up the necessary papers."

Arthur opened his newspaper.

"Before you start reading, there's something else," Mildred said. "I spoke to Mr Drummond about your court case."

Arthur's expression changed. Mildred quickly continued. "Before you say anything, I just wanted his advice on the matter. I'm not going to employ a solicitor, although I will happily do so if you wish."

"Nay, I'm not doing that; I said not." His tone was assertive.

"Very well, I respect that. Well, I explained the situation to Mr Drummond and he said he would speak to the magistrate about you and your friends. He said he would put in a good word."

"How will that make a difference?"

"I don't know, but he said he was a friend of the magistrate; it can't do any harm."

"Aye, 'appen it can't."

Just then Agnes came from the kitchen holding an envelope. "I'm just going to post a letter; I won't be long."

"Who are you writing to?" asked Mildred as Agnes put on her shoes.

"Oh, nobody," said Agnes and hurried out of the parlour before further interrogation.

Earlier, Agnes had cut out the advertisement from the newspaper and wrote a short letter explaining her interest in attending the audition. She hoped it wasn't too late; the closing date was the following day. She checked the address again. *'Mr Cameron Delaney, promoter, Hippodrome Theatre. Keighley'*. She was in good time to catch the last postal collection.

On Wednesday morning, two letters arrived at the bakery. Agnes was in the baking shed collecting some more baps to put on the shelves; Grace had taken delivery. Both had 'Oakworth' franking marks. One was clearly in a woman's hand and addressed to Mildred; the other, the writing was untidy with letters sloping different ways. It reminded Grace of her father's hand; he had poor handwriting. She looked at the envelope; it was addressed to Grace Marsden. "Freddie!" she exclaimed.

She quickly put the letter in the pocket of her overalls just as Agnes returned with a tray of bread rolls.

"I have a letter for mam; I'll just take it upstairs."

Grace went upstairs to deliver the letter but couldn't resist taking a peek at her own. She stopped halfway up the stairs and took out the envelope. The light was not good and she had to squint to read the contents. The scribbling script didn't help.

'My dearest Grace, I have not been able to settle since your visit at the weekend. I was caught by your beauty the moment you fell into my arms. I was hoping you felt the same way. Please write to me. I would like to hear from you very much. Yours in anticipation, Freddie.'

Several of the words had been misspelt; this was not the work of an educated man but, none-the-less, someone speaking from the heart. Grace clutched the letter to her bosom for a moment before putting it back in her apron pocket and then completing the three remaining steps to the parlour.

"Mam!" she shouted. "Letter for you."

Mildred came out of the kitchen, wiping her hands with a towel.

"Thank you dear. Is the shop busy today?"

"Aye, mam, as usual. Sithee later."

Grace left the parlour with a myriad of thoughts in her head all involving Freddie; she hoped he had liked the letter she had sent him. She would write again after work.

Upstairs, Mildred opened the letter; she guessed it was from Kitty with an Oakworth postmark.

She sat down at the table and started to read.

'My dearest Mildred, it was so lovely of you to write with such wonderful words. It was a delight for me to make the dresses for you and the girls. I am so glad you liked them. I would dearly like to take up your offer of visiting. I have several commissions I am busy with, but I can call on

Saturday afternoon about four o'clock. I hope that is suitable for you, but please let me know if it is not convenient.

You were correct about Grace and her affection for Freddie. He received a letter yesterday, which I assume is from her. I have taken heed of your advice and hidden it from him, although it goes very much against my nature. I have not thought to read it. Yours respectfully, Kitty.'

Mildred was pleased to receive Kitty's letter and immediately started composing a response, confirming the Saturday visit.

Agnes was singing during a break in customers, a point not lost on Grace. "Tha seems in a content mood, Agnes. I've not heard tha sing so much."

"Aye, I feel very happy. Norman's taking me to the picture house this evening."

"Oh aye, what to see?"

"Robin Hood and Maid Marian; it sounds so romantic."

"He was an outlaw, I learned."

"Aye, but with a good heart, all told, and he loved Maid Marian with all his being."

"Aye, depending on what story you believe."

"Don't be so cynical, Grace."

Grace laughed. "Cynical, now that's a good word; you can tell you've been in the company of an educated man."

"Aye, 'appen so; I love hearing Norman speak, so grand, so wise."

"Aye, with words tha don't know, I warrant."

"Don't be teasing Grace, just because you haven't heard from Freddie. I know you have eyes for him."

"Aye, 'appen I have, and I have heard from him, so there." Grace took out the letter from her apron pocket and held it up for Agnes to see.

"Oh my, and what does he say?"

"He has feelings for me right enough. I knew he had."

"And what are you going to do about it?"

"'Appen I'll see if he wants to meet me. Say nowt to mam, will tha?"

"Aye, your secret's safe with me." Agnes continued singing until the clang of the shop door broke her refrain.

Her singing continued as she strode through the park to meet Norman.

Her favourite artist was Marie Lloyd. In fact, one of the acts at the theatre on Saturday night sang one of her songs, *'Every little movement has a meaning of its own'*. She had watched intently as the artiste engaged the audience, making the song come alive.

Unfortunately, Agnes couldn't remember the tune, and there was no means of learning the lyrics; they had no gramophone at home. There was a song, though, that she did know; it was very popular the previous year, and the music and lyrics had appeared in the 'News of The World' - *'You made me love you'*. Agnes knew all the words. She didn't know if Marie Lloyd had sung it or not, but it didn't matter; this would be her chosen song for her audition; if she were lucky enough to be selected.

Friday morning, Agnes was getting anxious. She had not heard anything back from the Hippodrome; she was beginning to think the worse and felt a sense of rejection.

Nevertheless, it had been an exciting week for her. The trip to the Picture House was as romantic as she had hoped. She and Norman had held hands throughout the performance and, in particularly amorous parts, he had squeezed her hand, sending feelings like electric shocks through her body. The alleyway next to the butcher's had again been put to good use.

Later, the postman arrived with two letters. One, locally posted, with elegant script, addressed to Agnes, the other, in rather scruffy handwriting, addressed to Grace, postmarked 'Oakworth'. Grace was at the serving counter and took the letters. She pocketed hers and called Agnes from the baking shed.

"Agnes, there's a letter for you."

Agnes rushed into the shop, the beaded curtain unceremonially swished in all directions.

Grace gave her the letter. "I'm just going to the privy," she said then walked through the beads towards the baking shed.

There were no customers in the bakery, and Agnes quickly opened the letter. It was on headed notepaper, 'The Hippodrome Theatre'. Agnes read the contents.

'Dear Miss Marsden, I have received your request to perform at the forthcoming audition here at the Hippodrome.

Accordingly, I would like you to attend the said audition on Saturday 25th July at 11.30 a.m. prompt. A pianist will be available. If you have sheet music for your performance, you should bring this with you. Please announce yourself at the box office and my assistant will direct you. Yours sincerely, Cameron Delaney, Promoter.'

Agnes gasped. Only now did she realise the enormity of her decision. She hadn't told any of the family and wasn't sure whether she would do that. She read the letter again; '*sheet music*'. She had no idea where she would get that. She would ask Norman.

Meanwhile, Grace had locked herself in the outside toilet. It had a lift-up latch and a draw bolt which she secured. It was quite dark; the only illumination was coming from the daylight intruding through the gaps at the bottom and top of the door. There was a small hurricane lamp on the shelf beside the toilet and a box of matches, but she wouldn't bother as it took too long to light.

She took the letter from her apron and scanned the handwriting on the envelope, but with her best endeavours, it was impossible to read. She left the toilet and walked around the side, out of sight from the baking shed. She ripped open the envelope and started reading.

'My dearest Grace, not a moment goes by when I am not thinking about you, I grow impatient for a reply to my letters. I hoped upon hope that you shared the same feelings. I intend to take a trolley into town on Saturday afternoon and I will wait for you in the park at two-thirty. If you do not come, then I will know your mind. Affectionately yours, Freddie.'

Grace read it again, as much to decipher the handwriting and spelling as to understand the message. She was confused; she had sent him two letters, her original letter, and a reply to the one she had got from him. She couldn't understand why he had not mentioned them, but no matter, he was coming to see her. Her face lit up.

The bakery closed for lunch as usual at one o'clock; Arthur had already left for the Malt Shovel. Grace went upstairs to the parlour, still thinking about her meeting with Freddie. She decided not to say anything; she would be teased mercilessly by Agnes.

Agnes left for the short walk across the park to meet Norman; her letter about her audition was in her pocket.

Norman was waiting at the usual spot and stood as she approached. The grey skies that had been threatening rain all morning had chosen this time to deliver, just a gentle shower but sufficient to start darkening the footpath. With the low cloud cover, the clanking of the mills and the thrump of the foundries seemed amplified.

"Hello, Agnes, I think we need to find some shelter. We can go to Martha's Tea Shop; it's not far."

"Aye, I know it," she replied.

They linked arms and walked the length of Rotten Row where it joined Marshal Street. On the corner was Martha's Tea Shop. It was a squat building with bulging bottle-bottomed glass bay windows and looked much older than some of the adjoining buildings. The rain was increasing in intensity.

They reached the entrance. The top half of the door was wooden-trellised, painted white, with small thick glass squares; there was a hanging sign saying 'open'. Norman pushed the door, there were two stone steps down, which presented a potential hazard for the unwary.

"Mind the step," said Norman as he took Agnes's hand and led the way inside.

Given the time of day, it was busy; three waitresses in Victorian uniform were flitting between tables, taking orders, and delivering food and drinks.

There was just one spare table in the corner and Norman ushered Agnes to the seat. There was a strange smell of coffee and damp attire as they walked through. They sat down, and Agnes surveyed the café's interior. The quaintness from the outside was replicated inside. With just two bay windows, it made the room quite dark, particularly with leaden skies. Several faded variety hall posters were hanging on the wall, which immediately had Agnes's attention.

A waitress approached and took their orders. They settled for two teas and two fruit buns. The rain was now quite heavy, sending droplets chasing down the windowpanes.

Another couple entered, shaking their clothes and hair to

expel the rain, creating small puddles on the floor. With no free tables, they were asked to wait until there was room.

Agnes was anxious to share her news with Norman and took out the letter from her pocket.

"I've had a reply about the audition."

She passed him the letter and he quickly read it.

"But this is good news," he said. "Tomorrow? That doesn't give you much time."

"No, but I know the song I want to sing; I just don't know where I can get the music from."

"Tooley's," said Norman.

"Tooley's?"

"Yes, it's a music shop just off the High Street; they sell pianos and violins and the like. My father buys music from there for the organist."

"Oh, you are so clever, Norman. Thank you." She gripped his hand and squeezed it. "I will go directly after I've finished work."

"Have you told your mother?" asked Norman.

"I have a mind to, but I don't know what she will say. She may not want me to go."

"Would it help if I accompanied you?"

"Would you?"

"Of course, I'm not doing anything."

"That is so sweet of you, Norman. Yes, I will feel safer with you with me, and I know mam will be happy." She paused, mulling things through. "I think I will have to say something; I'll need Molly to work in the shop while I'm away. She won't mind."

"That seems the most appropriate course of action," said Norman. Agnes loved hearing him speak; he seemed to have so many words at his disposal.

Their refreshments arrived and they started eating their

cakes. Agnes wiped a crumb from the corner of Norman's mouth with her finger. She smiled at him, warm and caring.

Norman consumed his food and took a sip of tea to wash it down.

"I, too, have some news," he said.

Agnes looked at him, realising she had been all-consumed by her audition. "Please tell me."

Norman moved closer and spoke in almost a whisper. "My mother would like me to invite you to tea on Sunday afternoon; please say you will come."

"Sunday? Why, yes, of course. I would love to."

"We always have tea at four o'clock sharp on Sunday as father has evensong at six. So if you can come around three-thirty."

"Yes, yes, of course. I will look forward to it." She squeezed his hand again.

Agnes and Norman consumed their drinks and left the café. The rain had eased now, and the pair walked quickly along Rotten Row and stopped at the Solicitor's for Norman to return to work. They kissed on the doorstep.

"I will meet you at The Hippodrome at quarter-past-eleven tomorrow, and I'll tell mother you will join us on Sunday."

"Thank you, Norman, for your kindness. Yes, and I will go to the music shop after work."

Agnes's euphoria was even higher, if that were possible, as she walked through the park. Although the rain was only slight now, large drops cascaded from the trees released by the wind; Agnes's hair was quite wet. She didn't care.

Grace was preparing shelves as Agnes reached the bakery. She saw her sister enter. "You best dry thar hair, tha's all wet."

"Aye, I'll be back directly."

Agnes went upstairs to the parlour. Mildred was seated at the table, an empty plate with a few scattered crumbs was in front of her.

"Are you alright, Agnes, dear? You're all wet."

"Aye, mam, it's been raining." She went to the kitchen and returned with a towel and started rubbing her hair.

"I've something to say, mam."

Mildred looked at her. "What's that, dear?"

"I am going for an audition tomorrow at the Hippodrome; Norman is taking me."

"An audition?" She looked at Agnes incredulously. "What for?"

"A variety show, the advertisement was in the News."

Mildred appeared lost for words, momentarily, undecided about the appropriate response.

Agnes continued before she could respond. "I've always wanted to sing, and going to the theatre on Monday has turned my mind."

"Yes, yes, I can understand that my dear. But it is not all lights and glamour."

"Aye, mam, but it's something I've always wanted to do."

"What does Norman say about it?"

"He's happy for me; he's offered to accompany me to the audition."

"Has he indeed? Well, that says a lot about the lad, I'll say that. And when is this audition going to take place?"

"Tomorrow, eleven-thirty."

"What about the shop? Grace can't manage on her own, especially now with all the queues."

"Aye, I'll ask Molly to work; she won't mind."

Agnes had finished drying her hair, but it looked a mess.

Mildred stood up and started combing it with her fingers. "There, that's better. Put your bonnet on; it won't show."

"Thanks, mam. I need to go to Tooley's after work to buy some music for the pianist."

"Very well. Come up before you go and I'll give you some money."

"So you don't mind then?"

"If it's your ambition, then no, but be prepared for some heartbreak; that's all I will say."

Agnes went back to the shop. It was now open and there was a queue.

"Where hast tha been?" asked Grace as her sister put on her apron.

"Sorry, I had to dry off." Agnes turned to the next customer. "What would you like?"

By three-thirty, all the bread had gone, and Arthur came into the bakery and closed the door.

"Arthur, I have an appointment tomorrow morning. I will ask Molly to work in my place," said Agnes.

"What appointment?" asked Arthur. Grace looked on inquisitively.

"Just an appointment. I've told mam; she said it was ok."

"Have tha asked Molly?"

"Not yet, I'll do that when I get back. I just need to do some shopping. I won't be long."

Arthur looked at Grace and shrugged his shoulders. "Aye, go on then," he replied.

Agnes went upstairs to change.

Since acquiring the dresses from Kitty, which they would keep for best, Mildred had bought many more clothes for the children. There was a large haberdashery store on the High

Street which had expanded to sell clothes, and Agnes now had three different outfits from which to choose. The large wardrobe was bulging with frocks and underwear.

Molly and Freda had returned from school and were also in the bedroom as Agnes changed from her working clothes. Seeing her sisters, Agnes decided to take the opportunity of ensuring her work cover.

"Molly, will you work in the shop tomorrow morning? I have an appointment," said Agnes as she put on one of her new dresses.

"Aye, 'appen I can use the money," replied Molly.

"What am I going to do?" asked Freda.

"You can attend to some schoolwork," said Agnes. Freda folded her arms.

"I'll be going about quarter to eleven, but I will have to get ready, so I'll need you to cover for the morning; I should be back before closing."

"Aye, I can do that," said Molly and continued with some more embroidery. It was something that seemed to be dominating her spare time, and she was showing signs of real skill.

Agnes walked back into the parlour and Mildred was waiting. She gave Agnes a sixpence. "That should see to it, the music," she said and smiled.

The earlier rain had stopped completely and the pavements were drying. There was the usual pervasive smell of horse manure as Agnes left the bakery. It always happened after a shower and was something the residents had grown accustomed to.

Agnes had a vague recollection of where Tooley's Music Shop was, less than a ten minute walk following Norman's directions.

233

The side road was cobbled with evidence of horse-traffic everywhere as Agnes made the turn into Colston Lane off the High Street. There was an alley which ran the back of the High Street and next to it, Tooley's Music store. It had large plate-glass windows with several pianos on display, with a magnificent grand piano taking pride of place. The window-display contained smaller musical instruments, harmonicas, ukuleles, and banjos on stands.

She entered the shop; someone was playing on an upright piano. Seeing a customer, the pianist stopped and stood up.

"Good afternoon, miss, can I help you?"

The man would be in his forties. Tall, with dark, swept-back hair and elegantly dressed in a suit and tie. He was sporting a neatly trimmed moustache, giving him a military bearing.

"Yes, please, I have to sing at an audition tomorrow and I need some music."

"Yes, certainly, we have a wide range over there."

He pointed to a large rack, running the length of the wall, which appeared to be bulging with sheet music. "What did you have in mind?"

"I don't know who sings it - *'You made me love you'*. Do you know it?"

"Yes, of course, miss. It's one of our most popular songs. It's by Al Jolson; here, let me show you."

He escorted Agnes to a section headed 'Popular Songs'. He thumbed through about fifty titles and pulled out the chosen music.

"There you are," he said and handed it to her. She looked at it.

On the front, there was a colour drawing of a glamourous young lady with what looked like tears on her cheek. The heading 'Al Jolson's terrific Winter Garden hit' was above, then underneath, in block capitals, *'You made me love you' (I didn't want to do it)*, written and composed by Jo McCarthy and James V Monaco, price 6d.

Agnes opened the inside. The musical staves with their black dots stared at her, but she could follow the refrain which was helpfully set out under each note.

The man could sense her unease. "If you don't mind me asking, is this your first audition?"

"Aye," said Agnes still reading the words.

"At the Hippodrome, by any chance?"

"Aye," said Agnes still not properly concentrating.

"Well, that's a coincidence, I've been hired to provide the accompaniment."

"So you'll be playing the piano?" She looked up at him; he had her complete attention.

"Yes... And this is your first time, you say?"

"Aye, it is."

"Would you like me to run through it with you? I'm not busy at the moment."

Agnes's eyes lit up. "Oh, would you, that will be so kind. I've never sung with a piano before."

"Yes, it will be my pleasure; let's go to that one over there." He pointed to the one he was playing when she arrived.

He took the sheet from her and placed it on the music rack in the middle of the upright, above the keys. He started playing the opening bars.

"I will nod when you come in."

"Oh, yes, I'm ready." She coughed and cleared her throat.

"What key do you sing in?" asked the man.

Agnes looked at him. "I don't know, I just sing it."

"Alright, let me play the first verse and let's see how it goes."

The man played a four-bar introduction and then nodded. Agnes started the verse and gave it everything.

"I've been worried, all day long; Don't know if I'm right or wrong."

After the refrain, she went into the chorus with the more familiar, *"You made me love you, I didn't want to do it, I didn't want to do it."*

She was trying to imagine how Marie Lloyd would sing it.

The pianist stopped after the first chorus. "Well, I have to say you do have an excellent voice, so powerful."

"Thank you, Mr...?" Her question indicated an introduction was required.

"It's George, George Tooley, I'm the proprietor."

"Mr Tooley... I'm Agnes, Agnes Marsden."

"Agnes... Nice to meet you. Very well, let's go through it again from the top, Agnes," he instructed.

Agnes sang it again all the way through with George giving her tips on the three 'Ps' - phrasing, projection, and presentation. She soon realised she had a lot to learn; she had no idea it was so complicated.

With no customers, the proprietor was content to give Agnes more coaching until he was satisfied she would be able to perform the song satisfactorily.

"Just imagine feeling the words, not just saying them; this is a really romantic song and you should present it as such," he counselled.

He handed her the sheet music and dropped down the lid to the piano. They walked back to the counter with the cash register.

"Well, Agnes, I look forward to hearing you again tomorrow."

"Thank you, Mr Tooley, you have been most kind, and

most helpful. I will practise what you have told me this evening."

She handed over the sixpence charge and said her farewells. She was buzzing with excitement as she walked back to the bakery, singing as she walked.

The family were together in the parlour when Agnes arrived back; Arthur had returned from the Malt Shovel and was reading his newspaper at the table. A small box of pamphlets was beneath it.

Agnes put her sheet music down on the table. She had been clutching it the whole way home.

"Eh up, what's this, Al Jolson?" asked Arthur, seeing the cover "Who's he?"

"Oh, nothing, it's for some singing."

"Did you get what you wanted?" asked Mildred.

"Aye, thank you."

Agnes took off her hat and sat down. Grace was immediately intrigued, picked up the sheet music and started singing. *"You made me love you..."*

"What's this for?" asked Grace after she had completed the first line.

Agnes felt cornered; she needed to explain. "I have an audition at the Hippodrome tomorrow, for a variety show."

"An audition?" asked Arthur. "What do tha want to be doing one of them for?"

"I want to sing. There's no harm in that, is there?"

Thinking it as some sort of criticism, she walked to the table, retrieved the music, and stormed out of the parlour.

Mildred looked at the family. "Now then, be kind to Agnes. She wants to sing and we should support her."

Arthur had lost interest and carried on reading, but Grace followed Agnes to the bedroom.

Agnes was looking upset and Grace put a consoling arm around her.

"Agnes, don't take a mind to Arthur, tha knows what he's like. Tha has a lovely voice, tha should sing. Come, let me help you."

Agnes gave Grace the music and stood up. She smiled and then launched into the song complete with the movements that the music shop proprietor had suggested to her.

"You made me love you. I didn't want to do it; I didn't want to do it."

Chapter Thirteen

After they had eaten, Arthur left the bakery; he'd had enough of the caterwauling coming from the bedroom.

Now an active member of the Labour Party, he had offered to distribute the leaflets containing details of the Party's pledge to voters, promising social reform, and equality. The destination was the vicinity where he and his pals had been arrested, identified by the local constituency as a prime target area. It was a poor part of town containing rows and rows of terraced properties. How many tenants were actually entitled to vote was open to conjecture.

Wilfred was waiting for him outside the bakery.

They walked down James Street past the Malt Shovel where they would be going after their deliveries. The earlier rain had given way to brighter conditions.

"Have tha heard any more about court case?" asked Wilfred as they headed towards their assigned territory.

"Nay, 'appen I was thinking we could end up in Armley."

"I don't know what I'll do about t'shop. The girls can serve alright, but none can properly cut t'meat."

"Maybe tha'll have to employ someone."

"Aye I might, but takings won't stand another wage; nor do I knows one I would trust. 'Appen I'll have to show 'em what to do."

"Aye, mebbie magistrate might take that into account."

"Aye, let's hope. Hast tha spoke to Sam or Henry?"

"Nay, Wilfred, they were working earlier; 'appen they'll be there when we've finished."

It was gone ten o'clock and dark before Arthur and Wilfred had completed the drops. It had taken longer than

s

r

q

p

o

n

m

l

k

expected due to an unscheduled stop at the Queen's Head on Napier Street. It was ostensibly for the call of nature, but while they were there, it was only polite to enjoy a pint of their best.

With all the leaflets posted, the pair headed back to the Malt Shovel. Samuel and Henry had just arrived having completed their respective shifts.

Arthur and Wilfred collected their pints and joined them.

"'Ow do, Sam, Henry, how's tha doing?" said Arthur as they sat down.

"Aye, not bad," replied Henry. "Union's still arguing wi' bosses, but they'll not listen. 'Appen there'll be more trouble."

"Aye, I'd heard," said Arthur taking a large gulp of ale.

"Are tha still having trouble with t'flour?" asked Samuel.

"Not so much, at the moment, but it's costing a bob or two," replied Arthur.

"The reason I asked, I was talking to one of the stockmen this morning, and he reckons the government is buying up all t'grain."

"Aye, I heard similar, but what can us do?" replied Arthur with a concerned look. He took another swig.

"Aye, it makes you wonder what's going on though; Tom, behind the bar, keeps going on about a war."

"Aye, said the same to me; but I can't see that; I still say the politicians are just lining their pockets like t'mill owners. Probably selling it off to Russians at a tidy profit I wouldn't wonder,"

"Aye, tha could be right," said Henry. He finished his ale. "Best be off, six-till-two tomorrow."

Saturday morning, five-thirty, Arthur was outside taking some air and waiting for his flour delivery; the large baking oven was already lit and ready for the morning's production.

There was the usual trundle of Buxton's wagon as it bounced along the side road from James Street and parked outside. Arthur went to greet the miller.

"'Ow do, Arthur," said the friendly driver as he stepped down from his cab. "'Ow be tha?"

"Aye, Edward, fair to middling, fair to middling. Can tha do us the usual today?"

"Aye, well, I can let tha have two bags, but 'appen I'll need another shilling a bag. T'price of wheat at the wholesalers has gone up again."

Arthur looked at the miller. "A shilling more!? Tha'll have us bankrupt at this rate."

"Aye, Arthur, lad. I'm sorry, I really am, but there's nowt to be done about it."

"Aye, go on then," he said with a sigh of resignation. "But I need three today Edward. Can tha manage that?"

The miller considered Arthur's request.

"Aye, go on, Arthur, seeing it's tha." He went to the trailer and started lifting the heavy sacks while Arthur went into the shed to collect the money.

Buxton finished his delivery and Arthur paid him for the three bags.

"So, tell us, Edward, what do tha make of it all? Why's everything getting dearer?"

"'Appen things're going on we don't know owt about; that's my reckoning. Rumour has it Government's hoarding grain to put price up, then sell it us back at a profit."

"Nay, you think?"

"Aye, I can't see what else."

"Some was saying in t'Shovel there's gonna be a war, but there's nowt in the news about it. I think Government's just wanting to keep working folk in their place. I don't trust

Alan Reynolds

Asquith and his gentry crowd a jot."

By seven forty-five Molly was helping Grace get the bakery ready for the customers. A queue was already starting to form outside. Arthur had delivered the first batch of bread.

Meanwhile, Agnes had hardly slept due to her excitement. She had rehearsed the song so many times she could sing it in her sleep. The presentation had been perfected with the help of Grace the previous evening, trying to give the song a 'Marie Lloyd' treatment or at least how Agnes imagined it. She was ready to give the audition her best shot.

Mildred had made her some breakfast, but she hardly touched it.

"You must eat something, Agnes dear, you can't sing on an empty stomach," she warned, but Agnes's appetite had deserted her.

Freda was up and seated opposite Agnes at the table. "Can I help you get ready?" she asked.

"Aye, Freda, I'll be happy for you to."

Mildred came in from the bedroom carrying a box, which she presented to Agnes.

"What's this?" asked Agnes.

"Well, I went to Cappers yesterday afternoon; you need to look your best for your audition."

"Oh, mam!" Agnes cried, opening the lid, and examining the contents. "They are so fine. Thank you, thank you."

"Let me see, let me see," said Freda and picked up one of the black leather booties.

"All the rage, according to Mr Capper," said Mildred.

"Oh, aye, I've seen them in magazines." She took out the other from the box and examined it closely.

"You best try them on. Wait, I'll find you some stockings." Mildred went back to the bedroom and returned a few minutes later carrying a pair of black stockings.

Agnes was in her nightclothes still admiring the new footwear. She hitched up her nightgown and Mildred helped her put on the hosiery.

"Now try," said Mildred.

Freda passed Agnes the two booties and she slowly slipped her feet into them as Mildred pulled the backs up over her heels. Agnes stood up, stamped down, and they were in place. Mildred tied the laces loosely.

"Try walking," said Mildred.

Agnes walked across the parlour and back.

"How do they feel?"

"Very comfortable, truly."

Agnes looked down at her feet. The shiny booties pinched slightly, but she would put up with that. She would soon get used to them. "Thank you, mam, thank you." She went across to her mother and hugged her.

"Well, we want you looking your best, don't we? Come into the kitchen, and I'll help you wash your hair."

By ten-thirty, Agnes had washed her hair and towel-dried it. She was seated at the table in her underwear with Mildred's makeup box open in front of her. Freda was kneeling opposite watching her mother apply the final touches.

"There, put your dress on and let's have a look at you," said Mildred after a few minutes.

Agnes was wearing her 'Kitty' dress. She put it on and Mildred handed her a small clutch handbag. "You can borrow that," said Mildred. "There are a few threepenny bits in there for the cabbie."

"Thank you, mam," said Agnes and picked up her sheet music from the table, folded it up and managed to squeeze it into the bag.

Agnes stood up and Mildred held a mirror for her to check her appearance.

Her makeup was much more vivid than she was used to. "You don't think I look too common, do you?" she asked.

"No, Agnes, if you want to be on the stage, then you need the right makeup," replied her mother.

"You look like a picture in a magazine," said Freda as Agnes turned one way, then the other. Agnes kissed her sister.

"I best be off then," she said nervously, after a few last-minute adjustments.

Mildred hugged her. "Go on, Agnes, just do your best and don't forget to enjoy yourself."

Agnes put on her hat. She looked outside across the park from the parlour window; it looked dry; she would not need an umbrella. The trolleybus wires, which stretched across the road from the building to the stanchions on the other side, were still.

After her farewells, she left the parlour and walked down the stairs; her boots making a clomping noise. The pinches became more apparent, but she would manage.

The bakery was full, and Grace and Molly were working flat out. One or two women had noticed Agnes and started whispering.

"Good luck," shouted Grace seeing her sister walking to the door.

When her taxicab pulled up outside the Hippodrome, Agnes could see Norman waiting, pacing up and down outside the entrance. He saw the cabbie arrive and went to open the door for Agnes. She paid the fare and the taxi drove away.

"My, Agnes," said Norman, looking at her, first closely then at arms-length. "How wonderful you look."

"Thank you, Norman, you're looking mighty handsome yourself."

Norman was wearing his best suit again with a white shirt and its detachable collar.

She looked up at the building and the large sign, then took a deep breath. Who'd have thought; she was going to sing at the Hippodrome.

She linked his arm. Saturday morning and it was busy, several people stopped and stared as the pair entered the theatre, wondering who the glamorous couple were.

Inside, they headed for the box office. Agnes retrieved her letter from her bag and went to the small window. A woman in her later years was sorting tickets and looked up as Agnes approached.

"Hello dear, come for the audition have we?"

"Aye, Agnes Marsden."

The woman checked a piece of paper. "Ah, yes, eleven-thirty. Wait there and I'll take you through to Mr Delaney."

She pulled down a blind and a moment later appeared at an adjacent door. "Follow me," she said assertively.

The pair followed the woman along several corridors and arrived at a door with a notice, '*Stage Entrance - Performers and staff only*'.

Agnes was really nervous now; her legs were shaking as the woman opened the door and led the pair to the stage area.

Pieces of scenery were piled in the corner. Curtains, ropes, lights of every description and colour; Agnes looked up, trying to take it all in. In front of her were rows of seats, balconies, and boxes where the more privileged would sit. In the glare of the spotlights, they would look glamourous, but this morning, without them, the place looked surprisingly drab.

She was still holding Norman's hand and he squeezed hers. "I'll wait here," he said as the box-office woman walked towards a man standing in the centre of the stage.

"Mr Delaney, this is Agnes Marsden, your eleven-thirty." She turned and left, leaving Agnes to introduce herself to the promoter. "Hello, I'm Agnes," she said anxiously.

"Ah, yes, I've been looking forward to meeting you. George Tooley was speaking well of you... Cameron Delaney, promoter."

"Thank you, sir," replied Agnes.

The promotor was an imposing figure, probably in his late forties/early fifties; large, with a portly frame. He was flamboyantly dressed in a garishly green suit, patterned with bright brown squares, the very essence of someone in showbusiness.

Just then, another figure appeared from the back of the stage and joined them. "Hello, Agnes," said the man.

"Hello, Mr Tooley," she replied nervously and held out her hand in greeting. "I've remembered the music."

"That's very kind, Agnes, but the one you are singing, I know very well."

"I understand you are a fan of Miss Lloyd," said the promoter.

"Oh yes," replied Agnes.

"A wonderful performer; she has worked for me many times."

Agnes was star-struck. "You know her?"

"Why yes, she is a good friend." Agnes couldn't think of a suitable reply.

"Well, shall we get on? George will be at the piano; I would like you to stand in the middle of the stage. I'm going to sit in the front row. That clear?"

Agnes nodded.

"What song are you going to sing?"

"You made me love you."

"The Al Jolson song?"

"Yes."

"Hmm, it's normally a man's song. This will be interesting... Very well, I'll give you the cue when I'm ready."

The promoter walked along to the side of the stage and down a set of stairs adjacent to the orchestra pit, then into the centre of the front row.

George had arrived at the piano and started playing a refrain as a warmup. He turned to Agnes. "Are you ready?"

"Yes," she called; then took a deep breath.

George played the opening bars, and Agnes launched herself into the song.

"I've worried all day long, don't know if I'm right or wrong."

Of course, as he had said, the promoter had heard the song performed many times before but, more normally, by a male singer in the style of Al Jolson. Agnes gave it a woman's touch with more emotion, a completely different feel.

For Agnes, all her nerves had mysteriously disappeared; she felt like she owned the stage, and by the second chorus, her confidence was sky-high. She could hear her voice echoing around the grand theatre. It was a sensation she had never experienced before.

She gave a dramatic bow as the song ended; Delaney was off his feet applauding. George Tooley left the piano and walked towards her. "Well done, Agnes, that was really excellent."

She turned and could see a smiling Norman waving to her. She waved back.

Moments later she was joined by Delaney with a huge grin on his face. He was out of breath as he reached her.

"Well, young lady, I'll say this, you can really sing. There's some work to do on presentation, but your voice is very accomplished. I've not heard one as good for some time. Do you know any more songs? I would like to hear you do another one."

"Well, I haven't learned any."

"Can I make a suggestion?" asked the pianist. "I have a selection of popular songs you may know. Why not look through and choose one and you can sing with the music."

"Aye," said Agnes. "I can do that."

The three walked back to the piano and George produced a large leather briefcase stuffed full of sheet music.

He took out the bundle and started to flick through with Agnes looking over his shoulder.

"I know that one," said Agnes. " '*Waiting at the church*', but I don't know all the words."

"You can hold the music," said the promoter. "The words are printed."

So Agnes sang the song reading the lyrics from the sheet music while George accompanied her. It wasn't perfect; she had difficulty reading the words as fast as George was playing, but when she had finished, the pianist looked at Delaney, who was leaning against the piano, and smiled.

"Agnes, I think you have a bright future ahead of you," said the promoter.

"Thank you," said Agnes. "But I don't know what the audition was for."

"No, no, we've not discussed that. Well, I'm putting together a variety show to tour the North this autumn, Similar to the one that was playing here recently; that was one of my promotions. There will be about fifty dates in total, starting at the beginning of September and we're due to finish at the end of November. I'm still finalising the last three venues. We start preparing for the pantomime season after that. I need a solo vocalist as part of the programme. I pay top money; a pound a night."

"A pound… goodness," said Agnes. Her weekly wage at the bakery was eight shillings and sixpence.

"We will, of course, take care of all accommodation and travel expenses. Rehearsals start in two weeks in Bradford, the new Alhambra Theatre. I do have another person to see this afternoon, so I can't confirm anything at the moment, but I will write to you and let you know on Monday."

"Thank you, Mr Delaney?"

Norman was still at the back of the stage and Agnes looked at him and indicated with her head for him to join them. He walked over.

"Oh, this is my beau, Norman," she said as he approached.

"Hello, Norman, Cameron Delaney, at your service." They shook hands. "A mighty talented girl you have there if you don't mind me saying."

"Yes, she is, thank you."

They said their farewells.

"I'll write to you on Monday Agnes," confirmed the promoter as Agnes and Norman turned to leave.

They left the theatre via the stage door and started walking arm-in-arm back to the bakery. Agnes was still on a high from her performance and hadn't noticed the chafing of her new boots.

"So what did you think Norman?"

"I think you have the voice of an angel; the promoter and pianist seemed impressed too."

"Mmm, let's hope so."

"Did I hear him mention something about a tour?"

"Yes, a variety show, all across the North, he said. He's paying a pound a night, and he's taking care of the train and lodgings an' all."

"A pound? Well, he'll be expecting a lot for that money."

"Yes, but I don't want to get my hopes up. He's seeing another singer this afternoon; he might prefer her."

"Not if he's got any sense," said Norman.

Back in the bakery, Grace was anxiously watching the clock, waiting for her meeting with Freddie.

Agnes returned to the bakery with Norman at ten-to-one and she invited him into the shop. The boots were now causing her a great deal of discomfort and she was limping slightly. She couldn't wait to take them off.

"Come and say hello to Grace and Molly."

There was just one customer; the shelves were almost empty, just a couple of baps and a large loaf were left. The customer was served and left the shop.

"Hello, Agnes, Norman, how was the audition?" asked Grace. Molly was starting to wipe down, ready for closing.

"She was wonderful," said Norman. "She's so talented." Agnes was blushing.

"Aye, 'appen you're showing favour, Norman," said Grace.

"No, I mean it, and the judge seemed impressed too," he added.

"Judge?" said Grace.

"Aye, the promoter, Mr Delaney," clarified Agnes.

"So, did you get the job?" asked Molly, looking up from her cleaning.

"I don't know yet, 'appen he's got another to see. He's going to write to me on Monday."

Norman left to take a taxi back to Utley and Agnes went upstairs to change, still buzzing from the performance. Mildred came out of the kitchen where she had been baking with Freda.

"So, how was the audition?" she asked, wiping her hands with a towel.

"Aye, mam, the promoter was pleased," Agnes replied, removing her hat, then undoing her boot laces. She slowly eased her feet from their confines. Both heels were red raw and bleeding; congealed blood mingled with her stockings.

"Oh dear, those look painful; let me bathe them with some saltwater," said Mildred and went into the kitchen to fetch a bowl and a towel.

Freda and Mildred listened intently as Agnes gave a full account of her performance. Mildred was bathing Agnes's feet in warm water. She explained about the tour.

"Fifty shows? My, and a pound a night?

"Aye, mam."

"Goodness! And you are certain this is what you want to do?"

"Aye, mam, it is."

Later, Grace and Molly had cleaned the shop and joined Mildred and the girls in the parlour for lunch; Arthur had gone to the alehouse, having shown no interest in Agnes's audition.

All the chatter was about Agnes's experience of performing on stage. Grace's mind, however, kept drifting. She had decided not to say anything to her mother about the meeting. There was something in the way she had spoken about Freddie that suggested she might not approve.

By two-twenty, Grace had changed into her 'Kitty' dress

and was wearing a touch of makeup from Mildred's box. She walked into the parlour. Her mother and Molly were in the kitchen cleaning up; Agnes was sat reading. She looked up from her book.

"Look at tha in tha best frock. Where's tha going?" asked Agnes.

"Just shopping."

"'Appen you're seeing a fancy man, I warrant."

Hearing Grace, Mildred came in from the kitchen and she'd caught the remark.

"Don't be teasing your sister, Agnes," said Mildred.

Grace took one last look at herself in a hand mirror and kissed Mildred on the cheek."

"I'll be back shortly."

"Don't forget, Kitty is arriving at four-thirty for tea."

"Aye, mam."

Grace had forgotten; she wondered if Freddie had said anything to his mother about the meeting.

Grace left the parlour and the bakery. The weather was still fine, bright blue sky with fluffy clouds. The clanking of the mills in the distance was less prevalent. She felt a touch nervous as she crossed the road and entered the park. She had no idea where Freddie would be; he'd not indicated that in his letter. She walked across towards the main road opposite the trolleybus stop.

The townhall clock said two-thirty.

She walked along the footpath. Saturday, early afternoon, and the park was busy. A trolleybus stopped and disgorged its passengers. Agnes looked around. Most of the benches along the path seemed to be taken with old men and women with young children. One family were having a picnic. She stood and scanned the park and started walking back towards the solicitor's offices where Agnes and Norman would meet.

She was beginning to think she had been stood up when suddenly there was a voice from behind her.

"Grace?"

She turned around and there he was. "Tha came."

"Aye," said Grace.

She looked at him dolled up in his Sunday best, so different from his gardening attire. Her heart skipped a beat.

"Let's find a seat," she said, and they walked further into the park and sat at the first available bench. The back was covered in bird droppings, and Grace was careful not to dirty her dress.

"I didn't know if tha would come, not hearing from tha," said Freddie.

"But I sent two letters. Did tha not get them?"

"Nay, 'appen postie must've lost 'em."

"Aye, but I was careful with address, Blossom Cottage, Oakworth."

"Aye, that's right enough. There's not another in Oakworth."

"Well, I can't understand why tha's not got them. Tha's been on my mind Freddie, I have to admit. It were grand getting tha letters knowing how tha felt."

"Aye, me an' all; I can't stop thinking about tha since tha fell into my arms."

"Ha, ha, yes, I did, too, good and proper. I have in mind I wanted to stay there in your arms forever and tha never let me go."

Freddie looked at her. She'd not been this close to him; but she could see he had grey eyes, a rare colour, like her father's, what a strange coincidence. But her father's eyes were too often angry and bitter; Freddie's were soulful and warm. She couldn't move from his gaze; she was transfixed like a rabbit in a torchlight.

For a wonderful moment speech became superfluous. Grace's hands were folded on her lap. Freddie slowly reached across and held them with his right hand, large and rough-skinned from years of toil, calloused at the base of his thumb and index finger. She shivered as they became enveloped. She started stroking the back of his hand, her fingers long and dainty.

"So, what's to be done, Freddie?"

"I don't know, but I would love to take thee out."

"Aye, I would like that, but what would tha mother say about it."

"I'll say nowt, 'appen she doesn't encourage me with girls."

"Glad to hear of it." Grace laughed.

"What about thar mam?" asked Freddie.

"Aye, she an' all. Reckon we should keep it to ourselves for now. What say tha?"

"Aye, it makes sense; no point in causing trouble."

"Would tha fancy a walk, Freddie?"

"Aye, tis a grand afternoon."

"We could go down by the river; it's nice there."

"Aye, not been for a while."

The couple got up from their bench. Freddie spotted some dust on the back of Grace's dress and brushed it away with his hand, accidentally touching Grace's more private area.

"Sorry," he said straightaway. "There was dust on t'back of tha dress."

"Thank you for your thought, Freddie. Pay no mind; 'appen we're getting to know each other very well."

She giggled and took his hand.

It was a glorious afternoon, ideal for a stroll and many others were doing the same. They passed the railway station and headed along Low Mill Lane where a footpath dropped down to the river.

The Worth was not wide at this point, maybe thirty or forty feet from bank to bank, as it meandered down towards the larger Aire, which it would join a few miles away.

They reached the riverside which was flanked by trees in full leaf. Sunlight breaking through the canopy created mottled patterns on the gentle-flowing water. Grace felt Freddie squeeze her hand as they walked along the narrow footpath; she reciprocated.

A bird flashed across the water, a vivid aquamarine. "Did tha see that, Freddie?" said Grace.

"Aye, a kingfisher, beautiful birds, after a stickleback I wouldn't wonder."

They reached a large elm; the trunk was set back from the footpath, but its branches reached across the river, almost to the other side. The path was deserted. They stopped and Grace turned to Freddie; their eyes fixed, they moved closer, then closer still; their lips met. That first uncertain contact, soft, warm, and sensual.

Grace could feel his arms around her waist. She felt an irresistible urge inside; she wanted him to touch her again, but lower, where he had removed the speck of dust. The kissing continued; still, the path was empty. They were alone in the world. She pushed his hands down until he was cradling her bottom and he instinctively pulled her towards him. Her hat became dislodged and fell to the ground. She would leave it there; she didn't want to stop.

After several minutes, she broke away, more to catch her breath. Her face was flushed. His grey eyes seemed transfixed, a longing stare which stirred emotions in her she had never experienced before.

Grace needed to regain her composure. She picked up her

hat and shook it before placing it on her head. "Let's walk some more."

"Aye," said Freddie and took Grace's arm.

They continued chatting; Freddie describing life in Oakworth and the mill, Grace her work in the bakery; mundane things but part of getting to know each other.

"We're moving to the new house soon, Freddie. You'll be able to visit me often there, I think. Say you will."

"Aye, 'appen I will."

The stream to their left babbled gently onwards over smooth stones and gravelled bottom. A water vole made a tentative appearance, entered the water, and swam downstream before disappearing among tree roots that had infiltrated the water.

There were more stops in secluded places where intimacy was possible, or what intimacy was permitted in these conservative times. They reached a small arched bridge over the river. Beneath, it was dark; with just enough headroom to stand. The kissing was getting more passionate; Grace wanted more but resisted her desires.

Just then, a distant clock struck four bells.

"It's four o'clock, Freddie, 'appen we need to get back; thar mam's coming to tea."

"Aye, she said she were coming."

"Wish we didn't have to go; I want to stay here forever," said Grace.

"Aye, me an' all," said Freddie and started kissing her, gripping her bottom again. Grace responded, but after a minute broke away.

"Nay, Freddie, we best be going."

"Aye, tha's right."

Freddie let go and Grace calmed herself.

"But we can meet again," said Grace repositioning her

dislodged hat.

"Aye, I would like that."

"Aye, me an'all," said Grace.

They returned to the footpath and retraced their steps in silence. Both wanted to say more, but words didn't come.

It took over twenty minutes to reach the park, holding hands, lost in thoughts. It had gone four-thirty.

Suddenly, Freddie stopped. "Look, it's me mam." They had reached the footpath opposite the trolleybus stop.

They hid behind a tree as Kitty walked along the pathway through the park towards the bakery.

"Did she see us?" asked Grace.

"Nay, I wouldn't think so. 'Appen she's just got off trolley."

"Aye, I best go, Freddie; it has been lovely."

"Aye, it has. Will tha write?"

"Of course I will, I will write this evening."

"Aye, me an' all. I hope I can see tha again."

"Aye, Freddie, I want that very much."

With Kitty well out of sight, Freddie and Grace kissed again, oblivious to all around them. One or two passers-by looked at them, envious of the emotions on display. Kissing passionately in public was not normal behaviour.

Grace turned and walked back towards the bakery while Freddie crossed the road to catch the next trolleybus back to Oakworth.

The family were in the parlour waiting for their visitor, except Arthur, who was still in the Malt Shovel. Mildred wasn't expecting him back before early evening for his meal. Grace was still shopping, and her mother was a little concerned; she expected her to have returned by now.

Agnes, Molly and Freda had been helping their mother

make fruit scones which had just come out of the range. There was a wonderful smell emanating from the kitchen.

Mildred was looking through the parlour window and noticed Kitty walking through the park towards the bakery; she went downstairs to welcome her.

As Kitty approached, Mildred opened the shop door with the familiar clang.

"Kitty, so lovely to see you; do come through."

The seamstress followed Mildred upstairs where the three girls were waiting. There were warm hugs all around.

"Please make yourself at home. I don't know where Grace is; she went shopping two hours since and hasn't returned yet. I'm sure she will be here directly."

"No mind, it's a lovely afternoon, maybe she went for a walk."

Kitty suddenly had a thought; she hoped she was wrong.

"Please make yourself comfortable; I'll just go and get the tea," said Mildred and went into the kitchen.

"Let me help you," said Kitty and followed her. The girls were still sat at the table.

"Mildred," she whispered. "Freddie came into town this afternoon. You don't think they met do you…Grace and Freddie?"

Mildred thought for a moment. "I don't know; I wouldn't think so. She's not received any letters that I know about."

Chapter Fourteen

Mildred was still in the kitchen with Kitty making the tea when Grace arrived back at the bakery following her meeting with Freddie.

"Where have tha been?" asked Agnes as Grace entered the parlour. "Thar dress is all creased."

"Just been shopping," replied Grace as she removed her hat. "I'll go and change."

Kitty and Mildred entered the room. Kitty was carrying cups and saucers, while Mildred had a tray with a milk jug, sugar, and the teapot.

"Hello, dear," said Mildred as she put the tray down on the table. "You've been a long time; did you get what you wanted?"

"Nay, mam, 'appen I didn't see anything I liked... Hello Kitty," she said, greeting the seamstress, as she removed her shoes.

"There's mud on thar shoes, Grace," said Agnes. Grace looked down. They were covered with mud.

"Aye, it's from footpath in t'park; I'll change them."

She took off her shoes and headed for the bedroom. Kitty looked at Mildred, both wondering the same thing.

Mildred went back to the kitchen and returned with the scones on a large plate, then started pouring teas. "Help yourself to a scone, Kitty."

Kitty took a plate and scone; the three girls did the same.

Kitty addressed the two youngest. "So, you two have finished school now?"

"Aye, yesterday," said Molly. "'Appen I'm not going back next term."

"And what will you do?"

"I have no mind at the moment," replied Molly. "'Appen I'll serve in bakery, but I would like to work with fabric and the like."

"She does show a skill for embroidery," interjected Mildred.

"What about you, Freda?" asked Kitty.

"Aye, I'll be going back in September."

Kitty lifted her cup and took a sip of tea; she had a thought.

"I have an idea, Molly, how would you like to learn to be a seamstress? It would be of help to me with my dresses; I am so busy just now?"

Molly's eyes lit up. "Why, yes, 'appen I would like that very much."

Mildred intervened. "Are you sure, Kitty?" she said, looking at the seamstress. "That's very generous of you."

"Well, I can't afford to pay more than an apprentice's wage to start with, but if she has the skill, I can teach her so she can start getting her own customers. She can work at the cottage with me in the studio."

"Well, that sounds like a wonderful opportunity."

Just then, Grace returned from the bedroom, dressed in more appropriate clothing.

"Ah, Grace, help yourself to tea and scones," said Mildred. Grace poured herself a cup of tea. "Kitty has just offered to take Molly on as an apprentice seamstress."

Grace looked at Kitty, then at Molly. "Aye? 'Appen tha'll be good at that; tha's always been good with tha hands."

"Aye," replied Molly, the excitement of a new career, plain for all to see.

The chat was convivial. Agnes was asked to recount her audition experience for Kitty, which she was only too pleased to do. She even gave an impromptu performance which was keenly appreciated.

The scones and several cups of tea were consumed. Nothing more was said about Grace's absence or her muddy shoes and dishevelled appearance.

By six o'clock, it was time for Kitty to leave and catch the trolleybus back to Oakworth. She and Mildred exchanged farewells with a promise of reciprocity once the house move had been completed. The week was going to be very busy.

Arthur returned from the alehouse around twenty minutes later. He stumbled through the door carrying his newspaper.

Mildred and the girls had finished clearing up; the four daughters were in the bedroom.

"Where have you been, Arthur? I thought you might have had the courtesy to join us with our guest," said Mildred as she came out of the kitchen.

"Aye, 'appen I prefer company of my own sorts."

He was trying to undo his bootlaces, but his coordination was poor. The smell of alcohol was overpowering.

"Look at you, Arthur. Can't you see what you are doing to yourself? You'll end up just like your father; I've told you before."

"Aye, tha did."

"Oh, Arthur, why are you so angry at the world?"

"'Appen I have cause."

"You have no cause, Arthur Marsden," Mildred's voice was raised. "You are more favoured than most. You have a respectable profession, you are appreciated around here, and you are not poor like so many."

"Aye."

"So what more do you want? You are free to follow your causes, but why upset your family in so doing?"

Arthur's eyes were glazed and unfocused; he was unable to respond with any coherence.

"Go and sit at the table and I'll get you something to eat. I have a hotpot in the oven for you."

Arthur managed to stagger to his feet, having removed his boots. He slumped at the table and opened his newspaper. The headlines continued to be dominated by the problems in Ireland; the situation was deteriorating, and various commentators offered their opinions.

In the bedroom, there was a lot of whispering between Agnes and Grace.

"So did tha see him then?"

"Who?" replied Grace innocently.

"Freddie of course, you had a letter from him, I know."

"Aye, I did, but say nowt to mam, promise? I have a mind she doesn't approve."

"Aye, I'll not say owt, but how was it? Pretty passionate judging by the look of tha when tha got back."

"Aye, t'were wonderful."

She clasped her arms around herself, imagining they were Freddie's arms.

"Did tha let him kiss tha?"

"That would be telling."

"Aye, it would, but 'appen t'were more than kissing if tha asks me."

"Nay, nay, just kissing," said Grace and smiled broadly. "Aye, same as tha and Norman, I warrant."

"Maybe," said Agnes, defensively.

Laid in bed that night, Grace couldn't sleep thinking about her afternoon with Freddie. She could feel his hands around her bottom, pulling her onto him. She could feel other things too, pushing against her private area. Oh, how she wished she could touch it; his manhood which seemed so keen to be let loose.

After consuming his hotpot, Arthur changed and went out again. He and Wilfred had arranged another visit to the Picture House. However, it wasn't a resounding success as, once the lights had gone out, Arthur fell fast asleep and didn't wake up until the film had finished. Wilfred had to nudge him, much to Arthur's embarrassment.

The family were at least united for the Sunday morning visit to church. Arthur was, unsurprisingly, nursing a sore head.

Agnes left for Utley around two forty-five, for her afternoon tea invitation. Grace was in the bedroom, composing another letter to Freddie.

Agnes had dressed in her best outfit and was feeling slightly nervous again meeting Norman's family in a more formal setting than the garden party. As she sat in the taxicab, she fiddled with her fingers.

Norman was waiting outside the house as the cabbie pulled up. It was a warm afternoon, but he was dressed in his suit and waistcoat.

Agnes paid the cabbie and Norman held her hand for her to alight.

"Hello, Agnes." Norman greeted her and leaned to give her a kiss on the cheek.

"Hello, Norman, what a beautiful afternoon."

"Yes it is, and your presence makes it more so."

"Well, Norman, that is good of you to say." Agnes loved hearing Norman speak, always with the right words.

"Come through; mother is in the sitting room; we always have tea there."

Agnes followed Norman through the heavy wooden front door and into the hall.

"Through here," said Norman and they retraced their steps from the garden party.

It was the room that overlooked the patio, but it appeared much different with the furniture in place and the windows closed. She noticed a piano in the corner which she couldn't recall from her last visit. A large sideboard with sepia photographs in frames placed on top took up most of one wall. There was a wooden mantel clock in the middle with a bronze dial and ornate mahogany case. It struck the three-quarter hour, Westminster chimes.

Mrs Hoskins was seated on a large settee which was flanked by two equally large armchairs. They were facing the patio and the view of the garden. To the side, there was a wooden hostess trolley with a large teapot, a jug, and cups and saucers on top. Below were two shelves with items covered with tea towels.

"Hello, Agnes, lovely to see you again," said Mrs Hoskins and got up to greet the guest. "Norman's been telling us about your theatre audition, how exciting. You must tell me all about it. Come and sit down and make yourself comfortable. Norman, can you take Agnes's hat?" Agnes took it from her head and passed it to Norman.

She felt a sense of relief; she had been worried about how Norman's mother would view her ambition to be an entertainer.

"Yes, thank you." Agnes sat on one of the armchairs. Mary moved closer; Norman had left the room with the hat.

"Charles won't be a moment; he's just attending to some church matters."

Norman returned and his mother moved up so he could sit on the settee next to Agnes.

"So, Agnes, tell me all about the theatre; Norman was most complimentary."

"He is very kind. Yes, it was very exciting; I felt so nervous though."

"You wouldn't have thought so," said Norman. "You seemed very self-assured."

"Thank you," replied Agnes, who was starting to blush.

"And what's this about a tour, I hear?" asked Mary.

"Well, if I'm chosen, there's a tour of northern towns, but I don't have all the details."

"My, my, and what does your mother think of you being away on your own all that time?"

"Aye, she seemed right enough."

"Norman will miss you, won't you dear?"

"Yes, of course, but I have my studies to keep me busy; we will be well enough."

He turned to Agnes and smiled.

Just then, the vicar arrived. He was formally dressed in a light coloured suit and wearing his dog-collar.

Agnes went to stand. "No, don't get up, my dear. Lovely to see you again."

The vicar walked to her and they shook hands. Agnes had the daintiest of handshakes.

"Agnes was just telling us about her experience on stage yesterday," said the vicar's wife.

"Yes, most exciting, Norman was telling us," responded the vicar.

"Thank you, sir," said Agnes.

"It's Charles, please call me Charles. It's far less formal."

"Thank you... Charles," replied Agnes.

"You must come and sing at my church; I'm sure the congregation would really appreciate it."

"Yes, I would be pleased to."

"Thank you, I will speak to the organist. I can ask Norman to pass on a message."

Agnes looked at Norman. "Aye."

Once everyone was settled, the vicar's wife started distributing the teas from the hostess trolley then removed the towels to reveal plates of sandwiches and cakes.

"Oh, I wanted to mention," said Mary, "We did enjoy your bread, most excellent. I will get Norman to place another order."

"Thank you," said Agnes.

The afternoon tea proved a great success for Agnes. Her relationship with Norman had not only been accepted, but there was also a distinct feeling of encouragement, especially from the vicar's wife. After the food had been consumed, Norman and Agnes walked the garden. Without the various stalls which had taken a great deal of lawn space on her last visit, it seemed much larger with beautiful flowers and shrubs along the borders - hollyhocks, roses, hydrangeas, foxgloves, and delphiniums, all adding colour to the summer's afternoon. It seemed to define the very essence of Edwardian 'Englishness'.

Back in the bakery, that assessment would not have been shared by Arthur.

Following his association with the Labour Party, he had become increasingly interested in the plight of the mill and foundry workers. While Agnes was being entertained by the vicar and his wife, Arthur was in a small meeting room in the annexe of the Central Hall with twenty other party members discussing support for those workers still on strike. Sunday meetings were common, as attendance tended to be higher, but this was Arthur's first. A blue fug hung over the room from the numerous Woodbines being smoked.

There was a break and he struck up a conversation with a fellow member, Stanley Robson, who was seated next to him. He was carrying a copy of *Das Kapital*.

"What's that about?"

"You've not heard about it?"

"Nay, can't say I have."

"It's by Karl Marx."

"What's it about?"

"Class conflict and revolution. The ruling classes against the working classes."

"Sounds like my sort of book."

"Aye, the Committee keep copies, if tha has a mind to read it."

"Aye, 'appen I might."

The meeting concluded with a collection for workers' families affected by the strikes.

Tuesday 28th July 1914, was the start of the domino tumble that led to Great Britain sleep-walking into war. The Balkan conflict held little interest in the popular newspapers but the Times that day detailed the 'feud' between Austria and 'Servia' and the present tensions between the two states. The following day it was announced that Austria had declared war on Serbia.

In Keighley, the international events unfolding elsewhere had little bearing on day-to-day life. Agnes was eagerly awaiting a letter from the promoter; Grace hoping to hear from Freddie.

In the baking shed, Arthur had his own concerns, the price increases for his flour supply, his pending court case, and the plight of the striking workers, topics that dominated the conversation at the Malt Shovel. The pending move of house had not been discussed. He had not revealed to his drinking pals the change of fortune for the family following his father's demise.

It was around eleven o'clock when the postman arrived at the bakery with three letters, one for Mildred in wonderful flowing script, one for Agnes with 'The Hippodrome' stamp, and one addressed to Grace in almost indecipherable handwriting, postmarked 'Oakworth'. It was a testament to the post office's sorting skills that the letter had been delivered at all.

Both Agnes and Grace were serving customers. It was Agnes who spotted the postman first. He leaned across a customer, with no apology and put the letters on the counter in front of her.

She spotted the Hippodrome letter straightaway and her heart started racing. She grabbed it and put it in her pocket. A woman in an old raincoat and hat was waiting to be served. Grace ignored her and picked up the two remaining letters. She put the Oakworth one in her apron pocket.

"Agnes, can you see to this lady; I'll take this up to mam," she said, waving Mildred's letter.

There were three other customers in the shop and there were looks at each other with tuts of annoyance as they watched Grace disappear through the beaded curtain.

Grace called her mother and left the letter on the table, then returned to the shop. She was dying to read Freddie's letter but decided to wait until lunchtime when she could take her time.

Mildred came into the parlour from the kitchen wiping her hands with a towel cloth. She picked up the letter and slit it open with a knife. The letter from the solicitor had been posted the previous day and not hand-delivered by Norman.

'Dear Mrs Marsden,
I wanted to write to you on two issues.

You may have read about the recent falls in the stock market in the newspaper. By way of reassurance, with good foresight, we successfully transferred your shareholdings into Government bonds before the downturn and the value of your portfolio remains secure.

I can also advise you that we have made arrangements to withdraw sufficient funds from your holdings to complete the purchase of Springfield Hall on Monday in time for completion the following day, in line with your instructions. I understand you intend to move on Tuesday 4th August by which time the transaction will have been completed and the property yours.

I remain at your service,

Nevil Drummond'

Mildred read it through again. She had no knowledge of the workings of the financial markets and was pleased that Mr Drummond had taken good care of her interests. She would write again and thank him.

Back downstairs, the queue had gone and the bakery was empty. Agnes kept fiddling with the envelope in her pocket.

"Well, go on, Agnes, tha must open it," said Grace as Agnes took it out of her pocket.

She took one of the bread knives and slit the envelope open and held her breath.

'Dear Miss Marsden

I am writing following your recent audition at The Hippodrome. I am pleased to inform you that you have been chosen for a position with my tour company as a solo vocalist. We start rehearsals on August 24th at the Alhambra Theatre rehearsal rooms, Bradford. I will write to you with *your contract and further details shortly.*

I would like to add, you were the outstanding performer and I am looking forward to working with you.

Yours sincerely

Cameron Delany (Promoter)

Agnes's knees nearly gave way. "I've been chosen, it says," she managed to gasp and leant back against the bread shelves to steady herself. There were no chairs in the shop.

"Really!?" exclaimed Grace. "But that's wonderful."

"Aye, I don't know what to think, 'appen my mind is everywhere. I can't wait to tell Norman." She clasped the letter to her and sighed again.

The joy was quickly curtailed as the 'clang' of the door opening indicated another customer entering the shop.

Arthur locked the shop at one o'clock and within a minute, Agnes was through the door and crossing the road to the park to see Norman. Arthur made his customary trip down to the Malt Shovel.

Grace, meanwhile, with the shop empty, took out her letter from Freddie. She kissed the envelope and then opened it with a bread knife. She squinted to try to make sense of his scrawly writing; it resembled a child's hand.

'My dearest Grace, I have thought of little else since our meeting yesterday; my mind is in a whirl, my heart lost forever to you. I wish we were still down by the river; I never wanted it to end. I am hoping we can meet again soon. I thought we could go to the pictures if you would like that. There is an afternoon show on Friday if that is suitable. I hope you will write back and let me know.

There is still no news about work. The unions are keeping us away while they have more meetings with the mill owners and I am spending more time in the garden.

Well that is it for now. Please write back.
With my deepest love
Freddie.'

Grace read it again, ensuring she had understood the scribble masquerading as handwriting. She would write to him this afternoon and make the evening letter collection from the post box outside the grocer's.

Earlier that morning in Oakworth, Freddie was in the garden, tying up some runner beans when he spotted the postman walking along the top lane. Kitty was in her studio, working on one of her commissions.

Freddie stopped his travail and went to the top of the garden path to see if he was stopping. Sure enough, the man rounded the corner and walked down towards the cottage.

"'Ow do, Freddie."

"'Eh up, Sidney, has tha anything for us?"

"Aye, Freddie, 'appen it's another from the young lady for tha. It's the same handwriting in any case. Never forget handwriting in this job." The postman handed it over.

"Another?" queried Freddie.

"Aye, 'appen there were two last week."

"Oh? Aye. Ta, Sydney." The postman went on his way.

Freddie stared at the envelope. Two, he pondered; he couldn't understand. Grace had said she had sent two, but there was nothing delivered, at least his mam had said nothing. He went back to his bean sticks still thinking, then opened the letter.

'My dearest Freddie, I want to say you have fair turned my head you have. I have not been able to think about anything else. When I lie in bed, I can feel your arms around me. The time by the river was so wonderful. I can't wait to see you again. I read your letters again and again; I have

271

kept them safe in a special place and read them before I go to bed when no-one is looking.

Sending you all my love
Grace'

Freddie read it again, and again. He hoped she had received the letter he had sent and would be able to meet him again as he had suggested.

Freddie found it difficult to concentrate on any gardening. He was excited by the receipt of Grace's letter and buoyed by the thought of seeing her again, but he was also considering the lost letters. From his conversation with the postman, they appeared to have been delivered, but why had his mother not said anything? He needed to speak to her.

It was gone midday and he had completed the work he had planned for the morning and returned to the cottage for some refreshment.

Kitty was preparing some sandwiches as he walked into the kitchen.

"Hello, Freddie, how was your morning?"

"Aye, managed to get the beans finished. Should be a good crop this year, flowering's strong."

"That's excellent. I've made a cheese sandwich with some of last year's pickle," she said and handed him a plate with two pieces of bread, roughly cut, filled with the said ingredients.

"Mam, did you see any letters for me last week, private letters in a girl's hand."

Kitty hesitated.

"Letters? No, er... I can't say I remember any. I would have given them to you."

"Aye, that's what I thought. It were the postie, he said he delivered two such last week. 'Appen they were from Grace.

She has written to me again." He took out the envelope from his pocket and showed it to his mother.

"I see. And why is she writing to you?"

"'Appen we are fond of each other."

"I see, and you have feelings for her?"

"Aye, that I do."

Kitty was in a real dilemma; she could feel her world was about to come crashing down.

"But you don't know anything about her."

"Aye, but I do, mam."

"No, Freddie, you don't. She is much more worldly than you. I don't want to see you get hurt."

"Why so, mam? Grace would never hurt me."

"She might, she's a handsome girl; I expect she will have had many admirers."

Freddie hadn't considered any previous liaisons that Grace may have had. He looked down in thought. His appetite had momentarily deserted him.

Kitty thought quickly; she continued. "You mentioned two other letters last week? Maybe they got mixed up with my business correspondence; I had many last week, but I don't remember seeing any. Do you want me to check?"

"Aye, mam."

Kitty got up and went to her studio. Having had the delivery confirmed by the postman, there was little to be gained from withholding the letters; it would raise suspicions. She hoped the explanation would hold; she did not want Freddie to find out she had deliberately hidden them from him.

She retrieved the envelopes from her box and returned to the kitchen.

"Yes, it was as I thought; they were caught up among my business letters. I haven't got 'round to opening them yet; I have been so busy."

Freddie thought for a moment. His mother was fastidious when it came to correspondence; it seemed unusual, but he didn't question her explanation. He took the letters and put them in his pocket.

Kitty felt a sense of relief; she was pleased she had not opened them. It could have been a different outcome. It still did not resolve the wider issue, however. How could she cool down their blossoming relationship? She needed to speak to Mildred urgently.

Freddie took a bite from his sandwich then looked up. "When you went to see Mrs Marsden, did she say owt more about a gardener?"

"No, she didn't; I can ask her again. I'm going to visit her this afternoon."

"This afternoon? You didn't say owt."

"Well, I want to discuss young Molly with her. I've offered to take her on as an apprentice. I have been so busy; I could do with someone to help me."

"Oh, aye, 'appen it's a good idea, mam."

Freddie returned to his garden. He had read the two letters from Grace which again declared her affection for him. He had been pondering his mother's remarks. It was true that she was beautiful and would be desired by many a suitor, but her letters were clear that she had strong feelings for him. Should he be worried or trust his judgment? It would exercise his mind for a considerable time.

By two-thirty, Kitty was on the trolleybus travelling into Keighley. She was not inclined to visit anyone unannounced and without an invitation, but she felt sure Mildred would not mind, given the circumstances.

Kitty arrived at the bakery around three-fifteen. The shop

was closed having sold all its bread for the day; Grace and Agnes were cleaning. Kitty knocked on the glass door, and Agnes went to open it.

"Kitty, how are you? We weren't expecting you."

"No, true enough, but I was in town to do some shopping so I decided to call and say hello to your mother, I had some time before the trolley back."

"Aye, of course, come in; it's nice to see you. You know your way?"

"Yes, thank you, Agnes."

Kitty walked through the beaded curtain and up the stairs to the left.

"What did Kitty want?" asked Grace as Agnes returned to continue the cleaning.

"She says she was doing some shopping."

"Oh, aye." Grace thought it unusual. Kitty didn't seem like someone who would call unannounced, but she let it pass. Her mind wandered again; what was Freddie doing at that moment?

Kitty reached the door to the parlour, knocked, and went in.

"Hello… Mildred?" she called.

Mildred came out of the kitchen wiping her hands with a towel.

"Kitty? What a nice surprise. Would you like a cup of tea? You'll have to excuse me, I've been baking."

"That would be lovely, thank you."

Kitty sat at the table and waited while Mildred made the tea.

"So, tell me, how is everything?" asked Mildred as she returned a few minutes later with the teapot and cups. "I've got some scones; if you're hungry," she added.

"Thank you, yes, I will."

Mildred fetched the scones and milk jug.

"So, what brings you into town?"

Kitty had poured the tea and took a sip, trying to work out what to say.

"Hmm, I wanted to talk to you; it's Freddie and Grace."

"Ah, I wondered if that was it."

"Yes, Freddie intercepted the postman this morning and he had a letter from Grace. Of course he then asked me about the others."

"Others?"

"Yes, the two delivered last week; I hid them."

"I see, and what did he say?"

"Oh, I made an excuse; I said they had got caught up with some other correspondence, but that's not the problem. It seems they do have real feelings for each other. I just don't know what to do; I'm at my wits end thinking about it."

Mildred was deep in thought. "I really don't want Grace to find out about her father; God rest his soul."

"No, of course. I don't know how Freddie would react either if he learned the truth."

"It won't be favourable, that's for certain. Of course, when we move, she'll be even closer to him."

"Hmm, yes, that's a point. He asked me this morning about the gardening and if you would hire him."

"Yes, that is also a consideration."

"And I do want to honour my offer of an apprenticeship to Molly."

"Yes, that's most kind of you, she's done nothing but talk about it since your visit. She's been doing a lot of embroidery of late, to practice she said. I have to say she does show some talent in that regard. In fact, she has just gone to the drapers with Freda to get some more silks."

"She does seem quite keen," said Kitty.

"Yes indeed."

There was another pause. "What about sending Grace away somewhere?" asked Kitty.

"You mean a finishing school or some such?"

"Well, you have the means now."

"Hmm, I don't know; I hadn't considered it. I'm not sure what she would say."

"It was just an idea; I can't think anything straight."

"It is something to put a mind to."

Kitty took another sip of tea and then picked up a scone and took a bite, her mind mulling things over.

"Do you think that they've met; in private, I mean? It seems a coincidence that they were both missing on Saturday."

"Yes, I suppose that is a possibility; I did wonder that too. It is so worrying…" Mildred paused and took a drink of tea. "And I'm sure, from what you've said, that Grace will have received correspondence from him too. The postman always leaves letters with the girls, so I wouldn't know."

There was a long pause. Kitty looked up again. "What if we do nothing?"

"Nothing?" questioned Mildred.

"Yes, it might be that their ardour might slow in time."

"It's an action not without risk. What happens if their feelings deepen even more?" asked Mildred.

"I know, but I can't tell Freddie not to correspond with Grace; he would ask too many questions, and I'm sure your Grace will do the same."

"Yes, that's true. Actually, the more I think about it, the more I have a mind to send Grace away somewhere. I will make some enquiries; it could solve our problem. She's always said she wanted to travel and now Agnes has got her position with the theatre…"

"Really?" interrupted Kitty.

"Yes, sorry, I didn't tell you. She had a letter this morning confirming it; she starts rehearsals next month."

"Oh, that is such wonderful news. You must ask her to speak to me if she needs any dresses."

"Yes, of course."

"Sorry, I interrupted, you were saying about Grace and her desire to travel."

"Yes, she's always dreamt of going to Paris. She saw some pictures in a magazine and fell in love with the city. I can ask Mr Drummond where I might find such information; he'll be able to guide me."

"Yes, and in the meantime, we must hope that things don't go too far."

Just at that moment, Grace and Agnes walked into the parlour having completed their cleaning of the shop.

"Hello, again," said Kitty. "Agnes, your mother tells me your audition was successful. What wonderful news."

"Yes, it is, I've not been able to put my mind to anything else," replied Agnes.

The discussion was interrupted by the arrival of Molly and Freda.

"Hello Molly, Freda," said Kitty.

"Hello Mrs Bluet," replied Molly.

"Been buying silks, I understand?" said Kitty.

"Aye," replied Molly.

"I was just telling your mother you could start on the Monday after your move. How does that sound?"

"Aye, sounds most acceptable." Molly was clutching a brown paper bag containing her purchases from the drapers, crunching it up hardly able to contain her excitement.

"More tea, Kitty?" asked Mildred.

Chapter Fifteen

Kitty left to catch the five o'clock trolleybus back to Oakworth with a lot on her mind. She was pleased she had made the journey; a joint approach with Mildred was going to be essential if the family secret was going to remain secure.

After dinner, Grace was getting ready in the parlour; she had another suffragette meeting. Mildred was concerned that it might be an excuse for a liaison with Freddie.

"So, where is the meeting tonight?" Mildred asked.

"It's at the Meeting Hall as usual," replied Grace.

"And who is going to be there?"

"It's just the local committee and members and a guest speaker from Leeds. There'll be about thirty all told."

"You will be careful, won't you?"

"Aye, mam, of course. Don't fret, it's just a regular meeting."

Mildred had nowhere else to go with her enquiry without creating suspicion about her motives.

The following morning, Mildred sent Agnes to the solicitors around nine o'clock with a letter to secure an appointment with Mr Drummond. Norman answered the door as usual.

"Why, Agnes, so lovely to see you." The delight on his face as he saw Agnes standing there was plain for all to see.

"You too, Norman. I've a letter from my mam. She would like to see Mr Drummond this afternoon if that's possible. I can't stop, I need to get back; the shop is busy. Can you call and let me mam know?"

"Yes, of course, I'll see she has a reply before midday."

He appeared to be grinning.

The appointment would not pose a problem; the solicitor appeared willing to drop everything to see Mildred. Subsequently, the necessary letter was composed to confirm arrangements for three-thirty.

Norman was, as usual, the messenger, and around eleven o'clock, he made the journey across the park; he had another, more important motive. This was the opportunity he was waiting for.

As he entered the bakery, there was a queue of about six women waiting to be served. Norman attracted Agnes's attention.

"May I see your mother? I have a message from Mr Drummond."

Agnes excused herself from the customer and opened the counter flap to allow him through.

"Do you know where to go?"

"I've not been before."

"Through there and up the stairs." Agnes pointed to the beaded curtain and went back to the customer. Norman made his way up to the parlour.

He knocked on the door at the top of the stairs, took off his cap and waited.

The sound startled Mildred.

"Come in," she called.

Norman opened the door and walked in. Mildred was at the table drinking a cup of tea.

"Oh… Hello Norman, you gave me quite a fright."

"Sorry, Mrs Marsden. I didn't mean to disturb you; I have a message from Mr Drummond." He handed Mildred the letter. "He says he will be free to see you at three-thirty."

"Thank you Norman, that's most kind. You didn't have to come up; one of the girls would have done that."

"Ah, yes, but my motives were two-fold; I had another reason to see you." He was anxiously clasping his cap in his hands, switching it from right to left, then back.

"Oh," said Mildred, wondering what Norman was going to say.

He cleared his throat and continued to fiddle with his cap anxiously. "The thing is... As you know, I've been courting Agnes for some weeks now and I know in my heart of hearts that she is the girl I want to marry."

"Marry... My, that's all a bit sudden."

"Yes, it would seem so, but I know my mind. I love her dearly, and I want to devote my life to her."

"Have you spoken to your parents?"

"Yes, I have, and they agree. They like Agnes very much and would welcome her warmly into the family."

"You know she will be going away shortly?"

"I do, which is why I want to get engaged now. Then we can plan our wedding when she returns."

"I see... and you would like my permission?"

"Yes, Mrs Marsden. I will make Agnes a good husband. I am hard-working and I care for her more than words can say."

"How will you provide for her, may I ask?"

"I have good prospects. I will be qualified as a solicitor in two or three years and my parents would always support me if necessary. They are not without money, my grandfather left them well-provided for."

"Hmm, I see."

"I have thought about nothing else these past days, Mrs Marsden. I know I will make Agnes a good husband. I do not smoke or drink and I am mild in temperament."

Mildred paused to give the impression she was thinking the request through, but inside she was very happy with the match.

"Very well, I have no idea of Agnes's thoughts on the matter, but I know she is fond of you and. if she agrees, then you have my permission."

"Thank you, thank you. I promise I will look after Agnes; I won't let you down."

Agnes had no idea of Norman's intentions as she crossed the park for their usual lunchtime meeting. It was a warm, bright day with no threat of rain. She could see Norman waiting on the bench in his work suit and cap. He stood as she approached.

"Good afternoon, Agnes, a fine one too."

"Aye, that it is, Norman." Agnes sat down next to him and they held hands. After a brief catch up on the morning's events, Norman posed a question. "What time do you finish this afternoon?"

"Oh, I couldn't say that for certain. We've not much bread left, so maybe two-thirty. Arthur always closes the shop when we've run out; we get angry customers otherwise."

"Can we meet here again at about three o'clock?"

"Aye, 'appen I can; there's nothing wrong is there?"

"No, no, no, nothing's wrong, far from it. I've some urgent work I need to finish that's all."

Agnes looked at him; he seemed anxious. He was clasping his cap tightly, fiddling with his fingers and unable to make eye-contact. Something didn't seem right.

"Are you sure you'll be able to get away then?" asked Agnes.

"Yes, I've asked Mr Drummond and he has indicated I can take an hour off later, but it does mean I need to return now."

"Aye, if that's what you want." She looked at him closely.

"Are you sure nothing's wrong?"

"No, no, of course not. I will see you at three o'clock."

He smiled.

They parted with the plan to meet again as arranged. Agnes was intrigued by this request and Norman's behaviour. He was always such a confident, self-assured young man, but today he seemed anxious.

She returned to the parlour. Mildred was at the table reading the Keighley News.

"Agnes, dear, you're back early."

"Aye, mam, 'appen Norman had some work to finish; I'm meeting him later."

"I see, and did he say anything to you?"

"Nowt special, just said he was busy and we should meet later at three o'clock."

"Oh, I see."

Mildred continued reading her newspaper, but inside she had a sense of excitement, a wedding in the family, indeed.

Agnes's predictions about the bread supply proved correct, and by a quarter-to-three, she was back in the parlour with Grace having completed the cleaning. She changed out of her work clothes and was putting on her shoes, ready for her meeting with Norman.

Mildred came out of the kitchen. "Are you meeting with Norman?"

"Aye, mam, shan't be long, I wouldn't think."

"You take as long as you like dear. Enjoy the moment."

Agnes thought it was a strange thing to say but dismissed the comment.

"Aye, mam, sithee."

Agnes left the bakery and walked the short distance

through the park. She spotted Norman waiting outside the door of the solicitor's office and walked across to join him.

"Hello Agnes, you look so beautiful today."

"Thank you Norman."

"I thought we could go to Martha's Tea Shop again."

"Aye, that'll be nice," replied Agnes, still concerned about Norman's behaviour.

She was beginning to think that he might have tired of her and wanted to break off their relationship, so, she too, was starting to feel slightly anxious. They walked down to the corner in silence. They reached the café and Norman held open the door.

There were several tables free and Norman led Agnes to one by the window. Sun was streaming through, the glass cruet set creating shadows on the table, so different from their last visit. The café seemed much brighter as a result. Agnes looked around at the clientele, mostly older women, gentry-looking, taking afternoon tea.

A waitress took their order.

"It's a lovely afternoon," said Agnes in an attempt to break the silence.

"Yes, it is," said Norman, who appeared to be fiddling with something in his jacket pocket.

The waitress brought two cups of tea on a tray.

"Norman, what's the matter? You're starting to worry me. I've not seen you like this before."

"I'm sorry, Agnes, I don't mean to worry you. I have something to ask you."

Agnes took a sip of her tea. "You can ask me anything, you know that."

Norman rummaged around again in his jacket pocket and pulled out a small box and put it on the table in front of her.

"What's this?" asked Agnes.

"It's for you; please open it."

Agnes picked up the box and flipped the lid. For a moment she was speechless, a beautiful antique ring, gold with a setting of six diamonds around a larger one.

"It belonged to my grandmother... I'm asking you if we can be married. I want you to be my wife."

Agnes stared at the ring, then at Norman. "I don't know what to say; I really don't."

"Just say yes. I've had thoughts since I first set eyes on you but the visit to the house at the weekend made up my mind. My parents adore you, as do I. My mother gave me the ring so that I may give it to you, and this morning I asked your mother and she's given me her permission to propose to you."

Agnes was stunned. This announcement had come completely out of the blue. There had been no talk about any long term commitment; marriage was not on Agnes's mind. Her pending career as an entertainer had consumed her thoughts.

"Oh, Norman, you have taken me by complete surprise; it has fair taken the wind from my sails."

Norman sensed the hesitation. "You do not feel the same. It is clear."

"Norman, yes, I love you well enough. It's just..." She looked at the ring one last time, closed the box, then passed it back to Norman.

"Just what?" said Norman, totally crestfallen. He had expected an immediate acceptance.

"It's too big a step for me just now. I've not yet turned nineteen and I have my career I want to make... and you have your studies to consider. We can't live on a clerk's wages."

"We'll be fine for money; my parents will always help."

"No, Norman, I cannot allow that. I'm sorry it's just not the right time. Why can't we continue as we are? It suits us both, surely."

Norman picked up Agnes's hand and kissed it. "Agnes, I love you more than life itself. I want to spend every waking moment with you. Please say you will marry me."

"I love you too Norman, but, as I said, this is not the right time. Maybe in six months, if we still feel the same, I could give you a better answer."

Norman picked up the small box and slowly wrapped his hand around it, then placed it in his pocket. Agnes could see tears welling up in his eyes. "Please don't be upset, Norman; I still want to step out with you, It's just..." She didn't know what it was and couldn't finish the sentence, but something was holding Agnes back.

Norman got up from the table. "I best be getting back; I told Mr Drummond I wouldn't be long. I'll pay for the tea."

"Wait, Norman, wait." Agnes went to stand but noticed several customers looking at her. Norman put his hand in his pocket, pulled out a sixpence and gave it to a passing waitress. Then he was gone.

Agnes finished her tea with as much decorum as an abandoned girl could. She was replaying the last few minutes in her mind and questioning herself. Was she being too harsh on Norman?

Agnes walked back to the bakery; she passed the solicitor's office and wondered about Norman; she hoped he would understand.

As she approached the shop, her mother was just leaving for her appointment with Mr Drummond. Agnes almost ignored her, totally lost in her thoughts.

"Hello, Agnes, are you alright?"

Agnes looked up. "Aye, mam, I'll be fine," she replied. Mildred was holding the door open for her, but there was no acknowledgement.

Mildred sighed. Something wasn't fine; she had an idea that the proposal had not gone to plan.

Mildred was a few minutes early for her appointment and sat on a bench for a moment to gather her thoughts. Grace's liaison with Freddie had dominated her mind since the discussion with Kitty. She was sure she was doing the right thing in sending her away, although what Grace's reaction would be was anyone's guess.

Just before the allotted time, she walked to the front door of the solicitor's office and rang the bell.

Norman was acting doorman again.

"Hello Norman, how are you?" said Mildred cheerily.

"Mr Drummond is ready for you, please take a seat; he will be with you in a moment," replied Norman formally, with just the merest of eye-contact.

"Thank you," replied Mildred. By his behaviour, she guessed that Agnes had turned him down but decided it was not the right time to say anything.

The door to Drummond's office opened.

"Mrs Marsden, always a pleasure, please do come in."

He held the door open and Mildred took her usual place in front of the desk where a tray of tea was waiting.

The solicitor went to his seat. "To what do I owe this pleasure?" he asked as he dispensed the teas.

"I need some advice, Mr Drummond."

"Of course, I am at your service."

Mildred picked up her teacup and took a sip, merely to consider her question.

"I have a mind to send one of my daughters, Grace, the

eldest, to a finishing school or the like, Paris or Switzerland perhaps. She has talked often about travelling and I have read about such places in magazines. She could finish her education and travel at the same time. My question is… well, I have no knowledge of such establishments and I would value your thoughts on the matter."

The solicitor also took a sip of tea before answering and peered over the top of his spectacles in the manner of a schoolmaster.

"Hmm, can I ask you a question?"

"Of course," replied Mildred.

"What do you know about the political situation in Europe at the moment?"

"Why, nothing at all, Mr Drummond, only what's in the Keighley News."

Drummond picked up a folded newspaper which was in his letter tray and opened it. "This is today's Times newspaper."

He flicked through a few pages of the broadsheet, then read the headlines. "It appears Austria has declared war on Servia."

"Servia?"

"Yes, it's in the Balkans." Mildred looked blank.

"Let me explain. There's been a lot of unrest in the area since the Archduke was murdered."

"Archduke?"

"I won't clarify, it's a long story."

"I don't understand; what has this got to do with Paris?"

"Yes, a good question, Mrs Marsden; the answer is… everything. Russia is an ally of Servia and has started to mobilise troops, according to the report here." He was scanning the newspaper as he spoke.

Mildred still looked blank, unable to connect the

relevance.

"You see, if Russia gets dragged into the conflict, then Germany could get involved on the side of Austria."

Mildred was listening intently, holding her teacup with the saucer positioned underneath in her other hand to catch drips.

"If that happens, then France will almost certainly side with Russia... They are allies," he clarified.

"So, what are you saying, Mr Drummond?"

The solicitor turned a page.

"Not to put too fine a point on it, The Times, here, talks about a grave situation. There's a strong likelihood of a European war. The stock markets have already reacted badly as you will know from my letter."

"Yes, yes, I can see that."

"So, at present, it would not be a good time to consider sending your daughter abroad, not until the situation is clearer. Now, it might not affect Great Britain at all. Earl Grey is meeting heads of governments to try to reach agreements to stop the situation from escalating."

Mildred was looking anxious. "Earl Grey is a politician, Foreign Secretary," he explained seeing the disconnect.

"What do you think will happen, Mr Drummond? You seem very knowledgeable in such matters."

"Hmm, I wish I had a crystal ball, Mrs Marsden, but everything depends on what Germany does. If they stay out of the conflict, then the hostilities might be confined to Austria and Servia, but with Russia mobilising their troops, that changes things most seriously. It really is on a knife-edge."

"But it won't affect us, surely?"

"That's difficult to say, let us hope not, but it is wise to take precautions."

"And this is in The Times, you say?"

"Yes."

"I think I should buy a copy. I had no idea this was happening."

"No, it has not been widely reported in the provincial newspapers."

"That could account for the cost of flour. Arthur was saying that the miller had heard a rumour that the government was stockpiling grain."

"Hmm, I've not seen anything about that, but it could be right."

"What do you think we should do, Mr Drummond?"

"Frankly, Mrs Marsden, there is nothing to be done. We can only rely on politicians to resolve the situation."

Mildred had finished her tea. "What about the house?" she asked.

"I wouldn't worry about that; you continue with your plans and let's hope matters are resolved without any need for conflict."

But Mildred <u>was</u> worried. She thanked the solicitor for his counsel, and the solicitor escorted her to the door. There was no sign of Norman.

Mildred took a detour across the park to the top of James Street. There was a newsagent the other side of the grocer's store. She bought a copy of The Times and headed back to the bakery.

Archie Slater was outside calling the headlines.

"Foundrymen's strike called off," he trilled to anyone who would listen.

The threat of war had come out of the blue and merely added to Mildred's worries. She was no further forward in resolving Grace's liaison with Freddie. Sending her to a finishing school was not now an option.

In the parlour, Molly was working on her embroidery, Freda was reading. Grace and Agnes were in the bedroom. Arthur was at the table reading the Keighley News; the smell of alcohol seemed to emanate from his pores.

Mildred put The Times down on the table.

"What's this?" he said, looking at his mother as though she had stepped in something unpleasant.

"A decent newspaper with real news."

"Nay, that's gentry news, that's all."

"So, you've not heard about the war then?"

"What war?"

"It's in there… Austria and Servia. I've just come back from seeing Mr Drummond. He says we could be going to war as well. That's why the price of flour keeps going up."

"Nay, that's the government stockpiling to line their pockets."

"I think that's because they're trying to protect us more like."

"You're even talking like the gentry, mam. You should listen to thaself."

"Arthur, do not be so disrespectful."

Molly looked up. "What's this about a war?"

"Nothing to worry about, dear," said Mildred. She left the paper on the table and went to the bedroom to change. She looked in on the two girls.

"Is everything alright, Agnes? You seemed upset earlier."

Agnes was sat on the bed with a very sullen look.

"Aye, 'appen Norman's asked me to marry him."

"Hmm, I wondered if that was it. He asked my permission this morning."

"Aye, he said… And yet you said nowt?"

"Of course not; I wouldn't dream of spoiling the surprise.

And you've turned him down? Am I right?

"Aye, I don't want to be getting married just now. I've got my career to consider."

"I know, Agnes dear, but Norman is a good catch; you won't find many better."

Mildred sat down on the bed next to Agnes. "So, what's going to happen?"

"I don't know, mam. We were in the café and when I said no, he just walked out... 'Appen he won't want to see me again."

"But he's very fond of you, Agnes; I'm sure he will once he's had a chance to get over the disappointment."

Agnes wasn't convinced; her mood, not improved.

Mildred noticed Grace had been writing; there was a letter on the top of the dressing table in her handwriting.

"You've been writing?" said Mildred, looking at Grace.

"Aye," she replied but didn't clarify. Mildred had a good idea who the recipient was.

Arthur, despite his condemnation of the newspaper, had taken an interest in his mother's comments and was scanning the pages. He winced when he read an article about the Grouse Shooting prospects; 'patchy', it said, but the reports of the Balkan crisis did concern him.

That evening, Arthur attended another Labour Party meeting, called by the local membership to discuss the recent return to work of the foundrymen. About eighty men had congregated into the Meeting Hall. Arthur was joined by his two drinking pals, Henry King, and Samuel Tanner. During the walk to the meeting, Arthur discussed what he had read in the newspaper.

"This was in The Times?" said Henry.

"Aye," said Arthur.

"What are you doing reading that Liberal filth?"

"Me mam brought it home, but it's right, sure enough. We could be heading for war; that's what it said."

"'Appen it's a Liberal plot," said Samuel. "Keep the working class in their place."

"Aye, you could be right," said Arthur.

They reached the Meeting Hall and the atmosphere was belligerent. There was still much unrest among the members with accusations of a sell-out. This was not far from the truth. The workers had capitulated having been almost starved into submission.

The anger was plain for all to see, and the chairman had difficulty in keeping any sort of order. As speaker after speaker denounced the call to return to work. Far from resolving the long-running dispute, the agreement to call off the strike had merely fanned the flames for further unrest. There was anger aimed at the union leaders for giving in. Industrial relations between workers and the bosses were at an all-time low.

The last item on the agenda was 'any other business', and the chairman invited questions. Arthur stood up.

"What's the party's thoughts on a war in Europe?"

The local leadership were seated on the stage behind a trestle table on wooden chairs and were relieved to get a question not connected with recent local disputes. The chairman stood up and addressed Arthur's question.

"The general view is that the reports circulating in some national newspapers are scaremongering. The hostilities are localised and have nothing to do with hard-working folk in Great Britain. You will be aware that the last annual conference we passed a resolution condemning militarism and war."

"So you don't think there will be a war then?" Arthur was still stood.

"It's unlikely, and we would never support one in Parliament."

Arthur sat down. "Well, that's told tha Arthur lad," said Henry.

"Aye, it did," replied Arthur, and after a couple more questions, the chairman closed the meeting.

The following morning, Thursday, another letter arrived for Grace, postmarked Oakworth. She was serving in the bakery. She excused herself and headed for the outside toilet.

'My dearest Grace, I am not writing with good news I am afraid. All the lads have been called back to work; the strike has been called off. It means I cannot take you to the Picture House on Friday as I had hoped. It makes me feel so wretched. I hate working at the mill, can you see if your mother will employ me as a gardener? I will work very hard and I know about plants and the like. We could meet on Sunday again if you would like. Take a walk by the river if the weather is fair. Please write and let me know. Yours forever

Freddie'

Grace had managed to decipher the letter and was overwhelmed by disappointment, but the setback had merely served to fan the flames of ardour even more. She would ask her mother at the earliest opportunity.

Agnes, meanwhile, was also feeling emotional. She had not slept well thinking about Norman; she was having second thoughts; maybe she should marry him. She liked him well enough, and as her mother had said, he was a good catch. But then her thoughts turned to her new career; she would be away for the best part of three months and would have no time for anything else, let alone planning for a wedding.

She would talk to Norman again at lunchtime and see if they could come to a compromise.

But Norman wasn't there. It was a nice day with fluffy white clouds and bright sunshine as she walked across the park to their spot. The distant thrump of the factories echoed around the valley. She sat on the bench and waited. Occasionally, she stared across at the door to the solicitor's office and wondered if she should call and see if he was there. Twenty minutes went by, still nothing. The longer she waited, the more she urgently wanted to speak to Norman.

She looked at the offices again; Norman would be inside beavering away over some ledgers or files no doubt. Was he deliberately avoiding her? There was only one way to find out.

She got up from the bench and walked over to the front door, hesitated, then rang the bell.

But it wasn't Norman. It was a woman of mature years, greying hair, dressed smartly with a string of pearls around her neck.

"How may I help you?" she said, eyeing up the visitor.

"Can I speak to Norman, please?" asked Agnes nervously.

"He's not here. He's taken the day off."

"Oh, oh, I see. Never mind, thank you."

The woman shut the door without further formality, leaving Agnes wondering what to do.

She walked back to the bakery and climbed the stairs to the parlour, where her mother was talking to Grace.

Grace turned to Agnes as she came through the door. "Do you think Freddie should be our gardener at our new house?"

"What?" The question threw Agnes completely; her mind was elsewhere. Mildred interrupted before Agnes could answer.

"It's not up to Agnes. I just said there are a lot of considerations before I can make a decision on any staff. I need to think about the costs involved."

"You just don't like Freddie; that's it, isn't it?" said Grace and got up from the table and stormed out of the parlour towards the bedroom.

"Wait, wait," said Mildred, but she had already gone.

"Why can't Freddie work for us?" asked Agnes as she took off her hat and sat down.

"I've not said he can't. I just don't want to make any commitments, not just yet, not until we are in the house. Anyway, what are you doing back? You're usually meeting Norman."

"Aye, but 'appen he's taken the day off."

"Oh, I see. Do you want something to eat?" asked Mildred. She stood up from the table and headed towards the kitchen.

"I'm not hungry, mam. Can you give me some money for a cabbie, please? I will go and see Norman after we have finished."

"Yes, of course dear." She picked up her handbag, which was hanging by its straps from one of the chairs and took out her purse. "Here's a shilling that should cover it." Mildred handed Agnes the coin.

Mildred had her own journey in mind; she needed to visit Kitty.

Arthur was opening the bakery at two o'clock as Mildred came down the stairs; a queue of around ten women poured into the shop as the latch was dropped and the door opened with its customary 'clang'.

She looked across at the girls behind the counter. Grace gave her a frosty response and continued to serve the first customer. Mildred walked out and crossed the road to wait for the next cabbie with a heavy heart and no answer as to what she should do.

Forty minutes later, the taxi pulled up outside the village shop in Oakworth. Mildred had a call to make before she continued her journey to the cottage. She paid the driver and arranged to be picked up at the cottage at three-thirty.

She entered the store and recognised the proprietor straightaway.

"Can I help you madam?"

"Mr Jessop?"

"Aye."

"My name's Mildred Marsden. I'm the new owner of Springfield Hall."

"Oh aye... Wait... I remember. Tha was looking for Blossom Cottage if I recall correctly."

"Yes, that's right. You have a good memory."

"Aye, never forget a face."

"Well, I require a daily help and I understand that your good wife used to perform that task for the late owner."

"Aye, aye, she worked for Mr Springfield a short while; last year it were."

"Do you think she would be interested in working for me?"

"Aye 'appen she might, under my feet here she is, since she left." He chuckled to himself.

"That's excellent, excellent. Well, we move in next Tuesday and there will be lots to do. Is she here now?"

"Nay, you've just missed her, took the trolley into town she has."

"Oh dear, that's a pity, I didn't want to make another journey."

"Well, tell you what, why don't I ask her to come and see you at the house on Tuesday, say lunchtime?"

"Yes, that will be most acceptable; we will be at the house by then, I am sure."

Chapter Sixteen

Mildred thanked the man and left the store. Five minutes later, she was at the front door of Kitty's cottage. There was no sign of Freddie in the garden.

Mildred knocked and waited for a few minutes before knocking again. Kitty would be in her studio. A couple of minutes later, the door opened. "Mildred, how lovely to see you. Have you been knocking long, only I don't always hear it in the studio?"

"No, only a couple of minutes. Sorry to call unannounced."

"No matter, you are always welcome. Please do come in."

Kitty moved to one side to allow Mildred to pass.

"Is this about Grace?" said Kitty as she led Mildred to the sitting room.

"Yes, it is."

"Would you like a drink?"

"A cup of tea would be very nice, thank you," replied Mildred.

Kitty left Mildred and went to make the tea, returning a few minutes later with the drinks and some homemade biscuits.

"I don't know about you, but I get a bit peckish around this time of day."

Kitty sat down and started to pour the tea.

"So, what's the latest news then?"

Mildred described her visit to the solicitors. "He thinks there's going to be a war."

"Well, I've not heard anything about it," said Kitty.

"No, me neither, but he showed me in the newspaper, The Times. It doesn't look very good. So, there's no means of sending Grace away somewhere, not abroad anyway."

"So what's to be done?" asked Kitty, nibbling on a biscuit.

"I'm at a loss, I really am. Grace is pressing me to take Freddie as a gardener at the new house."

"Yes, he's said it to me on a few occasions."

"I just don't know what to do, Kitty, I really don't, and I have problems with Agnes too," Mildred explained the rejection of Norman's marriage proposal.

"Maybe we should just let things take their course, as we discussed, and see how it goes. With the move, I guess she'll be preoccupied and now Freddie's back at work, there's going to be less opportunity for them to meet."

"Yes, you could be right," said Mildred, taking the last sip of her tea. "But what about the gardener's position? Grace is not going to let that go."

"Hmm, well, it's your house and you can employ whoever you wish."

"Do you think I should employ Freddie?"

"Well, if Grace is working in town, I can't see it will do much harm. At least you can keep an eye on things."

"Yes, you could be right, and in different circumstances, I wouldn't have thought twice. Looking at your garden, I can see the lad's got talent."

"Yes, he certainly has a gift with nature."

With matters still not resolved, Mildred said farewell to Kitty and left the cottage. The cabbie was waiting to return her to the bakery.

Meanwhile, while Mildred was on her way back, Agnes was heading to Utley to see Norman. She didn't like the way the conversation had ended the previous day. Things needed to be said.

She arrived at the rectory and asked the driver to wait;

she was unsure of the reception.

She went to the front door and jerked the pull-down cord, which sounded a bell inside. There was a rustling, then the door opened.

"Hello Mrs Hoskins, is Norman at home?"

"Oh, it's you, you're the last person we expected to hear from. No, he's not. He's gone into Bradford, and it's all your fault."

"What do you mean?"

"Rejecting his proposal indeed. Is he not good enough for you, a baker's daughter?"

"That's not fair; that's not the reason at all. I'm just not ready for marriage; that's all there is to it."

The rector's wife looked at Agnes coldly and with much anger.

"I never meant to cause no harm. I am very fond of Norman," Agnes added.

"So this is how you treat people you are fond of, is it?"

"I came to put things right between us."

"Well, he's not here and because of you he won't be here for a long time."

Mrs Hoskins closed the door, leaving Agnes with more questions than had been answered. What did she mean by he won't be here for a long time?

The answer came the following day in a letter.

It had been hand-delivered and Agnes discovered it on the floor beneath the bakery letterbox at eight o'clock when she was opening the shop. After clearing the initial rush for bread, Agnes took a short break to read it.

'My dearest Agnes,

My mother told me you had called this afternoon; I am sorry I was not there to greet you. The thing is I have decided to sign up for the army. There was an advertisement in the newspaper for officer training so I went to the recruitment office in Bradford earlier and I have been accepted. I have handed in my notice at the solicitor's, but I intend to return to my studies when I have served my country.

I have been given the title of 'temporary gentleman', a strange name indeed. This is because I did not go to public school, nor can I say my parents are from the gentry class, so that is the name by which they address us. Once I have completed my training I will be a Second Lieutenant.

I will be leaving on Sunday so this is goodbye for a while, but I hope you will allow me to write to you from time to time.

With fondest love
Norman'

Agnes put her hand to her mouth in a state of shock. Then the tears started to fall.

Earlier, Arthur had been in discussion with the miller. Over recent days, Buxton's had been able to supply the bakery with all the required flour without Arthur having to resort to the more expensive wholesaler. The topic of continued supply was at the foremost of Arthur's mind.

"So, what do you think, Edward? Have tha heard owt?" asked Arthur, having described the articles in The Times.

"Nay, can't say that I have, but it would explain why price of grain has gone up."

"Aye, but it makes tha wonder what'll happen if there is a war. I mean, will us get any flour at all?"

"Who knows, but they can't let us starve, can they?"

"I wouldn't trust Asquith and his lot as far as I could throw 'em. Just in it for the'selves. 'Appen they want us to have a war just to put us working class in us place. There'll be a revolution you mark my words."

"You mean like the French? Guillotines and such?"

"Aye, I'd willingly pull the handle and that's no lie. Watching the heads of the gentry class rolling into baskets, now that's a sight to consider."

The atmosphere in the bakery was dreadful. Agnes's letter from Norman and Freddie cancelling the picture show had cast shadows over the two girls. The normal polite service was missing, a point noticed by several regulars.

Agnes had talked to Grace of the rejected proposal and Norman's decision to join the army; in turn, Grace had told Agnes of her desire for Freddie and her aim to have him working at the new house.

In the parlour, Mildred was busying herself with household chores, but her mind was being pulled in many different directions, mostly concerning her children. Only Freda, the youngest, seemed content and had not given Mildred a moment's worry. The priority was still to try and resolve the issue of Grace and Freddie; disclosure of the truth was difficult to contemplate; the fallout could split the family. Mildred couldn't afford to let that happen.

Her thoughts were being drawn to appoint Freddie as the new gardener. It would keep Grace happy, and with her working in town at the bakery, there would not be too many opportunities for her and Freddie to develop their relationship. A naïve thought as it would transpire.

There was another, more pressing issue. With only five days to go until the house move, nothing had been properly resolved about Arthur. The transfer of the business was progressing but, as the solicitor had explained, due to Arthur's age, it would have to be placed into a trust until he was twenty-one. It would take several weeks to complete everything. Then there were the staffing issues. As Arthur had expressed, with Grace and Agnes based in Oakworth, they would not be able to reach the bakery for seven-thirty, their usual start time. Mildred needed to raise it with him.

After lunch, she had walked up James Street to the newsagents to buy the day's edition of The Times. Following the discussion with the solicitor, she was anxious to know what was going on. She returned to the parlour and sat at the table with the newspaper open wide. It did not make good reading.

She turned the pages and the news was grim; it seemed Mr Drummond's prediction was proving correct. Under the heading, *'On the brink of war'*, it described the increased tension between Russia and Germany; both countries were in the process of mobilisation. According to the Prime Minister, who was addressing a hushed parliament, *'the issues of peace and war hang in the balance'*.

Mildred continued to scan the pages; the topic of war had now confined the 'Irish problem' to 'other matters'. There was no indication that Great Britain would become embroiled and it was hoped that Earl Grey's shuttle diplomacy would bring the two superpowers back from the brink, but the uncertainty was worrying.

Suddenly, Mildred felt quite alone. Her priority was her children; she would protect them at all costs, but for once, she wished she could share her burden. She needed to call on Kitty again; at least she understood.

Molly and Freda had been shopping, Grace and Agnes, cleaning in the bakery, when Arthur returned to the parlour.

"You're early," observed Mildred as he walked in and started removing his boots.

"Aye, 'appen most of me pals are working. Wilfred's back at butcher's."

"Well, that is most fortuitous. I want to talk to you about arrangements for next week."

"What arrangements?"

"For the bakery, after we move. It's not long now."

Arthur put his head in his hands. Ostrich syndrome – what you can't see, is not happening. A familiar characteristic Mildred had noticed before, just like his father, who would drown his troubles by looking at the bottom of a glass.

"You can't ignore this, Arthur, it's not going away. You have the staffing and your housekeeper to consider."

"What staff? I have Grace and Agnes."

"You have Grace, but in a few weeks you won't have Agnes, and what are you going to do about opening if the trollies aren't working?"

"We'll manage; 'appen they could get a cabbie. It seems to be their usual travel these days. Just like the gentry they are."

"Well, we can't afford cabbies every day."

"So, what say tha?"

"I don't know, but something needs to be done. You could change the opening hours."

"Nay, we can't do that; it's been eight o'clock since grandad's day."

"Yes, but things change."

"Aye, that they do."

"What about Wilfred's sisters?"

"They're working in is shop."

"What, all of them?"

"Aye, I think so."

"And what about someone to look after the house for you?"

"I've not thought."

"What about Mrs Stonehouse?"

"Wilfred's mam?"

"Yes, she used to do cleaning and the like until her husband passed away."

"'Appen she has her day filled looking after Wilfred and his lot."

"Yes, but they're growing up now; they can look after themselves. How many hours will you need?"

"I have no idea."

"Well, we'll have to work something out."

Arthur looked forlorn. To Mildred, he was still a child, and in many ways, he was. Responsibility had never sat well on his shoulders. He was a good baker, but anything else was a challenge.

"What say I go and see Mrs Stonehouse and ask her? It'll do no harm, and I'd sooner have someone we know than a stranger."

"Aye, if that's what tha think."

"Well, I'll go and pay Mrs Stonehouse a visit. There's something to eat for you in the kitchen if you're hungry."

A few minutes later, Mildred was walking up James Street to the butcher's shop. It was still open and doing a steady trade. Wilfred was in his striped butcher's uniform and straw boater; the front of his apron was smeared with blood and bits of meat from the labours of the day. He noticed Mildred walk in.

"Hello, Mrs Marsden, what can I get for tha? I've a nice piece of topside I've just cut, very lean and tender."

"Thank you Wilfred. I need to speak to your mother if she's available."

"Aye, 'appen she's upstairs. Do tha know tha way?"

"Well, I've not been before."

"I'll get one of the girls to take you up… Lilian, can tha take Mrs Marsden up to see mam?"

One of the three girls that were working put down her cleaning cloth and walked towards Mildred.

"My, how you have grown, Lilian," said Mildred as she approached.

Wilfred continued serving customers as the girl escorted Mildred to the upstairs rooms.

The layout of the first floor was very similar to the bakery, although it was slightly larger, with three bedrooms.

"Mam, it's Mrs Marsden for tha," shouted Lilian and then returned to the shop.

Violet Stonehouse came in from the kitchen, wiping her hands with a towel. She was a round, quite wholesome woman, her dark hair now increasingly greying. She was wearing a bright pinafore over a day-dress.

"Hello, Mrs Marsden. Please take a seat. To what do we owe this pleasure?"

"Hello, Mrs Stonehouse, thank you for your time. Sorry to call unannounced." Mildred sat down on the large settee which dominated the room.

"You're always welcome."

"Thank you, well, I'll get straight to the point; you may have heard we are shortly to be leaving the bakery."

"Aye, Wilfred did say; Oakworth, if I'm not mistaken."

"Yes, that's correct, Springfield Hall. Unfortunately, we find ourselves in a bit of a situation. Arthur has decided not to move with us so he can stay close to the bakery. It was not an easy decision, as you can imagine."

Violet sat down opposite her guest.

"No, I can imagine, Wilfred said Arthur didn't want to go. Something about becoming gentrified or some such thing."

"Yes, well… The thing is, Arthur can't look after himself, and I quite remember you used to be in service not long since… before your husband passed on."

"Aye, that's true, Lady Austwick, Fieldfare Hall… Silsden way," she clarified. "I had to give it up when Edgar died; I needed to be here for the children."

"Well, I've been talking to Arthur this afternoon, and I have a mind to employ a housekeeper for him, not full time, a few hours a week. I'm happy to discuss suitable times, and of course, appropriate recompense."

Mildred was becoming more and more adept at her 'gentry-speak' since her regular meetings with the solicitor.

Mrs Stonehouse thought for a moment. "Well, aye, extra money with these mouths to feed is always to be welcomed."

"Yes, seven, is it?"

"Aye; there's Lilian, she's thirteen; Gladys, fourteen; Phyllis, nineteen; Ivy, twenty; then there's the boys, Wilfred, he's twenty-one; Ernest, fifteen, and… then Ronald, he's twelve."

"My, I don't know how you manage to remember them all, and Wilfred's running the shop now?"

"Aye."

"What about the rest of the girls? Are they in the shop?"

"Aye, and Lilian is helping as well during the school holiday. The trouble is there's not really enough work for them all."

"Really? Now that's interesting. It so happens I may have a vacancy."

"In the bakery?"

"Yes, I don't know if you have heard from Wilfred, but Agnes is going to be leaving quite soon."

"No, he's not said owt."

"Yes, she's got a new career as a singer."

"A singer? Goodness, how wonderful."

"Well, yes, it's a dream she's had. She's just been for an audition at the Hippodrome."

"The Hippodrome?"

"Yes," Mildred replied proudly. "They liked her and she starts rehearsals in a few weeks so she'll be leaving the shop."

"Well, I don't think it's right for Gladys, she's only just started, but Ivy I'm sure would be interested. She's been working in the shop for six years. She keeps going on how she wants a change, even talked about going to one of the mills."

"Well, that seems an excellent solution. Can you speak to her and if she's interested she can talk to Arthur…? And would you be happy with the housekeeping position?"

"Aye, although I'll need to discuss hours. I have plenty to do here."

"Yes, of course. Why don't you come down to the bakery after you close tomorrow? Shall we say about three o'clock? I'll make sure Arthur's available."

"Aye, right you are, I'll bring Ivy with me."

Mildred returned to the shop pleased with herself that she seemed to have resolved the potential staffing problems.

Her arrival in the parlour startled Arthur who appeared to be reading the Keighley News. The Times was also open on the table and looked like it had been disturbed. He didn't want to give the impression he had been reading the Liberal standard-bearer.

"Ah, Arthur, I've been talking to Mrs Stonehouse and she has offered to be your housekeeper."

"Housekeeper? 'Appen only gentry have housekeepers."

"It's just a name, Arthur, someone to do your cleaning,

cooking, and washing. You'll be paying wages so it's not like it's charity or anything. It's what I've been doing for you for twenty years."

Arthur looked at his mother, mulling it over. Mildred could see his unease.

"Look, Arthur, your working class principles are all well and good, but the fact remains, you can't look after yourself."

"Aye, alright."

"The other thing, according to Mrs Stonehouse, Ivy's looking for a change. I thought she could take over from Agnes. You know her right enough."

"Aye, she's good with customers, so Wilfred says."

"Well, I've invited them both here tomorrow afternoon at three o'clock to discuss matters, so make sure you're back from the alehouse and not smelling of beer."

Arthur was scanning the newspaper again. "Aye, I'll be here."

Whilst outwardly giving the impression of indifference, inside he was pleased that his mother had taken control; it had been something that had been haunting him in those times in the small hours when sleep alluded him.

Saturday, August 1st 1914, a normal working day in the Marsden household.

Agnes was still contemplating her broken relationship with Norman; it had left a gaping hole in her life and she was trying to come to terms with her loss. Singing would be her salvation, she resolved.

For Grace, however, things couldn't be more different. She had received another letter from Freddie confirming he would be coming into town on Sunday afternoon to meet her. A walk by the river was suggested, and she sighed every time she thought about it.

During the morning, Arthur had a visitor. It was Herbert Radcliffe, the secretary of the local Labour Party. The shop was its usual mayhem for a Saturday morning and he had to wait for a few minutes before he could attract the attention of one of the girls. It was Grace who attended to him.

"Eh up, I've come to see Arthur, if he's about."

"He's 'round the back in the baking shed. If you go out of the shop and just down West Street, you'll see the entrance."

The man checked his bearings, vacated the shop, and turned left. The road was covered in horse manure; luckily, the narrow footpath was clear and a few moments later he had reached the yard and the back of the shed. He could see Arthur mixing another batch of bread.

"'Ow do, Arthur, lad."

Arthur was in a dream and the greeting made him jump. He looked up at the visitor, but with the bright background, didn't initially recognise him.

"It's Herbert Radcliffe."

It was like being visited by royalty. Arthur left what he was doing and started wiping his hands on an old cloth. His hair was dishevelled and white with flour dust.

"Aye, eh up, Herbert, nice to sithee. What brings thee round?"

He gave his right hand one last wipe on the back of his trousers then offered it to the visitor to shake. It was warmly reciprocated.

"I shan't keep thee, I know tha's busy. Have tha heard about the demonstration in London tomorrow?"

"Nay, can't say I have, Herbert."

"Aye, it's to protest about the war in Europe, and I know tha mentioned it at the meeting."

"Aye, it's not good, looking in t'papers."

"Nay, that's a fact; they're full of it today. Have you read The Herald this morning?"

"Nay, I've been in here since five."

"Ah, aye, of course… Well, there's a demonstration tomorrow in London to support the workers against the war. Ramsay MacDonald will be speaking, and all the National Executive will be there."

"Well, it's good to know someone's doing summat," said Arthur.

"Aye, well, there was an emergency meeting of the local committee last night, and we've managed to arrange a special train to take members down to London to support the protest; show solidarity, like, for the working class. Would tha be interested in joining us?"

"Tomorrow, tha say? Aye, 'appen I might," said Arthur without a moment's thought.

"Can tha get some others to join us, pals and that?"

"Aye, possibly, what time?"

"Train leaves at six tomorrow morning. We're expecting a good turnout. There's about a hundred already said they'd come."

"Aye, ok, how much is it?"

"It's just half a crown."

Arthur was thinking; few of his pals in the Malt Shovel could afford that. He would speak to his mother.

"Aye, I'll be there and 'appen I can bring a few pals too."

"Good… well, I shan't take up any more of tha time. Sithee in the morning."

They shook hands again and Herbert left to find more potential protestors. Arthur returned to his baking. A trip to London, indeed; he'd not been further than Bradford before. He felt a twinge of excitement.

At lunchtime, Arthur made his usual trip to the Malt Shovel. Most of his regular pals were working, but he mentioned the London trip to Thomas Fielding, the landlord, as he was waiting for his pint.

"Train leaves at six o'clock, it'll cost half a crown."

Fielding placed the pint in front of Arthur and watched as his first gulp took almost half the glass.

"Half a crown? Hmm, not sure there'll be too many takers at that price; I don't think there's much of an appetite for protesting after what's been going on around here."

"Aye, Tom, tha could be right, but mention it if tha has a mind. I'll be in tonight, see if anyone's of interest."

With the shop now closed, Grace and Agnes had finished cleaning and were in the parlour eating when Arthur returned. He put his cap on the side and started taking off his boots when Grace confronted him.

"Hey Arthur, what's this about a housekeeper? Getting a bit gentrified if tha asks me," she teased. She turned to Agnes and giggled.

"It's just a bit of cleaning; that's all," he replied indignantly.

There was a copy of The Times on the table; Mildred had made the trip to the newsagents earlier. Arthur finished taking off his boots and picked it up to read.

"Now then, Grace, stop teasing," said Mildred as she walked into the room with a plate of sandwiches for Arthur.

"It's cheese and pickle; I called in at Granger's earlier," she said, placing the plate in front of him.

"Ta," he replied without looking up.

His mother joined Grace and Agnes on the settee; the two youngest were in the bedroom. After a few minutes, Arthur looked up from the newspaper. "Has tha read the news mam?"

"Yes, I have."

"Says here they're calling for the troops to be made ready. It's not right, it's not right."

"No, Arthur it's not, but it did say the King has sent letters to the Kaiser, and the Tzar, maybe they'll see sense. They <u>are</u> related."

"Nah, there's profit to be made somewhere, you mark my words."

"I don't think it's profit, more pride if you ask me."

"Anyway, 'appen I'm off to London tomorrow, to protest."

The three women looked up in astonishment.

"London!?" exclaimed Mildred. Grace and Agnes looked at each other in disbelief.

"Aye, Labour Party's trying to do something about stopping the war. There's going to be a big rally; all the Executive will be there, including MacDonald. Summat's got to be done."

"But… London, you did say London?" said Mildred.

"Aye, there's a special train local committee's put on."

"But what will you do when you get there?" asked Mildred still trying to take in the implications.

"Protest, I expect," he replied and carried on reading.

"Well, you just mind yourself. You know what happened the last time you protested and I can't be going all the way down to London to bail you out."

"Aye, mam, don't fret, I'll be careful," he said, without looking up from his paper.

He eventually found a reference to the proposed rally he would be attending, just three or four lines. "Typical," he said to himself.

Then underneath there was another paragraph detailing a

speech by the Labour MP, Kier Hardy, proposing a motion in the House of Commons. '*We stand by the efforts of the international working class movement to unite the workers of the governments concerned to prevent their governments from entering upon war, as expressed in the resolution passed by the International Socialist Bureau*'. This was going to be the mission of the rally, it stated.

Arthur felt inspired; he was looking forward to joining the protest.

He was disturbed by his mother. "You've not forgotten this afternoon have you?"

Arthur looked up. "Forgotten what?"

"Mrs Stonehouse is calling at three o'clock." The clock on the mantlepiece said two forty-five.

"Oh, aye."

"Well, when you've finished your sandwich, get washed and changed. You don't want to be meeting her like that. You've got flour in your hair."

Arthur finished his lunch and went to change; merely to please his mother. His appearance was of no consequence to him. Clothes were just a means to protect modesty; anything else he considered a vanity.

Just after three o'clock, there was a rap on the shop door.

"That'll be Mrs Stonehouse," said Mildred. "Grace, can you let her in? I'll just clear the plates. Agnes can you lend me a hand?"

Mildred and Agnes gathered the lunchtime dishes and took them in the kitchen while Grace went to attend to the visitor.

There were footsteps up the stairs and then the parlour door opened. Mrs Stonehouse and her daughter, Ivy, entered.

Arthur was still at the table scanning The Times but folded it up as the guests arrived. Grace and Agnes went to the bedroom.

"Mrs Stonehouse, and Ivy," said Mildred. "How nice to see you. Do come in. Take a seat on the sofa, would you like a drink at all? I can make some tea."

"No, we're fine thanks," replied Mrs Stonehouse and the pair sat on the settee. Arthur got up from the table and sat in 'his' armchair; the one his father used to use.

"You know Arthur, of course."

"Aye," said Mrs Stonehouse. "Wilfred's always telling us of what he's been up to."

"How are you, Ivy?" asked Mildred.

Ivy was more her father's daughter, facially similar, and taller than her mother. She had yet to fill out as substantially as her mother had. She was wearing a smock with her dark hair tied back in a bun.

"I'm fine, thank you, Mrs Marsden," she replied demurely.

"Your mother says you might be interested in working at the bakery."

"Aye, there's nowt much to do at butcher's now Gladys has started work."

"Do you want to ask any questions, Arthur?" said Mildred.

"Nay, I've seen Ivy in t'shop, 'appen she'll soon learn bread," he replied. Ivy looked down; she appeared to be blushing.

"Would you like to have a look around, Mrs Stonehouse?"

"Aye, if tha don't mind."

Mildred got up and took the woman into the kitchen, leaving Ivy and Arthur. Ivy was looking around; Arthur appeared disinterested.

"Nice room," said Ivy after an uneasy silence.

"Aye, ta," replied Arthur.

"When's tha want us to start?" said Ivy, gradually gaining in confidence.

"Anytime tha likes, Agnes won't be leaving for a while, but 'appen you can learn what to do."

"Monday, then?"

"Aye, if that suits. Will Wilfred mind?"

"Nay, he'll be happy right enough; 'appen there's no work for all of us."

Mildred completed the tour of the upstairs with Mrs Stonehouse and pointed out areas that would need particular attention.

"We'll be leaving all the furnishings," she confirmed. "We are amply provided for at the new house."

"Aye, it sounds very grand."

"Yes, it's comfortable enough," replied Mildred but didn't elaborate further.

She looked at Arthur. "So, Arthur, have you decided?"

"Aye, Ivy will start on Monday."

"That's excellent; it will give her a chance to learn the ropes before Agnes leaves."

"Aye."

"What about hours... for Mrs Stonehouse?"

"I don't know, mam; what's tha think?"

"Well, I could probably spare three hours a day," interrupted Mrs Stonehouse. "Will you be wanting me to cook a meal?"

Arthur looked at Mildred; only now was he beginning to realise the enormity of the change ahead.

"Aye, if tha has a mind," said Arthur.

"Well, that will be extra, and you'll need to pay for what tha needs me to cook."

"Aye, I can give thee brass for that."

"Well, that's settled then," said Mildred.

"Aye, very well, when's tha want me to start?" asked Mrs Stonehouse.

"Well, we'll be leaving on Tuesday morning; I've ordered a van from Hayden's for nine o'clock. If you come after that, that would be most suitable. I will pay you for additional hours if you can spare the time. There could be some tidying to do."

"Aye, I can do that. I may bring Lilian with me; she's been helping in the shop, but she's under my feet most of the time."

"Yes, as you see fit, Mrs Stonehouse."

With the working and payment arrangements agreed, Mildred escorted the visitors to the front door with a sense of relief.

Arthur was back at the paper with mixed feelings. The change was coming at him like a runaway train and there was nothing to stop it now; he was considering the implications.

Chapter Seventeen

Later, Arthur was back at the alehouse drumming up support for the trip to London. As the landlord had predicted, there were not many takers. Most were griping at the half a crown cost which represented almost a day's wages for many of the mill-workers. Arthur had called on Wilfred to see if he would join him, but he had declined the offer as he would be busy in the butcher's preparing meat.

Arthur was sat with Samuel and Henry. He had agreed to pay for their fares, mainly because he wanted some company for the journey. Neither had been to London before so there was much excitement at the prospect. But there was a more sombre note to their discussion. It was Henry, looking as smart as ever, who broached the subject.

"Arthur, has tha been giving some thought t'court case?"

"Aye, Henry, it's never far from my mind."

"What do tha think? Will they send us to Armley?"

"Aye, it's a possibility. There were a bunch of lads in court this week and they were all sent down."

"Really? I never saw that. For how long?"

"For most, it were a fortnight, but one or two it were longer. One of them got twelve months. Mind you he did knock down a copper."

"Never!"

"Aye, it were right enough."

"So, this time next week 'appen we won't be drinking in here then?"

"Aye, I very much doubt it, Henry."

Samuel was listening to the discussion but didn't feel able to contribute. He suddenly had an urgent need to visit the outside toilet.

The following day at five-thirty, Arthur was at the station waiting for his two drinking pals. He checked his father's watch, not for the first time. Mildred had made some sandwiches which he had managed to cram into the side pocket of his suit jacket creating a large bulge. The sun had been up for over an hour and it was a bright summer's morning. He had already called at the ticket office and purchased three tickets.

It was ten-to-six before Arthur spotted the two pals hurrying down the road. The station entrance was packed with protestors filtering through the turnstiles to reach the platform, many carrying union banners; there was a great deal of shouting and singing.

"'Ow do, Arthur," said Henry. He was wearing a smart suit with a white, collarless shirt, leather boots, and his best cap. He was holding a brown paper carrier bag.

"Eh up, Henry, Sam; I thought tha wasn't coming. We best get to platform and get a seat; train'll be packed judging by this lot. I've got tickets."

They made their way down the wooden stairs from the ticket hall to the waiting train, where around two hundred other demonstrators were trying to get on board. Steam from the engine seemed to create a fog along the platform; there was the distinctive smell that steam trains emit.

The carriages were fairly basic with five-seat benches on either side of each slam-door compartment. The three walked along the length of the train and managed to find some empty seats towards the back.

Others piled in and the carriage was soon full. There were nods of acknowledgement to fellow passengers. One or two were carrying large banners which they rolled up and placed on the luggage rack above them.

The train pulled out on time, and Arthur felt a sense of excitement as the engine took the weight of the carriages with a roar of smoke and steam. It was only his second time on a train and by far the furthest he had ever travelled from Keighley. It was a similar experience for his pals and, as they soon would discover, for the rest of the compartment as well.

After an uncomfortable few minutes of silence, the atmosphere relaxed and the banter grew between the ten passengers. All were from the mills or the foundry and swapped tales of mistreatment and poor conditions. Arthur felt a sense of guilt that his occupation was comfortable by comparison.

The topic of the local demonstrations soon came up. As with Arthur and his two pals, three of the passengers were also due to attend court the following Friday having been arrested protesting outside the foundry gates.

"What do tha think's gonna happen?" asked Henry with some concern.

The foundryman introduced himself as Alf Sedgewick. He, like Samuel, worked at the foundry but in the machine shop and they hadn't met before.

"I don't know. One of the lads was talking to someone from the court and he was saying that if we plead guilty, they'll go steady on us, like."

Arthur was listening with interest. "But we never did owt," he remonstrated.

"Aye, but it's tha word against the police and no one's going to believe the workers. The magistrates have been told to be hard, that's what I heard."

Samuel had his head in his hands. The mood in the compartment changed.

The train passed through Leicester taking the old Great Central line down to London. Seeing the station pass by, one of the other passengers looked in horror. "Is this train gonna stop? I'm dying for a piss."

"Aye, me an'all," said Samuel.

Arthur too, was feeling the need.

"'Appen not, we'll have to hang out the window," said Alf.

It broke the sombre mood as each passenger took it in turn to stand on the seat next to the carriage door, put one leg on each side and, standing astride, lower the window by the leather strap, then relieve themselves. The strength of the wind at forty-five miles an hour took the stream of liquid to the right with some force, spraying the window of the adjacent compartment. Some blow-back into the carriage was unavoidable, and the floor next to the door soon resembled a urinal. It didn't make the rest of the journey very pleasant.

Every so often a stream of yellowish liquid would wash the outside of the compartment window as men in the next carriage did the same.

They eventually arrived at St Pancras at around midday and the mood seemed buoyant as the passengers exited the train, boisterous and anxious to let off steam having been cooped up for six hours,

Arthur was amazed at the sight of the station, the architecture, the buzz, the sheer size; it was like nothing he had experienced before. Samuel and Henry stared in wonderment.

"So where do we go?" asked Henry.

"I have no idea," said Arthur. "'Appen we'll follow this lot."

Just then, the sound of a brass band could be heard coming from the front of the train. As passengers piled out of the carriages, they lined up behind in a long chain and started moving out of the station. Banners waving, shouting, and singing, the men marched down the road towards Trafalgar Square some three miles away with the band at the head.

Onlookers in their finery watched the protestors with a look of incredulity; then walked on, hoping they hadn't been contaminated in some way.

Arthur and his pals were taking it all in; the cars, the buildings, the people; it was a different world.

As the protestors reached their destination, Arthur and his pals couldn't believe their eyes. Police estimates would later place the numbers at over ten thousand. Mounted constabulary were everywhere trying to maintain some sense of order.

"Is there an alehouse anywhere 'round here? I don't know about tha, but I'm getting very thirsty," said Henry.

"Aye, me an'all," said Samuel.

"Tha joining us for a drink, Alf? 'Appen there's an alehouse across yonder," said Arthur having spotted a suitable hostelry.

Others from the carriage had gone their separate ways, so it was the four of them that walked into The Queen's Head just opposite Nelson's Column. Arthur looked around. The pub had a different feel to the Malt Shovel; it lacked something. It seemed to be where people drank, not socialised.

Arthur went to the bar to get the beers. The place was heaving, with other demonstrators also taking the opportunity for some serious imbibing. Smoke was hanging in the air in a blue fog.

Arthur eventually got served and managed to carry the four glasses and return to his pals to distribute the ale.

"Eh up, 'appen they speak different down here; I couldn't understand a word of what t'landlord were saying," said Arthur as he handed out the beer.

They were forced to stand in the corner to consume their drinks; the crush was relentless.

"Eh, I've not seen owt like this," said Alf, looking around the saloon as he sipped the top of his ale.

Alf swilled the mouthful then looked at the beer suspiciously.

"I don't know what this is, but it's no beer I've tasted afore; it's like cat's piss."

The others took sips and analysed it like seasoned beer-drinkers.

"Aye, thar not wrong there, Alf," replied Arthur. But they would persevere in the absence of any alternative.

Arthur shared around his sandwiches. Unfortunately, they had been flattened in transit and were not particularly appealing but were consumed without protest. At just before four o'clock, and many pints later, the pub emptied and everyone headed towards Nelson's Column to listen to the speakers. There were, by this time, several thousand in the crowd around the giant monument, but, surprisingly to Arthur and his pals, not all were sympathetic to the cause. There was almost an equal number in the gathering bent on disrupting the demonstration.

Someone tried to unfurl a large red flag banner, the socialist symbol, which was greeted with derision by a vociferous group. The rejoinder came at once as several men rushed forward and replaced it with a Union Jack.

The refrain of 'The Red Flag' echoed around the crowd, but this was drowned out with the National Anthem and 'Land of Hope and Glory'. There were some minor scuffles but nothing that had disturbed the watching police who appeared content to let them get on with it. Arthur and his pals were trying to make sense of it all. He noticed several foreigners among the demonstrators, including many

Germans and French. With news having filtered through that Germany had declared war on Russia the previous day, Arthur thought it strange.

It was nearly an hour before the politicians and other participants started their speeches, each espousing their anti-war rhetoric. The main speaker was Kier Hardie, the MP and fierce anti-war campaigner. Despite the rumour, the leader of the Labour Party, Ramsay McDonald, didn't make an appearance, much to Arthur's disappointment. He had become an inspiring figure. Unfortunately, from Arthur's vantage point, the content of the speeches was almost inaudible, drowned out by boos and hisses from the 'pro-government' protestors.

At five o'clock, a resolution was declared supporting international solidarity and peace and the meeting concluded. As the crowd dispersed, there were more scuffles as rival factions attempted to settle scores. A breakaway group marched off towards Admiralty Arch and held a patriotic rally of their own. Arthur could see what was happening.

"Eh up, Sam, Henry, 'appen there's going to be trouble; let's get out of here. Are tha coming, Alf?"

Alf turned. "Aye, tha's not wrong. Can tha remember the way back?"

Arthur looked at the buildings and the streets. They all looked the same.

"I have a mind it were in that direction," he said, pointing to one of the junctions.

They broke away from the throng just as more fighting was breaking out. The guest speakers were nowhere to be seen, having been whisked away in chauffeur-driven cars.

After asking several people for directions, who seemed to have difficulty in understanding Arthur, he and his pals arrived back at St Pancras just before six which gave them enough time to buy refreshments and find seats for the six-thirty departure.

There was a sense of pride and satisfaction at their participation as they walked down the train looking for a vacant compartment. As Alf had said, "at least we can say we were there."

After some searching, they eventually managed to find a carriage that wasn't awash with urine.

"'Appen a few aren't going t'make it," observed Arthur, looking at the numbers on the station; far less than had travelled down.

The return journey was long and boring; there seemed to be little appetite for discussion, with the pals trying to catch some sleep as the engine slowly ate up the miles.

It was gone midnight by the time they arrived back in Keighley, and the hordes of demonstrators poured from the train.

Arthur, Samuel, and Henry said farewell to Alf and wished him good luck for the forthcoming court appearance before setting off to their respective homes.

Arthur was in a reflective mood as he walked back up James Street, inspired by the day and the experience; it would stay in his mind for a long time. Whether it would make any difference in preventing all-out war, though, was open to debate.

Earlier that Sunday, the family, minus Arthur, had attended church as usual. Like most churches in Britain, prayers for peace were said. Grace's mind, however, was on matters not remotely godly; her meeting with Freddie was dominating her thoughts.

Mildred had bought a copy of the Sunday Times on the way back to the bakery, anxious to catch up on the latest news about the situation in Europe.

It did not make good reading. As had been feared, Germany had declared war on Russia, entered Luxemburg and crossed the French border without any provocation. All eyes were now on France who was an ally of Russia and had been selling arms to Serbia. In the Houses of Parliament, there were calls, especially from the Labour Party, that Britain should remain neutral to the 'schisms on continental Europe'.

With the house move now only a couple of days away, Mildred had ordered a dozen tea chests from Granger's. Several of his staff were involved in carrying them down James Street to the bakery and negotiating the stairs to the parlour. It had taken an hour to finalise the delivery. Despite stacking them on top of each other, there was hardly room to move.

Mildred tried to put political machinations to the back of her mind by busying herself organising the packing. In a few minutes, the parlour resembled a battlefield with containers, clothes, and bed linen strewn everywhere. Mildred had spent an hour or more and a great deal of money in the draper's shop buying sheets, blankets, pillows, towels, and other items they would need in the new house. It was stretching Mildred's supervisory skills. The children were involved, but that only served to add to the stress. Grace, however, seemed to be distracted. She had a Suffragette meeting that afternoon she had told her mother.

Grace had arranged to meet Freddie at two-thirty and

walked across the park towards the trolleybus stop and sat on a bench in good view. She was anticipating another stroll down by the river; maybe Freddie would be even more passionate as he had been in her dreams. She tingled at the thought.

The two-thirty trolleybus arrived and she stood up to see the people getting off. The excitement caused her breathing to quicken; her heart was racing, her mouth felt dry. The passengers dispersed but there was no sign of Freddie. Grace walked towards the stop to have a closer look but it was now deserted, the passengers having dispersed to their destinations. She checked around the park, the usual promenaders, families, old men smoking their pipes, but still no sign of him. She went back to the bench and retrieved Freddie's letter to check she had got the right time.

'I will arrive in town on the two-thirty trolley; I will meet you in the park'.

There was no mistake. The clock on top of the Town Hall said two-forty. Something was wrong; she felt a sense of rejection.

Earlier that day, Freddie had slept until eight o'clock, two hours past his normal pattern. Not that he felt particularly refreshed. Two days of twelve-hour shifts at the mill had left him exhausted. His sleep, though, had been fitful with the anticipation of meeting Grace.

His mother was in the kitchen preparing breakfast, the smell of cooking hanging in the air.

She greeted him cheerily as he walked in. "Morning Freddie, you're late today."

"Aye, working back at mill fair done me in; the sooner I can leave that place the better."

He stifled a yawn and sat down at the table while Kitty

brought in a plate of fried bread and eggs and a pot of tea.

"Are you clearing that turnip patch today over by the fence?"

"Aye, I'll do that this morning; I'm going into town this afternoon."

"Town? Why do you need to go into town?"

"No reason, 'appen I fancied a change that's all. Have a look 'round."

Freddie and Grace had agreed to continue to keep the tryst a secret for the moment and he wasn't about to break that trust.

Kitty's mind was racing. A meeting with Grace; it had to be. She thought quickly.

"Well, if it's no reason, I have a thought. You know Mrs Marsden moves into Springfield on Tuesday."

"Aye."

"Well, I was thinking we could go across there this afternoon and tidy up the front. It must be so overgrown. I don't suppose the garden's been touched these past two months. It may put Mrs Marsden in mind of you being the gardener. It's what you said you wanted."

"Aye, that's true."

Kitty continued to embellish her idea. "Well, imagine Mrs Marsden's face when she sees what a good job you've made... I can help too; I could do with a break from the studio."

Freddie was regretting not being more specific with the excuse for his journey to town, but it was too late to change his story without exposing the true reason.

"This afternoon?"

"Yes, we can go after we've eaten, about one o'clock. You'll be working tomorrow."

"'Appen I could take the day off."

"No, no, no, you can't do that. You've only just returned to work; there'll be questions asked."

Freddie was beginning to waver. He thought of Grace waiting for him at the trolleybus stop; it would mean disappointing her, but, he reasoned, if he were able to work as the gardener in the new house, there would be plenty more opportunities ahead.

Kitty could see Freddie thinking it over. "It's what you've wanted… a gardener's job."

"Aye, that's right enough."

He finished his breakfast and took a drink of tea.

"Aye, go on."

Freddie felt rotten, not just the disappointment at missing the meeting, for which he was eagerly awaiting, but also letting Grace down. He would write to her immediately to apologise and explain the situation.

Back at the trolley stop, Grace was getting concerned. She had waited half an hour for the next trolleybus just in case he had been delayed, but there was still no sign of him. She feared something was wrong but had no idea what. The disappointment started eating away inside her; perhaps his feelings for her had waned. She wiped away a tear then headed back to the bakery to write to him.

"Everything alright, dear?" said Mildred as Grace walked into the parlour.

Mildred and the other three girls had been gathering their belongings and packing them up ready for the move.

Grace's face was flecked with tear stains.

"Yes, mam, just going to lie down."

Monday morning, August 3rd, 1914, five-thirty.

It was a bank holiday so Arthur would be opening the

shop as usual but closing at one o'clock. He was preparing for the morning's baking but feeling the effects of the previous day's journey to London. He felt light-headed and every movement was laboured. The rattle of Buxton's lorry did little to ease his condition.

The miller had some bad news. Although he had the three bags Arthur had ordered, the price had risen by five shillings, almost a twelve percent rise. Arthur would have no option but to increase the price of a quarter loaf by one penny.

"'Appen it's the government," said the miller.

"Aye, it will be them right enough; no thought of t'working class."

The miller unloaded the three bags and Arthur paid up.

"They'll have us bankrupt, you mark my words," said Arthur as he handed over the money.

"Aye, true enough. Mind you, if what I've heard this morning's right, it'll be the least of our worries."

"What say thee, Edward?"

"I heard Germany's declared war on France."

"Nay, never?"

"Aye, it's what I heard... and they've marched into Belgium."

Edward wouldn't be drawn on his source, but he had always been proved reliable.

"What'll that mean?"

"Have no idea, but 'appen it'll be war, if tha asks me."

The miller left. Arthur was pondering his comments, then trying to equate it with the messages from yesterday's speakers. The power of the working classes was not going to be enough, it seemed.

Around seven-thirty, Mildred appeared in the baking shed with some breakfast for Arthur. He was leaning on his shovel, half asleep. He had finished mixing the dough for the first batch and it was in the oven.

"Are you alright, Arthur? You look very pale."

"Aye, Mam, 'appen I need a bit more sleep."

"Yes, I didn't hear you come in."

"Nay, it were gone midnight."

"How was London? You must tell me all about it later."

"Aye, I will; it were very busy."

He picked up one of the sandwiches and took a bite. "Are tha seeing t'solicitor today?" he said with bits of bread flying from his mouth.

"Yes, this afternoon."

"I thought it were bank holiday."

"Yes, but he will be there this afternoon especially so he can give me the keys to the house. Why do you ask?"

"'Appen we were talking about t'court case with some other lads and they said they will go easy on us if we say we were guilty."

"Do you want me to ask?"

"Aye, I'd like to know, like."

"Yes, I'll ask him."

"The thing is… it don't feel right. I mean, we didn't do owt; we were just walking home."

"Yes, but, as I said, I'm happy to get you one of those lawyers if it will help."

"Nay. If my pals can't have one, then I won't either. It's the principle of the thing."

"Very well, but the offer is there."

Mildred turned and returned to the parlour deep in thought.

It was Ivy Stonehouse's first day at the bakery. She was excited and a little anxious at the prospect of a new career.

She tapped on the front door at ten-to-eight, wearing a light-brown smock, having made the short walk down James Street from the butcher's. Grace and Agnes were already preparing the shop and Agnes went to open the door; the first customers had started to form a queue.

Arthur delivered the first batch of bread to the shop a few minutes later and greeted the new arrival. Grace seemed distracted and was not in the most amiable of moods.

"Ignore her, she's a bit mardy this morning," said Agnes as she gave Ivy her pinafore. She explained the different prices and how to work the till, which was the extent of Ivy's induction.

Upstairs in the parlour, Mildred was continuing to get everything ready for the move. She had two errands to run, a visit to the grocer's, which was also open half-day, to replenish the shelves of the pantry for Arthur, then collecting the keys from the solicitor at three-thirty. She would get Granger's to deliver the goods; she wasn't about to struggle with heavy bags down James Street as she had done in the past. Those days were behind her.

The shop was hectic as usual for a Monday morning, especially since it was shorter opening. Ivy had settled in quickly and had impressed the girls with her confidence with the customers, many, of course, she knew from the butcher's and there were several comments concerning her jumping ship.

Just after eleven o'clock, Grace suddenly noticed a young man walk in. Her heart skipped a beat. It was Freddie.

She quickly finished serving her customer and went to the end of the counter.

"Freddie! What are you doing here?" she exclaimed.

"I came to see you; I wanted to explain about yesterday."

"But what about work?"

"I told them I've been taken sick."

"But you will lose your job."

"Aye, 'appen I might, but, if that is the way, then so be it. There are plenty of other mills."

"Wait a moment." She walked up to Agnes and whispered. "Agnes, I'm just going out for a few moments, don't say anything to mam, will you?"

Agnes looked at her, then Freddie. "No, your secret's safe with me."

Grace took off her pinafore and lifted the counter flap into the shop to join Freddie.

Leaving the bakery, they crossed James Street and walked into the park. Grace chose a bench in the middle. It was a cloudy day with the threat of rain, but at the moment it was dry. There were not many people around.

Grace was looking ahead not really knowing what to say. She had hardly slept. Partly worry, partly anger at having been stood up.

It was Freddie who broke the ice. "I am really sorry about yesterday; I hope tha's not angry with me. 'Appen I had to make a decision which I hope will be to our advantage. The thing is, me mam suggested that we go to tha new house and tidy the garden for thar mam. She thought it might persuade her to take me on as t'gardener. I was desperate to see tha, but it was hard to say no; I hope tha understands."

"I was so worried; I thought you had had an accident. Then I thought you had lost affection for me," Grace replied, not letting him get away with it that easily.

"No, no, no, never. I love tha too much. I could never lose affection."

She squeezed his hand. "You really love me?"

"Aye, ever since you fell into my arms."

She smiled. "Yes, I remember that well. It wasn't deliberate, you know."

"Ha, I know that."

"I am glad you were there to catch me." She looked at him. "Look, I can't stay long, we are busy in the shop. Will you be here at one o'clock? We close then for the day; it's bank holiday. We can go for a walk."

"Aye, I'll wait for thee here."

Grace made her way back to the bakery, relieved that her relationship with Freddie was back on track. She opened her handbag and took out the letter she had written to him and tore it up. She would dispose of it later.

She returned to the shop and put on her apron. She turned to Agnes who was serving.

"Will you and Ivy be able to clean when we close today?"

Agnes finished attending her customer.

"Aye, I don't see why not. Are you meeting Freddie?"

"Aye, but not a word to mam, eh."

"What shall I say if she asks?"

"Tell her I've gone shopping."

"'Appen all the shops are closed. It's bank holiday."

"Oh, aye... Just say I've gone for a walk."

"Aye, 'appen her minds on the new house. She'll not be bothering."

The mood in the shop changed dramatically. Grace continued to smile the whole time and even joked with some of the customers. Ivy was proving to be a quick learner and both Grace and Agnes commented favourably on her progress.

At one o'clock, Arthur closed the shop. He was dead on

his feet and decided to give the Malt Shovel a miss and catch up on his sleep. He paid no attention to Grace who seemed to be in a hurry to leave the shop.

"Grace is going out, Ivy and me will see t'cleaning," said Agnes to a rather bemused Arthur.

Grace almost ran across the road to the park, anxious to see Freddie. He was waiting at the same bench as before and stood up to greet her.

"Would you like to go down by the river?" he said as she approached.

"Aye, I would like that very much."

As with the previous visit, they were able to find a secluded spot. The mutual desire was increasing, the kissing more urgent. Grace could feel Freddie's hands in places where they shouldn't be, but she did nothing to stop him, just moaned in acquiescence.

After almost an hour, they left the riverside and made their way back to the bakery, totally unfulfilled but nevertheless happy.

"'Appen we'll be able to meet more often if tha can persuade thar mam to use me as her gardener."

"Aye, I'll speak to her again."

As they reached the bakery, it started to spot with rain. She squeezed his hand, then watched as he made his way towards the trolleybus stop. She wanted to go with him.

Grace let herself in; the shop was empty. Agnes and Ivy had completed the clean-up.

In the parlour, Agnes and the three girls were eating as Grace returned. Mildred was just coming out of the kitchen, having heard footsteps coming up the stairs.

"Ah, Grace, there you are. Would you like something to eat?"

"Aye, Mam, just a sandwich, thank you."

"Agnes said you've been for a walk. Did you go anywhere nice?"

"Nay, just needed some fresh air."

Mildred returned to the kitchen and didn't pursue the matter further. She had more pressing things on her mind.

The visit to the solicitor was going to be a pleasurable duty for Mildred. At three-thirty, as she crossed the park, she ignored the drizzly rain which had been falling for the last hour; the aqueous sky was grey and threatened further showers; the thrumping industrial noises from the mills were rumbling away in the distance. Despite all the shops being closed and the damp conditions, the park was quite busy with people taking the air. Gaily covered umbrellas were out in force.

She reached the solicitors, rang the bell, and waited under her umbrella for the door to open. She was so used to Norman and his greeting and was taken back by the middle-aged matron who presented herself.

"Yes," she said abruptly.

"Mrs Marsden, for Mr Drummond," announced Mildred in a superior tone; she was not about to be out-gentrified by a solicitor's assistant.

"Yes, come in; he is expecting you."

Mildred collapsed her umbrella, which was now dripping on the floor of the reception area. The woman looked at the small puddle with displeasure.

"Take a seat," she said and walked into the office area and sat down behind a large typewriter. There appeared to be no-one else in the office.

Moments later, Drummond's door opened.

"Ah, Mrs Marsden, do come in. I hope you didn't get too wet in this inclement weather."

He allowed Mildred to pass and closed the door,

"It's supposed to brighten up later," he said as he walked to his seat. The usual tray of tea was in front of him.

Mildred removed her white gloves and composed herself; the solicitor poured the tea.

"I'm so grateful for you to be available this afternoon especially for me."

"It was of little consequence, Mrs Marsden, glad to be of service. I occasionally come into the office on bank holidays if we are particularly busy."

"I hear Norman has signed up," she said, continuing the conversation.

"Yes, it was all a bit sudden, but I do admire the young man's courage. He will make good officer material; there's no doubt."

"Yes, he was always so polite."

"Well, down to business. I received confirmation from the bank and estate agents on Friday that the purchase has been completed and you are now officially the owner of Springfield Hall. Congratulations," he said, handing Mildred her drink.

"Thank you, Mr Drummond, yes, this is indeed a joyous occasion."

There was a convivial exchange and then Mildred had a request while they drank their tea.

"Can I ask a question, Mr Drummond?"

"Of course."

"I have been speaking with Arthur, my son, about his court case, which is due this Friday coming. Were you able to put in a good word for him? He has been most concerned."

"Ah, er, well, er, I do intend to." He shifted uncomfortably in his chair. "It so happens, I'm meeting the chair of the magistrates at a Law Society dinner tomorrow evening; I most certainly will express such sentiments."

"Oh, thank you, that is most kind. He also asked me for your opinion on whether he should plead guilty or not."

"Guilty? Hmm, well, the courts, in my experience, do tend to take a lighter view of those who confess their wrongdoings."

"But Arthur is adamant he and his friends were just walking home and were set upon by the police."

"Yes, that is most unfortunate, but, you see, it's just his word against the police. I would strongly recommend he finds a good lawyer. I am happy to suggest such a person."

"Thank you, Mr Drummond, that is most kind, but Arthur wants to be treated the same as his pals and will not countenance such a thing."

"I see, very well, I will do what I can, Mrs Marsden."

"Thank you, Mr Drummond, that is most kind," she repeated.

The solicitor looked at her benevolently.

Mildred finished her tea and placed the cup and saucer back on the tray.

"What do you think will happen, Mr Drummond… about the war, I mean? You hear all sorts."

"Hmm, it's not looking promising, if I might say. You have heard that Germany has declared war on France and is threatening Belgium."

"I heard something about that, yes."

"Well, Great Britain has treaties with Belgium."

"And what does that mean, exactly?"

"Well, basically, if Belgium is threatened, then Great Britain will become involved."

"In war, you mean?"

"Yes… Although in my opinion, if it did come to that, I don't think it will last long."

Alan Reynolds

"Oh dear, it is so worrying."

"I would try not to worry, Mrs Marsden. You must look forward to moving into your new house. I wouldn't think a war will affect you in any way."

He reached into his drawer and pulled out a large, heavy envelope,

"These are yours, Mrs Marsden. Congratulations again."

Mildred looked inside, the keys to the new property. She viewed them with a mix of pride and excitement.

Chapter Eighteen

Tuesday 4th August 1914, was a momentous day for the Marsden family and, as it would transpire, for the world. With no exaggeration, life would never be the same again.

Arthur was more refreshed, having managed to sleep the whole of the previous afternoon, despite the chaos surrounding him as the girls completed their packing ready for the move.

At five am, Buxton's lorry arrived with the flour delivery, but the mood was sombre; the uncertainty of what lay ahead cast a dark cloud over the usual banter. It was just the three sacks again; it seemed a long time since his daily delivery was double that.

"It don't look too good," was the miller's response to Arthur's enquiry about the latest news.

As Arthur mixed his dough, his mind was still unable to comprehend what was happening around him. In true character, he had ignored the implications of the family's departure. Having lived in close proximity with his mother and siblings all his life, he still had not fully appreciated the loneliness and feeling of isolation which would ensue.

Then there was the court case. It was another issue that had been sealed away in the recesses of his mind. Every time he was reminded of the event, he felt sick to the stomach. Talking about it with his pals on the train had given him a degree of catharsis. Still, with the date drawing closer, the possibility of him being incarcerated caused him more and more anxiety. Who would look after the bakery? That was just one of the practical implications. How he would cope with prison was a lesser consideration and one he hadn't challenged himself with providing an answer.

Upstairs in the parlour, Mildred was regimenting everything with military precision.

It had been decided that Agnes and Ivy would be working in the shop; Arthur was happy that Ivy could cope despite only having half a day's experience. Grace, Molly and Freda would go to the new house to help Mildred unpack and clean. Grace was keen to be part of the advanced party in the remote hope she would see Freddie.

Hayden's, the removal people, had been booked for nine o'clock.

By eight o'clock, the queues waiting for the bakery to open stretched almost to the butcher's as rumours of shortages circulated. Arthur had once again imposed rationing, which had, in turn, led to numerous complaints.

Half an hour later, the bakery was still busy as Mrs Stonehouse arrived with her daughter Lilian, the youngest of the Stonehouse girls, to start cleaning. There were complaints from waiting customers as they moved to the front of the line to get into the shop.

"I'm not buying; I'm working here," she remonstrated in reply to angry comments.

She pushed through the crush and waited at the counter flap for Ivy to let them in.

Upstairs, it was pandemonium as they entered the parlour.

"Oh, hello Mrs Stonehouse, it is so good to see you. Please excuse the mess," greeted Mildred.

Tea chests littered the room with barely enough space to pass.

"Have no mind to it, Mrs Marsden, I am pleased to be away from the shop... You know Lilian?"

"Yes, of course. Hello Lilian." She looked at the girl, definitely her mother's daughter, dressed in her smock ready to work.

"Where would you like us to start?" asked Mrs Stonehouse.

"Well, everything for the move is in here, so the bedrooms and kitchen are ready."

Mildred opened her purse and took out some money. "I hope this will cover today; I will see that Arthur pays you in future."

Mrs Stonehouse looked at the two half crowns. "Thank you, that is most generous."

Arthur was finishing another mix when Hayden's van pulled into the yard next to the baking shed. Mildred had arranged this to avoid taking tea chests through the shop, away from prying eyes.

It was not a large van by any means, more a delivery vehicle but sufficient for today's duties. It was in a chocolate and cream livery with the name F. Hayden & Co, Removals, in flowing white script on the side. It had an open front with a long steering column and four white-walled solid rubber tyres.

The proprietor, Frank Hayden, climbed down from the driver's seat. A dapper, humourless man, wearing brown removal man's overalls, flat cap, and sporting a white moustache and sideburns which ran almost to his chin. He resembled a storeman. There was a younger version next to him whose attempt at garnering facial hair had not yet materialised into anything recognisable. Arthur approached the visitors.

"Eh up," greeted Arthur. "Tha come to take stuff t'new house?"

"Aye, Frank Hayden at tha service." He took off his cap and went to shake hands.

"Best not, covered in flour," said Arthur, wiping his hands

343

on his apron.

"Aye, of course… er, this is my son, Cyril."

Arthur looked at the lad, about fifteen-years-old; he seemed far too skinny for lifting a lot of furniture. He took off his cap and nodded.

"'Ow do," he said by way of greeting.

Arthur led the pair along the short corridor then up the stairs to the parlour.

"Mam, the men are here," said Arthur as he entered the room. Mildred was in the kitchen supervising Mrs Stonehouse.

She came into the parlour and greeted them. "Hello, Mr Hayden. These are all that need to go. Will you have room for everything?"

Frank looked at the dozen or so tea chests. "Aye, 'appen I have, and more besides," he replied.

Negotiating the stairs was tricky, but between them, they completed the task of loading the van in an hour or so. The young Cyril, defying his appearance, was incredibly strong and made light work of the precious cargo. The parlour looked empty once the containers had been removed. The apartment was now the sole domain of Arthur. He had decided to take over his mother's bedroom and Mildred had moved all his clothes into the wardrobe.

"Now, Mr Hayden, you know where to go?" asked Mildred, half question, half statement, after the final box had been taken to the van.

"Aye, Oakworth… Springfield Hall."

"Yes, that's right. My daughters and I will take a taxicab and meet you there."

The three girls said goodbye to Agnes and Ivy, who were still busy with customers, while Mildred walked down the corridor to the baking shed.

Arthur was by the oven, waiting for the next batch of bread to finish.

"We're going now, Arthur, I've moved your clothes into the bedroom, and Mrs Stonehouse is cleaning. Agnes will be joining us later after she's finished in the shop. I've given her some money for a cabbie."

"Aye, sithee," said Arthur and opened the door to the oven without any further acknowledgement. Mildred sighed.

They left the bakery and walked across the road where a taxicab was parked. Before getting into the cab, Mildred took one last look at her home for the last twenty-two years with mixed emotions. Most of the bad memories had been eroded by the excitement of what lay ahead.

Just over half an hour later, the taxi approached the entrance of the Springfield Hall estate with the two impressive horse chestnut trees, their flowers white and abundant. The gate had been opened by the removal men. They drove through along the short driveway and there it was, their new home. Mildred stared at the building bathed in the morning sun. She sighed.

Then she noticed something.

"My, just look at the garden; someone's been here; see how fine it is. It must be Mr Drummond's idea. I must thank him for his thoughtfulness."

Grace was dying to say something but decided not to reveal the source of the industry. Her mother would discover the benefactor soon enough.

Hayden's van was parked outside the front door. The two removal men opened the back of the vehicle on seeing the approaching cabbie.

It was a dry and sunny day. Mildred, Grace, Molly, and

Freda exited the taxi and Mildred paid the driver. There had been much excitement among the two younger girls who had chatted incessantly on the journey from the bakery, arguing over who would have which bedroom.

Mildred took another long look at the magnificent frontage hardly able to believe what was happening. She took out the keys from her handbag and opened the 'front door' – a description that was totally inadequate to describe the large carved oak entrance.

They walked through the small portico into the hall. The girls tagged along behind their mother and just stared at the reception area. It was larger than their parlour. Fittingly, rays of sun shone through the windows. There was a musty smell from being shut up for two months or more, but that would soon go.

"Where do you want the tea chests?" asked the elder Mr Hayden, breaking the moment.

"Just put them down there for now," said Mildred indicating the centre of the hall.

The three girls ascended the staircase to the right to explore the first floor, while Mildred headed for the kitchen. She opened the windows and looked out across the extensive lawn with its shrubbed borders. The grass looked as if it had been recently cut. There was a large patio in front of the sitting room window adorned with stone garden ornaments and flowerpots.

Mildred looked at the range again, strange, and unfamiliar; that was going to take some time to get used to. There was a scullery to the left which contained the pantry and had an access door to the patio. She took her keys and tried them until she found the one that opened the door. She hadn't explored the garden when she visited with the land agent; she had just looked through the window.

The question of a gardener again crossed her mind. Grace had mentioned Freddie several times and it was something she would need to give careful consideration.

She left the door open and returned to the kitchen. She could see the removal men; they had brought in the tea chests and she went to supervise the distribution. She had no intention of carrying the heavy containers up the stairs.

Apart from three which contained items for the kitchen and a few ornaments and nick-nacks, the remaining chests, were for the bedrooms. The three girls had returned downstairs and were checking through them. They had chosen their respective bedrooms and directed the removal men accordingly.

"Mr Hayden, would you like a drink?" asked Mildred after the men had finished. "I have water or I can make some tea."

"Just water," said Hayden. "'Appen we have another job on when we've done here."

Mildred found two glasses from one of the tea chests and went to the sink. How different everything was from her old kitchen, a real tap with no pump. She returned with the drinks and paid the men for their labours and included a generous tip. The water was consumed in one gulp.

"Would you like another?" asked Mildred.

"Nay, thank you, Mrs Marsden. Best be off, busy day today. Thanks again... Oh, afore we go, have tha thought about tha empty chests?"

"No, I can't say I have," replied Mildred.

"I can call back for 'em later if tha wish, after we've done; about five-ish, if that suits."

"Could you? That would be such a service, thank you."

Mr Hayden senior put the two glasses down on the hall table and appeared to push the young Hayden through the door. Mildred closed it behind them.

Now the sorting out would begin.

Mildred checked each room in turn. The ground floor looked empty, especially the library having had its bookshelves cleared and the paintings removed. There were lighter areas on the wall where they once hung.

The sitting room was magnificent with its views across the garden. There was a three-piece suite, a sideboard, a small table with two chairs, one standard lamp and two occasional tables which looked like they once supported plant pots judging by white water stains on the top. The carpets and curtains, as one would expect, were of excellent quality. There were signs from the carpet shade that some items of furniture had been taken away, but Mildred couldn't remember what they were.

There was a large fireplace which had been cleaned of ashes; it had an impressive ornate marble mantlepiece and surround. Mildred made a note to check on the coal stock. With the exception of the kitchen, all the downstairs rooms had fireplaces. Mildred's bedroom was also similarly heated. With the present weather, the need for a fire wasn't urgent.

The study, a smaller room, was neat and tidy with just two chairs, a writing desk, and a table. Molly had already claimed it as a sewing room. It, too, overlooked the garden. The library and dining room were at the front of the house and would be unused for the moment. She would cover the furniture with sheets in due course, to prevent dust.

It was just turned midday when there was the sound of a bell ringing. It was their first visitor. Mildred answered the call.

"Good day, Mrs Marsden? Daisy Jessop, I understand

you're seeking a housekeeper."

Mildred looked at the woman. She was slim and smartly-dressed, wearing a fashionable hat over tied-back fair hair. She would be in her late forties. She did not match Mildred's idea of a housekeeper, so different from Mrs Stonehouse, but immediately made a favourable impression. There was an urgency about her that suggested she would stand no-nonsense.

"Yes, that's correct, please do come in."

She entered the hall and looked around. "My, this looks so different without the paintings, so bare."

"Yes, I'm sure it does," said Mildred. "Come through to the kitchen."

Mrs Jessop took off her hat and followed Mildred, appearing to take everything in.

"Would you like tea at all?"

"Yes, if that's not too much of an inconvenience."

"No, not at all, you can help me work the range."

"It's straightforward enough. Do you have a kettle?"

"Yes, somewhere."

Mildred rummaged through one of the tea chests and retrieved the said item. It was still wrapped in a paper bag with its spout protruding from the top. She had bought a new, lighter version, from the hardware store on the High Street specifically for the new gas range. She had left her old 'heavy-duty' model for Arthur.

Mrs Jessop took off her light jacket. She had a hessian carrier bag with her which she opened, took out an apron and put it on.

"Give it me, I'll show you," said the woman in authoritative tones. She removed the wrapping, went to the sink, and filled the kettle with water. She placed it over one of the gas rings on the range.

"These knobs control the burners," she explained. "Have you got a match stalk?"

"No, I don't think so."

"Wait a moment."

Mrs Jessop went to the top drawer next to the sink. It appeared empty, but she put her hand in and rummaged around. At the back was a small box.

"Ah, yes, here they are. Always kept a packet here."

She went back to the range and showed Mildred how to switch on the gas and light the burner. In a second the flame was heating the kettle.

She rattled the matchbox. "And make sure you don't run out of these." She replaced the box back in the drawer. Mildred made a mental note.

The coaching continued. "Be careful, it's much quicker than your normal range; you'll need to keep a watch on it or the kettle will boil dry. Have you got milk and tea?"

Mildred searched around in another box and pulled out a packet of tea, a bottle of milk and a teapot and tea strainer. "The girls are upstairs. I'll see if they want a drink."

Mildred went upstairs, thinking about the prospective housekeeper. She had already made a good impression.

The three girls were too busy sorting their rooms to be disturbed. There seemed to be a fascination with the new toilet which appeared to be in constant use. Mildred returned to the kitchen where Mrs Jessop was just pouring the tea.

"My, my, that _is_ quick," observed Mildred.

"Now, as soon as we've drunk this, I'll get on. Where would you like me to start?"

Mildred was taken by surprise at her forthrightness. "Er, well, you could help me unpack these tea chests and perhaps you could explain one or two things; this is all new to me."

"Very well, and how many hours a week will you need

me?"

"I hadn't really thought about it; what do you recommend?"

"Well, when I worked here, I did five hours a day, but Sir James took a lot of looking after. A frightful man he was. I left after three months, about a year since. I couldn't stand him and his ways. Just because he was a knight of the realm thought it gave him the right to take all manner of liberties."

"Really?"

"Yes, only demanded that I bathe him; I told him right out it was not part of a housekeeper's job. I gave him short shrift, I don't mind saying. Do you know, he always seemed to be staring at me? Had these beady eyes, he did. I was glad to see the back of him. This world is non the poorer for his passing."

"Well, I never… Hmm, I'm not sure I'll need that many hours; there won't be that much to do, but let's see how this week goes and we can decide after that."

"Yes, very well, that suits."

The cooking utensils which were hanging on hooks when Mildred viewed the house were still there and she added some that she had brought from the bakery. She also brought her box of cooking ingredients, flour sugar, herbs and so on. She had left sufficient food supplies for Arthur to keep him going for a couple of days.

"Would your husband deliver some supplies, Mrs Jessop; if I gave you a list?"

"Yes, of course, he will be glad to, He does several deliveries to the farms hereabouts."

They soon had all the tea chests emptied and the contents put away, Mrs Jessop started cleaning the kitchen with a bar of soap from her bag of materials.

Mildred, meanwhile, went upstairs to check on the girls.

They had helped each other make their beds and were busy comparing rooms. There were three bedrooms and the bathroom at the back overlooking the lawn. Grace and Molly had chosen back rooms; the master bedroom also faced the gardens. Freda and Agnes would have the front rooms with a spare available which Mildred hoped might be Arthur's one day.

She returned to the kitchen and was pleasantly surprised to see the results of Mrs Jessop's labours. She was at the sink washing some glasses from one of the tea chests ready to be placed on the shelves.

"Ah, Mrs Marsden, I need to explain the hot water system," she said, seeing Mildred return.

She wiped her hands on a towel.

"Thank you, yes, I wasn't sure about that. I meant to ask Mr Drummond."

"It's easy enough, but you will need to have the fire lit in the sitting room. It heats the water in the tank in the airing cupboard. It's ingenious."

"Airing cupboard?"

"I'll show you."

With the vagaries of the heating system explained, they returned to the kitchen where the three girls had descended seeking food,

Mildred introduced the girls to Mrs Jessop. "You sit down, I'll make a sandwich. Do you have any bread, Mrs Marsden?"

Mildred retrieved one of Arthur's loaves from the breadbin and handed it to her. While Mrs Jessop prepared lunch, Mildred demonstrated the gas cooker for the benefit of the girls who had difficulty taking it all in.

With lunch consumed, the girls left the kitchen to explore

the garden. A few minutes later there was another ring at the front door.

Mildred answered it. "Kitty! What a lovely surprise, please, do come in."

The two women hugged, then Kitty looked around the hall. "My, this is so grand."

"Thank you," replied Mildred.

"I've brought you a present to welcome you to Oakworth."

"A present? Why thank you. That's very thoughtful of you."

Kitty handed Mildred a small carrier bag.

"I baked it this morning," said Kitty as Mildred viewed the wonderful sponge cake contained therein.

"Come through to the kitchen. You must meet Mrs Jessop."

"Daisy? I've known Daisy for years."

Mildred and Kitty walked into the kitchen where Mrs Jessop was washing the plates from lunch.

"Hello, Daisy, how are you?"

"Kitty, lovely to see you."

"And you are starting back here again?"

"Yes, Mrs Marsden has kindly agreed to employ me."

Kitty looked out of the window to the garden.

"It looks like Freddie made a good job on the grass, Mildred," Kitty commented.

"Freddie?"

"Yes, he came over on Sunday, spent most of the day here."

"Really? I didn't realise it was Freddie; I thought it was something Mr Drummond had organised. He has done a fine job, I must say. Please tell him how grateful I am."

"Yes, of course... Well, he does have sights on becoming your gardener," said Kitty.

Mildred looked at the garden again. "And he did all this on Sunday?"

"Yes, he used my old lawnmower; we don't use it anymore since he dug up the grass and planted potatoes. He was able to get in; he climbed over the wall and opened the gate."

"Resourceful as well, it would seem."

There was a ten-foot-high brick-built boundary wall accessed by a wooden door next to the house. It had a metal latch and was bolted from the inside.

"Yes, he can turn his hands to most things in the garden."

"I think there's a lawnmower in the shed," interrupted Mrs Jessop. "A large one, the previous gardener, Jed Dewhurst, used to use it."

"Well, I must have a look. Would you like to join me in the garden, Kitty; it's such a nice afternoon."

Mildred led Kitty through the scullery and out onto the patio. There was a bench to the right of the sitting room window. Mildred sat down and spoke to Kitty in no more than a whisper.

"So, what do you think about Freddie working here? I am unsure what will be for the best," said Mildred.

"Yes, it has been on my mind too. I can't see how we can prevent them from meeting. At least if Freddie is working here we can keep a better eye on them."

"Yes, that's true."

Kitty looked up at the bright sunshine and closed her eyes.

"Have you a thought what would happen if he was to find out the truth?" asked Mildred.

"Yes, it's been on my mind lately and frankly speaking, I don't know how he would react, particularly now he has an eye for Grace. Mind you, I don't think they've met alone, to my understanding anyway, but, of course, they have been writing," replied Kitty without opening her eyes.

"Oh dear, it is such a worry. Mind you, he has done a remarkable job; I will say that."

"Yes, he has shown a passion for gardening and the like."

"Hmm, I really don't know, I'm still unsure, but I do have a mind to ask him. As you say, we can keep an eye on things and hope that matters don't get out of hand… I know, maybe you can tell him it's on a trial basis; a month, say."

"Yes, that seems a sensible course of action."

"Yes, yes," said Mildred, feeling a load had been lifted from her. "In which case, you better ask him when he can start."

"Very well, I'm sure he'll want to start straightaway; he dislikes his job at the mill intensely."

They walked the garden for a while, which allowed Mildred to check the gardener's hut, which required another key from the large ring. It needed a sharp tug as Mildred pulled open the wooden door, which had warped in the sun. They were confronted by a pungent smell of decaying grass but looking around, there was an impressive array of equipment and, in the centre, an industrial-size lawnmower.

"I'll mention that to Freddie; it will save him bringing his tools from home," said Kitty.

They walked back to the kitchen. Mildred was still uneasy about Freddie; she would say nothing to Grace for the time being.

"Hello Molly," said Kitty, seeing her sat at the table.

"Hello, Mrs Bluet, I wanted to show you what I've been doing."

Molly produced a raffia basket and opened it. Inside were numerous embroideries. Molly took them out and opened them onto the table one by one.

Kitty picked up the first one and examined it with a seamstress's eye. Mrs Jessop also took an interest.

"Oh my, Molly, but these are magnificent. You show such talent for someone so young. You know you could sell these; there are people willing to pay for such quality."

"Really?"

"Oh, yes," said Kitty holding them up to the window.

"We can talk about that on Monday. I have many clients who would be interested, and at a good price, I warrant."

Molly returned the embroideries back to the box. "Thank you, Mrs Bluet."

"It's Kitty, please call me Kitty."

"Aye, Kitty, thank you. I'll see tha Monday."

Molly, buoyed by Kitty's comments, was almost walking on air as she left the kitchen and headed for the study to arrange her sewing room.

"Well, Mildred, what with Agnes's singing and Molly's needlework, you have such a talented family."

"Thank you, Kitty, that's most kind of you to say. Grace also has a gift for organising. You know she's a member of the Suffragettes?"

"No, I can't rightly remember you have said such."

"Oh yes, she goes to all the meetings. She's quite a principled young woman. She could make Prime Minister one day."

"Mmm, let's hope so. I believe women could make a far better job of things. We wouldn't be going into war, that's for certain."

"No, you're right there. Have you heard anything today?"

"I spoke to Daisy's husband at the store and the newspapers are full of it. Could happen at any moment, he reckons."

"I wonder what will become of us," said Mildred.

"I hope it will all blow over once everyone has let off steam."

"I do hope you're right, Kitty."

Mrs Jessop made the family more tea and Kitty's sponge cake was consumed with relish.

Kitty left the house around three-thirty with the promise of a return the following day to advise on Freddie's decision.

Agnes arrived at the house in a cabbie a few minutes later and was introduced to Mrs Jessop before exploring the house with her three excited sisters. She was quite happy with the choice of bedroom; the thought of her own room filled her with such joy. Then she had a thought, maybe they could get a piano; she could learn to play. She would mention it to her mother. It would take her thoughts off lost loves. Norman was still on her mind; she missed him more than she realised.

Daisy Oswald left around four with a list of items for her husband to deliver in his van later. Before leaving, she had lit the fire in the sitting room, which was now uncomfortably hot. Mildred had open the patio door to let in some air. It was a small price to pay; at least they would now have running hot water. All the girls had indicated they would be having baths before retiring to bed.

Mildred was in her bedroom sorting out her clothes and arranging the furniture to her liking. As well as the large bed and fancy headboard there were two high-back armchairs, a long dressing table and stool, a large wardrobe, and tallboy. The view over the back garden and distant hills was breath-taking, especially on a day like today.

Grace walked in to see what she was doing, then asked the question.

"Mam, did Kitty say anything about Freddie?"

"Well, we have talked about it, yes, and I have suggested we give it a try… for a month. Kitty is going to ask him if that is suitable."

"Oh, it will, it will. He will be so good; I know he will."
She giggled like a schoolgirl and left the bedroom.

Grace's reaction concerned Mildred, but she let it pass.

Earlier, back at the bakery, Arthur had closed the shop
at two-thirty, having run out of bread. He had left Ivy and
Agnes to clean the shop and made his way down James
Street to the Malt Shovel.

The alehouse was unusually quiet with most of the
clientele now back at work. Arthur spent some time chatting
with the landlord. There was only one topic of conversation.

"So, what do you think's going to 'appen?" asked Arthur,
having consumed half his glass in one gulp.

"Your guess is as good as mine, Arthur, but judging by
t'papers, it's not looking good. Mind you if t'Germans are
invading Belgium, then I think we should go over there and
give them a bloody nose. Show 'em they can't go 'round
bullying smaller countries; it ain't right."

"Aye, that's a point of view, Thomas, but 'appen if all
t'working classes across Europe were to rise up against the
war, then that would give them politicians summat to think
about."

"Aye, tha maybe right Arthur, but 'appen it's too late for
that now. Most of the folk in here want to give the Kaiser a
swift kick up the arse."

Arthur finished the rest of his drink in another gulp.
"Stick another in there will tha, Thomas?"

By five o'clock, Arthur was staggering up James Street
swaying from side to side. As he crossed West Street by the
bank, he felt something soft and squidgy under his feet, a
recently deposited pile of horse manure. He ignored the mess

on his boots and stumbled to the front door of the bakery.

He rummaged around in his pocket to find his keys and after several unsuccessful attempts managed to locate the lock and open the door with an almighty clang. He closed it behind him and walked through the shop and the beaded curtains, then up the stairs to the parlour, leaving a trail of horse dung behind him.

He looked around; the place was deserted. There was no noise, no bickering voices, no laughter, just the occasional vehicle outside and the clip-clop of a horse-drawn wagon.

He looked at his feet and, ignoring the offending mess, took off his boots. They fell on their side with bits of straw and horse excrement caked on the soles.

Mrs Stonehouse had left and the parlour was clean and tidy. But it was not just the dust and grime that had been removed; the soul of the parlour had gone.

Although he was standing still, the room continued to move, spinning around uncontrollably. He shuffled to the sofa and collapsed in a stupor.

It was just turned five-thirty when the removal men collected the empty tea chests which had been stacked in the hall awaiting collection. Then, around six-thirty, a delivery van pulled up outside Springfield Hall. Mildred had heard it arrive and went to open the front door. The vehicle was the same model as Hayden's van. The name 'O. Jessop & Co, Oakworth Store' had been painted on the side in a similar script.

Seeing it was her provisions delivery, Mildred called the girls together to help carry the boxes and bags into the kitchen.

As well as meat and food supplies, at Mrs Jessop's suggestion, Mildred had also ordered soap and soda crystals.

She had also remembered several boxes of matches. A copy of The Times was on top of one of the bags; Mildred was anxious to catch up on the news.

The four girls helped Mildred with the unpacking and placing items on the shelves. The pantry in the scullery was almost full.

Grace had offered to help Mildred prepare the evening meal and between them, they managed to master the controls of the new cooker. There was a new joy within the family.

It was to be fleeting.

After finishing eating, the girls went out into the garden and were running around the lawn, letting off steam while Mildred washed up. Fresh air and space was a totally new experience.

As they came in, Grace approached her mother. "Mam, 'appen we should get a croquet set. Now we're gentry."

"And a piano," added Agnes, picking up an apple from the fruit bowl and taking a bite.

"All in good time, all in good time," said Mildred, feeling slightly overwhelmed.

As it started to get dark, Mildred turned on the light in the kitchen. The illumination lit every corner of the room.

"Goodness, it's so bright," observed Molly, who had been helping her mother.

After she had finished with her chores, Molly returned to the study to continue arranging it into her sewing room.

By ten o'clock, the family were exhausted and enjoying their first night in the new house. Having their own bedrooms was something that, only a few weeks ago, was the stuff of dreams. There was even a queue to use the new bathroom.

The house was quiet, not a sound. Mildred was in bed contemplating the day, reading by a bedside lamp. The occasional bat skittered past the bedroom window, searching for insects that had been attracted by the light. An owl hooted outside but not loud enough to awaken the sleeping occupants. Mildred switched off the light and was soon falling asleep.

Suddenly, a peel of bells echoed around the village. Mildred woke with a start, hearing the sound. She was initially confused in her new surroundings but managed to find the switch to her bedside lamp. She looked at her small carriage clock on the bedside table.

Ten minutes past eleven.

Chapter Nineteen

The peeling bells had also sounded in Keighley. Arthur was still asleep on the sofa after almost six hours. The noise woke him; he tried to get up but was totally disorientated. His head hurt and he was in desperate need of the toilet.

The parlour was in darkness; streetlamps outside the window gave off a dim light. He managed to get to his feet but stumbled and fell back on the sofa. The bells continued; then shouts and hoots added to the clamour. It resembled the protest march a few weeks earlier.

He steadied himself and went to the window. He looked across towards the park; the wires and stanchions used by the trolleybuses impaired the view.

The ringing continued, echoing along James Street and across the park. As his eyes began to focus, he looked down at the pavement and could see people milling about.

Arthur managed to light one of the gas lamps in the parlour. He put his hands on his knees in an attempt to recover, then went to the bedroom to relieve himself in the chamber pot under his bed.

He returned to the parlour and put on his boots. The mess on the soles had dried to a crust which broke off leaving residue on the floor. Arthur didn't notice.

He walked gingerly down the stairs, clutching the wooden bannister for balance, then headed through the bakery and into the street. There were dozens of people, some were shouting, several were singing the National Anthem. Arthur went up to the nearest bystander.

"Eh up, what's going on?" he asked.

"It's war, we've declared war on Germany. We'll show them sausage-eating Krauts a thing or two... God Save The

King," he yelled at the top of his voice.

Arthur was trying to take in the news. He noticed his pal Wilfred standing outside the butcher's and walked up to meet him.

"'Ow do, Wilfred."

"Eh up, Arthur, tha heard t'news?"

"Aye, bloody war."

"Aye, what'll happen do tha think?"

"'Appen a lot of working-class folk are going to get killed."

Another bystander heard the comment. "Nah, it'll all be over by Christmas. Once we get over there with the French, we'll soon have them Germans on the run."

"Aye, 'appen he's right Arthur."

"Well, we'll have to wait and see, I'm off to my bed... Sithee Wilfred."

Arthur turned and walked back to the bakery. The bells had stopped, but there were still many people about chanting and singing.

He reached the parlour then went into the kitchen and poured himself a glass of water. Then refilled the glass and poured another; he was desperately thirsty. He was trying to take in the news; it filled him with dread. He had never responded well to change; he liked routine and order. What would the implications be?

Arthur turned off the light in the parlour and retired to his bedroom. Next to the bed on the small table was the clockwork alarm clock, He wound it up and noticed the time, almost midnight. The alarm was set for four forty-five.

Having just slept for almost six hours, his metabolism was all over the place; he couldn't sleep and, without food since lunchtime, felt hungry. He got out of bed, returned to the kitchen, and opened the door to the pantry. It looked strange; all his mother's pickles and all but one of the jams had gone, just a few tins and some bread. The butter dish was still there. He lifted the lid; the butter was almost ghee, having melted during the day, no matter.

He took out the bread, butter, and the remaining jam jar, then placed them on the kitchen table. Within ten minutes, he had consumed three strawberry jam sandwiches. His head was still sore, but the food had helped to relieve some of the symptoms of his drunkenness.

Arthur left the kitchen and walked into the parlour. The noise from outside had gone; an eerie silence had descended. He took another look outside the window; James Street and the park were deserted. He turned off the gas lamp again and went back into his new bedroom. It seemed so strange without his sisters close by.

Only now was he beginning to come to terms with the isolation of living on his own and the dependence he had on his mother.

At four forty-five, the tinny trill of the alarm clock woke Arthur. The noise caused him to tumble on the floor, narrowly missing the chamber pot, which he had not pushed back under the bed.

His shirt, underclothes, and trousers were in a pile on the floor where he had left them the previous evening. He picked up his underclothes and trousers, and holding onto the bed, managed to put them on. He completed his dressing, left the bedroom, and went into the kitchen. The range had not been lit, so there was no hot water. He went to the sink and poured himself a glass of water, then went back into the parlour to put on his boots which were still showing the evidence of the previous day's mishap.

He continued to experience the effects of his alcohol

consumption, and his fitful sleep, as he opened up the baking shed and lit the fire to the oven.

It was starting to get light, the beginning of a new day. It was a cool morning but bright; there appeared no threat of rain.

War, he suddenly remembered. He looked around the baking shed and the yard. It all looked the same, but something had changed. He made use of the outside toilet, then returned to check the oven.

A few minutes later came the familiar sound of Buxton's wagon trundling down West Street.

Edward Buxton descended from his cab, there seemed to be far fewer sacks of flour on the trailer.

"'Ow do, Arthur," said the man, his expression seemed grave.

"Eh up, Edward, it's a grim do alright."

"Aye, that's for sure."

"Have you heard owt?"

"Nay, not much, there's no one about."

"What's going to happen with flour?"

"I wish I knew, Arthur. Price of grain's going through t'roof, if tha can get any."

"How do they expect people to eat?"

"'Appen they don't know what's going on."

"Aye, and they'll be looking for cannon-fodder soon enough, you mark my words... So what can tha do us?"

"Look, I can do two, and that's more than I should."

"Two?"

"Aye."

"That's no use, I need three at least. What about Ruskin's?"

"Nay, I sent my lad over there at three this morning; they've none either... Sorry, Arthur, it's best I can do. Price is up a shilling an' all."

"A shilling?" Arthur exclaimed.

"Aye."

Arthur heaved a huge sigh of resignation. "Aye, alright, if that's best tha can do, I've no choice, have I?"

Buxton carried the sacks into the baking shed and left. Arthur was thinking about how he would cope with the demand. It would have to be more rationing.

At seven-thirty, there was another visitor at the shed.

"Eh up, Arthur, I've been knocking on t'door, but 'appen no one could hear."

"'Ow do, Ivy. Nay, sorry, can't always hear when I'm mixing."

"As it happened, I wanted to ask a question."

Arthur checked the bread baking in the oven, then leaned on his shovel and gave her his attention.

"Aye, what's it about?"

"I've been talking to me mam. With all of us at butcher's, there's not much room, especially as Ronald and Lilian are getting bigger. There's a lot of arguing."

"Aye…? Wilfred's not said owt."

"Nay, he's scared of me mam, that's why."

"So, what are you asking?"

"I was wondering if I could rent thar spare room. I could do the cleaning for tha by way of payment. I would be no trouble," she quickly added.

Arthur thought for a few moments; it made a great deal of sense. "Aye, I don't see why not. 'Appen tha would be a bit of company an' all."

"Aye, if tha's happy. I can collect my things after work."

"Aye, aye, do that… Is thar mam coming today?"

"Aye, she'll be here later."

"Right, tha best get ready, bread's almost done. Can tha

get the baskets?"

Ivy walked across the shed and collected the large wicker containers for the finished bread and placed them by the side of the oven. She looked at Arthur who was staring inside the furnace.

"'Appen there'll be trouble today. Folk're already queuing up at Granger's Store, and at butcher's. There's a few women outside here too. What time's Agnes arriving?"

Arthur turned. "She said she was catching first trolley. Grace is coming an' all."

"Wilfred said there's going to be a war."

"Aye, it's already started."

"I heard the bells ringing last night, but I went back to sleep. What'll happen do tha think?"

"Who can tell. 'Appen a lot of folk'll get killed."

Just then there was a rattle at the front door. Arthur opened the oven and looked at Ivy. "That'll be them. Best let 'em in; bread's almost ready."

Ivy went through the corridor to the shop. It was Grace and Agnes, but behind them there was a large gathering of women, most with shopping bags.

"Hello Ivy," said Agnes. "Looks like we're going to be busy."

The three girls put on their aprons and prepared the shelves. Arthur brought in the loaves and baps.

"We're going to have to ration again today; there was only two bags of flour; that'll mean half a loaf each."

"Half a loaf?" exclaimed Grace.

"Aye, 'appen it'll all've gone by lunchtime. Miller's got no flour."

"There'll be a riot at this rate," said Agnes.

"Well, there's nowt to be done. If tha gets a problem, come and tell me."

At Springfield Hall, Mildred was up early. After the noise of the bells, she had slept soundly in her new bed. She woke Grace and Agnes at six-fifteen ready to catch the trolleybus; it was a twenty minute walk to the stop outside the store. Mildred made them some tea and sandwiches for breakfast while they were getting ready.

With the fire in the sitting room not yet lit, there was no hot water in the bathroom, but the girls didn't seem to mind. Running water was a luxury they were still getting used to.

Once they were away, Mildred made herself some breakfast, using her frying pan for the first time on the new range. She couldn't believe how quickly everything cooked.

At ten o'clock, the soft clanging of the doorbell echoed around the hallway. Mildred was in her bedroom and made her way down the staircase to answer it. She was expecting Mrs Jessop, but it was a young man instead.

"Freddie!?"

"Aye, good morning Mrs Marsden, mam said tha wanted to hire me as gardener."

Mildred was momentarily in shock at the unexpected arrival. She viewed the lad, slim, trousers held up with braces, white shirt, hobnail boots and flat cap.

He took off his cap and clutched it to him.

"Well... yes... we did discuss it... on a month's trial, if that suits."

"Aye, 'appen it suits very well. I've been t'mill and told them I weren't coming back. I've brought some things; I can start straight away."

"Alright, very well. I'll open the gate for you."

Mildred could see a wheelbarrow with some gardening tools lay across it parked on the forecourt behind him.

Mildred closed the door and walked through to the scullery and opened the door to the patio, still wondering if she had made the right decision. The end of the house was to the left, a short distance from the scullery door. The high brick wall surrounding the grounds continued around the perimeter. The latch gate provided access. Mildred pulled back the bolt and opened the door. She wondered how Freddie had managed to scale the wall on his last visit; it would have taken some athleticism.

Freddie was waiting with his wheelbarrow still holding his cap.

"Your mother said you did some work here on Sunday."

"Aye, that I did."

"Well, I must say you did a splendid job. Tell me, how on earth did you get into the garden?"

"It were no bother, propped barrow against t'wall and pulled meself over."

"Really? How clever of you."

"Aye."

"Let me give you the keys to the gardener's shed; there are quite a few tools in there and a lawnmower."

There was a light brown gravel path traversing the lawn and running below the patio, past the scullery, to the boundary wall. They walked along about twenty yards to the shed. Mildred had her collection of keys; she found the right one, removed it from the ring and opened the shed door.

They were greeted again by the unpleasant aroma. Freddie's eyes lit up as he scanned the impressive display of tools.

"By 'eck, there's some fine things in here," he said, touching the collection of spades and forks.

Mildred looked at him and was suddenly reminded of her late husband. The facial likeness, his eyes, the shape of his nose, even some of his mannerisms. It was uncanny; it was like a resurrection.

"I'll leave you to it Freddie… Oh, but we've not discussed your hours. Have you a thought?"

"Aye, 'appen I could work till five o'clock if that suits."

"Every day?"

"Aye, if tha needs… Not Sunday, though."

"No, of course, naturally, or Saturday for that matter. I would think five days would be sufficient, don't you?"

"Aye, very well."

"That's settled then, and I will pay you by the hour, the same rate as the mill; that would seem to be fair."

"Aye, aye, more than fair," he said, still holding his cap to his stomach.

Back at the bakery, Arthur's prediction of a riot was not far from the truth. When the announcement of a half-loaf ration was announced, word quickly spread and there was a huge wave of anger. One or two women started banging on the window, which was threatening to break. Grace called Arthur, who had to come out and remonstrate with them.

By mid-morning, the clamour at the bakery had died down, but it was pandemonium at Granger's store at the top of James Street as women bought as much tin foods as they could carry or afford. George Granger also had to impose rationing on certain items.

There was a strange atmosphere in the town, a great deal of uncertainty; nobody quite knew what to do. There was a huge demand for newspapers to get the latest news, but apart from mobilising the troops and navy, there was not a great deal of information.

Just before eleven o'clock, the postman arrived at the bakery with a letter addressed to Agnes. He handed it to her and she recognised the writing straight away. With Ivy and Grace now coping with the queue, she made an excuse and went outside the baking shed to read it.

'*My dearest Agnes, I hope this letter finds you in good heart. I think about you every minute. I'm not allowed to say where we are but the training is going as well as it could be. The commanding officer seems pleased with my progress. Tomorrow we are moving to a new camp in case there is a war. Have you any more news on your tour? Oh how I wish I could hear you sing again. I hope you will write to me. There is an army post office address via the G.P.O. which I am assured will find me. Sending you all my love, Norman.*'

Tears started to fall from Agnes's face. If only she hadn't been so selfish, he would still be working at the solicitors, and they would be meeting every day in the park. She missed him so much.

Agnes composed herself. As she walked through the baking shed, Arthur noticed she was upset. "Eh up, our Agnes, is there owt wrong?"

"Nay, Arthur, it's nowt," she replied and returned to the shop.

Just before eleven-thirty, there was more upheaval on James Street as the battalion from the local garrison marched down the street on the way to the station. All the traffic came to a halt and people cheered as they paraded by.

A few minutes later, Mrs Stonehouse appeared in the baking shed. Arthur was mixing his last dough.

"Arthur Marsden, I need a word."

Arthur looked up. "'Ow do, Mrs Stonehouse, how be tha?"

"Never mind 'how be tha', what's with all the horse muck on the floor upstairs? Did yer Mam not teach tha to clean yer boots before you walk into the parlour? And I've emptied the piss-pot this time, but I expect tha to see to that in future. I'm not here to mollycoddle tha. What time do tha want yer lunch?"

Arthur was taken aback, nobody had spoken to him like that before, not even his own mother. No wonder Wilfred was frightened of her.

"Er… sorry Mrs Stonehouse, 'appen I weren't thinking straight."

"Aye, the ale, I bet. It killed yer father… 'appen it'll do for tha. If tha's got any sense tha'll give it a miss. Now, what time do you want lunch?"

Arthur just stared for a moment. "Aye, well we close the shop at one."

"One o'clock it is then. I'll get some supplies in; you can pay me later."

Arthur was going to explain his normal routine visit to the Malt Shovel but, in view of Mrs Stonehouse's comments, didn't feel it would be well received.

"Aye, ta, I'll be there."

"I'll do the girls something too."

She left Arthur and walked back along the corridor. She put her head through the beaded curtain and attracted Ivy's attention in the shop.

"I'll do tha something to eat when tha shut t'shop. I'm going to Granger's to get a few things. I'll see Wilfred and get some meat for tha tea an' all."

"Aye, ta mam," said Ivy and returned to the dwindling queue of customers.

Back upstairs, Mrs Stonehouse took off her apron and put on her hat, then left to collect the shopping.

By one o'clock, the bread had all gone and Arthur closed the shop. He would not be reopening today; there would be a lot of disappointed people.

Mrs Stonehouse was waiting as the three girls from the shop arrived for their lunch. Arthur joined them a few minutes later.

"Take yer boots off, Arthur," shouted Mrs Stonehouse as he entered the parlour.

Arthur complied. The parlour was tidy and the floor cleaned.

"So, thar happy with our Ivy moving in?" asked Mrs Stonehouse as she brought in a tray of bread, cheese, and pickle.

"Aye, it suits well enough," replied Arthur.

"What's this Arthur?" enquired Grace.

Mrs Stonehouse interrupted before Arthur could reply. "Our Ivy's renting t'spare room. It'll help us out at butcher's; it's getting very crowded there."

Grace looked at Arthur "Aye, 'appen it makes good sense. Tha'll have someone to keep an eye on tha Arthur. Make sure you don't get up to mischief."

Arthur scowled. "Nay, there's nowt of the sorts."

"So what's going to happen about this war, Arthur?" asked Agnes. "'Appen Norman's going to be fighting, I reckon."

"Aye, and there'll be more besides, you mark my words. We should never have got involved. It's the politicians; I blame them."

Agnes took little comfort from Arthur's evaluation and continued eating her lunch in deep reflection.

"I need some money for the food, Arthur, after you've eaten," said Mrs Stonehouse, changing the subject. "Mind you, Granger's hardly had owt left, there were queues up the High Street, but I got our Wilfred to give tha some meat and there's fresh vegetables from the greengrocer's."

"Ta, Mrs Stonehouse, I'll see to it."

"Aye, and I don't know if tha'll be needing me after today. Ivy can well look after tha?"

"Aye," said Ivy, looking up from her cheese and pickle. "'Appen I can."

Arthur paid Mrs Stonehouse for the provisions and her services for the day. He wasn't unhappy to be rid of her; she was far too domineering for his taste. Ivy was different, much more placid, and polite.

After cleaning the shop, Grace and Agnes crossed the park to catch the trolleybus back to Oakworth; Ivy went back to the butcher's to collect her things.

Arthur retired to the Malt Shovel.

Grace and Agnes reached Oakworth and alighted the trolleybus outside the store, then walked the mile and a half to the house.

As they reached the gravel drive, Grace noticed a wheelbarrow next to the side gate to the garden. The entrance was open and the lawn visible beyond. Her heart skipped a beat. "Freddie," she said to herself.

Instead of using the front entrance, the girls headed for the gate.

"Looks like the new gardener's started," said Agnes and looked at Grace with a knowing smile.

"Aye, seems so."

They walked into the garden. To the left along the footpath, the door to the shed was open. Grace scanned the lawn but couldn't see him. In the far corner, a good hundred yards away, was a compost heap where the grass cuttings and other garden waste was gathered. To the right was the entrance to the orchard, a small copse of about twenty apple trees. Then there he was. He had discarded his shirt, his trousers suspended from the braces.

Grace wanted to shout at the top of her voice, but just waved. Freddie waved back and started walking towards them. "I'm going in," said Agnes.

"I'll be there in a moment; I just want to say hello to Freddie," replied Grace.

The door to the scullery was unlocked and Agnes went through to the kitchen where Mrs Jessop was baking.

"Hello, Mrs Jessop, fine day."

"Oh, hello, Agnes, yes it is. Your mother's upstairs and Molly's in her sewing room. I've not seen Freda, probably in her bedroom. Would you like some tea?"

"Aye, thank you, I'll just go and change. Grace is talking to Freddie."

"Right you are," replied the housekeeper and left her baking to make the tea.

Freddie had reached the footpath and approached Grace. His body glistened from his labours.

"My, but tha looks so pretty, Grace, tha really do."

"You're looking mighty fine yourself, Freddie Bluet," replied Grace, eyeing up his physique. "Would you like a drink?"

"Aye, a glass of water would be very welcome; it's warm work."

"I'll bring it out directly; will tha be in t'shed?"

"Aye," replied Freddie with a wink. "'Appen I will."

Grace went through to the kitchen, where Mrs Jessop was filling a teapot. "Hello Grace, would you like some tea, I've just made a fresh pot?"

"Thank you, Mrs Jessop. I'll just take Freddie a drink. It's thirsty work in this weather."

Grace picked up a drinking glass from one of the shelves,

filled it from the tap, then returned to the garden through the scullery.

She was still wearing her work clothes, but she didn't think Freddie would mind.

She reached the shed. Freddie had put on his shirt and was leaning against the lawnmower.

"Your drink," said Grace, entering the shed and handing it to him.

He downed it in one gulp. "Would you like another?" asked Grace, seeing the degree of thirst.

"Aye, but in a moment." He took Grace's hand and pulled her towards him.

In a moment, they were locked in a kiss that almost took her breath away. More and more urgent, Grace could feel his hands holding her buttocks and pulling her onto him as he had at the riverbank. Grace's breathing increased.

Suddenly a voice. "Grace... Grace, are you there?"

"It's me mam, I best go?" said Grace.

"Can I see thee tonight?" asked Freddie.

"Aye, if I can get away."

"Eight o'clock by the trolley stop; I'll wait for thee."

"Aye, I'll try," said Grace and she took the glass from him and walked back towards the scullery door. Her face was flushed.

Mildred was waiting. "Ah, there you are... Mrs Stonehouse has made some tea for you."

"I've just taken Freddie some water; 'appen he was thirsty."

Grace felt like a guilty schoolgirl.

In the Malt Shovel, Arthur was enjoying his second pint as Wilfred walked in.

"'Ow do, Wilfred what'll tha have?"

"Eh up, Arthur, a pint'll be grand."

Arthur went to the counter and ordered the drink. He returned with the beer and another for himself.

"So what's the latest?" asked Wilfred.

"It's grim," replied Arthur, finishing his remaining pint, and starting on the new one. "I was talking to Thomas. 'Appen they've nationalised t'railways."

"Aye? Well that's no bad thing. Maybe they'll run on time."

"Aye, there is that," said Arthur.

"What about t'war?"

"Nowt much's happening at t'moment, according to Thomas. France's going to war with Germany so it'll be them and us versus the Krauts. They've invaded Belgium apparently."

"Nay, so what's gonna happen? I mean we nearly ran out of meat today and I've no idea if we'll get another delivery tomorrow."

"Aye, same as bread, no flour according t'miller."

"Did tha hear about the problems up at Granger's?"

"What were that?"

"'Appen he had to call out constabulary this afternoon. Some women started looting."

"Nay."

"Aye, I were chatting with one of the girls."

"Eh, I don't know what's to be done, Wilfred lad."

Arthur returned to the bakery in a slightly better state than the previous day. He was greeted by Ivy.

"Eh up, Arthur, I'm cooking us some tea, why don't you have a wash down and a nap. Tha'll feel better for it."

Arthur looked at Ivy, fresh-faced and with the benefit of a trace of makeup.

"Aye, 'appen I'll do that. Summat smells good."

"Aye, mam got a piece of steak for us. I'll do us some onions and potatoes to go with it."

"Aye, that'll be grand."

Ivy's presence had changed the atmosphere; Arthur felt less isolation. His mood changed completely.

It was seven-thirty in Oakworth, Freddie and Mrs Jessop had long since completed their work and had left; it was just the family. Grace and Agnes were helping in the kitchen with the washing up after the evening meal. With further direction from the housekeeper, Mildred was feeling more comfortable with the new cooker and announced her intention to use the oven to do some baking the following day.

"Aye, if tha can get flour," said Agnes, who explained the difficulties at the bakery.

Grace had finished her chores. "It's a lovely evening, 'appen I'll go for a walk and have a look around. I could do with some air."

Mildred was on alert. "Why don't you go too, Agnes? It will do you both good."

Grace gave Agnes a look.

"Nay, I want to rest up and read for a while. I've been on my feet all day."

Mildred tried another tack. "Do you have to go, Grace? I was hoping we could play some games, as a family."

"I'll not be long."

"Well, mind you are. It'll be getting dark shortly."

Grace had already washed and changed into more comfortable attire.

The large entrance hall was beautifully decorated with wood panelling and there was a small cupboard integrated into the décor next to the doorway. It had been designed to store shoes and umbrellas. She opened the door and removed her booties.

In a moment she was through the door and walking at a brisk pace along the drive.

The sun had set and dusk was easing towards darkness as Grace reached the village store. She could see Freddie waiting on the corner.

"Sorry I'm late," said Grace as she approached.

"Pay no mind; it's just good to see tha," said Freddie.

"I can't stop long; me mam wants to play some games with t'family."

"Aye, I'm just glad tha's here."

There was a track next to the store that led to a farm about half a mile away. The whole area was deserted. There would be little traffic this time of night and the last trolleybus had gone.

There were high hedgerows on either side. They reached a four-bar gate which led into a field. Freddie opened it and Grace followed. They were immediately locked into another passionate kiss. Freddie took off his jacket and lay it on the ground.

"Nay, Freddie, not here. I need to be getting back."

"Aye, I'm sorry Grace. I meant no disrespect. I love tha with all my heart."

He picked up his jacket.

They kissed again. "Aye, pay no mind, Freddie, I want that too, but special."

"Aye, me an' all... What shall us do?" asked Freddie.

Although it was quite dark now, Grace could see Freddie's face quite clearly. She stroked his cheek. "I want us to be married. Now there's a war, I worry they might take tha away from me. Tha may need to go and fight."

Freddie kissed her again.

"Aye, that's right enough. I want that too."

"I need to get back. I'll try and get more time tomorrow."

"Aye," replied Freddie and they left the field and walked back to the store.

They kissed again and went their separate ways.

Grace's mind was buzzing as she walked back to the Hall. It was a dry, warm night, and without street lighting, there seemed more stars in the sky than she had ever seen before. A good omen, she thought. She couldn't wait to be with Freddie again.

Back at the bakery, Arthur and Ivy had eaten their meal. Ivy had proved to be an excellent cook. While she was cleaning the dishes, Arthur was at the table reading the Keighley News, but there was little information on the war. Unusually, he had decided not to go to the Malt Shovel.

After finishing the chores, Ivy went into the bedroom.

Earlier, she and Arthur had dismantled one of the two beds and taken it to the baking shed to be disposed of. They had also removed the dividing curtain that had separated him from his sisters for so many years. The room had been transformed, with much more space, and Ivy was now arranging everything to her liking.

A little later, she said goodnight to Arthur and retired for the night. He too was feeling the effects of the day and decided he would also go to bed.

Ivy tossed and turned. Not only was she in a new bed, but this was also the first time in her life, she had not shared with someone, albeit separated by a bolster.

It was gone eleven o'clock. She picked up her pillow and left the bedroom. Slowly, she opened Arthur's bedroom door and walked to the bed. He was snoring.

"Arthur, I can't sleep; can I get in with you?"

"Eh… what…?" he muttered.

"I've got my pillow; I'll not disturb thee."

Arthur was still in a deep sleep. Ivy lifted the covers and crawled in, separating herself from him with the pillow.

Chapter Twenty

Thursday morning, the noise from Arthur's alarm clock reverberated around the bedroom. It woke him with a start. He sat up in bed trying to focus and suddenly became aware that he was not alone.

He looked at the face on the pillow next to him. "Ivy? What are tha doing here?"

She roused and squinted. "'Appen I couldn't sleep. Tha don't mind, do tha?"

He wasn't sure how to answer the question; he didn't know what he felt. "But tha shouldn't be here."

"Aye, but I couldn't sleep. I'm not used to being on my own."

"Aye, well, I don't have time to discuss it now. Bread needs baking. Miller'll be here shortly."

He got out of bed and started dressing. "I'll sithee downstairs later," he said and left the bedroom.

Ivy went back to sleep.

In the baking shed, Arthur lit the oven as usual and waited for Buxton's lorry. Six o'clock and there was still no sign of the miller; Arthur was getting anxious.

Just before seven o'clock, Ivy walked along the corridor to the baking shed. She was carrying a plate with a fried egg and a slice of bread in one hand and a cup of tea in the other.

"Arthur," she called. He was outside looking for signs of the Buxton's lorry.

He turned and walked back to the shed.

"'Ow do, Ivy."

"I've brought tha a spot of breakfast. 'Appen tha'll be hungry. I've fired up the range and made tha a drink an' all."

"Aye, ta, that's very good of tha." He took the plate and

started eating.

"Where's all the bread?" asked Ivy seeing the empty mixing bath.

"Buxton's not here yet. Looks like we may be closed today."

Arthur finished his breakfast just as the sound of a lorry echoed around West Street.

"That'll be him now," he told Ivy.

The lorry pulled into the yard, and the miller jumped down from his cab.

"Eh up, Arthur, sorry I'm late, been out since three trying to get grain."

Arthur looked at the trailer; there was even less than yesterday.

"'Ow do, Edward, what's tha latest? Have tha got t'flour?"

"Aye, but not much. 'Appen it's one today, Arthur; it's all I have."

"I can't supply folk with that; it'll all be gone by eleven. What's to be done?"

"Sorry, Arthur; it's best I can do. One or two bakers say they're starting to mix their bread with potato flour."

"Nay, can't do that; customers won't have it."

"They'll have no choice if war stops grain coming in from America."

Ivy was listening to the conversation. "Bake what you can, Arthur; we'll sort out t'customers, don't tha worry."

Arthur felt a sense of resignation; there was little alternative.

Agnes and Grace arrived just after seven forty-five; Ivy explained the problems with the flour delivery. "'Appen we'll need to ration again; just six ounces a customer."

"Six ounces?" queried Agnes.

"Aye, it'll be fairest way. Miller's got no flour."

Back in the baking shed, Arthur had started mixing; it would be just one batch today. His mind suddenly switched to other matters. It was just a day to go before the court case. The thought had a purgatory effect, and he had to make a dash for the outside toilet. He started wondering if he would be able to make any bread again.

In Blossom Cottage, Freddie had woken early and was feeling on a high following his meeting with Grace the previous evening. He had replayed every moment in his mind. Her suggestion of marriage was a joy; it was something he had thought of but hadn't plucked up the courage to ask. He couldn't wait to marry her and consummate their relationship. He was ready for another day at Springfield Hall.

The smell of cooking from the kitchen permeated up the stairs and was extremely appetising. He was feeling hungry.

He joined his mother, who was at the range frying eggs and sausages.

"Good morning, Freddie, how was your night?"

"Fine, mam... Something smells good."

"Sit down, I've done you a fry up; set you up for the day."

Freddie sat down and a few minutes later, Kitty served the food.

"Looks like it'll be a nice day, Freddie, what will you be doing at the house."

"Working in t'orchard; it's not been touched for years."

He cut off a portion of sausage and put it in his mouth.

"I want to ask a question."

"Of course, what is it?"

"Well, you know I've been corresponding with Grace."

"Yes, you've told me."

"Well, 'appen I've feelings for her... and she for me."

Kitty stopped eating. "I see."

"Aye, 'appen we want to get married."

"Married? No, no you can't; that's impossible," she said before she could stop herself.

"Mam, why do tha say that? I'm old enough... and so's Grace."

Kitty looked down. It was the moment she had been dreading, but she could see no way out.

"Freddie, there's something I need to tell you. It's going to hurt you and I'm sorry."

Her serious expression concerned Freddie. She was always bright and positive.

"What is it?"

"Years ago, I worked at the bakery where Grace lived."

"Aye, I know that; tha told me."

"Mr Marsden, Grace's dad, was the baker... and I'm ashamed to say, he took advantage of me."

"What do tha mean?"

Now it was Freddie's turn to look anxious. He had put down his knife and fork.

"I became pregnant."

"Pregnant!?"

"Yes, I had to leave the bakery... I was fortunate, Mr Marsden gave me money to take care of myself; not every man honours their responsibilities."

"So, why didn't tha tell me before? What happened to the child?"

Tears started to fall down Kitty's cheek.

The penny dropped.

"Oh... nooo!"

"Yes, Freddie, I'm sorry. You are that child."

"But you told me my father was dead, years ago."

"Yes, I did, I wanted to protect you... at school. I told

everyone I was a widow."

"So, Grace... she's my... sister?"

"Yes, half-sister... I'm so sorry, Freddie, I'm so sorry. I had no idea you would ever meet Grace, let alone have feelings for her."

Freddie pushed his plate away; the half-eaten sausage was covered in congealed egg. He got up from the table and left the kitchen.

"Freddie where are you going? We need to talk about this."

Freddie ignored his mother and went to his room. Kitty sat for a moment, composed herself and started clearing the plates.

Upstairs, Freddie was in despair; his future had just come crashing down. He needed to think.

He picked up his purse and jacket; he checked his pockets for his keys. He needed to get out of the cottage.

Kitty heard him coming down the stairs; she could see he was wearing his jacket.

"Freddie? Freddie where are you going? Don't rush off, we need to talk."

Freddie ignored his mother and left.

He made the short walk to the store and the trolleybus stop where only a few hours earlier he and Grace were locked together in passion.

Ten minutes later the bus arrived and he got on. He had no idea where he was going.

Kitty cleared up the kitchen, more to keep busy. She was wracked with worry. She had envisaged this situation and how she would handle it, sensitively and caring, carefully explaining the events in a way Freddie would understand. She thought she could handle the shock and disappointment he would feel by keeping talking and reassuring him. She hadn't factored in any emotional attachment he might feel towards Grace. She needed to speak to Mildred.

She picked up her hat and handbag and left the cottage. There was no one at the trolley stop; the bus had already left. Twenty-five minutes later, she was walking up the drive of Springfield Hall. She was hoping the side gate would be open, but it wasn't. Maybe Freddie was taking out his frustrations on the orchard; a forlorn hope as it would transpire.

She reached the front entrance and rang the bell.

"Kitty, how lovely to see you, come in, come in. Would you like a drink?" greeted Mildred.

Kitty didn't reply but followed her through into the kitchen. Mrs Jessop was just finishing cleaning.

"Hello, Daisy, how are you?" said Kitty.

"Very well, Kitty, thank you for asking."

"I need to speak to Mrs Marsden in confidence, do you mind?"

"No, of course, I'll clean upstairs." She left the kitchen. Kitty closed the door.

"Whatever's the matter, Kitty?" asked Mildred.

"Freddie told me that he and Grace want to get married."

"Oh dear, I had no idea it had got that far... You don't think they... you know?"

"I don't know to be truthful. I do hope not."

"So what happened?"

"I told Freddie the truth." Kitty started sobbing.

"Oh my goodness..." Mildred stopped and put her hand on Kitty's shoulder. "What happened?"

"He went upstairs, then came back down wearing his jacket and left the cottage. I was hoping that he had come here."

"No, I've not seen him."

"I'm worried, Mildred. I don't know where he's gone or what he might do," said Kitty. "Do you think he's gone to see Grace?"

"Hmm, that's possible, I suppose," replied Mildred. "I think it's best I go into town and see her. Even if he's not spoken to her; I think it's time she knew. Now it's out in the open."

"Yes, of course you're right. I'll go back to the cottage and wait in case he comes back."

"Stay for a cup of tea; it will do you good."

"Yes, I will, Mildred, thank you."

It was another hour before Mildred was ready for her journey into town. Unfortunately, there was no cabbie stop in Oakworth or means of calling one, so Mildred was faced with a walk to the store and a ride on the trolleybus.

It was approaching noon as Mildred walked across the park to the bakery. She was surprised to see the door shut and the 'closed' notice displayed.

Agnes was cleaning the front of the counter and saw her mother approach. She opened the door with a clang.

"Hello, mam, what brings tha into town?"

"I want to speak to Arthur and see how he is. Why is the bakery closed?"

"We've run out of flour, bread's all gone. It's the war, Arthur says."

"Hello Grace, hello Ivy," she called seeing the two girls behind the serving counter. They both acknowledged her greeting.

"I'll just go and speak to Arthur; I'll be back shortly."

Arthur was cleaning the mixing vat and looked up as she entered the shed.

"'Ow do, mam, what brings tha here?"

"I wanted to see you about tomorrow, to make sure you were alright and to ask if you would like me to come with you to the court."

Arthur wiped his hands on a towel and walked over to his mother.

"Aye, I would be glad of that."

"What time do you have to be there?"

"At nine-thirty, it said on t'letter. I don't know what time I'll be in front of t'magistrate. There'll be a few to see, I'll warrant."

"I will make arrangements to be here before then. Have you thought about the bakery?"

"Aye, I think about nowt else. I don't know what to do. 'Appen there'll be no bread if things carry on. Buxton's only delivered one bag today."

"Can't you get any more?"

"Nay, Edward was up at three this morning trying to get some grain he told me."

"What about Granger's?"

"Nay, they'll not have any. 'Appen they got looted yesterday. Constabulary were called an' all sorts, according to Ivy."

"Really? And Ivy, how is she settling in?"

"Aye, well enough." He looked down. "I don't know what to do if they put us away. Who will look after t'shop?"

"Well, Grace can mix the bread she's done it before."

"Not on her own, she hasn't; and how will she get here for five in the morning from Oakworth? There're no trolleys and cabbies won't come out at that time of day?"

Mildred could see his point. "Well, if you can manage tomorrow morning, then Grace can take over. There will be time before you have to be there. You know, the court may treat you leniently. You are a master baker after all, and not one of those ruffian mill workers; have you thought of that?"

"Aye, but as I see it they'll treat us all the same. They say we're all tarred with same brush. T'were in papers."

"Well, there's nothing to be done today, and don't spend all day in the Malt Shovel. Drowning your sorrows will only make matters worse and you'll need a clear head tomorrow."

"Aye, mam, tha's right enough."

"I just need to speak to Grace. I will call in before I leave."

Mildred walked back to the shop; the girls were still busy cleaning. One or two women had been knocking on the door wanting to know what was happening and why they weren't open.

"Grace, can you leave that for a moment? I need to speak to you."

Grace put down her cleaning cloth and followed Mildred up the stairs.

"Is this about the baking tomorrow? I spoke to Arthur and said I can do it."

"No, Grace, it's something else." They reached the parlour. "You best sit down; I have some news which you won't take kindly to."

Grace sat down at the table and Mildred sat opposite.

"I've heard that you and Freddie have discussed getting married."

"Who told you that?"

"It doesn't matter, the point is, you can't."

"What do you mean, I can't?"

Mildred looked down trying to pick the right words.

"The thing is… Freddie's your brother, well half-brother."

"What? Nay, that can't be right."

"I'm afraid it is. I only found out myself after your father died. It seems he had an affair with Kitty for a short while and she fell pregnant with Freddie."

"No, no, you're just saying that because you don't like him."

"No, I like him well enough and, but for the circumstances, I would have given the union my blessing."

Grace had gone very pale. "Does Freddie know?"

"Yes, Kitty told him this morning when he announced his intentions."

"I must see him." Grace started crying.

"No one knows where he is. He didn't come to work at the house."

Grace's face was ashen. Mildred continued. "I need to ask you a question. Have you and he engaged in any, er, intimate things?"

"Nay, but I wish we had. I wish I didn't know this."

"Yes, well, when you've had chance to think on it, you'll have a different opinion."

Grace took out a handkerchief and blew her nose. "Where's Freddie, where's he gone?"

"I don't know. Kitty said he left the cottage when he heard the news; she's not seen him since."

Grace went quiet while trying to come to terms with the news. She stood up.

"'Appen I'll finish cleaning," she said and walked out of the parlour.

Out of habit, Mildred got up and went into the kitchen to make a cup of tea. The fire in the range had gone out. She started the process of relighting it.

Having cleaned down the baking shed; Arthur went upstairs to see his mother. "Would you like a drink, Arthur?

I've just made some tea," she said as he sat down.

"Nay ta, I need to go down to t'Shovel."

"Well, remember what I said. Don't get worse for drink; you'll need your wits about you tomorrow."

"Aye, mam, don't fret… What's up with Grace? She was crying when I saw her in t'shop."

"I'll let her tell you," replied Mildred and sat down with her tea.

But Arthur was too wrapped up in his court case and never pursued the matter further. He was unaware that he had a half-brother.

Mildred continued. "So, I'll be here tomorrow morning before nine o'clock. Make sure you're not late, otherwise, nothing's going to save you."

"Aye, I'll be ready."

Agnes and Grace had finished the cleaning and were preparing to leave. Mildred offered to take them back to the Hall in a taxicab. Ivy went up to the flat to change and start cleaning.

Freddie was totally bereft to the extent his mind wasn't functioning in any logical way. He couldn't remember how he'd reached the park opposite the trolley stop or what he was doing there. He still couldn't see Grace as a sister. They were going to be lovers, get married; it was something he'd dreamed of.

Just then, he was distracted by the sound of music. He looked to his right and another bus was approaching. It was festooned in banners: 'Men of Yorkshire - Do your duty'; 'Your country needs you'; 'Fall in; Answer now in your country's hour of need'. On the top deck, a brass band was playing. The banner across the front read; 'Army Recruitment Bus'.

People on the roadside and in the park were watching with interest, some were waving handkerchiefs. Men in khaki were waving back at the bystanders. Every man they saw they beckoned towards them. One soldier appeared to be gesturing to Freddie.

Freddie stood up and walked along the pathway. The bus had stopped outside the Town Hall.

There were at least twenty men crowded around the entrance to the bus where an officer in an immaculate uniform was talking to them. Some, he ushered inside, others, which from their appearance were in advanced years, he expressed his gratitude and then politely sent them on their way.

"Don't worry, sir, there'll be plenty of work to do here," Freddie heard him say to one disappointed silver-haired gentleman.

Freddie joined the line and twenty minutes later he was being ushered inside.

There were six soldiers, answering questions and a lieutenant sat at a makeshift table taking details. "Next," he bellowed. It was Freddie's turn.

"Name?"

"Freddie, er, Frederick Bluet."

"Age?"

"Nineteen."

"Address?"

"Blossom Cottage, Oakworth."

"Right, Freddie, sign here." He pushed forward a form containing a significant amount of words, some of which Freddie didn't recognise. He signed.

"Right, tomorrow you need to report to the Town Hall in Bradford where you will undergo a series of tests to confirm you are physically fit to join the army. Do you understand?"

"Yes, sir," replied Freddie. "What time?"

"Ten o'clock onwards."

"What happens then?"

"If you're passed as fit, you will be taken to one of the army training camps… Next!" he bellowed. He put Freddie's form on top of a pile of others.

Freddie left the bus considering the enormity of what he had just done.

Freddie caught the next trolleybus back to Oakworth. As he entered the cottage, his mother, on hearing the door open, rushed from her studio.

"Freddie, Freddie, where have you been? I've been frantic with worry."

"I've been into town." They walked into the kitchen and Freddie sat down.

"To see Grace?" said Kitty.

"Nay, 'appen she'll not want to see me, will she?"

"Oh, Freddie, I can't imagine what you must be feeling right now. If I could turn back the clock, I would."

"Aye, mam, I knows. I needed some time to think."

"Yes, I understand, I realise that Freddie. Give it time; the wounds will heal." She put her hand on his forehead in a comforting way.

"I've joined the army."

"You've done what!?" Kitty almost collapsed on the nearest kitchen chair. "Oh, dear Lord, no."

"Aye, 'appen they're going to need good soldiers to fight the Germans."

"This is all my fault."

"Aye," said Freddie. "'Appen it is." She ignored the remark.

"So, what's going to happen?"

"Tomorrow, I've got to go into Bradford to Town Hall;

summat to do with tests, and then I'll go to training camp."

"Oh, dear Lord," she repeated. She put her hand over her mouth.

"I'm going to my room; I need to get things ready."

It was almost four o'clock.

Kitty left the cottage and hurried to see Mildred. She reached the Hall and rang the bell. Mrs Jessop opened the door.

"Kitty, lovely to see you. Mrs Marsden's in the kitchen."

Mildred had returned from her visit to the bakery.

"Kitty, is there any news?"

"Yes, Freddie's just got back."

"Where did he go?"

"Into town… he's signed up."

"What do you mean, signed up?"

"Joined the army, while he was in town."

"Oh dear Kitty, I'm so sorry."

"I don't know what to do, what if he gets killed?"

"Don't be thinking about that; they say in the papers it will all be over by Christmas. Maybe it will do him good to get away for a while."

Unable to reply, Kitty sat down, her face pale and drawn; her hands were shaking. "Did you speak to Grace?"

"Yes, I did, she was very upset, I don't mind saying. She's upstairs in her bedroom. She and Agnes came back in the taxicab with me. Hardly said a word since she's been back. Agnes is with her."

"It's good she has someone to talk to. Freddie doesn't have anyone."

"No, it's going to be difficult for him," said Mildred.

Having heard Kitty's voice, Grace came into the kitchen. She looked at Kitty. "How could you do this to us?"

Mildred intervened. "Now, Grace, Kitty never meant any

harm."

"It's alright, Mildred. Grace has a right to be angry. In her situation, I would feel the same." She looked at Grace. "If it's any consolation, I'm angry with myself, but I never thought for one minute that Freddie would have feelings for you, Grace."

"Aye, well, it's too late now, what's done is done. Where is he now?"

"He's back home."

"Can I see him?" said Grace.

"I'm not sure that's a good idea. He's busy getting his things together. I was just telling your mother, he's joined the army," replied Kitty.

"Joined the army?!" exclaimed Grace. "Oh no, not that." She turned to her mother. "Mam, I want to see him."

"It will only upset both of you. It's for the best, even if it doesn't seem like it now," said Mildred.

Grace burst into tears and went back upstairs.

Back in town, Arthur had left the baking shed and had returned to the Malt Shovel with Wilfred. Henry and Samuel were still working but would meet up later.

"So what's gonna happen tomorrow?" asked Wilfred, as he supped his pint.

"I've no idea, Wilfred. 'Appen I may have to shut bakery."

"Nay, it won't come to that, surely. What're folk going to do?"

"I don't know. We had just one sack of flour today and miller reckons it's going to get worse."

"Aye, same with t'meat. Them at slaughterhouse are rationing."

"Well, if we get sent to Armley, there's no one to make t'bread."

"I thought tha Grace was learning."

"Aye, she were, but she don't know owt yet."

The atmosphere was solemn.

Arthur returned to the bakery around four-thirty. Having taken heed of Mildred's warning, he'd restricted himself to just two pints. Ivy was cleaning in the kitchen. There was a smell of cooking.

"Arthur?" called Ivy, hearing the parlour door open.

"Aye," said Arthur as he took off his boots and placed them neatly in the corner. Mrs Stonehouse's words had left an indelible mark.

Ivy came in from the kitchen. "I'm making a rabbit pie; Wilfred had a couple in today from one of t'farmers. It'll be ready in an hour; why don't you take a bath and have a sleep? It'll make tha feel better. There's plenty of hot water."

Archie Slater's soprano voice was audible from the street below. "War latest, get the war latest," he trilled. Arthur was carrying the newspaper and placed it on the table. He thought for a moment.

"Aye, alright; 'appen I will."

He went down to the shed and collected the bath. Then took an old sheet from the bedroom cupboard and laid it down in front of the hearth in the parlour. In the winter, the fire would be blazing, but it was a warm day and wouldn't be required. Ivy appeared from the kitchen carrying a steaming bucket from the range and poured in the boiling hot water.

"I'll just bring a couple more, that ought to do it."

The bath was now half full. Ivy added another bucket of cold water and checked the temperature. "Aye, that's just right. I'll top it up when there's more hot water. I'll be in kitchen."

Arthur returned from the bedroom with a towel wrapped

around his waist, checked the temperature, and slowly lowered himself in. Then remembered he had forgotten the soap.

"Ivy, can tha fetch us some soap?" he shouted.

A few moments later, Ivy walked in with a large block of carbolic. Arthur was covering his privates.

"Nay, don't be shy Arthur; I've seen it all before. I've got brothers remember," she teased. "Can I have t'water after tha? It'll be a shame to waste it."

Arthur took the soap from her. "Aye, I'll give thee a shout when I'm done."

She returned to the kitchen and Arthur completed his ablutions. Having finished, he gingerly stepped out onto the towel and started to dry himself. Ivy was watching from the kitchen door. She was no stranger to the male anatomy but was fascinated by Arthur. He had a lean physique, skinny even.

"Do tha want me to give tha a hand, Arthur?" she called. Arthur looked around; he could see her watching.

"Nay, 'appen I can manage, ta."

Arthur finished drying and walked back to the bedroom. "I've done," he shouted as he walked past the kitchen. Ivy was at the range.

She left the cooking. "Have tha a towel, Arthur?" she called.

"Aye, give us a minute."

Arthur left the bedroom, wearing his underclothes and rummaged around in one of the cupboards.

"There," he said, handing her a large sheet. "Tha can use that."

Ivy undressed and got in the bath. The area around it was wet.

Arthur came into the parlour. Ivy covered herself with

her arms.

"Just get me paper," he said and retrieved it from the table, then returned to the bedroom.

Ten minutes later, Ivy had finished and had dried off. She wrapped the towel around herself.

"Arthur," she called. "I've finished. Can tha give us a hand?"

Emptying the bath was not an easy manoeuvre. There were two handles, one on each side and they lifted the tub, which was still half full. The water sloshed around as they carried it slowly to the kitchen.

Arthur used the bucket to take out some of the water and then the pair raised it slowly to the sink and poured the remainder down the drain. There was an amount of sediment in the bottom which Ivy washed out with a cloth.

"I'll tidy up," said Ivy. "You take the bath back to the shed."

Arthur was not used to this directing but complied.

By seven o'clock, the pair had eaten and Ivy was in the kitchen, washing the dishes. Arthur had changed into his going out clothes.

"I'm off t'Shovel. I won't be long," he called to her from the kitchen door.

"Aye, Arthur. I'll finish off here."

As Arthur was walking down James Street, he started thinking about Ivy. She was good company and very organised; she also had a calming effect on him.

The alehouse was busy, his two pals, Samuel, and Henry, were seated at one of the tables and waved to him. Arthur went to the bar and ordered three pints.

The atmosphere was more akin to a wake. The court case

loomed over the three like the sword of Damocles. In fact, the bar was unusually quiet; the landlord had commented on it. There were several others among his customers who would be appearing before the magistrate the following day.

"What's news on t'war?" asked Henry, as Arthur joined them.

"Nowt much in t'paper, but 'appen summat's up. No grain to be had. Reckon all working class are gonna starve," replied Arthur. There followed a long and ill-informed conjecture between the three about the possible future of the war.

Back in Blossom Cottage, Kitty was still trying to come to terms with Freddie's news. She considered it some divine punishment for her sins. Earlier, she and Freddie had eaten together, but there was little conversation, despite Kitty inviting questions. She wondered if Freddie regretted his hasty decision to join up but didn't challenge him. Tonight sleep would not come easy.

Grace was lay in bed trying to resolve the events of the day. To be told that Freddie was her brother and then that he was going to war was a double blow. For her, too, sleep would be elusive.

Arthur had returned from the Malt Shovel just after nine o'clock. Ivy was on the sofa reading the evening paper, the gaslight barely giving off enough illumination for the purpose. Outside it was quite dark.

She got up. "Eh up, Arthur, I've made tha a sandwich for supper. Sit down, I'll get it."

Arthur was momentarily taken aback. "Aye, ta." He went to the sofa and retrieved his newspaper and sat at the table. Ivy brought in a plate of cold rabbit and pickle sandwiches.

"There's no bread left," she said as she put the plate down in front of him.

"Aye, and I don't know if there'll be owt more either."

"Don't say that Arthur, wait till miller comes tomorrow; it'll be alright. If you show me what to do, 'appen I can help tha; I'm a quick learner."

"Aye, alright, let's see what Buxton's come up with."

"And don't go mithering about t'court case either. I've a feeling everything will work out."

Half an hour later, Arthur was just getting into bed when Ivy appeared at the door.

"Is it alright?" she said.

"Aye," replied Arthur and she got in beside him.

She put her arm around him. "And don't tha give a thought to flippin' magistrates, tha'll be right enough, tha mark my words."

Arthur felt a significant stirring in his loins as Ivy's hand moved downwards. She held his swollen member.

"'Appen we should make the most of the time, don't tha think?" she said.

Chapter Twenty One

Arthur's alarm clock again heralded the start of a new day, one that would change his life forever. He turned and saw Ivy sleeping peacefully next to him. He had no idea how someone could sleep through such an almighty sound.

This morning he felt different; he was a real man now. It gave him a sense of fulfilment and the strength to cope with what lay ahead.

It had been his first time with a woman and it was rushed; he wasn't even sure what was expected. Ivy seemed much more knowledgeable in such matters and guided him.

She stirred.

"What time is it?" she asked.

"It's ten to five."

She got out of bed and reached for the chamber pot under the bed, and without a moment's hesitation or inhibition, started to relieve herself.

"I'll fire up the range and make us some breakfast; you see to shed," she said.

"Aye, let's hope Buxton's have got some flour or else we might as well go back to bed."

Fortunately, the Government had released more grain supplies and for the first time in some while, the miller had almost a full load.

"Eh up, Edward, that's a sight I thought I'd never see again," said Arthur, looking at the trailer.

"Aye, I were at mill at four; we had a big delivery. I can let tha have three, if it suits."

"I'll take as many as tha can spare."

He looked around. "Say nowt, I'll let tha have four."

"Ta, Edward. Same price as yesterday?"

"Aye," replied the miller.

The sacks were stacked in the corner and paid for.

"Good luck, Arthur, for later," shouted Buxton as he clambered into his cab.

"Ta Edward. 'Appen I might need it."

Buxton's wagon trundled out of the yard to its next delivery.

Ivy arrived with a cup of tea and a fried egg a few minutes later. Arthur was starting his first mix. He put down his ladle and joined Ivy.

"Tha best show us what to do," she said, handing him his breakfast and drink.

Arthur made short work of the egg.

"Aye, I'm just about to start t'mix."

Arthur explained the oven and the temperature. "T'coal's over there," he explained, pointing to a bunker in the yard against the wall next to the shed.

He then went to the mixing vat and explained the ingredients and the right proportions. Ivy looked on intently as Arthur, using the skill of a master baker, mixed the dough. Once it was the right consistency, from years of practice, he ladled it into the moulds and then placed them on his baker's shovel. Then it was into the oven. Ivy loaded the next batch.

By seven-thirty, the first supply of bread was stacked into the two large baskets ready to go through to the shop. Ivy started on the second mix under Arthur's watchful eye. He seemed pleased with her progress; she <u>was</u> a quick learner.

A few minutes later, Grace and Agnes arrived. They were putting on their aprons as Arthur carried one of the baskets into the shop.

"Eh up, should be a better day today. Miller's got us four bags, 'appen we'll be busy once word gets out."

"Four bags?" said Grace. "Who's going to make t'bread while you're at court?"

"'Appen Ivy can. I'm just showing her what to do."

"Ivy? But she knows nowt about baking."

"Aye, which is why I'm teaching her."

Grace looked at Agnes. "If you say so, Arthur."

"Aye, but you can help keep an eye on her."

Grace had not slept well; she was still grieving over her relationship with Freddie. Her mood reflected her frustration.

"Aye, if I've got time. Once folk know we've got bread, they'll be queued up the street again."

"Aye, I knows that. Just do what tha can."

Grace and Agnes started to unload the basket and put the bread on the shelves. There was already a line starting to form outside. Women were pressing their heads against the shop window to check the activity inside. The news of bread would soon be passed on.

"What'll us do if tha gets sent down?" said Grace.

"I don't know. Mam's coming to court, 'appen we'll get chance to arrange summat."

Arthur went back to check on Ivy. She was kneading the dough as Arthur had demonstrated. He checked the consistency. "Just a bit more water," he advised, and poured in two ladles full from a bucket and checked again. "Try it now."

Satisfied the dough was the right texture, he supervised the filling of the moulds and the loading of the shovel. He checked the oven as she pushed the long shovel inside. "Keep an eye on t'coal; don't let fire go out or tha'll have to start again."

"Aye," said Ivy, pleased with her efforts.

As soon as the bread was ready, Ivy carried it through to the shop. It was heaving with women, grappling to get their hands on a loaf. Grace was having to keep order and threatened to close the shop if they didn't behave.

"Eh up, Ivy," said Agnes, "Got thaself a new job I hear."

"Aye, Arthur's showing me what to do in case he gets sent down. There's a lot to learn."

"'Appen Grace knows about it," said Agnes.

"Aye, but tha'll be in Oakworth and tha won't be getting here for five in t'morning."

Agnes looked at Grace. "Aye, she makes good sense."

Another customer barged to the front; it was chaos.

Ivy went back to the baking shed. It was time for Arthur to get ready.

At Blossom Cottage, Freddie had packed a few things into a small suitcase. He was wearing his only suit as he went downstairs. Kitty was waiting at the front door. "I'll walk you to trolley stop," she said, and collected her hat from the small table in the hallway.

The previous evening had been emotional, but Freddie was gradually coming to terms with the situation. Having been brought up by Kitty, there was a strong bond between them and, despite the revelations, that connection was still intact. He had regrets about his decision to sign up. He knew it had upset Kitty, but he couldn't stay in Oakworth in the present circumstances.

Kitty hugged Freddie, then opened the front door.

"Here, take this," she said and pushed four half-crowns into his hand.

"Thanks mam," he said, and the pair left the cottage.

The trolleybus was waiting at the stop; there were five minutes before it would leave. There was no-one else waiting, and the driver was leant against the cab pulling on a cigarette.

"Going on tha travels?" asked the man seeing Freddie's suitcase.

"Yes," said Kitty before Freddie could answer, "He's going to do his duty for King and country," she added proudly.

"I take my hat off to tha," he said and doffed his cap reverentially. "It's a brave thing tha does. Good luck to tha, son. There'll be no charge for tha."

"Thanks," said Freddie.

"That's very kind of you," said Kitty.

The driver checked his fob watch. "Climb up, son, we'll get going."

There was another hug and Freddie boarded the bus. It pulled away with Kitty waving her handkerchief until it rounded the bend and was out of sight. She sobbed uncontrollably.

She couldn't face going back to the cottage; she needed some company.

The walk to the Hall took about fifteen minutes. The sky was overcast and there was a threat of rain in the air. The scented honeysuckle gave off a pleasing smell as she walked down the drive to the front door.

She rang the bell and a few moments later, Mrs Jessop opened it.

"Hello Daisy, is Mildred in? I'm sorry to call unannounced," said Kitty.

"No, she's gone into town. It's her son's court case."

"Of course, oh dear, I had forgotten."

"Would you like a drink? I've just put the kettle on."

"Yes, yes, thank you that would be most welcome," replied Kitty.

"Was this just a social call?"

"Yes and no. I've just seen my son off to war; I just

needed some company."

"Oh dear, I'm sorry to hear that; it must be a terrible worry."

"Yes it is."

"Mind you, I have to admire their bravery."

"Yes, that's true, I suppose," said Kitty.

Mildred had arrived in town around eight forty-five and made the short walk from the trolleybus stop to the bakery. She was amazed at the queue which snaked up the street almost to the butcher's. She walked past the waiting women into the shop to a great deal of protest. Grace spotted her mother and opened the flap for her to enter. Arthur was in the parlour getting ready.

Mildred spoke briefly to Grace and Agnes, but little more than a quick 'hello' as both were focused on their customers.

Upstairs, Arthur was trying to fasten his tie when his mother entered the room.

"Eh up, Mam, can tha give us a hand with this knot; it keeps coming undone?"

Mildred completed the task. "Let's have a look at you," she said, standing back and checking his appearance.

"What's happening downstairs? There's a queue a mile long," she asked.

"Aye, I've four sacks of flour this morning. 'Appen words got out that we've got bread."

"What about the baking?"

"Ivy's doing it."

"Ivy?!"

"Aye, 'appen she's managing; I'll check on her again before we go. She's a quick learner, I'll say that. She watched me do the first batch and she's done t'rest. Folks won't tell the difference, I warrant."

"Oh, that's something at least."

The pair left the parlour just after nine-thirty. Arthur checked on Ivy; she was at the oven waiting for another batch to finish baking.

"Eh up, Ivy, how's it going?"

"Aye, 'appen I'm getting the hang of it. Next batch is in t'oven."

Arthur opened the front of the oven and looked inside.

"Thanks Ivy, that's grand. Well, I'm off now. I don't know if I will see tha or not later."

Ivy went over to him. Her hair was covered in flour dust. "You make sure you get back here, Arthur Marsden, there's folk depending on tha." She leaned up and kissed him on the cheek.

"Aye, ta."

He walked out of the baking shed and into the shop where his mother was waiting for him.

"Come on, Arthur, you don't want to be late."

Agnes and Grace wished him good luck, and the pair left for the twenty-minute walk to the courthouse.

As they approached, Mildred looked in horror. It was pandemonium, with maybe a hundred people congregating around the entrance. Several Black Marias were parked with a line of policemen patrolling the area.

Mildred remembered the time with Grace and the Suffragettes, but this was much worse.

Arthur and his mother jostled their way to the front and into the building. Again, it was packed with people. Some Arthur recognised, including Alf from the train. Arthur approached him.

"Eh up, Alf, how be tha?"

"'Ow do, Arthur, what a palaver."

"Aye, you're not wrong. Have tha been up yet, Alf?"

"Nay, eleven they reckon. There's a backlog, or so they say."

"Have tha seen anything of Samuel or Henry?"

"Nay, not seen 'em."

"Well, if tha sees 'em, tell 'em I'm here."

"Aye, will do. Good luck."

"Aye, you too, Alf."

Arthur re-joined his mother, who had held back while Arthur engaged with his pal.

"That was Alf. We met him on the train to London; reckons there's going to be a wait. Have tha seen anything of Wilfred?"

"No, but it's nearly ten o'clock; I expect he'll be here somewhere."

Arthur went to the enquiry window and reported to the clerk of the court who checked his manifest. Arthur was forlornly hoping against hope that there had been some sort of mistake, but he was to be disappointed.

"Yes, you're on the list. Your case should be heard by midday."

Arthur took out his fob watch and checked the time, nine fifty-six. Just then, he spotted Wilfred looking confused.

"Eh up, Wilfred."

"'Ow do, Arthur, what's to do?"

"Have tha registered?"

"Nay, I've just got here."

"Come with me."

There was a row of seats along the corridor which were all taken. Mildred waited for one to become available. The clerk called five names, and two of the seats were vacated. She immediately sat down before anyone else could use it while Arthur took Wilfred to register.

It was just a case of waiting. Arthur was becoming more and more anxious, pacing up and down and making use of the toilet on several occasions.

Back at the bakery, the queues continued but were now more of a steady flow than the earlier crush. With the supply of flour at more normal levels, the rationing was raised to one loaf or four baps per person.

Ivy continued to churn out the bread, and even Grace commented favourably on her loaves. After the initial success, Ivy was becoming more confident and enthusiastic in her endeavours.

At eleven o'clock, the postman barged his way to the front of the queue and handed a letter to Grace. It was addressed to Agnes. The printed lettering, 'The Hippodrome', appeared next to the postage stamp.

"There's a letter, Agnes. I'll manage customers if tha wants to read it."

Agnes wiped her hands, took the letter, and walked along to the baking shed. Ivy was busy mixing.

Agnes opened the letter.

'Dear Agnes,

I regret to inform you that due to the recent announcement of hostilities, I have had no option but to cancel the forthcoming tour as several of our male performers have answered the call to the colours.

I am sorry for this disappointment but I am sure that matters will be resolved by Christmas and we can look forward to the pantomime season. I have a part in mind for you.

Yours sincerely
Cameron Delaney,

Promoter, Hippodrome Theatre'

Agnes read it again and her heart sank, the disappointment palpable.

"Are tha alright?" asked Ivy. "Tha looks upset; not bad news I hope."

"Just a disappointment, I'll get over it," replied Agnes. She put the letter in her apron pocket, composed herself and returned to the shop.

Back in the courthouse, the tension was mounting. They witnessed several women returning from the public gallery in tears, having heard their menfolk had been sent down. Any thoughts of some sort of reprieve were quickly evaporating. Arthur was stood by his mother and suddenly felt the need for the toilet once again. Then, the clerk walked into the corridor and called out four names: Wilfred Stonehouse, Henry King, Samuel Tanner, and Arthur Marsden.

Henry and Samuel had been at the far end of the corridor and had not spoken to Arthur. They approached him. "Eh up, Arthur, how bin tha?" said Henry.

"Been better, Henry, I have to admit."

Samuel nodded, unable to speak; words would not come out.

They were joined by Wilfred, and the four of them walked into the courtroom. Mildred made her way up a flight of stairs to the public gallery. The court was crowded with smartly-dressed men, some wearing wigs. Several policemen, with their batons prominent at their side, were also present looking suspiciously at the defendants.

The clerk checked their names again on his list and they were escorted by one of the officers to a door which he opened. There was a short flight of stairs which they ascended, then they were in the dock facing three men who were seated opposite. Behind the person in the middle, there was the royal coat of arms on the wall.

The clerk of the court read out their names.

The Chairman of the Magistrates looked at the four. "Gentlemen, you have each been charged with affray, contrary to Common Law. How do you plead? Wilfred Stonehouse."

"Guilty, sir."

"Samuel Tanner."

"Guilty, sir"

"Henry King."

"Guilty, sir."

"Arthur Marsden."

There was a pause. "We didn't do owt, sir. We were just walking home."

There were murmurs in the public gallery.

"Silence…" admonished the Chairman. "How do you plead?

"Guilty," whispered Arthur.

"Louder, I can't hear you," shouted the Magistrate.

"Guilty," replied Arthur more audibly.

The three magistrates conferred. There was a hum of whispered conversation coming from the watching public.

The discussion seemed to last for several minutes. Arthur's need for the toilet was becoming desperate.

Then the Chairman addressed them.

"Very well, you have, all four, pleaded guilty to the charge, which is to your credit, but let me say this, the right to protest is enshrined in the basic freedoms of our society; the right to violate property and injure members of our loyal constabulary is not. The charges against you that have come before this court are serious indeed, particularly in these troubled times. A custodial sentence would rightly be the appropriate punishment. However, I note that you are of previous good character and you, Mr Marsden, are a master baker and provide a valuable service to the community. I have taken this into account." Arthur's legs were about to give way. The Magistrate continued. "I have decided in the circumstances and taking everything into account, to give you a conditional discharge."

There were more murmurs from the gallery. The Magistrate continued.

"The condition is that you leave this courtroom and proceed directly to one of His Majesty's armed forces' recruitment centres and sign up to serve your country for the duration of the present conflict. With your capacity for violence, you will be a valuable addition to our country's brave soldiers. I have spoken to the commanding officer of the Bradford Battalion, and he has agreed to accept you despite the serious charges against you. Failure to comply with this condition will be deemed a contempt of court and will attract an appropriate additional sentence. You are free to go."

He slammed his gavel down onto its wooden block making loud crack; it made the defendants jump.

Arthur was unable to move and was pushed along by Samuel. They left the dock and huddled together in the corridor.

"What's it mean?" asked Henry.

"'Appen we've been called up," replied Arthur.

Mildred descended the stairs in a state of shock. She saw Arthur and his pals stood together in the corridor and walked towards them.

"Arthur," she called.

"Mam... I need the privy; I won't be a minute."

He walked along the corridor; he was not the only person in need of a comfort break.

Mildred looked at Wilfred. "What about the butcher's; what will you do?"

"Appen I don't know. Ernest's just left school, but he knows a bit, and Phyllis can bone a steak. We'll manage somehow."

Arthur joined them. "So what are you going to do?" asked Mildred.

"Well, we need to get to Bradford and sign up."

"But you will come back surely; you'll need to collect all your things."

"I'll speak t'clerk and see if he knows."

Arthur approached the clerk who was rounding up the next batch of men to face the court.

"Excuse me sir, but what happens when we sign up? We have all our things to collect and arrangements to be made."

"Ah, yes, I recommend you explain that to the recruitment officer. My understanding is you'll be allowed home once you have passed the tests and signed up. Then you will need to report back in the morning." Arthur thanked the man and returned to his pals.

"He says we need to go to Bradford and sign up, then we'll be allowed back to collect our things and go back in t'morning. 'Appen recruitment officer will tell us."

"Where do we go?" asked Samuel. He was stood in a daze hardly able to take everything in.

"I heard it were the Town Hall," said Henry.

"Aye, that makes sense. We best be going," said Arthur.

Mildred went to Arthur and hugged him. It felt strange; his mother had rarely shown this level of affection.

"Take a cabbie; I'll give you the fare." She broke away from the hug and took out her purse and handed Arthur a ten-shilling note. Arthur noticed a tear in her eye.

"Don't fret none, mam, 'appen they'll look after us all right."

Arthur and his pals left the courthouse and went to the taxi rank across the road. Mildred also decided to take a cabbie back to the bakery.

It took nearly an hour to reach Bradford Town Hall. There were large signs outside the building advertising the recruitment centre and a queue of men around twenty deep had formed waiting to sign up.

It took another half an hour before the pals were inside. A soldier in khaki uniform approached them. "Come this way," he said, authoritatively.

They followed the private into a room where an officer and two assistants were seated behind a trestle table. The lieutenant looked up at the four lads.

"We've just come from t'court in Keighley. Magistrate said we had to sign up," said Arthur.

"I see," said the officer. "Yes, he said he would be sending over some volunteers. Right, my orderly here will write down your details and then take you to the medical room for examination... to make sure you are fit to join," he clarified.

"We've got no stuff with us. 'Appen we've come straight from Magistrate," said Arthur.

"Yes, that's alright; we won't be leaving for camp until O eight-hundred tomorrow morning. You will need to be here for then."

The pals followed the orderly along another dingy corridor. There was a door with a temporary sign saying 'medical' on it. The soldier knocked on the door.

"Come," said a voice from within. The orderly went inside, then returned a couple of minutes later holding a number of forms.

"Right, I'll take down your details while one of you is being examined."

"You, what's your name?"

"Samuel Tennant, sir." The orderly checked the spelling and wrote Samuel's name on the first form.

"Right, Tennant, you go in and I'll take down the details of your pals here. Then I can do yours when you've finished."

The testing process consisted of a physical examination, a medical questionnaire, and an eye-test.

After completing the questionnaire, the doctor directed Samuel to walk up and down the room smartly two or three times; then to hop across the room on the right foot; and back again on the left. Then he was halted, and told to stand upright, with his arms extended above his head while the medical examiner walked slowly around him, carefully inspecting the whole surface of his body looking for scars, swellings or any other abnormality that might preclude him from serving in the army.

Satisfied Samuel met the required standard, he was dismissed.

Arthur went next.

It wasn't a large room but sufficient for its purpose. There was a table with various forms, ink pads and stamps, untidily scattered across the top. In the middle, there was a pen, inkwell, and blotter. Behind the table there were two wooden lathe-back chairs. In the corner, also behind the table, was a screen. There was a sash window, open at the top, which had been half-covered by a sheet of paper to deter onlookers.

An officer was sat on one of the chairs and peered at Arthur over his spectacles. His pen was poised over a new form.

"Name?"

"Arthur Marsden?" The officer wrote Arthur's name.

"Occupation?"

"Master baker."

He looked up from his form. "Hmm, a master baker, eh? We could use your skills at the front. The men are going to need feeding."

"Aye, sir," replied Arthur.

"Age?"

"Nineteen."

"Nationality?"

"British."

"Right, Marsden, Captain Lawton, here, will take your weight and height and check your eyesight. Have you any medical conditions we should know about?"

"No sir."

Another officer was standing on the other side of the room fiddling around with the eye-test equipment. Arthur's eyes were tested and height and weight checked. Then he was asked to do the hopping procedure.

"You're a tall lad, but a bit on the skinny side; you could do with fattening up. The army will soon sort that out for you," said the officer as he walked around him.

The formalities completed; Arthur was sent back to the corridor to wait while Henry went through the same process.

Wilfred was last to go. Ten minutes later; he was back, his face was grim.

"What's up, Wilfred?" asked Arthur.

"'Appen eyesight's bad; he said I wouldn't pass."

"What're they going to do?"

"When I told them we'd been sent by t'magistrates, he said I were not to worry. He just signed t'form."

The orderly returned. "Right, gentlemen, follow me."

They walked down more corridors and into another room. Men were milling about everywhere, some in uniform, others, like Arthur and his pals, looking confused and lost.

"Just the last formality, you will take the King's oath and sign the papers."

The four were each handed a bible. The orderly read the oath.

"Do you swear to faithfully defend His Majesty, his heirs and successors against all enemies?"

"I do," replied the pals together.

"And do you also swear to obey the authority of all generals and officers set over you?"

"I do," they said again.

Each signed their 'call-up' forms. They were now officially members of His Majesty's armed forces.

"What happens now?" asked Arthur.

The orderly gathered the documents together. "You'll be given leave of absence to return to your homes to collect your belongings, one suitcase only, and return here by seven-thirty tomorrow morning when you'll be provided with transportation to your training camp."

Back at the bakery, Mildred had returned from the courthouse with the news of Arthur's sentence. Grace and Agnes were still serving and had little chance to say a great deal, but Ivy felt devastated on hearing the news.

Grace closed the shop at one o'clock for lunch as usual. They would open again at two. Ivy had been able to continue supplying the shop with loaves and the shelves were reasonably full.

Grace walked along the corridor where Ivy was mixing, taking out her frustrations on more dough.

"Take a break, Ivy, tha's been on thar feet all morning. Mam's getting us something to eat upstairs."

Ivy left her mixing and the pair went up to the parlour and joined Mildred and Agnes. She brought in a plate of sandwiches and some tea.

"We need to talk about what we're going to do about the bakery," said Mildred as she poured the drinks.

"What's going to happen?" asked Grace.

"Well, we'll have to wait for Arthur to return and see what he says, but, as I understand, he'll need to leave early tomorrow. He won't have time to do any baking."

"'Appen I can make t'bread, Mrs Marsden, and Grace can help me, if she has a mind."

"Aye, but what about the customers? I can't serve them on my own," said Agnes.

"No, that's right enough," said Mildred.

"And I don't know owt about t'flour. I'll need money to pay Mr Buxton," added Ivy.

"Yes, of course. Well, Grace can look after the money; that won't be a problem."

The conversation stalled; Mildred was trying to think things through.

"What was the letter from Hippodrome tha had, Agnes?" asked Grace after they had finished eating.

"'Appen tours cancelled because of t'war."

"Oh dear," said Mildred.

"Aye, but they have a position in mind for me in the pantomime at Christmas."

"Well, at least that's something, but you must be very disappointed."

"Aye, mam, I am."

"What about getting a piano? You did mention it."

"Aye, that would be a wonderful idea. I can learn to write

my own songs."

"We'll go to see Mr Tooley next week."

At two o'clock, Grace reopened the shop. The hectic morning had taken her mind off Freddie; she wondered what he was doing now.

With footfall now down to just an occasional customer, Grace checked on the bread situation with Ivy.

"There's still a sack of flour left, shall us make some more?" said Ivy.

"Nay, we'll save that for tomorrow; there's still a few loaves in the shop. We'll not be busy now. I'll close up when that's gone. Tha can start cleaning up."

"Aye," said Ivy and started pouring water in the mixing vat. She was covered in flour.

Arthur arrived back from Bradford just after four o'clock.

Mildred was in the parlour with Agnes and Grace. Ivy had cleaned the baking shed and was in the bedroom.

"Arthur, thank goodness. How are you?" said Mildred.

"Aye, alright, considering," he replied.

"Sit down I'll make some tea."

Ivy came in from the bedroom. "Eh up, Arthur. It's good to see tha back. What's happened? Tha mam says tha's been called up."

"Aye, it's right enough. We've been told we can collect us stuff, but we've got to get back to Bradford for seven-thirty in morning."

The family and Ivy sat down at the table and discussed a plan that would keep the bakery going; at least while there was a supply of flour.

Ivy would continue living at the flat and agreed to open up

in the morning and meet the miller. Mildred would give her sufficient money to pay the man. Grace would help once she had arrived from Oakworth and Agnes and Mildred would serve the customers. Arthur was amazed at the support, especially from his mother who had once vowed she would not be seen dead serving in the shop; but needs must, she explained. At least it would keep the business going.

"Aye, that's grand," said Arthur once the strategy was explained.

There were tearful farewells at five o'clock when Mildred felt she needed to return to the house. She wanted to call in on Kitty to tell her about Arthur's news and see how she was managing after Freddie's departure. She needed someone to talk to. There would be plenty of other things to occupy her mind, not least the gardener's position. She would speak to Mrs Jessop for a recommendation. She remembered she had mentioned the previous gardener, Jed somebody. She would enquire if he were still available.

The parlour was empty. Ivy was in the kitchen busy cooking. Archie Slater's voice was again audible but Arthur hadn't bothered to buy a paper; there was little point. He sat at the table staring into space.

"Why don't you go wash and change, Arthur?" called Ivy. "I've got us some nice pork chops; I'll make us a casserole."

Arthur came into the kitchen. "Aye, 'appen I will."

Ivy completed her cooking and dished up a relative feast for Arthur. They sat down opposite each other at the table.

"Tha never knows when next tha'll get a decent meal," she said as they started eating.

With Arthur locked away in his thoughts, there was a comfortable silence as they ate their dinner. When they had finished, Ivy started clearing the plates to take to the kitchen; she turned to Arthur. "Tha will write to us while tha're away?"

"Aye, I'll do that," he replied.

Later, they again shared the bed and, this time, there was no uncertain fumbling. It was the soldier's farewell.

The following morning, the alarm clock sounded it's awakening call and Arthur started to collect his things together.

Ivy got dressed and headed down to the baking shed to open up. Arthur joined her to make sure that everything was as it should be just as Buxton's lorry arrived.

"Eh up, Arthur, how be tha?" said the miller in his usual manner.

Arthur related the court appearance and the arrangements for the continuation of the business. He also introduced Ivy.

"She'll be doing baking," he explained. The miller nodded to Ivy in acknowledgement.

"I can do tha another three sacks today, if that suits," said Buxton, walking towards his lorry.

"Aye, that's grand," said Arthur. Ivy watched and learned.

The miller unloaded the flour and was about to get back in his cab when he turned.

"Tha's a brave lad, Arthur. Mind tha keep safe." The pair embraced.

Arthur watched the lorry turn and trundle out of the gate. He suddenly realised there was a possibility he might never see Edward again. He was swept with sadness.

Arthur walked back to the parlour to finish packing and returned to the baking shed at six forty-five dressed in his suit, flat cap, and his best boots. He was carrying a small suitcase. He walked to the baking shed to see how Ivy was managing.

Ivy heard him come down the corridor and left her dough to say goodbye, wiping her hands on her overalls.

"Tha'll be alright, Arthur, tha make sure. I need tha to come back to me."

Ivy grabbed him and planted a kiss on his lips. Then flung her arms around him. "I wish tha didn't have to go. Tha will write won't you?"

"Aye, Ivy. I'll write."

Arthur and Ivy walked back through the shop to the front door. He looked up at the bell as it clanged and wondered if he would ever hear it's cheery sound again.

Wilfred was pacing up and down outside the shop looking anxious. As best pals, they had agreed they would go to Bradford together. Like Arthur, Wilfred was carrying a small suitcase.

"'Ow do, Arthur."

"Eh up, Wilfred. We'll take cabbie. Mam's given us money."

"Aye, right you are." Wilfred went to his sister who was stood in the doorway and kissed her on the cheek. "Sithee, Ivy."

Ivy waved as the pals crossed the road to the waiting taxicab.

"Bradford Town Hall," said Arthur to the driver. He turned and waved to Ivy then got in the back of the vehicle followed by Wilfred.

Arthur's war was about to begin.

THE END

'Arthur's War' – the sequel to 'The Baker's Story' is scheduled to be released by Fisher King Publishing, in autumn 2021.

Alan Reynolds

Following a successful career in Banking, award winning author Alan Reynolds established his own training company in 2002 and has successfully managed projects across a wide range of businesses. This experience has led to an interest in psychology and human behaviour through watching interactions, studying responses and research. Leadership has also featured strongly in his training portfolios and the knowledge gained has helped build the strong characters in his books.

Alan's interest in writing started as a hobby but after completing his first novel in just three weeks, the favourable reviews he received encouraged him to take up a new career. The inspiration for this award-winning author come from real life facts which he weaves seamlessly into fast-paced, page-turning works of fiction.